Runaway River

The Bitterroot Mountains Series,
Mountains of Montana Collection

Kim Taylor

Trilogy Christian Publishers
A Wholly Owned Subsidary of Trinity Broadcasting Network
2442 Michelle Drive
Tustin, CA 92780

For information, address Trilogy Christian Publishing
Rights Department, 2442 Michelle Drive, Tustin, Ca 92780.
Trilogy Christian Publishing/ TBN and colophon are trademarks of Trinity Broadcasting Network.

For information about special discounts for bulk purchases, please contact Trilogy Christian Publishing.

Manufactured in the United States of America

Trilogy Disclaimer: The views and content expressed in this book are those of the author and may not necessarily reflect the views and doctrine of Trilogy Christian Publishing or the Trinity Broadcasting Network.

10 9 8 7 6 5 4 3 2 1

Library of Congress Cataloging-in-Publication Data is available.

ISBN 978-1-64773-094-9 (Print Book)
ISBN 978-1-64773-095-6 (ebook)

To my husband, Glenn, for his unfailing support and timely nudges. You are, and always will be, my favorite person on earth.

Acknowledgments

To Carrie Fancett Pagels and Sarah E. Ladd for their unfailing support and hours of editing. I've enjoyed having you along for the journey. Thanks for allowing Kim Taylor and Beth Yates into your world. Beth's story wouldn't be the same without you.

To my husband, Glenn, for his countless hours of reading and editing. Many late nights, Mexican dinners, and cups of tea went into Beth and Ethan's story. I value your pastoral background, experience with people, and solid biblical knowledge; all three contributed greatly to the depth and spiritual threads in this story.

To Tamela Hancock Murray of the Steve Laube Agency, thank you for believing in me and in Beth Yates' story.

To R. C. Sproul Jr., for the following quotable thought:

> "Why do bad things happen to good people?
> That only happened once, and He volunteered."

Preface

Dear friend,

I am honored to have you along for Beth's journey. Her journey, like yours and mine, has had its ups and downs. My hope and prayer is that you will close this book knowing that hardship, trials, and trauma are so very dear to the heart of God. He is never absent or detached from our troubles and sorrows.

Whether pain be short-lived or never-ending, He is there at every moment. Whether you are angry or at peace, He is listening. Even when we can't see it or believe it, He is working. He is trying to reach those who hurt others, and He is healing those who have been hurt and never received apologies or restoration.

So many unanswered questions come with pain, but we can never understand "why" until we truly understand "who." God never fails at anything.

Healing is a journey. May you survive and continue to heal. May your story be instrumental in the lives of those hurting around you, not because of pat answers or churchy clichés, but because you stayed, you listened, and you prayed.

Please share Beth's story with a friend. It would mean a great deal to me. And be sure to join me as Sadie and Michael's story continues in *Stubborn Creek*, book two of the *Bitterroot Mountains* series.

He has made everything beautiful in its time. He has also set eternity in the human heart; yet no one can fathom what God has done from beginning to end.

—Ecclesiastes 3:11 (NIV)

Chapter One

May 1, 1897
Chicago, Illinois

The children were finally asleep. All fifty-six of them.

Holding her breath, Beth Yates took several careful steps and then paused to steady the tea tray in her hands. She smiled at her success. All of them into bed in forty-five minutes, ten minutes less than the night before. Floorboards creaked overhead, pulling her attention upward. She listened for the pitter-patter of tiny feet but heard nothing.

Peace at last, a moment all to herself.

But a sudden tug on the back of her skirt told her one little boy wasn't asleep. Understandably. Tomorrow, he would finally have a family.

She turned around. "Freddy, you should be in bed."

Freddy's eyes threatened tears. "What if they don't like me, Miss Beth?"

What would Mother say? *Something sweet*, she thought. "They won't like you. They'll *love* you." She smiled down at him, thinking of all of the undeserved beatings this small, redheaded, freckle-nosed boy had endured.

"Will they hit me and call me bad names?" His words voiced the fear his five-year-old emotions couldn't.

She hurried to one knee, smoothing his hair. "Of course, not. These are good, kind folks." Seeing the doubt and confusion on his tiny face, she added, "They've been wanting a little boy just like you for a long time."

He smiled, accepting her words. "Will I get my own room?"

She nodded hesitantly. She didn't know for sure. Surely, the couple from Wisconsin had some means since they had traveled by train several times to meet with Father. Of course, they would have a room for him, a room filled with toys.

Beth had a room of her own once, but that was before Father had to leave the university. Before he spoke his mind. She lacked the details but knew it ended badly.

Thinking of Freddy's drunken uncle, she decided to lower his expectations.

"Most children don't have their own room. Be thankful for a new family," She reminded gently, glancing upward in hopes Freddy hadn't woken any of the other children. "Some children are still hoping for a family."

"Can't I take Opy and Nixon with me? They been wanting a family awful bad."

Let him down easy, she reminded herself. "God has a specific family picked out for them."

In all honesty, she didn't know if God had anything to do with finding these children families and a home. Why had He abandoned them in the first place? But she hoped quoting Mother would suffice.

It could work out for Freddy, as dreams should.

"I don't want to go." Tears filled his eyes.

"Now, now." She pulled a handkerchief from her apron pocket. "Don't you worry. It will be wonderful. You'll see." She hoped it would be true for him, unlike her family's move from a glorious home in uptown to follow Father and Mother's dream.

Their dream, not hers.

She chastised her thoughts even as she thought them. It was right to care for orphans.

She stiffened with a renewed sense of duty, rallied her spirits in thought of the cup of tea to come, and covered Freddy's runny nose.

"Blow."

He tried.

"No, blow. Don't suck."

When blowing became impossible, he wiped his nose with his shirtsleeve.

She sent him back to bed with a sigh and the promise of a bright and happy tomorrow. It would be a bright and happy day, the first she'd had in years. She was to deliver Freddy to his new family at Union Station first thing. After that, a glorious day, free of duty and responsibility. She'd enjoy a café, visit the dress shops on the avenue, perhaps even buy a new dress.

Thinking of the days back at the university, she smiled. Father, a distinguished professor. Mother, head of various committees. She shrugged at the memories, considering the tiny amount Father had sacrificed for her to go downtown.

I'll buy a new hair comb instead.

Hearing no movement overhead, she organized the tea tray with Mother's finest china in the old butler's pantry, complete with the strawberry patch teapot, matching creamer and sugar bowl, and a single teacup. The set was the one luxury that had followed them in the move. Moving toward the kitchen, the tea tray wobbled and tilted in time with the sway of her hips, forcing the lovely teacup to rattle in its saucer.

Hot tea was a necessity on a cold night like this.

"Might even snow," Father had said.

Snow? At this time of year? She shook her head.

She slowed to a snail's pace, desperate to calm the hot tea from swishing side to side. Should've waited to pour the tea, but the ambiance of such finery got the better of her.

A tea party for one.

She sighed and decided to endure it as best as she could.

At twenty-three years of age, friends were long gone. They doted over husbands and raised well-behaved children now. And she was here. Stuck. Imprisoned by her parents' dying devotion to save the world, one orphan at a time.

If only she'd spoken her mind when she had the chance.

Maybe she'd be married and raising children of her own. She could've stayed behind. Worked as a nanny or a tutor to one of the university families. She wasn't so bad looking. Society would forgive her height for good behavior.

I possess a few qualities that might entice a—

Hot tea erupted from the mouth of the teapot and splashed onto her skin. Beth writhed at the burn on her hand and then shrugged. *I possess a few qualities that might humor a man*, she corrected. She stared at the tray, and the pool of tea accumulated in the saucer and tightened her grip to continue.

The moment she emerged from the kitchen, her brother Michael came barreling down the banister, feet first, sixteen-year-old frame second. It took less than half a wink to wipe her legs out from underneath her, upset the tray, and send Mother's favorite china into the air. Beth gasped, and her shoulders tensed as the tray hit the floor, followed by each piece of china, and then silence.

She froze.

Michael froze.

Seconds passed.

The rug hadn't softened the blow, shards of porcelain strewn about. Suddenly, it hit her, *not the teapot,* and she raced to the rescue.

But it was too late.

Tightening her fists, she glared at the ceiling. She had little patience when it came to Michael's thoughtlessness. *If he woke the children.* Her eyes lowered to meet his careless expression. She was still a couple of inches taller. *Grow up, Michael. I had to*, but the sleeping children kept her mouth closed.

"Sorry. My fault." Michael said as he slid Father's copy of *The Relations of Science and Religion: The Morse Lecture* to his side and behind his back.

Did he really think her a nitwit? That she wouldn't notice? Maybe words weren't necessary. Michael knew how she merely tolerated his fascination of books, his obsession with reading. His hunger for information kept him from getting chores done and made more work for her.

Sorry? An apology wouldn't bring Mother's precious china back to life.

Staring at the disaster at her feet, she frowned. Nothing could.

Muttering a rebuke under her breath, she bent down to gather the broken pieces. *Will nothing ever go right?*

She could hear Mother now, "My wedding china isn't meant for everyday use." How could they possibly afford to replace it? Father had recently taken a second job, what with donations low and the extra mouths to feed. On her hands and knees, she began to rehearse words of apology.

Michael knelt beside her and swept the porcelain shards into a pile with his hand.

"Stop" Beth put her hand over his. "You're going to cut yourself. I'll do it," she ordered.

He stopped short, smirked, and then continued.

"I said, I'll take care—"

A knock at the door made them both look up.

"Who could that be? At this hour?" Beth glanced at the mantle clock. *Eight o'clock.* Mother should've been home by now, but why would she knock?

Michael pushed himself off the floor. "Mother forgot her key again."

His overly confident answers annoyed Beth. She tossed the broken pieces onto the tray and slid the evidence underneath Father's tattered "thinking" chair. She'd work out the words of apology later.

At the window, Michael pressed his cheek against the glass. "It isn't Mother. It's Vance Carney." A hint of disbelief crowded his words.

Beth smiled secretly. She enjoyed Michael's miscalculations. He was too smart for his own good.

Another knock, a louder one.

She huffed, not wanting anything to wake the children, and she really wasn't in the mood for company tonight. "Coming." That gave her a few more seconds, enough time to scoot the last visible piece of porcelain under the ragbag coats hanging on the wall. She looked at Michael, his face still pressed against the window. Beth smoothed her apron and opened the door.

"Mr. Carney," she gasped. "Sir, you're bleed—"

Carney held up a large hand. "I need to speak with Mrs. Yates, your mother." His breathing skipped and heaved as he rubbed the back of his neck. He looked exhausted. "Please. Right away."

"She…she's taken Father his dinner—" Beth cut her explanation short, seeing more blood on the man's clothes. "Sir, are you all right?"

Carney nodded, but the red gash across his left cheek said otherwise. Michael joined Beth at the door.

"There's been an accident…a fire at the factory," he stuttered and then wiped his face, pausing to stare at the fresh blood on the back of his hand. He pulled his hat from atop his head and rolled it up like a scroll. "Your father is…" he trailed off, clearing his throat before shifting his gaze.

"Hurt!" Beth exclaimed, finishing his sentence.

"No." Carney swallowed hard. "Please." He lowered his head. "Your father is dead, miss. I'm sorry."

Beth blinked, and her body faltered even as Michael reached to steady her. The heat in her cheeks chilled as she fell against the door. *No.* Her breathing turned to gasping. A voice cried out inside her head. *It's not true. It can't be.* Her hand crept along the flat of one of the door's mahogany panels, and she held herself upright as she tried to gain control.

Behind Vance, a gust of wind rushed through the street. Specks of nature carried with it.

"Are you sure it was Father?" Michael asked, his eyes narrowing at Mr. Carney. "How?" He shot a look at Beth, muscles tensed on his neck. "Perhaps it isn't him," he stated, but not as confidently as Beth was accustomed to.

Carney assured them that it was.

Michael reached for Carney's forearm. "Take me to him."

But Beth couldn't move. Michael pulled his coat from the wall hook. It rebelled the first time. His jaw twitched, pushing back emotion. After this, nothing would happen as it should.

Don't leave me, Beth would've shouted it if she could. Something always seized her thoughts, held them captive, like the air she breathed now. *Don't leave me alone.*

With one boot on and still wriggling into the second, Michael pushed passed them, forcing Carney down a step.

"Wait. I'm coming too," Beth finally cried out.

"No, you stay here, in case…" Michael shook his head low then looked up, "…for when Mother returns."

Beth nodded. That's right. She had to stay here—must be here when Mother returns. Mother might have taken another route. And the children needed her. Her seven-year-old sister, Maggie, needed her. She choked back the painful lump in her throat and stared beyond Carney and Michael to the flickering streetlamp. Its candlelight snapped and sparked as she watched until it eventually went out.

15

"I'm very sorry, miss." Carney hesitated for a moment, and her gaze slowly returned to him as he joined Michael in the street. Wind gusts whipped at Michael's coat and hair as their eyes locked. Beth nodded, permitting him to run. The wind pushed against the door as Beth tightened her grip on the cold knob to close it.

With her face in her hands, she slid down the backside of the door to the floor. Tears stung her cheeks as fear seized her heart.

* * * * *

Opening her eyes, Beth looked around the darkened room and then wiped her wet face with the back of her sleeve. The clock hid its face. The fire in the hearth was nothing but slow-burning embers. She slowly rose to her knees, then to her feet. The clock chimed the late hour as she stood. Beyond the front window, smoke wafted through the street, softening the light of distant lampposts.

Michael hadn't returned. Mother hadn't come home.

The house might as well have been vacant. Not a sound was heard. How she longed to wake Maggie, but she knew her sister would need Mother when she woke.

Falling into her mother's rocking chair near the fireplace, she smoothed her hands down the armrests, a solid comfort in the silence, but only for a moment. Body coiled and tense, she rose to her feet.

I can't just sit here. I have to know.

She grabbed her coat. Mrs. Rothmire, their nearest neighbor, had sat with the children before. Surely, the hour wouldn't offend her, considering the circumstances.

* * * * *

Father was dead.

Any doubt she might've had now lay on the cold street beside her. Flames engulfed the sausage factory and had for hours. Half of the building had grown dark, but the other still lit the sky with flames. The horses and carts that normally crowded the intersection were gone. A second fire wagon had arrived, forcing an opening in the crowd.

The air was thick with ash. Not a star in the sky. The moon didn't dare show its face. It wouldn't be right if it did. Chaos surrounded her. Voices were muffled and monotone. Men yelled in the distance. People screamed, running in every direction.

In the midst, Beth grabbed Michael's arm with a backward jerk. "You can't do this. It's too dangerous!"

"I have to. Mother could still be alive." He pulled himself from her grip. "This is my fault."

"Michael, please." Beth tried to reach for him, but his stride quickly put distance between them. She fell to the ground and rubbed her eyes. They stung. They ached.

Sitting beside her father's body, she wondered. Would she lose Michael too?

She tried to warm her cold hands with her breath, but the smoke burned her lungs as much as the tears did her eyes. Reaching one hand into her coat pocket, she pulled out Father's pocket watch and dangled it before her eyes, slowly dropping it into her lap. Her fingers caressed its markings, its design untouched by flames.

How Father loved this watch.

Most of the men made it out in time, that's what Carney had said. Father's body was one of the first pulled from the blaze. They identified him by this watch.

Beth smoothed her thumb over the engraving on the back.

"In His time."

17

Why those words? They held no meaning. She flipped it open, her fingers trembling. Still ticking. She hugged it close, hearing Father's heartbeat with every tick. As long as she lived, it would hold him near, keep him alive.

"Twelve o'clock," the hands read. She hadn't heard from Carney for some time.

All she could do was wait and hope. Stand by as men, her brother one of them, fought the flames and battled falling debris in hopes of saving the remaining few.

She scanned the scene, searching for Michael but seeing only dead bodies. Several yards away, a doctor knelt beside a man while a woman assisted him. Beth purposefully adjusted and smoothed the wool blanket covering her father's body but didn't allow herself to touch him. This would be too real if she did.

Snapping the watch shut, Beth looked up into the gray sky when a sudden explosion forced her to shield her face. A plume of black smoke cut through the already dark clouds. Women screamed in horror, while men pulled back from the raging inferno.

Part of the building had caved.

"Michael!" She cried, jumping to her feet and running through the crowd toward the blaze.

"Get that girl out of here!" a man yelled.

Someone tried to stop her. Beth swerved and kept running.

"Get back!" another man warned, seizing her with a grip so strong, his fingers jabbed into her ribs. She wrestled to get free.

"My brother's in there. Let…me…go. I have to—"

"It's too late, miss."

She wriggled again. Pulling his arm away, she tried to uncurl his grip one finger at a time as she watched the south building collapse. The north end threatened to come down any second.

Suddenly, in the distance, amidst the smoke and inflamed backdrop, a silhouette emerged. Carney's large frame staggered, zigzagging to stay vertical. A limp body hung in his arms. Behind him appeared a second silhouette, smaller and more dear.

"Michael."

The man released her, and she ran. She reached them as the third floor collapsed into the second and leveled the building. Carney stammered and stumbled to the ground, releasing Mother's body to the street, limp. Beth rushed to her side.

"Is she…?" Beth steadied her trembling lips and swallowed hard.

Relieved that Michael was still alive, Beth reached for him, only to gasp as Mother drew an unexpected breath. Beth leaned in close and wanted to touch her but couldn't.

"Mother, I'm here." She squeezed Michael's hand. "We're here."

"She's alive!" Carney proclaimed and called for the doctor.

Michael tensed but didn't speak.

"Eli…zabeth."

"Yes, yes, I'm here."

Her mother struggled to reach out, her charred hand searching. Beth gently took her hand.

"Take care…" Mother swallowed and grimaced in pain. "…of Michael and…" With a rough cough, she closed her eyes and tried again. "Maggie needs…" She coughed again, her mouth gaping in search of air, unable to continue.

"Yes, Mother, I will. I promise. Be still now. The doctor is here," Beth murmured reassuringly, squeezing her hand.

Violent tremors seized Mother's weakened body, forcing Beth back as the doctor came in a rush between them.

Beth looked into the sky. Her hands and eyes moving to a position of prayer, of desperation.

Please, God, I beg you. Don't let her die. We've already lost so much.

She opened her eyes, and the sky blurred as snowflakes hit her eyelashes and cheeks. She opened her clutched hands to catch a bit of the graceful white falling around her, as if hope was on its way.

Staring at the snow melting in her hands, she heard the doctor whisper, "She's gone."

Beth gasped.

Michael lowered his head.

Mother's body relaxed. Her chest didn't rise again.

"No," Beth whispered, then cried. "No."

Massaging the blanket covering the body, Beth begged life to come back.

Chapter Two

A thick, familiar fog blanketed the cemetery, and a rainy mist sifted in from the north, making it difficult for Beth to keep her eyes open. *After three sunny days*, she thought, *it would rain today.*

Tall, tower-like cedars surrounded the old cemetery with round scraggly bushes set between them. An impenetrable fortress of green. Broken walkways cut the yard into quarters. Her parents' plots sat in the northwest corner, that much farther from home.

"The Lord is my shepherd; I shall not want. He maketh me to lie down in green pastures."

Reverend Biggs spoke with a confidence and strength that didn't match his frame.

Beth's eyes narrowed as she listened. Empty words, jeering words to haunt her pain.

"Yea, though I walk through the valley of the shadow of death, I will fear no evil: for thou art with me," Biggs continued.

Beth looked away, silencing both the man and his words, for clearly, God was as far away now as He had always been.

A small crowd of mourners had gathered on this dreadful morning, many with faces she didn't know. Most had sent condolences by post. Considering the severity of the fire, an open-casket ceremony was out of the question.

A shiver crawled up her back, and her shoulders twitched. Michael stepped closer, laced his arm through hers, and squeezed. Tears filled his eyes. He wiped them and cleared his throat.

Maggie gently tugged at Beth's coat, interrupting her thoughts. Her little sister's wet, red face begged Beth for a smile, one that would tell her everything would be all right. Maggie had been crying since breakfast.

Could a child comprehend death?

Beth offered a smile but knew in her heart it wasn't genuine. She pulled her coat tighter around her neck, as if hiding the deception as her thoughts raced. *I should have done something, said something. Maybe they would have listened. We could have stayed at the university. None of this—*

"Surely goodness and mercy shall follow me all the days of my life," Reverend Biggs paused, then added, "Thomas and Mary Yates, may you rest in peace." He solemnly closed the Bible and bowed his head.

Michael tried to control the tears. In the privacy of prayer, he wiped his eyes numerous times. She knew he wouldn't be able to control it much longer.

Beth looked around at heads bowed all across the cemetery as the reverend prayed. And for a single moment, she was alone. She couldn't pray; she didn't want to.

She'd prayed before. He didn't listen.

Michael and Maggie could pray if it brought them comfort though.

She drew Maggie closer as her tiny sobs grew louder. She stared at the two caskets before her. *I didn't even get to say goodbye. Father, Mother, I never told you, but...*

A collective "amen" brought movement back into the moment and stole her last words.

Michael erupted in tears and fell to his knees, sobbing uncontrollably, his muscles tense and his lips tight, which told Beth that he was trying to stop but couldn't. Maggie began to wail, the sound followed by the cries of numerous orphans. Beth pulled Maggie and some of the children closer, fixing an iron grip on her own emotions. She couldn't comfort all of them. She couldn't even comfort herself, but for their sake, she bit the inside of her cheek. The pain gave the necessary restraint…for now.

People shook her hand and patted her on the back, but she felt nothing. The few remaining mourners dissipated, and Beth saw the reverend and his wife aiding children into distant carriages. The mist had finally stopped, and a ray of sunshine sliced through an opening in the clouds. Maggie had joined Michael, both caressing the wooden coffins as solemn men stepped forward to lower them into the ground. Maggie rushed to push them away, and Michael rose to restrain her. Beth looked away, panicked.

This wasn't happening.

"Miss Yates, might I have a word before you go?" Reverend Biggs touched her arm as his wife gathered Maggie into her arms, urging her toward the carriage. Michael swallowed hard and, without a word, shook the reverend's hand.

Beth cleared her throat, hoping Reverend Biggs didn't intend to grace her with a lengthy eulogy about who her parents were and what they'd accomplished with an added promise of "they're in a better place." She couldn't handle that right now, and she wasn't about to make a scene in front of the children.

"You be sure to let us know your plans," Reverend Biggs said, gently taking Beth's hand.

Beth forced a tiny smile and a compliant nod.

Biggs continued, "God knows what you're going through, Beth. He cares. He knew of this day. Be assured, He will be with you as you grieve."

She had prepared herself for a cold, memorized scriptural explanation of death and life after but not this. Even so, her better judgment told her to keep silent.

"He didn't want this to happen," he continued.

Beth threw the palm of her hand into the air, silencing him as her thoughts screamed, *How dare you say God cares! I am living proof that He couldn't care less.* She waved her stiff hand and stepped back. *Where was God when Father was burning to death, and where was God when I begged Him to spare Mother's life? Is that the God you say cares for me?*

Beth clenched her teeth and tightened her jaw, determined to speak her mind.

"Don't tell me God cares. This is His fault. He has abandoned us. And now I must—"

Reverend Biggs interrupted her as he placed a gentle hand on her shoulder. Beth pulled away and managed only a simple, "thank you for the service," before allowing a shocked Michael to help her to the carriage.

"Beth, you shouldn't have said those things. It's not true." He prepared to continue.

Her pointed expression silenced him. Michael's saddened gaze stabbed at her already broken heart. She looked away, refusing to listen.

This was God's fault, and she would never forgive Him.

The carriage skipped and lurched with the unevenness of the street, contributing to her already pounding headache. As the driver pulled the carriage up to the front door, Beth looked back and counted the additional carriages in the procession. Reverend and Mrs. Biggs had insisted on making all of the arrangements for the orphans to attend the funeral.

She stepped out of the carriage with a heavy foot and acknowledged the driver. Michael reached for Maggie and let several other children down as Beth fiddled with the top button on her long black coat that refused to release. She gazed at the structure they called home. A broken shutter clapped loosely against the brick, the chimney was crumbling, and several roof tiles were missing. Her hands and arms fell to her side as she beheld the enormous task that lay before her.

A tiny hand reached for hers when a strange sound caught her attention. Out of the corner of her eye, she noticed a man in the shadows several doors down. She nervously fumbled with the key in her pocket and made her way to the door but couldn't stop her hands from shaking. Michael tried to help, but she pushed him away and glanced at the dark figure. "I've got it." She jiggled the key into the hole and relaxed when the key finally found its place. She hurried them inside, patting the last little one on the back.

The world outside held odd sounds and unfamiliar faces. Inside, they were all safe. Beth stuck her head out the door and looked around, quickly noting that the stranger was gone. She closed the door, secured the lock, and sighed. The house echoed the clamoring of tiny feet hitting the stairs. The fire in the hearth burned low and needed another log to make it comfortable. Michael took to the stairs slower than normal, just one at a time, and the children disappeared to the far-off corners of the house.

In the silence, Beth rubbed her hands together to remove the chill and leaned her weary forehead against the mantel. Staring at the dying fire, she poked its embers back to life while she thought. She honestly regretted her behavior with the reverend and his wife. She had always wondered how it would feel to truly speak her mind. Now she knew.

Chapter Three

Eastern Montana

Ethan Dawson didn't want a wife right now, especially that one.

He pictured the look on Miss Tucker's face when her father found them alone in the barn of the Tucker Ranch, her timing perfectly rehearsed. If Mr. Tucker had shown up one minute earlier, Ethan would be dead right now, or worse, married.

Ethan unbuttoned his shirt, laying it across the back of the chair. His shoulder twitched with a chill, since the guest room at the Tucker Ranch didn't possess the luxury of a fireplace. He plunked his nearly six-foot frame into the chair with a thud, hoping the noise didn't wake the house. With one leg crossed over his other knee, he bent to pull off his boot as he thought of Tucker's daughter. Sixteen years old, going on twenty, with a voice and hands as sticky as molasses.

As usual, he'd made a mess of things in the female arena. A muffled groan escaped as he shimmied each boot free. Why wouldn't women leave him be? They didn't need to find him. He'd find one...when the time was right.

And right now, it wasn't.

Ethan's socks were twisted and plastered to his swollen feet. He knew better than to try to break in new boots right then. Growing up on a cattle ranch, boots were either a man's best friend or a spit-in-the-eye enemy.

But he wasn't a cattle rancher, not anymore. That was Father's dream, and Peter's too. He was a horse breeder, at least that was his plan. A childhood visit to the Kentucky Derby, and his mind was made up. His dream began. An obsession, as some folks called it. He'd read every book, asked every question, saved every penny, and interned with the finest breeders and trainers on both sides of the Mississippi. Every horse within a twenty-mile radius of home knew his name. He had a reputation now.

It was the Dawson way.

Dawsons didn't do small. There were expectations. Theirs and his.

He thought of Missy May Tucker.

He knew better than to let his guard down. A wife and family would only hold him back.

If it were up to him, he'd have his ranch. His own land, his own barns, and his own horses. But it seemed that it wasn't up to him. No amount of money or hard work, no leaning on the family name, no expertise or know-how seemed to help. It was like there was some invisible force bent against him.

So for now, he worked for Marcus Daly, Copper King of the West, and one of the wealthiest horse ranchers this side of the Mississippi River. A slight delay, he promised himself. Someday, he'd give Daly some real competition.

Someday.

He shook his head at the countless setbacks, but then had to laugh. He was definitely a Dawson. He'd heard the stories. He knew his folks struggled in the early days too. Even Peter faced his challenges. Nothing came easy. Nothing had been handed to them on a silver platter. He had to work for it. Fight for it. Nothin's worth gettin' less it's hard.

He looked to the floor as if the devil himself had orchestrated the setbacks.

Bring it on. It'll take a lot more than a few roadblocks to stop me.

After he placed his boots and damp socks at the end of the guest bed, he finished undressing and then fell into bed. Didn't even crack the covers. Laid there, one foot still touching the floor. The aroma of supper's sweet ham and potatoes hung in the air. Thankful for a full stomach, he sighed. How long had it been since he'd had a home-cooked meal? Supper wasn't the same back at Daly's ranch. Hired hands ate at camp, not all fancy like with the family. No one knew exactly what Cook whipped up in that kitchen shack, or why his biscuits dulled a man's mind. Ethan licked his lips, happy to find a remnant crumb of Mrs. Tucker's biscuits.

His eyes adjusted as the night sky darkened the room. A lonely star appeared through the window, and he knew if he were to step onto the large veranda of Tucker's two-story farmhouse, a host of stars would present a grand finale, a show only the great state of Montana could perform. He lit the lantern on the bedside table and stared at the flower-papered wall. Wishing, praying he was in his own house on his own acres.

He reached behind his head, yanked out the extra pillow, and chucked it to the floor. Turning over, he pushed his face deep into the feathers. A growl, loud enough to satisfy him, reverberated in his ears. Time was not a friend. His mind raced with a list of things yet to do. He calculated the days left of his trip. This delay would put him a solid month behind in purchasing his own place, if not more.

He rubbed his forehead. What was he thinking to leave his future in the hands of the Johnston Brothers Real Estate Co? He should have hand delivered that land offer to Buck Reardon in person. It was a fair offer. That was his land. He'd claimed it already, despite the owner's well-known refusal to sell.

Reardon had a reputation.

Ethan had prayed about the land, sure, but God wasn't working fast enough. Depending on other people had caused Ethan too many delays already. He'd take matters into his own hands once he returned to the Bitterroot Valley. He didn't have time to wait. He needed that piece long before winter.

He pictured the land, situated perfectly with the Bitterroot River cutting right through the heart of it, water rights to feed field and hoof aplenty. The main road along the eastern border made for easy travel. Train tracks beyond that made for easy transport of livestock. Enough timber to build the house and barns with acres to spare. He'd already drawn up the plans, and yet here he sat on the eastern side of the state five hundred miles away.

He turned over onto his back and heard his father's words ring in his ears, *God's timing isn't our own. Don't try to get ahead of the Almighty.* He lifted his head and grabbed his pocket watch from the side table to check the time, then snapped it shut and stretched out his hand to turn down the lantern. This day was gone, like so many others.

He planned tomorrow's ride. He'd get going first thing, head west for Billings. The sooner he was on his way, the sooner he'd get back to what he really wanted. The trip had been successful. Mr. Daly would be pleased. *At least one man was getting what he wanted when he wanted it.*

His mind drifted, and he envisioned his own place the way he'd dreamed it up as a youngster. Thoroughbreds, Quarters, and Arabians running free across the grassy lowlands at the foothills of the rugged Bitterroot Mountains of Western Montana.

He rubbed his tired eyes to clear his mind.

"Lord, when?"

He turned over, not expecting a verbal response.

* * * * *

"You've got fine stock, sir," Ethan said, stretching out his hand to seal the deal with Tucker. "Mr. Daly will be satisfied with young Shilo for sure. And thanks for the bed and fine meal."

Tucker put a husky hand on his shoulder. "Ethan, I've known your folks for years. For the third time, call me Seth."

"Yes, sir, Mr. Tucker." Old habits die hard, even the good ones.

"Your ma and pa sure did a mighty fine job raising you two boys. Wishin' my boy had turned out so good." He rolled his eyes. "My daughter too."

Ethan gave an uncomfortable but respectful nod and slapped his leather gloves into one hand. Was Tucker apologizing for his daughter?

"How's this horse ranch of yours comin' along?" Tucker said.

So, Tucker had heard of his plans. News travels fast, or maybe it was the Dawson reputation. "Soon."

Tucker waved him off as if suddenly disinterested. "Why don't you stay for lunch? My Sarah's cookin' up a mighty feast. You'd think the whole town was comin' out for it."

"Wish I could, but I have to be on my way as soon as possible." Ethan thanked him for his generosity and threw the reins over Jax's head, giving his saddle a tug.

"Ethan, always a pleasure doin' business with you. We'll have Daly's stock ready mid-August." Tucker shook Ethan's outstretched hand with vigor. Leaning closer, Tucker offered. "Come on back when the timin's right. We'll get you a right fine pair of Anglo-Arabians. Don't be sayin' no word to your Mr. Daly. We'll keep that little fact between us. All righty?"

Ethan offered a second handshake. "Deal."

After tucking papers into his saddlebag, Ethan gave the buckle a tight pull as Tucker's wife crossed the yard, handed him a bundle tied up with string, and patted his cheek.

"Thank you for everything, Mrs. Tucker." He pulled himself into the saddle. "Let's go, Jax." Jax sidestepped with anticipation. He turned down the long dusty drive, tipping his hat in the direction of the veranda where Mrs. Tucker stood, waving her kitchen rag in the air. He stroked the bundle that contained some of that "feast" Tucker had mentioned. He wasn't hungry yet, but he would be.

Missy May Tucker stood next to her mother, leaning against a post with a half a smile and half a scowl on her face. Ethan tipped his hat in her direction. She whirled around, went back into the house, letting the screen door slam behind her.

"It's just you and me, girl, and miles of Montana dirt." Ethan murmured, leaning down to stroke Jax's neck. "Jax is hardly a name for a mare," his mother had said. An American Quarter horse with a bit of donkey, she believed. Granted, she never cared for Jax, said the horse was nothing but trouble, but Jax was a fine specimen of a horse. She was pure Quarter Bay, and a trusted partner, better than any woman ever could be. And boy could she herd cattle. Mother couldn't argue with that fact.

He swatted the dried mud on his chaps until dirt crumbled into the breeze and remembered the time Jax broke free, slipped through the back door of the kitchen, and nibbled at Mother's freshly baked bread. He smirked. She offered half loaves at the annual church bazaar that year, he remembered. His eyes narrowed. He'd never quite figured out how Jax wriggled free.

No, the name Jax was perfect. Just like the game of jacks. Starts out easy and gets more difficult as the game goes on, harder and more painful, if you play to win, that is. Training Jax was hard and painful, but she was worth it, the stubborn ones always are. No finer horse in all of Montana.

Ethan paused to glance back as he reached the line of trees that bordered Tucker's land. Mrs. Tucker still stood on the veranda, and Tucker crossed the field beyond the fence line in the distance.

Glancing north, he sighed. He was so close to his childhood home, he could practically smell the spiced corn bread baking in the oven. His family's ranch sat seventy-five miles or so north of Miles City, a day's ride.

"We'll go home next spring," he promised himself and his four-legged companion.

Reaching inside his coat pocket, Ethan pulled out his itinerary. Forsyth. Custer. Billings. He clicked the reins, and Jax picked up her feet. They had a good half day's ride ahead of them.

* * * * *

Warm wind hit his face and pushed back his Stetson.

All the hours in a saddle made him question his purpose in life. Pain and discomfort can do that to a man. Working as a foreman for Daly was a job, a place to wait. Hours were good. Pay was fair.

The Daly Ranch boasted over a thousand horses. What man in his right mind would pass up the chance to work alongside such fine men and stock? But the job bit with disappointment. As foreman, he spent more time scheduling ranch hands, writing paychecks, purchasing stock, and traveling for Daly than training and breeding horses.

Stuck, that's what he was.

He'd been in this place before. He wasn't a deskman. He was a dirt man, born and bred.

He adjusted in his saddle and lifted his hat to let the warm air comb through his hair. Two years now he'd worked for Daly, and this was his second trip this season. *Two long years.* He'd lost momentum.

Mother had hinted as much in her last letter.

Oh, she didn't mean to pressure him. She'd be proud to have him back home. Father too. But his father understood. Supported Ethan's drive long before he had a road. He sighed, hoping his folks and others didn't think of him as a failure. He'd voiced his plans and dreams too soon. He knew that now. How could he have known about Father's health at the time? And Peter's first wife. No one plans hard times. He replaced his hat and quickened their pace, happy that his father was back on his feet, and Peter had found happiness twice.

Daly insisted Ethan take the train for this buying spree, but Ethan convinced him that he'd cover more ground on horseback. As he adjusted his weary backside, he wondered if Mr. Daly was the wiser.

* * * * *

Forsyth, Montana, left nothing to the imagination. What a man wanted, a man got.

Ethan moaned as he dismounted and tied Jax to the post. The sun had set, pushing the town to an angle with its shadow. He pulled a "Jax-proof" knot and stroked her neck, a reward for a hard day's ride. "I'm hungry. How about you?" Jax whinnied and nuzzled her nose into Ethan's chest in response. "Well, let me see what I can find."

"Honey, I've got all you need to *find* right here," a woman's soft voice came out of the shadows as Ethan's boot hit the boardwalk. He faltered and nearly lost his footing.

He caught the sparkle in her eye as the lights from a nearby saloon illuminated her face. A memorized smile curled as if on cue, and she stepped close enough that the overpowering scent of her perfume took his breath away. "Miss." He put some distance between them and tipped his hat. An inherited gesture.

But before he looked up, her naked arms slithered around his neck, matching his own height with hers. "A man can get pretty lonely." Her tone crawled much like her arms did.

"Miss, I've no interest in…I'm not really…" The words scurried away like rats as he peeled her arms from his neck and stepped back, catching the back of his pants on a rusty nail protruding from a post.

"Oh, every man has interest in…" She waved the back of her hands down her bodice in a would-be hourglass figure.

Forcing his attention elsewhere, he turned to assess the damage to his one good pair of pants. Split clean through. He growled under his breath. *Women are nothing but trouble.* Were then and always will be. He forced a respectful smile as he turned to face her. She reached for him a second time, but this time her shoulder met a firm hand. "I…I have a girl." He looked down at his boots. It wasn't a lie exactly.

"Back home?" She didn't back away as he'd hoped.

"No, here." The shake in his voice would soon give him away. This could only go so far before he'd have to do something drastic, like run.

"You have a girl in Forsyth?" Her words hinted her disbelief.

He needed to put an end to this. "Yes. Now, if you'll excuse me, I am hungry." He tore himself away from her fingers as they combed his arm and back. He did have a girl. He had Jax. He could hear her muttering something about satisfying his hunger. The woman followed him as far as the light allowed, then she stopped as if some invisible line halted her from going any farther. He took a deep breath and glanced back at Jax, who seemed to smile in jest before chewing at the knot Ethan had secured.

A wooden sign at the end of the boardwalk welcomed him and his empty stomach. A plump middle-aged woman laughed wholeheartedly as he took a seat and ordered the day's special. "Today's special is as special today as it was yesterday." She shot a big smile toward the kitchen where a man slapped the bar several times, only encouraging the woman's laughter.

"And the day before that," the man called from the back.

Ethan smirked and looked at the woman. He could handle this kind of woman. She posed no threat. He forced a loud "thank you" as the woman retreated to the kitchen with a kiss and a pat to the man's cheek. Ethan chuckled to himself and then pulled the newspaper from a neighboring table, snapped it open to the date on the front page, and frowned.

Almost a month old.

He read the headline, "Factory Fire Threatens to Destroy Chicago Again." He remembered the great Chicago fire of 1871. Hundreds of folks lost their lives, and thousands lost their homes. He was a young boy at the time. As he read the current story of how the fire department, one man, and a boy recently saved Chicago from a repeated tragedy, he shook his head, thankful folks had been spared the heartache this time.

Within minutes, sustenance came, and the woman let him eat in peace. Murmurs hummed in the back room, and an occasional thud and burst of laughter resounded whenever the woman poked her head out to check on him. He licked the last piece of chicken from his fingers and tucked a payment under the plate. He adjusted his Stetson as the door slammed shut behind him, and the brass bell gave notice of his departure.

Ethan eyed the saloon and jumped the boardwalk two buildings before in hopes of avoiding Miss Trouble. Jax perked her head up as if she were up to something. A loud crash and a boisterous voice bellowed a melody as someone on the piano tried to find the singer's key and couldn't. Ethan quickened his stride. Darkness closed the door of every respectable establishment, and if the town didn't have a hotel, he might find himself sleeping under the stars tonight.

* * * * *

"Think this is funny, do you?" Ethan rolled out a blanket as close to the fire as he thought safe. Jax whinnied low, secretly poking fun at Ethan's cold, hard predicament. "But you don't have to sleep on the ground." He unbuckled his saddle and hung it over a nearby downed tree and scratched at the beard on his face. At least he'd bathed at the Tucker Ranch. It might be a few days before the hope of a bath would present itself.

He secured Jax to a tree and checked the knot a second time before retiring to the thin cushion beside the fire. He tossed and turned several times before sitting so he could uproot a pesky weed gnawing at his side. He grunted and looked up at Jax for sympathy. Jax turned away, clearly unable to appreciate the situation. Ethan fell back and closed his eyes.

"I want breakfast in bed tomorrow. Thank you very much. And good night."

* * * * *

"Jax. Jax!" Ethan called as he glanced around the area.

Jax was gone, and his boots were gone too. He threw back the blanket and jumped to his feet. A couple of steps announced the morning dew. "Jax." He shook each foot, but it was too late. The dew had soaked through. His fists balled at his side. *When I find her, I'm going to…*

He stopped. What if someone had taken her? What if someone had stolen his horse and his boots? He searched for other missing things and spotted his saddle nearby. He growled. Horse thieves who leave the saddle behind? He paused for a moment, considering his only option and headed for town. But as he walked out of the woods into the clearing, movement caught his eye.

Jax.

A scowl returned to his face as he marched into the sunrise, bootless and hungry. Jax took a nonchalant step as Ethan approached, then opened her mouth and let his boots fall to the ground with a sideways bounce. She took another step and bent down to nibble a blade of grass. *Lord, she knows how to aggravate me.*

He set the saddle on the ground and grabbed one boot, then the other. He saddled Jax in silence. Words weren't necessary. He'd win this argument. Despite Jax's current behavior, she was still a good horse…and bound and determined to make his life as interesting as possible.

No woman could ever do that.

Chapter Four

Chicago, Illinois

Beth stared at the darkness beyond the kitchen window. *Bedtime.* Something she'd come to dread. Michael and Maggie sat across the kitchen table while the Petrachelli twins played on the floor. Michael stirred his tea for the hundredth time, and Maggie moped, leaning from one elbow to the other. Perhaps she and Maggie could take a walk tomorrow. That would raise Maggie's spirits. Hers too, she hoped. She needed to clear her head, and the fresh air might do her a world of good.

What were they going to do?

She needed a job, but the past few weeks left little time to look. It was one decision after another. Decisions she'd had to make on her own. Funeral arrangements. Burial costs. Paying bills. Running the house. Caring for the children. Paperwork. She never understood the burdens her parents carried.

They were her burdens now.

"The Myers will be here on Monday to pick up Cece and Eldon," Beth told Michael and watched for the twin's response. They looked at each other with delight and began dancing about. How she longed for a reason to celebrate like that, a reason to smile again.

Beth and Michael shared a fatigued glance. The Schaumburg Orphanage had graciously taken the other orphans, and the Petrachellis were the last to be placed in a home. Beth rubbed her temples. It all happened so fast, yet the days seemed to drag on.

"Time for bed, children. You too, Maggie," she said.

"Me? Why?" Maggie dramatically slumped to the table, arms flat. "I'm so de…lib…itated."

Beth wanted to smile, but a heaviness remained. Maggie's altered vocabulary had returned at least. "To bed with you…and it's *debilitated*."

The Petrachelli children scrambled up the stairs. With a grunt, Maggie pulled from the table and climbed the stairs on all fours. "It isn't fair. I'm two years older. I'm sad too."

"I want you in bed and asleep in five minutes," Beth quoted her mother, and the words hurt.

Michael's gaze diverted. He was hurting too. He pulled a letter from his pocket and placed it on the table but held it, unopened, until the children disappeared upstairs. "We received another notice from the Chicago Savings and Loan Company."

She stared at the missive for a moment then looked at him. "I see." She'd been ignoring the post for more than a week, afraid of what unexpected bill might arrive.

"What are we going to do?" Michael said, shaking the letter.

Beth sipped her tea and forced a yawn. Another volunteered. "I don't know." It wasn't his burden to bear. "I'll figure something out."

"You're not sleeping, are you?" He eyed her, waiting for an answer.

She shook her head.

Michael folded his arms and leaned back in his chair. "I can take a job at the sausage factory. Carney said I could—"

"No," She interrupted him quickly, hands flattened on the table.

"They've started rebuilding the south building, and I know they are looking for workers."

Of course, they are. "Absolutely not, Michael." She tightened her fist on the table. "I cannot believe I am hearing this. How could you?" If she had her way, Michael would never work in a place like that. "That place is a *death* trap." Even as the words came out, she wanted them back. She hadn't been able to say the word since the funeral.

Death.

The thought brought tears to her eyes. She hadn't built a fire in weeks for the horrible memories that accompanied the flames.

"I don't think we are going to have a choice." He shook the letter in the air then paraphrased the first few lines, "Mr. Elias Sands requests a meeting and is politely..." He paused, raising an eyebrow, "...politely demanding payment on the mortgage immediately, or he will force a sale to pay the debt."

"Does it say how much we owe?" She asked, guessing an amount and bracing herself.

Michael read off the figure printed on the notice and looked up.

What? She grabbed the letter. "How can that be?" *I don't understand.* There must be some mistake, but there it was in print.

Michael shrugged. "I will take a job at the factory."

"No." She squeezed his arm. "No, and that's final."

Beth bit her lip. An impossible amount to repay. Little money remained in the "emergency" jar and not much more at the bank. She'd checked the donation box this morning only to find it empty. She had to do something—she was in charge of this house and this family now. She had to. Courage rose within her as she stiffened, pitched her chin, and rose to heat the tea kettle.

"I'll see this Mr. Sands tomorrow."

Over the next few minutes, she and Michael constructed a plan. They had no family, no money—nothing except the house, its contents, and each other.

"Selling the house is our only option," Michael stated.

She could see the wheels turning in that brilliant mind of his. "Slow down. I'll check with the bank to see exactly how much we have there, and then I'll see Mr. Vance about Father's wages."

Michael nodded and promised to take care of Maggie and the twins during her absence.

Before trudging off to bed, he turned. "Get some sleep. You've got a big day tomorrow."

Beth nodded and took another sip of lukewarm tea, hoping to calm her nerves. She wasn't a business-minded person. She wasn't much of anything. The teakettle finally blew its whistle, interrupting that train of thought. She pulled the over-filled kettle from the stove as it erupted with steam, spitting boiling water. She caressed her hand to remove the burn and scolded the kettle.

* * * * *

Beth tossed and turned, fluffed her pillow, flattened her pillow. Nothing helped. Finally, she sat up and threw the covers aside. Pushing her toes into her slippers, she stood and wrapped her mother's robe around her, finding some comfort there.

For years, she had despised her measly existence, sometimes hated her life. How stuck she felt, unable to change a single thing. She had no future. Duty, day in and day out. In fact, she nearly voiced her thoughts the day her parents died. Right now, she'd give anything to have it all, even the unchanging, never-ending daily routine of managing an orphanage. Wouldn't complain. Never give another thought to how grand life once was. She'd stay stuck for eternity if it would bring them back.

She cracked the window and heard the howl of the wind, the sound of broken shutters hitting against the house without any hope of rhythm. In the street, another moving wagon, heavy with furniture, hobbled slowly along, as if leaving in secret. Another family leaving the neighborhood. They wanted to leave.

She wanted to stay, have things the way they were before.

A lump choked her throat. She didn't want to cry, but the dull pulsing pain couldn't be helped. New and unfamiliar sounds now filled the house, noises that had always been there but went unnoticed. A creaking noise drew her attention, and she forced herself to ignore it.

Beth watched her sister sleep. "Finally," she whispered. She hoped tonight Maggie would sleep uninterrupted. She'd been waking in the middle of the night screaming. Could she blame her?

Sitting at a window bench, Beth reached for the quilt folded neatly beside her. Below, the milk deliveryman with his horse and cart parked several houses away. He'd soon be at their door. She calculated the cost and decided to cancel further delivery. Milk wasn't a necessity. Streetlights flickered, and a gust of wind knocked over a barrel, sending it tumbling down the street hitting everything in its path. Someone had fixed the lamplight that had gone out. It flickered high and bright.

Life was different now.

She had to be different. She had to be strong. *Stronger.* She thought of Reverend Biggs' mention of "her plans" and wondered if she really could do it. She had to have a plan.

You don't have a choice.

A long uncontrollable yawn took over, and she hoped it signaled a good night's sleep. Her eyes slowly shut just as Maggie sat up suddenly and screamed.

* * * * *

Beth smoothed her hands down the vested suit that once belonged to her mother and silently rehearsed the proposition she and Michael had discussed.

"Are you nervous?" Michael asked.

Beth shot him a look. "Should I be?" *Tell me no.*

Michael folded his arms. "No. He's a businessman. Keep to business."

Maggie hugged her. "You should cry, Beth. People always feel sorry for girls that cry." Maggie pulled away, practicing tears. Of course, Maggie would suggest drama.

"It's girls *who* cry, not girls *that* cry." *I haven't been a girl for some time now.* "I'm not going to cry. Be good while I'm gone."

Maggie's smile flattened. Beth glanced at the Petrachelli children hugging Michael's legs. Was she right to entrust their care to her brother? She pictured him fighting the blaze.

Michael roughed Maggie's hair and squeezed the twins. "We will be. Don't worry about us."

Beth gathered her coat and satchel and turned to add a "goodbye" and "wish me luck" but couldn't put two sensible words together as four orphans stared back at her, two of them flesh and blood. "I'll be fine," she added, trying to be brave. She reached for the doorknob, and Michael held it open.

"Lock the door behind me," she said.

"Keep to business," he said.

"Lock it," she repeated.

44

"Don't forget to cry," Maggie called out as Beth waved goodbye and turned in the direction of Chicago Savings and Loan.

* * * * *

"Is Mr. Sands available?" Beth stared at the familiar face sitting behind the secretary's desk. "Annie Parker?" Would her childhood friend recognize her? Beth should have called her Miss Parker. Her hands flinched.

Keep to business.

Sands' two-story office was simple and plain, yet terrifying. Brick walls on two sides without even a window to cheer it.

"Beth...how are you?" Annie rose and lost her footing, knocking over a box of pencils. Pencils rolled off the edge of her desk and onto the floor.

"Fine." Beth bent down to collect the pencils on the floor and collected her thoughts too. "And you?"

"Fine. I'm fine," Annie said.

"And you work for Mr. Sands?" What kind of question is that? Of course, she worked for him.

Annie dropped the last pencil back in the box. "Have a seat. I'll let Mr. Sands know you are here." Apparently, Annie was a business-minded person. She knocked on the windowless door, then opened it enough to slip in. Beth tried to get a glimpse of the man who held her future in his hands. Strained to listen. Was he a big man? Was he an old man? Would he be terrifying or sympathetic?

"Miss Yates is here to see you, sir." Annie's voice was muffled. "No, I don't have her on your schedule, but..."

Beth straightened and decided that Maggie's suggestion was definitely out of the question. Twenty-three-year-old women don't cry.

"Good day, Miss Yates," Sands offered as she entered an office lined with stacks of paper that nearly covered every inch of his desk.

Beth took a seat and tucked her hands between her legs, hoping Sands hadn't seen them shaking. "Thank you for seeing me today, sir. I know you are a very busy man." He wasn't as scary as she thought he would be. Looked like her grandfather might've looked. Plump, red-cheeked, and bushy brows with spectacles atop his nose, like old Saint Nick.

"Are you prepared to make a payment today, Miss Yates?"

He is a businessman. She cleared her throat. "Sir, we have a proposal to make, if you would—"

"A proposal?" He paused, leaned forward, and looked over top his round-rimmed glasses.

The silence itself killed her resolve. "Y…yes. My brother and I intend to find jobs and sell the house. If you will just give us a little more time, I'm sure we can bring our account current." They didn't come out as she'd rehearsed, but the words were out.

Mr. Sands leaned back in his chair, arms behind his head. "I see." He reached down and opened a drawer, pulled out a cigar, and snipped the end, then struck a match but didn't light his cigar. A thin line of smoke trailed upward. The flame snapped and crackled. She stared at the tiny flame.

"Miss Yates, you are three months behind on your mortgage. This is a financial institution, not a charity."

She watched the flame grow closer to his fingers. Three months behind? Father never…how could they be three months behind? Beth held her breath as the flame threatened his skin.

He finally snuffed the match before the flame reached his fingers. "What if I let every person down on their luck suggest a proposal?"

She let out her breath and looked up at him, her mind grabbing at the words jumbled in her head. Down on their luck? Is that what he called their situation? Heat rose up her neck then to her cheeks. Her hands clutched the coarse fabric of her skirt tighter. She had to hold her tongue.

His brows rose. "How would I explain this plan to my investors, Miss Yates?"

"Sir, all we need is a little more time," Beth said as she stood, her voice trembling.

"Miss Yates, you don't have a job, and you can't pay your mortgage. Your home will have to be sold." Sands stared at her and then her suit for a moment and added, "And even after the sale of your home, you will still owe a rather large sum."

What? Had she read the notice incorrectly? "Mr. Sands, surely, our home is worth more than we owe."

"Times are hard. Your father came to me for money on numerous occasions…just to keep those dear children clothed and fed."

"He did?" She couldn't do the calculations in her head. She needed Michael's sharp mind. "Father never mentioned it."

"Parents rarely share their financial hardships. I'm sure they didn't want you to worry. A lot of folks moving out. This area isn't as desirable as it once was."

"Exactly." She swallowed. "How much do we owe?" Beth took a deep breath and braced herself.

Sands swung around in his chair and opened a drawer behind his desk. More papers jammed into files. He lifted a file then slid the drawer close, shaking the floor beneath her feet. After thumbing through the sheets of papers, he scribbled various numbers on notepaper. Sands replaced the file and closed the drawer, giving the floor another shake.

He turned around and folded his large mushroom-like hands together on the top of his desk. "Sit, please."

"I'd rather stand. Thank you, sir."

"Miss Yates, including principle, interest, and past dues…" He read off the total then leaned back in his chair as she fell back into the seat. She knew immediately what fate awaited her. There's no possible way she could earn enough to keep the house from foreclosure and pay the balance. "Your home will be sold, Miss Yates."

Deciding Maggie's suggestion was absolutely necessary, she added, "We have no place to go." She forced out the first sob and the rest came voluntarily, much too voluntarily.

Sands pulled out a pressed handkerchief from his suit pocket and handed it to her. "Do you currently have a job?"

Beth shook her head and took the handkerchief to blow her nose.

"And your brother?"

She shook her head and blew her nose again.

"I see." He dawned an idea, tapped his temple with his index finger, and then began looking through piles of paperwork. "I am aware of a position that would be suitable to your particular situation."

Beth acknowledged his statement with a forced smile. Maybe he had a heart after all. He wrote down the name and address on a piece of paper and slid it across the desk.

"Cook?" she said. As she read the address, she noted his error and squeezed out a tiny smile. He wrote Hide Park instead of Hyde Park.

"Jobs are hard to find these days. You owe a debt you cannot pay. You don't want your brother working at the sausage factory, now do you?"

"No, of course not." *Hyde Park.* Was she dreaming? Evidence of her relief escaped. She was desperate. Now, lo and behold, someone offered her a job in the most illustrious area in Chicago. Her future seemed brighter at that very moment. After all the terrible things that had happened, a glimmer of hope.

"You and your family will have a place to live…and work. The establishment needs a cook and housekeeper. I have an interesting relationship with the manager. Work until your debt is paid. After that, you'll be free to go." He stood with hand outstretched, ready to shake on it and conclude the meeting.

Her stomach churned with excitement. She rose with hand extended. "All right, I'll do it."

He took her hand in a swift swoop. "You have until the end of the week to move, Miss Yates. I will have a man pick you up at six o'clock tomorrow morning to start work."

She nodded and smiled. Her stomach churned again. She blamed it on her nerves and lack of sleep. She had a job in Hyde Park.

And right now, that's all that mattered.

Chapter Five

Eli Sands motioned his new secretary, Annie Parker, inside his office. "What is it?" He grunted.

She had to stop interrupting him with petty questions. She had to stop wearing such ridiculous attire.

"A Mr. Donovan to see you, sir. Says he has an appointment, but I don't have him on your schedule." Annie apologized.

Eli checked the time. He had many unscheduled visitors. "Thank you, Miss Parker. I suppose I could see him now. Show him in," he said before she closed the door.

Annie ushered Donovan into his office. Eli didn't stand or welcome him but held up a hand to silence him and waited for the door to close completely.

He pulled his glasses down to the tip of his nose and looked over the top rim. He whispered low. "I've got another job for you."

"As interesting as the last, I hope." Donovan slumped into the seat with one leg draped over the arm of the chair.

Eli leaned back and pushed his chair far enough from his desk to rest his two short legs on top, one over the other. "It involves a particular family, one you might know."

Donovan dawned a sinister smile. "Ah, I do know the one."

Eli let his legs fall to the floor with a thud, sat up straight, and reached for his cigar and a piece of paper. He scribbled out instructions and slid it across his desk. "Now, get out of here. And next time, use the back stairs."

Donovan grabbed his hat and the piece of paper without reading it. "See ya 'round." He closed the door, muttered something to Annie, and then slammed the outer door.

Eli snipped the end of his cigar. Should he be celebrating this soon? He threw back his head. *Why not?* The Yates' house was his, and he'd got the girl in the deal. Everything was falling into place. It had taken ten long years, but he had finally done it, the last piece of the puzzle. He struck the match, lit the cigar, and leaned back in his chair.

Eleanor will be so proud.

"Miss Parker?" he called out suddenly, as if an idea had recently occurred to him.

Annie opened the door to his office with a pen and paper in hand. "Yes, Mr. Sands?"

"Cancel my appointments for today. I will be at home with my wife should anything urgent arise." He gathered several files and slipped them into his case. "And type up these notices. You may go home when you are finished." He held out the files.

* * * * *

Annie Parker thumbed through Sands' files and placed another sheet of paper in the typewriter. Her lips pursed, and she shook her head. *Eli Sands, you are a fake—a phony.* Sands' little beady eyes matched his tiny heart to perfection, and he smiled too much. She'd like to wipe that evil smile right off his big flat face—Annie shrugged—though that wouldn't bode well for job security.

The typewriter jammed. She grunted and ripped the paper out, crumpled it up, and threw it in the wastebasket to start over. She noticed the ink on her hands and skirt and frowned. Her ivory linen skirt laced with silver thread, pains-takingly hand-stitched, ruined. She'd worked on that leaf design for over a month.

She plunked her sore fingers across the keys with repe-tition. It was the same past due notice as usual. With every strike, she ruined someone's life forever, just like she'd ruined the Millers' life. She'd never forgive herself for that. And with Mrs. Miller expecting a baby any day. The Hanovers. The Carters. And now, the Yates family.

Her fingers stilled, and her gaze fell to the rug near the doorway. The powdery residue from falling mortar remained from Mr. Carter's slamming the door. She could hear her mother's words screaming in her head, *Eli Sands is a snake.* Annie defended him in the beginning but not anymore. She swung around in her chair, grabbed a stack of envelopes, and then returned to her typing. "How could you be so cruel, Mr. Sands?" Elizabeth Yates? Hasn't she been through enough already?

The typewriter jammed again. She pulled the paper free, crumpled it, and tossed it to the wastebasket but missed it completely.

* * * * *

Eli opened his wife's bedroom door, noticing the fact that she'd redecorated again. Not very different in color, but the added gold filigree threatened a headache.

"You're home early, Elias," Eleanor said and tried to sit up in bed. "Quiet day at the office?"

He nodded and turned to the nurse. "Sofia, you can go. I will be home for the rest of the evening."

"Yes, sir. Good night, ma'am." Sofia curtsied, gathered her belongings quickly, and closed the door behind her.

"Do you like it?" She raised a weary hand to circle the room. "I grew tired of the drab. The change in color was exactly what I needed."

He nodded his approval but saw very little difference. "You've outdone yourself."

"You know me, and I did it all myself." She laughed, softer and weaker than she once did. "Well, I might have had a little help." She teased as he helped her to a sitting position.

"How are you feeling today, my dear? You've got some of your color back." Eli fussed with the new billowy covers to sit beside her.

She offered a brief synopsis of her day, and he listened intently. "Oh, and Doctor Manning stopped by. He seemed pleased with my progress. I didn't hurt as much today."

His smile widened. *The medicine is working.* He leaned down, smoothed her hair off her face, and placed a kiss on her forehead, then her cheek. "I'm glad you are feeling better. Rest now. I'll have the kitchen prepare your favorite." After her afternoon dosage, he knew she'd sleep for several hours. Eleanor needed to. She had suffered for too long, bedridden long enough. Eleanor didn't know about the new treatment or the cost of it. Doctor Manning hadn't suspected anything.

Once this land project was finished and the money started to roll in, he'd be able to ease her suffering for the rest of her life. He massaged her weak hand and lifted it to his lips. "Rest now, dear Eleanor."

Eleanor gave a sleepy smile in return. "I am rather tired."

Chapter Six

A knock hurried Beth to the door. "You're early," she said.

Mr. Sands had said a man would arrive, but this wasn't the man she expected. His height matched the doorframe.

"I'll be ready in a few minutes. Please have a seat." She motioned to the front room, but he didn't move.

Michael grunted as he came down the stairs, his early morning hair sticking straight out to one side but rallied when he saw the visitor. "I'm Michael." He offered his hand in greeting, but the stranger refused.

Beth hurried into the kitchen, set breakfast on the table, and left a list of chores with instructions on the counter. "Michael," she called out, "I've left instructions on the table here—"

"That man has a gun," Michael suddenly whispered in her ear as if it were something she'd neglected to mention.

She jumped. "You scared me to—"

"He has a gun." His hands were on her shoulders now.

"All right, keep your voice down. It's probably for protection."

Michael cocked his head in disbelief. "Does he look like he needs protection to you?" Michael voiced louder.

"Shhh." No, he didn't. She motioned to quiet him again. "It will be all right," she whispered. "A lot of men carry guns—"

"Father didn't."

She stood in silence. Perhaps her employer was an important person, one in need of protection. Mr. Sands hadn't elaborated. She bit her lip and winced at the scowl on Michael's face. "It will be fine. I promise. This home is in a fine neighborhood. Perfectly safe. I'll be home sometime this afternoon, I think. Maybe this evening." She put her hand on his arm to calm him.

"There's a mean man in the living room." Maggie suddenly appeared in the kitchen, wearing only her undergarment, out of breath and pointing.

"Shhh." Beth motioned Maggie to her. "He's here to escort me to my new job."

Maggie came closer and whispered, "He's got purple hands...and I think he's a predi...tator. I can see it in his eyes."

Beth gave Michael a "don't patronize her" look. "He's a guest in our home, Maggie. Don't be rude. And for heaven's sake, go put some clothes on."

* * * * *

Michael helped her into the man's carriage since the escort made no effort to be a gentleman. Maggie stood at the top of the stairs in her nightgown, mouthing words that couldn't be found in a dictionary. Beth waved goodbye and smiled at Michael with confidence before facing her escort.

The man's eyes narrowed. Beth hoped a smile would suddenly appear on his face, but he only stiffened. From a side-glance, his eyes seemed to darken, his stare ice cold. She pulled her coat tighter around her neck and put as much distance between this cold, stiff stranger as possible.

You can do this. You have to, she reminded herself.

She straightened as they passed a notorious street sign, one she'd heard of but had never seen. A strange feeling came over her as her stomach knotted. She leaned over the carriage wall and stared at the row of wood and brick buildings lined up like mismatched cracker tins. This wasn't the Hyde Park she'd heard about her entire life. She tried to swallow several times and couldn't, not with the lump in her throat. No castle-like estates, no lush green lawns. "Sir, I don't think—"

He pulled the horses to a skid, and the sad creatures obeyed without ceremony. He nodded toward the building at her side. With some uncertainty, she stepped out of the carriage and stared at the large four-story brick building before her. He was already at the door, motioning for her to hurry. With one hand, she smoothed her coat, tucking a stubborn strand of hair behind her ear with the other. That's when she saw it. Large letters painted red as cherries above the doorway. "Hide Park." But Mr. Sands specifically said Hyde Park. She consulted her memory and couldn't take her eyes off the "I" in the word "Hide." It was worn and chipped. Had she been deceived, or was this the result of her ignorance?

Her first few steps were heavy and the climb to the top of the stairs laborious as she felt her expectations lower. He opened the door without knocking and hung his hat and coat on a wall hook.

She scanned the room. There was a fireplace on the farthest wall, but it didn't have a fire in it. The room was dark red, almost brown, with cushioned chairs and several small round tables scattered here and there. Burnt cigarette butts and empty liquor bottles lay in piles on the floor. At least the seat cushions coordinated in some fashion with the heavy drapes that pushed out the morning sun. Could she live here? Could Michael and Maggie live here?

She loosened her hat and hung it on a hook as her escort disappeared through a door on the left. The kitchen, she supposed. "She's here," Beth heard him say.

"Finally," a woman's hoarse voice replied.

Beth hung her coat and respectfully pushed through the kitchen door that was still swinging on its hinge. "I'm Kitty, and you already know Donovan. You'll meet the rest of the gang shortly. Get an apron. They'll be down in an hour."

So, her new employer was Kitty. Beth stared at the ceiling. The name alone made it difficult to swallow. She scanned the kitchen and found an apron hanging beside a mop and a broom.

"You can manage breakfast for twenty-five?" The question held a demand. Kitty was an older woman, dressed in a purple and black dress that offered too much cleavage, with a closed fan dangling from her wrist.

Beth nodded and watched Kitty and Donovan leave the kitchen. She opened several drawers, familiarizing herself with the layout. A quick walk through the pantry told her she had everything she needed. She stoked the fire in the stove, reached to open the icebox for the eggs, and caught a glimpse of Kitty and Donovan at the end of the hall. She hugged the fragile eggs, pulled herself back against the wall, almost invisible, and strained to listen. Only whispers. She frowned.

A noise in the hall made her jump. *Splat.* She gasped and stared at the slimy egg on the floor. She checked the kitchen door, moved the small crate of eggs to one hip, and bent down to collect the cracked goop with her apron. Never did she take an eye off the kitchen door.

The loss of one egg was a pity.

The loss of her job? Disastrous.

* * * * *

"There," Beth said, wiping her hands on her apron as her gaze moved to the clock on the wall. One hour. On the nose. She scanned the long kitchen table for the second time, leaned back against the kitchen counter as a girl, much younger than herself, wandered in and collapsed onto the bench, apparently not quite awake yet. Then a second young girl walked in. And a third. Each one as pathetic as the last. Beth said nothing but mentally counted. Twenty-five girls, none older than herself.

"May I please have some milk?" The girl had a soft sweet voice.

"Mallory, don't be so polite, and nobody wants to hear your sob story again either," an older girl snapped.

Mallory hung her head low and didn't respond. Beth hurried to pour the girl milk when an awkward silence came over the room, a silence so cruel. Minutes passed, and still no one uttered a word. Beth busied herself with filling plates and taking dirty dishes.

"This is pretty good," a girl dressed in a bright yellow lace gown finally broke the silence. "Not like that mud Dobbs used to make."

Beth stood a bit taller at that moment. No one had ever complimented her cooking before.

"Hey, where is Dobbs?" a girl at the end of the table asked.

"He's gone," Kitty announced as she entered into the kitchen like a gust of wind, and all the girls sat straighter and focused on their plates. "He had a little accident yesterday."

The girls looked up from their plates but said nothing. Mallory slumped and shoveled eggs around in the dish. Kitty snapped the girl's back with her closed fan. "Sit up, girl."

Mallory tensed, and her eyes threatened tears.

"Betsy, here," Kitty extended a hand of introduction, "is our new cook."

"It's Beth," Beth said nervously. "Beth Yat—"

"No last names. We've no need for 'em here," Kitty interrupted. "You're just plain Betsy."

Kitty yanked Mallory to her feet and led her into another room. "I've had just about enough of your shenanigans."

Beth froze, then turned around to face the kitchen window. "Father doesn't like nicknames," she mouthed the words. *Didn't...like nicknames.* He never liked the name Beth. He would have despised Betsy for sure. Her stomach churned. She clutched her hands together and pushed a fist into her stomach to hide the ache.

Outside, the early morning sun was up but hidden behind the clouds. Birds didn't sing, and children didn't play about in the streets.

Her hands trembled, and she tensed as she listened to the whispered conversations down the hall. Hearing several screams in the background, she cringed. This wasn't a private house of someone great and important.

This wasn't the magnificent Hyde Park. It was Hide Park, a brothel.

* * * * *

Michael opened the door as Beth trudged up the front steps to the house. She couldn't look him in the eye. He would know, or he would want to know. And he mustn't ever know that she worked at a brothel.

He closed the door as she slowly unbuttoned her coat. "Well," he said as he took her coat, "what was it like?"

If only she could lie down. "What?" Forget that this day every happened.

"Hyde Park. What was it like?"

You mean Hide Park, she wanted to say. "Fine."

"Was it—"

She stopped him with her hand. *Please. No more questions.* "I'm tired." She looked into his eyes, lowered her hand,

and took to the stairs. Her fingers gripped the rail and with each step, she dug her nails deep into its wood.

The front door burst open. Beth heard tiny footsteps. "Maggie, where have you been?" Michael demanded in a forced hush. "You can't run off like that."

"Beth! You're home."

"Shhh." Michael silenced her.

Beth heard Maggie's muffled cry but continued to her room without glancing back.

"Let her be," Michael said. The calm in his voice must have soothed Maggie.

Beth rolled her stiff shoulders and cleared the hallway of orphaned toys. She looked in on Cece and Eldon, who entertained themselves in a now-empty bedroom. Then she climbed a second set of stairs to the attic and threw herself across the bed. After a few minutes had passed, she turned onto her back and rubbed her eyes and her temples simultaneously. *What have I done?* She pulled her mother's red rose quilt from the end of the bed. She longed to feel safe.

She could work at Hide Park—what other choice did she have? But live there? The thought of Michael and Maggie living in a place like that made her sick. Surely there had to be another way. Mr. Sands could have the house. People didn't go to prison for debt anymore.

She sat up, putting her feet flat on the floor. She'd find a small inexpensive room for rent. It had to be in a safe neighborhood, for sure. They'd sell everything. She'd pay Eli Sands back, every last penny.

* * * * *

Ethan looked around the supper table, amazed at how familiar friends make a man realize what he's been missing.

To visit the Holt family on his way back to the Daly Ranch didn't seem like work. It was like being home.

Little Alice Holt jumped onto his lap, shaking his thoughts. She's a sweet little one, always had been. "Will you marry me, Ethan? I'm super smart, and I'm taller now." The little girl's eyes sparkled as she stared up at him.

"Alice Sue Holt." Mr. Amos Holt narrowed his eyes at the girl.

Shock and embarrassment reddened Mrs. Holt's already pink cheeks. The rest of the Holt family looked at each other around the dinner table, clearly shocked too. Ethan loved that about this family. Whatever they did, they did together.

"I'll wait for you." Alice smiled as she gathered Ethan's face in her tiny hands.

You'll be waiting a long time. He chuckled as he adjusted the six-year-old onto his knee. "Alice, you'll always be my favorite gal."

She threw her arms around his neck and squeezed. "So, you will marry me?" she confirmed.

Once Holt got to laughing, his wife and their six older children joined in. Ethan pulled Alice's face close and placed a kiss on her forehead before setting her down to finish his pork chop. "Mrs. Holt, no one makes pork chops like you do."

She hid her giggle with the back of her hand.

He licked his fingers and thumb to clean the last bit off. Traveling sure had its advantages, especially when it gave him the opportunity to visit old friends. Good people, good food. The pleasure outweighed everything else at that moment. "Thanks for a delicious meal."

She nodded and began to clear the table. Ethan turned to Holt. "How goes the breeding of these Swedish Warmbloods I've heard so much about?"

"Well, you will see for yourself in the morning. Your Mr. Daly will be surprised, I think."

"Oh, I'm not here at Mr. Daly's bidding, not this time. It's Mrs. Daly who's interested."

Holt smirked. "Well then, whatever the fine lady wants." His thick fist hit the table the moment his laughter hit Ethan's ears.

Mrs. Holt brought two cups of coffee to the table and pushed a large jar of honey in Ethan's direction.

"Thank you, Elsa." Holt downed his coffee. "What're your folks up to these days, Ethan? Still herding?" He pushed his chair out from the table, crossing his legs and long arms.

"Still herding," Ethan said as he stirred a large spoonful of honey into his cup. "They'll be cattle ranchers until the good Lord sees them home." The sound of his mama's words rang in his ears and brought a smile to his face. He lifted his cup to his mouth, swished its sweetness around, and swallowed. "You remember my brother Peter?"

Holt nodded, and Ethan continued, "Pete up and married a second McIntyre girl." A hint of doubt rumbled in his voice.

"Well, I'll be. You hear that, Elsa? Pete married another one of them McIntyre girls." Holt shook his head. "Two times the charm."

His words stung with truth. Peter was happier now.

"He and Ellie bought the adjoining acreage north of the ranch."

"And what about you? You still pining for that horse ranch of yours?"

Ethan took another drink, ignoring the renewed pressure of living up to his own words. "Until the day I die."

"And...any wedding bells in your future, son?" He winked in his wife's direction. "How about the other McIntyre girl?"

"Ah. Never." Ethan smiled, quickly tossed the remaining coffee down his throat. His empty cup hit the wooden table as several younger Holt children darted into the kitchen, weaving in and around the chairs and table, a welcome diversion from a subject he'd rather avoid altogether.

* * * * *

"Beth, look." Michael folded the newspaper in half and pointed to a large advertisement titled, "The Grandest Accommodations in the West." They misspelled the word "accommodations." She ignored the error and continued to read as Michael leaned back on the hind legs of a kitchen chair.

"Well, what do you think?" he asked.

"What do I think?" She cocked her head. "It's Montana, Michael. That's what I think."

"But look here." He leaned in, letting the front legs hit the floor with a thud and pointed out several important details. "Position includes lodging and meals." He threw his hands into the air as if he'd performed a magic trick.

"It's Montana." She raised both eyebrows.

"You said you wanted a different job. You said we couldn't live at Miss Kathryn's." She was happy not to have mentioned Miss Kathryn's real name but sad that she'd said too much.

I wish I'd never mentioned it now. "I know what I said. I'll find another job. There has to be something else out there." Beth let the newspaper fall to her lap into a crumpled mess.

"But we only have a few more days." Michael had to remind her. "There's always the sausage factory."

True and terrifying, she thought as she smoothed out the newspaper to read the advertisement a second time. "Grandest Accommodations in the West. Set in the beautiful

Bitterroot Valley. The Ravalli Hotel seeks to employ up to twenty young women in the newly appointed and luxurious dining room. Position includes training, uniform, lodging, and meals. For information, write to the undersigned. Thomas C. Riley, Manager of Operations."

She thumbed over the advertisement that displayed a large photograph of the hotel surrounded by tall evergreens. She pictured fine linens, shining silverware, and sparkling crystal. Fresh flowers on every table. Walls lined with colored paper and floors covered with luxurious carpet. There had to be numerous fireplaces. From the description in the newspaper, the owner spared no expense. "Owned by Mr. Marcus Daly," it read.

Beth leaned back in her chair and looked at Michael. "Montana?"

"Montana," he declared and pushed himself to his feet. "I'll get a pen and paper."

* * * * *

Eli Sands sat at his desk, thumbing through the owner's booklet for the new telephone in front of him. He pulled his spectacles down on his nose, hoping his eyes would refocus on the small print. "These newfangled contraptions," he muttered, turning the page. Picking up the handset from its golden base, he unwound the shoelace cord. Even his secretary had been able to figure out how to use the thing. Young people seem more agile with these modern conveniences.

The office doorknob turned, and the door cracked. He dropped the booklet into a drawer quickly, pushed his spectacles up his nose, and slid the telephone to its proper place.

"I'm sorry, Mr. Sands. I did knock," Annie apologized as she came in, her voice short. "I have, um, something of a somewhat personal nature I need to take care of this afternoon. It is of some urgency."

"If you must, Miss Parker. I am going home soon anyway. My wife is ill, as you know."

She nodded without compassion, which irked him.

"Go." He motioned her away. She slipped out and closed the door. Eli glanced at the telephone sitting on his desk and decided to leave it for another day. He couldn't get the confounded thing to work anyhow. With his briefcase in hand and several drawings rolled under his arm, he locked the door to his office and headed home.

"Home," he ordered his driver. The carriage lurched and rattled along the cobbled streets. Eli hugged his case and closed his eyes. He had foreclosed on every property from State Street to East Chicago Avenue with very little inconvenience to himself. Times were tough, and people fell behind easily. Only the Yates' orphanage remained out of reach.

Until now.

He adjusted his back and let his head rest against the plush velvet of his carriage. He didn't care about the size or condition of the Yates' building or its gothic adornments. It would be coming down. All that mattered was the location. That puny piece of land was the gateway to his lifelong dream and the last piece to the puzzle. He slowly smiled at the day's success and rubbed the long wrinkles across his forehead. After his meeting with Kitty and Donovan this morning, success was within his grasp.

Once the foreclosure was complete, his plan would move forward rather quickly. He looked at his watch. Two o'clock. A slow smile grew on his face. It had taken him years, but he, Elias E. Sands, had done it, done what people said he'd never do.

He'd finally made it to the top.

Chapter Seven

Beth wiped down the wooden block table and slid the flour and sugar canisters back against the wall. She had completed her morning duties with great haste and efficiency, hoping to escape the reality of working in a brothel as soon as possible. After tomorrow, it wouldn't matter. All this would be behind her. And with the Petrachelli children in their new home, she could finally do it. She could quit.

Wringing the dishrag in her hands, she leaned on the counter. She didn't have another job yet. But if nothing else, there was always the job in Montana.

She shuddered at the thought of her family living and working in this place. The men were vulgar, disgusting, and reeked of liquor. The women were thin and sickly, loud and crass. The whole place smelled like cheap perfume. Only in the kitchen could she escape.

Kitty rushed into the kitchen. "Room 17 needs cleaned up," She said, pointing toward the back stairs.

"It's two o'clock, ma'am. I was just leaving for the day." Beth swallowed and tried to appear confident. Kitty's girls didn't get dinner.

"You'll be done when I say you're done." Kitty swung her arm into the air with a snap. Kitty pushed her toward the stairs. "Git. Room 17."

For three days, Beth managed to keep to the kitchen after she discovered the awful truth about Hide Park. She stared at Kitty and decided the name, Kitty, fit her perfectly, for her nose was as flat as an alley cat's. Kitty yanked the mop and bucket from behind the door and shoved them into her arms when she didn't obey the order. "You'll learn to do what I say, when I say it, or I'll take it out of your pay, missy."

Beth nodded. "Yes, ma'am."

Beth lifted the mop and heavy bucket full of soapy water one stair at a time. *Room 17.* Heaven forbid that she forget the room number. She pulled the bucket down the hall, not caring at all that the soapy water splashed onto the floor and splattered on the wall. She bit her lip as she neared. A foul stench hit her nose as she pushed the door open. Vomit splattered across the floor. A small iron bed sat against the wall in the corner with white sheets and dark blue blankets hanging over the edge of the footboard to the floor in disarray. A woman's nightgown, or what there was of it, lay in a heap on the floor. A bottle of whiskey and two half empty glasses sat on the table in the other corner.

Beth covered her nose and mouth with one hand while trying to manage the mop single-handed with the other. *Good enough.* She pushed the bucket and mop into the hall, pulled the blankets and sheets over the footboard, and fluffed them to a smooth landing across the bed. If she stayed any longer, she was going to be sick.

"Well, well, well. What have we here?" a husky voice echoed behind her.

All the hairs on the back of her neck rose. *Donovan.*

She turned, lowered her head, and moved toward the door. "I've finished making the bed and cleaning up. I'll be going home now." She straightened and squared her shoulders, but he didn't move. She swallowed hard and took a step, but his hand was there to stop her. His "purple hand," as Maggie described. It was black and blue, not purple. It was burned. For a moment, the memory of that snowy night passed through her mind. Donovan's Adam's apple bobbed and drew her attention.

She sidestepped. He did too, his lingering stare making her insides shrink. "Please?" she choked out in a whisper. Her eyes began to well up. She tried to squeeze through what little opening there was between him and the door, but he swayed back and forth, blocking her every move. Her hands began to shake. "Someone, help me," she cried, but no one came. "Please. Let me go." Her voice was weak.

He stepped into the room, and she backed away, one backward step after another until she hit the table, and one of the chairs tumbled to the floor. He slowly closed the door behind him and flipped the lock. The sound of the metal lock pushing through the wood ignited a determination she'd never known before. Her hands searched frantically for the bottle of whiskey on the table and knocked over the glasses instead, giving her plan improper notice. Donovan came closer. She grabbed the bottle, turned it upside down, and held it up in the air, letting liquor run down her hand then her arm.

He let out a rooster-like chuckle.

"If you touch me, I'll"—she forced a scowl on her face to show on the outside what she lacked on the inside, but his hand came over her mouth before she could react.

"You'll what? Scream?"

She couldn't breathe. His hands smelled of grease and old leather. She could taste it. She tried to push him away but hadn't the strength. His eyes never left hers, even as he lifted the bottle of whiskey from her grasp and set it on the table. A cry from the depths came up and escaped her lips as he pushed her body to the wall and yanked the front of her blouse until the buttons popped off. She turned her face and closed her eyes. Each button hit the floor, singly, and his warm breath stuck to her skin.

It was now or never. She forced out a heavy sigh and shot her knee into his groin as hard as she could, paralyzing him and rendering him speechless. She grabbed the bottle from the table and struck him alongside of the head.

She froze and stared at the unbroken bottle in her hand as he slumped to the floor. It slipped from her hands, shattering into a thousand pieces. She frantically fumbled the lock until it came free. She hurried down the back steps, slipping on several, nearly losing her footing.

She yanked at her long dark coat hanging on the wall, and it ripped at the collar. She pushed through the back door, forcing it to slam into the railing. She heard it close and open again but didn't look back. The screeching sound of the back door hinges confirmed she was not alone in the alley.

"You get back here, you little whore!" Kitty screamed, "You are nothing, no good to anyone now, damaged goods! You hear me?"

Beth hastened her stride. Her heavy breathing pounded inside her head. She turned the corner and ran into someone carrying a basket full of market goods. Vegetables and bread loaves flew into the air. Cursing resounded in her ears as she ran. She ducked into an alley, back against the cold brick, wanting to silence her breathing.

Every few seconds, she peeked around the corner to see if Donovan or Kitty had come after her. Her blouse hung open, and her skirt clung to her body, drenched in whiskey. A sob escaped, and her fingers shook as she tried to push a remaining button through an eyelet on her blouse. She wiped her face with her sleeve, made sure the street was clear, and made herself a promise she'd never break.

She'd never trust men, never let a man touch her, never even look one in the eye. Never.

Never.

* * * * *

Beth snuck through the back door of her house, listening. It appeared that Michael and Maggie were gone. "Hello?" No one answered when she called out. They mustn't see her like this. A distant pounding came from the alley like someone knocking several houses down. She leaned over the sink and let the cool water run through her fingers. With a bar of soap, she lathered it thick and scrubbed the liquor from her skin, wishing the removal of the memory was as easy.

A knock at the front door made her jump. She shut the water off and waited. Her muscles tensed. *They've found me.*

Another knock.

Beth hesitated, frantically turned toward the back door, her only means of escape. Then it was quiet. She tiptoed across the kitchen floor and put her ear into the hall. She took a step closer. The floor creaked beneath her and she paused.

"Elizabeth, it's Annie...Annie Parker." The voice sounded muffled behind the thick mahogany door.

Beth crept closer.

"Elizabeth, I know you are in there. Please."

The plea in Annie's voice made Beth reach for the doorknob. Her hand trembled on the knob, announcing her.

"I knew you were home."

Beth sighed and then forced a smile as she turned the knob, opening the door enough to make sure Annie was alone.

"I must speak to you," Annie said as she glanced over her shoulder.

"I, um…" Beth stuttered and searched for an excuse to avoid company. "I am sick…ill. Might even be contagi—"

"Nonsense. Please, let me in." Annie put her foot between the door and the frame. "Mr. Sands has done something. I have to explain."

"Just give me a moment to…"—Beth pulled the top of her blouse closed and cleared her throat. "…to get a robe." She let the door swing open as she turned and ran up the stairs, taking two at a time. Like Michael always did. "Lock the door. I won't be long." Beth heard the door close and hurried to her room. She reached for her robe when she caught her reflection in the mirror. Her fingers traced the fabric where six or seven tiny buttons had been, the lace still soaked in liquor. She removed her blouse and skirt. The articles were poison to her now. She searched her closet for something, anything, that she hadn't worn to *that place.*

Pulling her best dress from the wardrobe, Beth shimmied it on, hiding the damaged person behind its simple lace and plain pleats. As she came down the stairs, the sound of clanging dishes came from the kitchen. She slowed. Annie wasn't in the front room. A hesitant glance into the kitchen revealed Annie at the stove, lifting a kettle of hot water.

"I hope you don't mind." It was a statement, but it held a question.

"No. No, of course not." The sound of voices made them both look toward the back door. A distant pounding continued.

"It's the least I can do," Annie said.

Sitting at the kitchen table, Beth sipped her tea. Its warmth, not to mention its strength, cleared her head.

"Elizabeth, for what I am about to tell you…you mustn't hate me. Please, promise me you won't hate me."

Annie's hazel eyes matched the ribbon at her neckline to perfection. Annie had always made her own clothes in school, probably still did. She looked so sophisticated now. Beth nodded and leaned in, feeling dirty and poor next to Annie's finer attire.

"Mr. Sands said that a man contacted him months ago about buying the orphanage, something about the man's willingness to pay a rather large sum, some kind of business venture or something." Annie named the price.

Shocked and somewhat relieved at the price, Beth held her breath. More than enough to pay off their debt. "That is wonderful."

"There's more." Annie squeezed Beth's hand. "Mr. Sands refused to let him buy it, said that it would ruin his plans." Annie shook her head. "And then, a Miss Kathryn came by the office yesterday morning," she added, but didn't finish her sentence.

Beth gave an understanding nod. "Yes. I work for, or should I say worked for Kitty…Miss Kathryn."

"Well, then you must know Mr. Donovan?"

Beth's eyes narrowed, trying hard to hide the connection. "Yes." In more ways than she cared to admit. Until this moment, she'd not considered Donovan's fate. Had she killed him? Maybe that is why he didn't come after her. Would the police come for her?

"I don't know all the details, but today, Donovan and Kathryn both came to see Mr. Sands, and your name came up in the conversation…often."

Beth held her breath. "What?" Confusion tried to answer the question. "Why?"

Annie nervously cleared her throat and spoke each word with perfect clarity, "Mr. Sands said you were pretty enough to make him a killing. He plans to…" Annie took a deep breath, "…ruin you."

Beth slumped in her chair, and her cup hit the table with a crash. She didn't have the heart to tell Annie she was too late. "Annie, do you know anything about my father borrowing money from Mr. Sands?"

"I don't know any of Mr. Sands' dealings before I came to work for him, but I did chance a peek into the files once. He'd dropped his keys, you see." She offered a cunning smile. "I couldn't even find the deed to the orphanage." A puzzled look crossed her face. "Just a lot of building drawings and maps." She gripped Beth's hand. "I know that it's none of my business, but, Beth, the deed wasn't there, and it should've been." A sudden noise in the street startled them both.

"I have to go." Annie scooted her chair out and stood, tears starting to fill her eyes. She emptied money from her satchel onto the table. "Take it. You mustn't go back to that place. Something awful might happen."

* * * * *

Beth dug through the pile of papers sitting on Father's desk and rustled files in his desk drawer. The pounding noise in the alley seemed closer. Louder.

She pushed and pulled papers in desperate search of a train schedule. Several books and small piles of paper fell to the floor, but she ignored them. *Found it.* She grabbed it up and unfolded the long, narrow pamphlet. Tapping her fingers on the desk, she memorized the departures.

A knock at the front door startled her. She panicked and hid behind the desk, her heavy breathing the only sound. She peered over Father's desk. Another knock sent her to the floor.

"Beth!"

She heard a familiar voice. *Michael?* She tiptoed to the front room window and peeked through the thin crack in the curtains, then slid the lock and opened the door. "Where have you been?" Her eyes scanned the street before shutting the door and securing the lock.

"Where have I been? I went to find you." Beth saw him grinding his teeth behind the formed smile. He looked down at Maggie, who tried to kick off her shoes.

"He's mean." Her left shoe rebelled, and Beth bent down to help.

"Keep your shoes on for now." She glanced at Michael. His foot tapped the floor nervously. She shot him a questioning stare. "Why don't you go make yourself something to eat, Maggie." Beth watched her go before she pushed herself from the floor. "Michael, what is it?"

Michael motioned her to the fireplace. "Two men came around earlier, said they were here to help you move. *You*, not us. They had guns, Beth. Guns." He rubbed his smooth chin and cleared his throat when Beth looked away. "Movers don't carry guns, Beth."

"How long ago did they leave?" They'd be back. She calculated how much time they had before Eli's men returned.

"They're still here. But don't worry. I took care of them," he whispered low. "I locked them in the cellar."

Confused, Beth checked the front window for any sign of them and then jerked. "Wait, our cellar?"

"Yes. Something wasn't right about them or you working for *Hide Park*." He lifted a brow.

Beth wondered just how much he knew about the establishment. There wasn't time for that conversation. She remembered the pounding. "Those men are still down there." She tried to recall the last time she'd heard the noise.

"I made sure of it." He rattled off details of how he convinced the men her belongings were down there. "They won't get out." He went on about steel bars.

She raced to the back door to check the alley. Sure enough, the double metal doors were barred shut.

"Who are we looking for?" Maggie joined her. Beth yanked her inside and locked the back door.

She paced back and forth with folded arms. Without preface or warning, she whispered, "Mr. Sands cannot be trusted."

Michael scrunched his face. "Something has happen…. what?" He joined her pace. "I knew it."

She shook her head. "We can't trust him. That's all."

"Those men are Sands' men."

She nodded, conveying more than she wanted to share.

He scratched the back of his neck. "We can't just leave them down there."

"Oh, yes we can." She forced the train schedule to his chest. "We have to get out of town."

Suddenly, gunshots rang out. Two and several more. Beth froze, but Michael grabbed Maggie and took Beth's hand, pulling them behind Father's desk. "Stay down. Don't make a sound." Beth tucked herself and Maggie under the desk as Michael disappeared. She called out for him in a whisper but only heard the front door open. Seconds later, Michael joined them behind the desk with his finger to his lips.

Maggie started to whisper, but Beth quickly clasped her hand over Maggie's mouth in silence. They listened. Nothing. Then a little rattle at the back door. A sudden crash of broken glass made them huddle closer. Hurried footsteps scurried up the stairs and down, rushing from room to room.

"She's gone," Beth heard a man say.

Footsteps halted at Father's office door. They held their breath.

"She'll be back," the man added.

"She hasn't been gone long. Left the door wide open."

Michael smiled. Footsteps grew distant. A muffled conversation followed.

Beth started to move, hearing them leave, but Michael pulled her back as he mouthed, "Wait."

The front door slammed shut. Still they waited. Seconds passed and Michael slowly peeked his head above the desktop. "I'll make sure they're gone," he whispered.

Beth nodded and hugged Maggie closer.

"They're gone." He returned and helped them to their feet. He handed her the train schedule. "There's an evening train."

Beth searched the train schedule and confirmed his information.

"Beth, are you thinking what I think you are thinking?" Michael said.

Beth nodded and together they mouthed the word, "Montana."

* * * * *

The cemetery was bleak. Distant streetlights flickered as the wind swayed the tree branches. Evidence of spring lay beyond its hedges but not within. The three of them stood for a few moments at their parents' graves. For Beth, tears wouldn't come. She couldn't let them. Every noise added to her fear. Michael said nothing. Beth watched as the muscles in his face and neck twitched and bulged, telling her he was holding emotion back.

Maggie knelt at the matted dirt mounds. "Will we ever see them again?" She looked up at Beth with wet, puffy eyes. "I mean, after Montana, when we come back home? Will we?"

Beth choked at Maggie's words and shook her head. "Maggie, you must say a very big goodbye. We are going away for a long time."

"Can't we take them with us?" Maggie put a hand on the dirt.

"They are in heaven now, Maggie, but they will always be with us in our hearts." Beth spoke softly, struggling to believe the truth she spoke. She didn't know what happened to a person after death—not really—only little pieces of conversations she'd overheard. But right now, a confused lie would have to suffice.

"I don't want to go then. I want to stay here." Maggie straightened and pitched her reddened chin into the air.

The sound of horses beating the street drew Beth's attention. "We must go." Beth looked at Father's watch. "And we have to hurry." She gathered the bags as Michael drug heavy wooden trunks along the broken sidewalk without complaint. Maggie also struggled to carry bags double her weight and size, all their worldly possessions. She tried to wave down a passing carriage, but the driver continued without notice.

Michael whistled loud, and the driver turned and pulled back. Assisting the driver, Michael loaded their belongings while Beth tried to comfort a distraught Maggie. Pulling her away from the graves tore at Beth's already broken heart, ripping deeper and cutting the pieces smaller.

She didn't want to leave them either, but she couldn't say it, wouldn't say it. She needed to be strong. "Maggie, we must go, please," Beth pleaded. "Please don't make this harder than it already is."

"Who will make my favorite toast?" Maggie whimpered. "Who will fix my broken things?"

"I will," Beth answered, fully aware that the driver had already checked the meter, and she hadn't counted the cost of getting to the station. The fact was, Beth had been making Maggie breakfast since she was a baby, and Michael had fixed nearly everything since then too.

"But you don't fix things," Maggie sobbed in disbelief.

"All right then, Michael will fix your broken things," she answered, annoyed at the time and yet concerned. "We are going to take care of each other no matter what. Do you understand me?" Wrapping her arms around Maggie, Beth lifted her tiny frame, tucking her sweet red face close.

Letting the iron gate close behind her was like cutting off her oxygen, the very air she needed to breathe. She pushed Maggie into Michael's arms and climbed inside the carriage.

"Michael, can a heart be a broken thing?" Maggie asked.

Beth pulled Maggie close, gave Michael a half smile, and leaned out the window, saying one last goodbye to all she'd known, and then motioned the driver. "Chicago Union Depot, please."

* * * * *

Beth took in a deep breath, relieved to have made it this far and overtaken with all the commotion. At least the crowd would conceal them if it became necessary.

The Chicago Union Depot hummed with anxious travelers. Wide marble steps led down into an expansive room with matching marbled walls and floors. Its columned ceiling echoed her voice and somehow announced her thoughts. Church-like benches lined both sides of the room, and the large clock stood like a guard in the middle of the room.

Beth adjusted the bags she carried, trying to keep her balance. "There." She pointed through the crowd to a long line of passengers. Michael headed in that direction without so much as a "follow me."

"Are we going to be boys forever, Beth?" Maggie scratched her head underneath her hat. Beth had forgotten that she and Maggie were dressed in some of Father's and Michael's old clothes.

"Of course not." She raised an eyebrow in Michael's direction, but he was too far ahead. "It's just a game. I'll tell you when it's over."

"But I like this game."

Beth tried to keep up with Michael and gently prodded Maggie to keep her between them for fear of being separated. "Michael, slow down. For every step you take, we have to take three."

Michael rolled his eyes, and Maggie covered up her giggle.

"Three tickets to Montana," Beth said after waiting in line so long that the clock tower screamed, "Sands is coming for you," with every movement.

With the tickets tucked securely inside her coat and their luggage bound for the loading dock, they pushed and shoved their way to the terminal entrance.

"Come on," Michael called to her.

Beth scanned every face, old and young, as they made their way down the long corridor to board their train, a train bound for the great unknown. An official in a dark suit strolled along the platform, pushing eager passengers back.

"Move on back. Keep on moving." His voice was long and drawn out and fell down a tone at the end of every sentence.

"I can't believe it," Michael said for the twentieth time.

Believe it, Beth wanted to say, and that would be the end of it, but she didn't. She looked over her shoulder to make sure they hadn't been followed.

"The St. Paul. Chicago to St. Paul, Minnesota. All aboard."

Maggie tugged on Beth's sleeve, "I thought you said we were going to Montana."

"We are," Beth hurried her, "but there are several states in our way."

The train car was full, every square inch occupied. Beth pushed through to locate the assigned seats. She and Maggie sat to one side, Michael across the aisle. Their bags took the space between them, for the overhead bays were filled to capacity. This would be quite a long journey. She wondered, as she tapped the thin pocketbook at her chest, if the printed time included scheduled stops along the way.

Beth adjusted to accommodate the small case on her lap as the official made his way through the aisle, validating each ticket. The whistle blew, much to Maggie's delight, and the train rumbled and lurched.

Beth looked out the window at the platform still scattered with well-wishers and let out a long sigh. Maggie had gripped the back of the seat and hadn't let go since she heard a man down the aisle say, "Here we go." Michael was taking in every detail of the train's interior.

Beth let her head rest against the side of the train car, finally beginning to believe they might be free of Mr. Sands and his men. She watched the end of the platform slowly come into view. Three men stood at its edge. She snapped her head back to view their faces.

One of the men was Donovan.

Chapter Eight

If ever a boy needed to be a man, it was now.

Michael Yates had never been so sore, and the frequent jostle of the train reminded him again. He'd slept for several hours during the night. Not well, but he'd slept. If it wasn't a baby crying, it was a man snoring or Maggie complaining.

He stirred and tried to stretch his long legs into the aisle but couldn't move. The train car was full, every last seat taken. Suitcases of various sizes and shapes surrounded him like too many books crammed onto a library shelf. His thoughts were crowded too. Two women across the aisle hadn't stopped talking for hours. "Nursed that baby till he was two years old," one woman said.

Michael cringed. *Of all the subjects, it would have to be this one.*

"That's when babies start bitin', you know. I said to…"

Forcing his mind to the weather, he squinted one eye open. Morning had arrived, and Beth had already shushed Maggie several times. With his little finger, he drew back the window shade and scanned the landscape. *Minnesota, or maybe North Dakota.* But how could he know? There wasn't a "welcome" sign to mark the state boundaries…unless he'd missed it. At least he'd put some physical distance between what he'd done…or not done. A sudden sway of the car unleashed a suitcase from the overhead compartment, landing on his head. He shrunk. "Ouch."

He'd battled that particular travel trunk one too many times. Should have been loaded, not stored anyway. He shoved the case into Beth's arms. "I can't breathe in here."

Her shocked expression was very much like Mother's.

"I can't even move." Michael stood and smacked his head on the brass bar. "Ouch." Massaging the sore spot, he looked at Beth and Maggie sitting across from him. By her tight lips, Beth was embarrassed. Maggie snickered. Beth hushed her again.

"Sit down, boy. You want to wake the dead?" a man hissed.

Beth grabbed Michael's hand, urging him to sit. "Michael," she whispered as she tugged. "People are still sleeping."

Like I should be. Agitation narrowed his eyes. "I'm going to suffocate in here, and if that woman..." he said, pointing without any pretense of being polite, "...says one more word about nursing, I'm going to vomit." With that, he shoved several cases out of his way and tore himself from her grip.

"Michael, please," Beth called and then offered an apology to the other passengers. "He's tired. It's been a long journey."

Beth's voice vanished as he stepped into the open air and pulled the train door closed behind him. *I am tired, and it has been a long journey.* That wasn't even the half of it. His body was as weary as his soul. He knew immediately he'd acted out and was sorry for it. *I'm not myself,* was his only apology.

With his back against the train, he slid down to the platform beneath his feet and ran his hand through his hair. Perhaps grief had finally found its place, or maybe it was the guilt.

The mechanical vibration of the train soothed him, numbed him of the responsibility he bore. It was his fault.

Beth had no idea, and maybe it was best that he keep it that way. The sound of iron scraping steel lulled him. With a knee to his chest, he listened to the rhythm.

He should be grieving. He'd lost everything. He should feel guilty. Mother and Father wouldn't be gone if he hadn't... The word "failed" seemed to fly by with the speed of the train. He stretched a hand beyond the safety of the iron bars and let a powerful blast of air soar between his fingers, stinging the tips. Although its force burned his skin, it was exhilarating. And alive. And somehow, forgiving.

He should've taken the job at the sausage factory when Father asked him to. At the time, Michael argued that his studies would suffer, that he'd sacrifice his place at the university, that he was the thinking kind, not the working sort. Now? He'd sacrifice it all to bring them back. He'd forget the university and his hopes of medical school in a heartbeat.

The ache of truth tightened his chest. He'd never be free of what he'd done.

Tilting his head, he glanced through the passage window at Beth's stunned and worried face then slumped to the floor. She was doing the best she could. He exhaled and shook his head. *You did this. You caused this.*

"You're the man of the house now."

That's what people told him. Sure, he knew what they meant, but until today, he'd ignored the meaning and the responsibility.

You broke it. Fix it.

Chicago disappeared hours ago, and only the great unknown lay ahead. He smirked. How *great* that unknown might be was yet to be determined. What he thought would be, would never be. That was a reality he'd carry with him for the rest of his life.

Massaging his sore eyes, he rose, preparing to brave the wrath of an older sister. The open door sucked him, and the noise of the train hushed as he slid the door closed.

Beth straightened. "I made some more room and borrowed a newspaper for you to read," she said. "Will it help, do you think?"

Michael hoped his smile communicated a "yes" and "I'm sorry" at the same time.

* * * * *

"Beth?" Maggie turned around and collapsed in her seat, shoving the book she'd been reading in Beth's face. "This book is so, so, so boring." Each word clung to the last.

Beth frowned. "There's no such thing as boring, just boring people." Her mother's words rang true. Beth stole the tiny book she'd specifically packed for Maggie's benefit and caressed the cover. "*Disorderly Girl* is a fine book, one of Mother's favorites."

Maggie pouted. "I want *Tom Sawyer* or *Treasure Island*. This book is for…girls."

Beth held the treasure close, remembering the fine memories of Mother reading it to her as a child. "You are a girl, Maggie."

"Well, I'm not a fancy girl."

"You're not?" Beth tightened her lips. "What sort of girl are you then?"

"I'm a regular girl," Maggie said with chin hoisted high.

A regular girl? "Well, you are too young for Tom Sawyer. Besides, we couldn't bring everything."

Maggie sulked.

Beth tucked the book into her bag. "Now find something to do. You have a couple of toys, you have a book,"

Beth said, motioning toward the window, "you could show some appreciation for the scenery."

Maggie cocked her head and squinted her big blue eyes. "And…what else?"

* * * * *

Beth squeezed her forehead. If only the man would close his mouth for five whole minutes. Exhaustion played with her mind. Voices were too loud, simple noises exaggerated and untimely, and the subject of conversation…unbelievable.

"Killin' is what them Indians do," he said.

Beth shot him a horrified look. "Sir, please. This is hardly appropriate." She nodded toward Maggie. "Not in front of the children."

"Why those Indians paid no mind at all. Women and children, slaughtered like pigs," still he continued, unmoved by her rebuke.

Beth scowled and turned to Maggie, who had hidden herself between several cases, pretending it was a fort. Maggie appeared unscathed.

"Why, back in seventy-six, I was…"

Beth drew a long breath and let it all out. Suddenly, a little boy ran down the aisle, tripping to his demise over cases bulging into the walkway. His father, quick at his heels, arrested him by the back of his trousers. The ruckus startled Michael. He flipped the corner of his newspaper to see but didn't linger, Maggie came out of her cocoon, and the now quiet baby several rows away began to cry again.

Beth rubbed her temples harder, looking first at her siblings and then glancing outside. *They've been so brave.* Braver than she would've been at their age. Beyond her reflection, she scanned the moving landscape. *Bare. No life at all.*

Refocusing on her image in the window, she had the same thought. *No life at all.*

At least the storyteller appeared permanently silenced. She checked to make sure.

The man slapped his knee. "Why, when my folks came out west with the wagon train, they brought a load of ammunition to fight off them Indians."

Beth scanned the train, several passengers listened.

"The wagon master told my pa to save the last bullets for hisself and us kids. Better to be shot dead than to suffer a bloody haircut."

Beth stood. "Sir, I beg you."

"Just tellin' it like it is, miss. Truth is truth," he continued his tale.

Beth fidgeted in her seat. She'd heard the stories but never supposed them true. Her mind visualized the scene like a theater play with actors and props bringing reality to life. A long line of wagons traveling across a landscape of dirt and weeds, thundering hooves and war cries erupting as painted faces and horses surrounded the now circled band of wagons. Gunshots and screams rang out.

Beth shook her head, mentally erasing the horrific scene.

"My pa wouldn't give up...fought them Indians until we was down to the last bullet," he added.

Several other passengers gasped. Beth joined them, albeit privately. Her eyelids began to twitch. Surely, it wasn't true. She seized her knees as her skin began to crawl. The tension in her neck pulled painfully at her spine.

It couldn't be true.

She'd been so determined to get them out of Chicago. Had they escaped the hand of Eli Sands only to fall into the dangerous and deadly hands of the wild frontier? "Sir, might I ask the location of this...these happenings," Beth asked, clearing her throat.

He scratched his chin. "Where you headed?"

"The Bitterroot Valley." Beth closed her eyes, bracing herself. *Please, don't say the Bitterroot Valley.*

He slapped his leg. "Ah, the Battle of the Big Hole."

She tensed. The very name sounded absolutely terrible. A quick look in Maggie's direction solidified the horror. Maggie was standing with her chin resting on her arms on top of several cases, ears intent on hearing every word.

He described the battle as the most deadly of battles. "There was a band of men, cavalry and officers, led by Lt Col George Custer."

Beth leaned in and swallowed. "Go on."

He paused, scratching behind his ear. "They didn't know what hit 'em."

Beth checked on Maggie. "And…then what happened?"

"It was an ambush. Complete annihilation. Nearly three hundred men died that day, including Custer hisself."

Beth gasped and jumped up. "I knew it." She frowned at Michael. "We shouldn't have come."

Michael stood to meet her. "Beth, you're overreacting."

Maggie scrunched her face. "I think it sounds exciting."

Beth covered her mouth. "We have to go back…now."

"Beth." Michael clamped his hands on her shoulders.

She focused on him, then pointed to the storyteller who sat with his arms folded and eyes closed. "He said there are Indians in Montana. They have brutally murdered men, women," leaning in so Maggie couldn't hear, she added, "and children." Her voice cracked. "It's not safe, Michael. We have to go back."

"You're jumping to conclusions," he replied.

Beth leaned in closer. "If we get off at the next station, we have just enough money to get us back home. We could still manage to—"

"Beth." He shook her. "You can't believe everything you hear." He nodded in the direction of the man.

The man smirked and winked before gathering his things and moving down several rows. Beth narrowed her gaze. Michael urged her to her seat. "Remember what Father used to say? We killed Indian men, women, and *children* too."

Beth nodded. Trying to calm herself, she stared at the swindler who'd already found his next victim and then turned to Michael. "How'd you get to be so smart anyway?"

Michael shrugged. "I was born this way."

* * * * *

"I can see it." Maggie exclaimed, a much-needed change from her hours of whining.

The conductor swept through the aisle. "Next stop. Billings, Montana."

Maggie pressed her nose against the window. "Is this it?"

Beth shared a smile with Michael. "No, we have a little ways to go, but we are getting close." She patted the Ravalli Hotel advertisement in her pocket.

Michael leaned in and whispered, "Where are all the Indians, Beth?"

Beth nudged him. "Where are all the mountains, Michael?" She pointed toward the window.

"They're there. Look." He put his arm around her and pointed straight out in front of her. "They're just hidden."

She scanned the land. Mountains surrounded them. Tall ones. Round ones. Clumped-together ones. All veiled. "Is it smoke that hides them?"

Michael shrugged.

Beth smirked. "You mean to tell me you don't *know*?" She grinned and enjoyed the feeling.

90

"Haze," a woman holding several children on her lap said.

"Thank you," Beth replied, smiling, as Michael glared. "It's haze, Michael." For once, she'd educate him.

Billings, Montana, was much larger than she had imagined. The horizon, enormous. Sky as far as the eye could see. Evergreens, dark and pale, dotted the distant hills. The train began to slow, offering lingering views of small farms and meticulous vegetable gardens. Larger trees popped up here and there. Homes came into view, and soon, structures took over every windowpane.

"It's a miniature Chicago," Michael said.

Beth had been thinking the same thing. Excitement hung in the air. She could feel it. The train pulled into the station, and people began to clear out. She inquired of the conductor as to the next departure.

"We have some time before the train leaves," she told Michael. "I'll get something to eat." Beth grabbed her coat. It was exhilarating to get off the train. Stretching her arms high into the air, she took a deep breath. A sweet aroma hit her nose, so she followed it to a bakery nestled in between a general store and post office.

Smoothing her hand over the letter in her pocket, guilt took its ugly toll. Annie Parker would understand. She, being the one person Beth could trust, would know what to do. The idea of those two men breaking into her home sent chills down her spine. Rotten men.

Strengthening her resolve, she headed straight for the post office. After posting Annie's letter and purchasing some fresh bread from the bakery, she stopped by a general store to get some cheese and salami. Beth crossed Main Street and headed for the small train station, feeling free. Free of Sands *and* his lot. Nearing the end of the boardwalk, her reflection in a window made her stop and stare. "A necessary disguise," she told herself. She stepped back to get a larger view and fidgeted with the shirt and trousers she wore. She adjusted her father's hat and several curls escaped.

Suddenly, a woman came around the corner and screamed, followed by the sound of thunder. A large horse jumped onto the boardwalk with a man running behind, waving her out of the way, but there wasn't time. It was like she was wearing Father's boots, much too big and far too heavy. The horse bolted past, pushing her to the edge of the boardwalk and into a summersault over the rail. Her arms flailed to grab a post, cheese and salami flying into the air. Landing hard on her side, she rolled over to watch her bread tumble into the path of the horses and wagons, followed by her father's hat.

Without warning, she was scooped from the street by the man who waved her down. "I'm sorry, miss."

With his mud-whiskered face only inches from hers, Beth pulled away and fought to be free. "Let me go." She pushed at him. "I mean it." Still, he didn't set her down until his foot hit the boards. "Put me down." Beth kicked her legs and squirmed.

Her feet touched the ground, and she shook free of him and the dirt. She hugged the pain in her arm and saw the torn shirtsleeve and blood. He returned with her hat, but the loaf of bread was lost forever. She searched the street as horse and carriage played tetherball with her meal. He flicked the dirt from her hat and handed it to her. "Are you hurt?"

She released her arm and took the hat with a clipped, "I'm fine." Beth averted eye contact. She was hurt; her arm was throbbing. Clapping her trousers and dusting off her sleeve, she pushed the pain away. Putting distance between them, she gathered her cheese and salami from the boardwalk.

"Miss?"

"I said I'm fine," she scolded.

He motioned toward her backside.

Beth scowled at him and then examined the damage for herself. "Oh, dear." Frantically, she covered the tear in the backside of her trousers with her father's hat.

"You *are* hurt." His hand grazed for her arm, and she jerked it away.

"Don't...you...touch...me." She couldn't help but notice his broad shoulders and stout frame, for he'd lifted her without a struggle. She'd be no match for him if he tried something. She sized him up to Donovan. His jacket and trousers were covered with clumps of dried mud and horse manure, but his eyes didn't gleam evil as Donovan's had. She eyed the train station.

"Your arm looks pretty bad. Let me see." He had her cornered between a post and wooden crates. His warm breath caressed her cheek. His touch sent a shock wave through her body. She pulled away and heard the whistle blow at the train station and calculated the distance. She'd run.

He gave her space. "I'd be happy to see you to the doc about that arm. I'll pay for the damages. Don't you worry."

"I said I'm fine."

He tipped his cowboy hat. "Yes, you did. Sorry about my horse. She can be a bit *stubborn*."

She scowled at the comment, hearing his tone perfectly.

Again, he tipped his hat before jumping the boardwalk. "Jax," he called to his horse standing near the general store, its tether dangling to the ground.

* * * * *

Ethan threw the reins over Jax's head, grabbed the saddle horn, and paused before mounting. He glanced over his shoulder as the young woman dressed as a boy hobbled down the boardwalk.

KIM TAYLOR

She fumbled on her heel, the salami falling onto the ground with a bounce, and she nearly lost the other package again. She bent to pick it up, splitting her trousers even farther. Ethan cleared his throat and looked away.

Pulling himself into his saddle, he glanced her direction again. "Jax, I think you've met your match." He turned toward the edge of town, bidding Billings, goodbye, and the Bitterroot Valley, hello.

* * * * *

Beth's cheeks burned as she climbed the stairs to the station platform. Glancing at the mangled cheese and salami she still possessed, she hoped it would be enough. She reached a soured Michael at the train. He raised an eyebrow and nodded to the large clock at the center of the platform.

"Sorry, I'm late," she said.

Maggie grabbed the package from her hands. "Did you buy any candy? I'm starved."

"*No*, Maggie, I didn't buy candy. Candy is a luxury we can't afford. Don't ask me again."

Michael and Maggie grimaced at Beth's pointed statement. Maggie slumped to the train car seat. "Now, I really am going to die."

"Don't say that," Beth and Michael said in unison.

As they took their places, Michael waved at the air. "What's that awful smell?" Michael examined her.

Beth shrugged. "I had some trouble in town."

"With what, a horse?" Michael tucked his nose into his elbow and produced a handkerchief. "Because you stink."

"Yeah, you stink," Maggie added.

"That's the least of my concerns." She considered her arm and her backside.

Beth was deep in thought when the train lunged from the station, and Micheal examined her arm. "Want to tell me about it?"

She met his gaze. "No. No, I don't."

"Tickets, please," the conductor's voice came down the aisle.

Maggie tapped Beth's knee incessantly, and Michael shouted, "Beth!"

"What?" Beth snapped out of her trance.

"Tickets?" the conductor asked.

Embarrassed and apologetic, Beth handed the conductor the tickets.

Michael took the returned tickets and put them in his pocket. "Sir, might there be a first aid kit aboard?"

Chapter Nine

Chicago, Illinois

"What's this?" Annie Parker asked as the young man slammed a heavy wooden crate full of papers on her new desk at Rice's Auction House. Why Annie even asked, she didn't know. A crate marked "Yates" stared back at her.

Eli Sands, you snake.

She smiled, however, at the outcome. Beth Yates had escaped Eli Sands.

Pulling the temporary marker affixed to the wood, she frowned, gritting her teeth at her not-so-triumphant outcome.

"It's the Yates' estate." The boy, ten years younger, smirked, apparently trying to impress her. Again.

"Yes, I see that. Thank you…" She couldn't remember the boy's name.

After resigning her position at Chicago Savings and Loan, Annie had little hope of finding a decent job. Sands was a powerful man. No one would hire her.

Here she sat, sorting through dead people's belongings, not at all what she imagined herself doing at this point in her life. She lifted a handful of documents from the crate. Trash mostly. Bills, receipts—meaningless papers.

The boy cleared his throat.

"Is there something else?" Annie asked. The boy straightened, grinning from ear to ear. Placing her hands on the desk together in prayer-like form, she added, "You've been most helpful. I can manage."

He hesitated but finally returned to the warehouse, leaving her in peace. At least working for Rice's Auction House kept her mother from hounding her day after day about marriage…and babies. If it weren't for this job, she'd be parading around like a desperate twenty-five-year-old at her mother's bidding. Annie refused to be desperate like so many of her friends.

Annie sorted through the stack of papers in front of her. Into the burn barrel with it. She tossed the bulk into the wheelbarrow beside her desk, and a plume of dust filled the room. Coughing to find her breath, she smoothed out her lace-collared jacket—her latest design. Completely inappropriate for Rice's Auction House, she knew, but perfect in every other way.

There was a well-worn Bible. She placed it aside, knowing it held responsiblity for Mr. Yates' dismissal at the university but didn't belong in the burn bin. Digging deeper into the crate, she lifted a sizable leather pouch. The weight of it forced her to stand. Such an official item. Annie stared at it for a moment and then dropped the mass on the desk. What could this be? Her gut told her it was important.

A door closed down the hall, and Annie looked up. She pushed the pouch aside and gathered another stack, tossing papers to the barrel one by one.

"I'm going home." Mr. Rice said, knocking along the wall without opening the door.

"Good night, Mr. Rice." Annie waited. Rice called to his men in the warehouse and then closed the front door. All was quiet again. Opening the door, she checked the hall and then gently pushed the door closed.

Rushing to her desk, she suddenly felt like a thief. Shaking her head, she untied the leather string and slowly pulled out a handful of documents.

"Good heavens." She thumbed through the paperwork, letting several more "good heavens" escape. *It can't be.* The door opened unexpectedly, and Annie jumped.

"We're lockin' up for the night." The warehouse man checked the clock. "It's quittin' time."

Annie nodded…much too fast. She tried to calm down and slowly tucked the papers into the pouch. "I'm done for the day." She rose and reached for her coat and satchel as the man turned and called to his men. Brushing the edge of her desk, she snatched the leather pouch under her arm.

Everyone else went home for the night, but Annie couldn't. Squeezing the pouch under her arm, she went in search of the one man who might be able to set things right for Beth Yates. Mr. R. C. Clemens. Clemens owned the Yates' mortgage before Sands. Surely, Mr. Clemens would know what to do.

Working for Eli Sands, Annie felt she'd ruined so many lives. The news of Mr. Carter's suicide solidified the task before her. She had to make this right, to right her wrongs and soothe her soul.

Several hours passed, and still Annie searched. Annie dare not show these papers to anyone but R. C. Clemens. She'd knocked on so many doors that she felt like a fool. But she had to do this. She and Beth were hardly friends. Their families rarely socialized, what with her father's disgrace at the university. Annie shrugged at the role her own father played in Yates' dismissal.

She'd make amends for that too.

Climbing the wide iron stairs to a set of giant doors, she sucked in the night air and knocked. A long day and an empty stomach toyed with her, for the lion-head handles seemed to roar with rejection.

The door opened, revealing a well-dressed thin butler.

"Is this the Clemens' residence?" she said.

Suddenly, an older gentleman stepped behind the doorman, his feeble hand wobbling on the head of his cane. "And just who might you be?"

"Are you a Mr. Clemens? Of Clemens Savings?"

He whispered to the butler, and the man left them alone. "What's this all about, young lady?" His brows furrowed as he leaned on his cane.

"Sir, do you remember the Yates family? Owned the orphanage on the corner." She pointed in the general direction.

"I do, indeed," Clemens said.

She smiled. "Then I am going to need you to help me with these." Annie handed him the deed to the orphanage and the Last Will and Testament of Mr. and Mrs. Yates.

* * * * *

"R. C. Clemens to see Mr. Elias Sands."

Eli straightened at the voice outside his office door. What business did Clemens have with him? He'd paid him off years ago.

Eli listened for his new secretary's response. "I'm sorry, but Mr. Sands is a very busy man." Eli rubbed his forehead. That whine in her voice would drive him mad, but at least she had gumption.

"No matter, I have an urgent matter to discuss with Mr. Sands. Tell him…never mind, I'll tell him myself."

A ruckus followed a "you can't go in there until I announce you."

Eli heard the clicking of Clemens' cane hitting the floor drawing closer. Eli rose and met him at the door. "Why, Mr. Clemens, come in, come in." Eli winked. "Caroline is new. You'll have to forgive her." Eli turned to her with a stern face. "I purchased Clemens' Savings and Loan a while back."

Caroline smiled nervously.

Eli held up a bottle of brandy, "Drink?"

Clemens declined. Eli indulged himself.

"Retirement looks good on you. Are you enjoying—"

Clemens slammed his cane on Eli's desk. "Sir, do you know the Yates family?"

Eli tried not to appear stunned. "Please have a seat." Eli leaned back in his chair, put both hands behind his neck. "Yes, the family owned the home for orphans." He softened his tone. "'Twas a shame, wasn't it? And such a tragedy."

Clemens' eyes narrowed. "Yes, that's the family. I understand you had dealings with the children of Mr. and Mrs. Yates." Eli adjusted and cleared his throat, disguising the lump. Clemens leaned in. "Do you know where I might find the oldest daughter, Elizabeth Yates?"

Eli looked up at the ceiling, calculating his words and his thoughts. "Miss Yates did come to see me, now that you mentioned it. Said they were moving out of state." Sands sat up and leaned in. "I don't have an address, but I might know someone who can locate the family." He tossed brandy into his mouth. "I'll see what I can do."

Clemens' jaw tightened. "Fine," he said and rose.

"Why, sir…do you wish to contact Miss Yates?" Eli said.

Clemens patted his jacket. "I've come upon some documents that concern Miss Yates—all the Yates children in fact."

"Documents?"

"A will and deed, among other things," Clemens replied.

"Might I have a look at these papers you've come upon?" Eli said. His knuckles popped as he tightened his fist.

"You be sure to let me know if you find Miss Yates."

Eli hesitated before rising. "Will do. Always a pleasure, Clemens."

"I'll do some of my own digging." Clemens dismissed Eli without so much as a wave or "good day."

When the door closed, Eli downed his brandy. Standing at the window, he watched Clemens hobble down the sidewalk, Eli's future success dangling in his hand.

* * * * *

Eli didn't care how it was done. The Yates' will and deed could sabotage his entire plan, ruin everything. He wasn't about to let that happen. Tapping his fingers, he threw his spectacles onto his desk. Investors were on the wire, and his reputation was at stake. He'd eliminated inconveniences before. He'd do it again. He picked up the telephone, still new and awkward in his hands, but at least he'd conquered its basic function.

The operator made the connection as Eli cocked his head to listen to Caroline's typing. Sounded like a child learning to play the piano in the next room. At least, Miss Parker knew how to stay busy and keep quiet. Time would tell if Caroline had it in her. He smirked. With that voice, he wondered if he could stand her long enough to find out.

The line clicked. "Vern. Sands here. I have need of your services." He smiled at Vern's response. "Meet me in the usual spot. I'll give you the details." Eli hung up the telephone.

Vern Larson had been in the forgery business for nearly twenty-five years. He was the best in the business and charged handsomely for his work and his silence. Eli didn't say as much, but he'd pay any price. He needed this problem gone. *Yesterday.*

Just like Elizabeth Yates—gone.

Once Vern forged the document, Elizabeth Yates will have unknowingly revoked her right to the property and released all interest to the bearer of the deed. Leaning back, Sands closed his eyes, tasting success. Suddenly, his chair tipped to one side, snapping a leg in half. "Ah." He grabbed at the desk but snagged the cord of the telephone instead. The telephone, along with a box of cigars and several large files flew at him as he plummeted to the floor.

There was a knock at his office door. Eli struggled to pull himself into a dog-like position and then to his feet but hit his head on the desk. The door opened. "Sir?" Eli panicked and climbed to his feet. "The investors will be here soon," Caroline said. "It's nearly four o'clock." A strange expression crossed her face. "Are you all right?"

He waved her away, dusted off his trousers, and straightened his tie. He'd been waiting for this moment. He was more than ready. He heard the outer door open, followed by voices.

Caroline rushed to greet them. "You are early. Mr. Sands is not yet ready—"

"Come in, gentlemen," he cut her off with a glare. "Come in," he welcomed them and pulled a large rolled case from atop his desk. Introductions weren't necessary. Every man had a reputation. They greeted each other as if old friends, but he was well aware of the rivalry and competition in the room. He conversed with each one, loud and pointed enough to convey a chummy relationship, targeting Laramie, Schwab, and Burns.

He gathered them around the large drafting table and slowly unrolled the blueprints. "This, my friends, is going to make all of us a lot of money." He laid out the plan as they huddled. Schwab, he noted, seemed to hold back. A big man from out west, Sands had offered to cover his travel expenses just to get the man here. He needed Schwab if expansion were to be a possibility.

Eli spread out the large drawings across the long wooden table and tapped his index finger to indicate the location. "Eight city blocks. Thirteen acres is all it takes. Gentlemen, here, we have a gated courtyard, country estate charm with all the finest amenities and modern conveniences, horse stables and a riding park, parks with walking paths, meticulously maintained gardens and well-manicured lawns, a play area for children, a gaming range and men's lounge."

Schwab's interest piqued, and murmurs rounded the table. He caught Schwab touching his lips and motioning for him to do the same. Eli ignored the odd gesture and continued. "A surrounding fortress of exquisite connected townhomes complete with a private motorcar garage. A private community, for which one would pay handsomely to be a member."

"Membership?" Larami questioned. Others joined him.

"Yearly dues and fees in addition to the purchase price." A quick understanding filled the room. "Luxury and convenience with a hefty price."

Questions erupted, and Eli fought to stay in control while presenting the confidence investors required. Several others stared at him strangely, but Eli refocused. "Additional plans include adjacent streets filled with dress shops, fresh markets, tea shops, and cafés."

Eli lifted the elevation drawings of a single townhome to the top of the pile and pulled out the floor plans. "Beautifully appointed estate homes built with only the finest materials." He laid out samples of granite, marble, walnut, and mahogany. The sales pitch continued as he gave an update on where the project stood in Chicago. "Imagine a community like this in *your* city. In fact, imagine several."

Silence befell the room. Sands coughed. Men began shaking hands, a sign of his success. "My office will be in touch" and "Count me in," filled the room. Rich men were an interesting group. He'd fit in well. Congratulations came to him from nearly every man except one. *Schwab.* He couldn't read the man as he could the others. He blamed the wild west. As men left with a promise of partnership, Eli closed in on Schwab.

"I'll be in touch." Schwab grabbed his coat and hat.

Sands wasn't about to let Schwab walk away, not when he was this close to sealing the deal. Might not have a second chance. "Schwab, you're a smart fellow, you seem—"

Schwab hesitated at the door but slipped away with a backward wave.

Eli stood at his second-story window as the men stepped in carriages to leave. *Now, they respect me.*

Caroline knocked and poked her head in the door. "Will there be anything else before I go?" She grimaced. "Sir, blood is dripping down your face."

* * * * *

Eli sat alone in his leather chair near the fire in the study, a glass of champagne on the table beside him. *You're on top now, Sands.* Laramie's words were ones he'd never forget. Eli closed his files and placed them carefully beside his drink. *Success.*

He reached for his glass, symbolically toasting to his own triumph. He'd always been an entrepreneur, a visionary. And today, his dream unfolded before his very eyes.

Chicago's real estate king, a toast. Chicago's own Vivian Italy cheered him. Taking another sip, he leaned closer to the fire.

"Sir, your wife is inquiring," Sofia said.

"Tell her I will be up shortly," he replied.

The maid curtsied and left the study as quietly as she'd entered.

Eleanor had been ill for the past twenty years. Doctors couldn't identify the cause, and no amount of medicine had been able to cure it. Even unconventional medicines had left them without hope. He'd worked hard in the early days just to make ends meet, but when Eleanor got sick, he had to do more—work harder, smarter.

He poured himself another glass of champagne. Worked three jobs until he met Carl McCane. "The Cane," as men called him, taught him how to get ahead. For McCane, it was all about money, but Eli wanted more. Money *and* respect. A job turned into a partnership and eventually a takeover when McCane died. Hiding McCane's unsavory business establishments, Eli took a few bold steps in real estate. Bought out several respectable firms, including Clemen's Saving and Loan.

Now? He owned more than half of the savings and loans.

How does it feel? Alexander Burns' voice rang in his ears.

Eli lifted his glass in a toast. "It feels good."

News of the day's success made Eleanor proud. She didn't know of his other profitable business dealings, nor the shady means of today's success. She would never know. He did what needed to be done so that she could live comfortably. He raised a glass. "To you, my dear."

Looking around his study at a myriad of unusual collectibles, he recalled vacations never taken. A fake bronze statue of a racehorse sat above the fireplace. He'd own a racehorse one day. Men of wealth owned race horses. *Someday,* he promised himself. For now, the items were meaningless trinkets purchased through the catalogue or left behind after evictions.

He finished the champagne and doused the fire. He needed to see his lovely wife before retiring.

* * * * *

Hamilton, Montana.

Ethan put his elbows on the desk and threw the pencil. *Maintain. That's all I ever do.* This wasn't the life for him, sitting behind his office desk at the Daly Ranch. He wanted his own desk. *Yes.*

And his own pencil.

Grabbing the pencil, he sketched out some dates on a piece of paper, occasionally looking at the calendar pinned to the stable wall. June 1897.

"You're back."

Ethan sat up and nodded to Mr. Daly's butler standing in the doorway, his attire shining by comparison. "Just rode in this morning."

"The family is expected on Friday with a possible list of ten additional guests. Are things in order for the races and at least one horseback excursion?"

"I'll finalize things today," Ethan said, mentally adding the duty to the day's agenda.

The butler gave a militant nod and forced his hands behind his back as he turned to leave.

Ethan let all of the air out of his lungs. Felt like a schoolboy standing in front of his master. He shook his head. He hadn't been a schoolboy for a long time. *Welcome home.* Ethan leaned back in his chair.

Daly was a businessman—intelligent, ambitious, handsome. *A lot like me.* Ethan smiled and sat up straighter. His father's humor, comforting.

Daly was a good man. Owned or partially owned nearly every business in town. Put Hamilton on the Montana map, people said. Daly owned the Big Mill and The Amalgamated Copper Mining Company, among other things.

A man of many talents and hobbies, but there was one hobby Daly loved more than anything. Horse racing. His prized thoroughbred named Tammany had put Daly in the winner's circle. Between the award-winning chestnut stallion and Daly's horse trainer, Sam Lucas, Daly's future in horse racing looked bright.

If Ethan could get back on track, his future would be bright. He'd get down to the land office first chance, but with the family coming back to town, he'd be too busy. After a short rest, he and Jax would head out to camp and check on the ranch hand and bring back a cow. He'd rode Jax hard, but Daly's kitchen would be in need of fresh beef for their guests.

"Ethan." A stable boy grabbed at the doorway, pulling himself in. "It's Jax. She's in Mrs. Daly's rose garden again."

Ethan jumped up and his chair hit the wall behind him. He grabbed his hat and hurried after the boy.

* * * * *

With Jax secured, Ethan went back to his office. Thankfully, the Dalys weren't home yet, and the gardener assured him that no permanent damage had been done.

Ethan plunked his sore feet on top the desk and planned the day's events. He'd get things squared away with the ranch hand, head to town to organize the race for Saturday, and meet the train and pick up Daly's new stock. If he worked hard enough, he might have enough time to get to the land office before it closed.

Ethan hoped to have his stock purchased and fields plowed by spring, but if Reardon didn't agree to his proposal, he'd be back to square one. Couldn't install the fences or the corrals, couldn't build the barns. He shook his head. Way behind schedule. He was not about to wait it out another winter, nor was he about to go back home a failure.

You're not in control, son. God is. His father's words annoyed him at times. He knew they were true, but Ethan didn't like them much. At thirty years old, he was way past his prime, at least by Dawson standards.

He took another sip of coffee. Realizing his coffee had grown cold, he gulped down the rest. Good thing Cook hadn't made the coffee this morning. A man got much more than he bargained for where Cook's brew was concerned. Mud, some said. Poison.

Ethan licked his lips, aware of the mustache and beard he now possessed. People always said he looked like his father. More now than ever, Ethan supposed, with the added warmth on his face. He caressed his father's watch as he slid it into his pocket and remembered the day he left home, his mother standing on the porch, wringing her hands. Father smiling, knowing Ethan's determination and drive needed a road. A road going nowhere fast.

"Ethan, when did you get in?"

Ethan looked up from his thoughts as Russ Miles, filled the doorway with his tall, muscular build. Ah, a familiar face. Russ was his right-hand man and a friend. In his early sixties, Russ could outwork, outsmart any man around. Been herding cattle and raising horses his entire life. But after his wife died, Russ sold his ranch near Darby and came to work for Daly. Didn't need to work but wanted to. Been working for Daly for more than ten years.

"Just got in," Ethan replied.

"I trust your ad…vent…eure was a success." Russ' fake French accent always made Ethan smile.

"Picked out a handful of good, steady workhorses. They'll arrive next month, and a lively young filly. She'll be coming in on the afternoon train."

Russ rubbed his lower back and stretched.

"I'll warn you, Russ. That filly sure gave me a run for my money. Said she'd been runnin' wild before they caught her. One of Black's bloodline."

Russ whistled. "Well, I'll be. Finally found that old son of a gun."

"She's a beauty all right. Dark hair, fine lines, and stubborn as all get out." Suddenly, Ethan remembered the young woman he had encountered and had to decide exactly whom he was talking about. "Had to get in there and show her who's boss."

"I'll bet she laid out a welcomin' mat." Russ clapped his thigh. "What was the score?"

"Let's just say I got a little dirt on my face." He pushed the thought of the young woman dressed as a boy away.

"Well, it seems to me, son, we could all use a little dirt on our face ever' once in a while. Keeps us humble. Anyhow, I was beginning to get a little bored 'round here. That one should liven things up a bit." Russ kicked his boot against the doorpost, and several clods of dirt and horse manure fell to the ground.

Ethan leaned against the desk and motioned Russ to come in. Russ stepped inside and closed the door. When the door clicked shut, Ethan whispered, "I'm going to buy ol' Reardon's place."

Russ let out a whoop and a holler but stopped. "Wait. Does he know about this?"

"If he doesn't, he's about to." Ethan grabbed his hat. "Come on. Let's check on camp and then get some breakfast in town before the train arrives. Dalys arrive on Friday. We've got a lot to do before I can get over to the land office. With so much to do in town today and in the morning, I'm thinking a hot bath and a bed at the hotel would do us a world of good."

"On Daly's time, on Daly's dime," Russ added.

They saddled their horses and headed to town. Ethan checked his pocket watch. "We should probably stop in and see Bella while we're in town." Ethan winked.

Russ leaned over, nearly lost his saddle, and struck Ethan's shoulder. "She won't be seeing you ten inches in her door till you shave that forest off your face."

Ethan stroked his beard. "Why, I was thinking it made me look older, more distinguished."

Russ shook his head. "Hardly, son. Hardly."

Chapter Ten

"All aboard. Passage to Hamilton, with stops in Lolo, Stevensville, and Darby."

The porter's announcement was muffled from inside the ladies' room. "Finally." She hadn't calculated the need to change trains in Missoula, Montana, or the additional cost. The train to Hamilton didn't run every day, so they'd slept the night at the station.

Beth stuffed Michael's old clothes in her case and checked her new appearance. Arriving at a new job in her brother's clothes would have been a disaster. Her mother's suit seemed fitting. Mr. Thomas C. Riley of the Ravalli Hotel was a businessman, and she wanted to approach him as such.

"Well, here we go." Beth exhaled. "Today's the day." After changing into a proper attire, she felt better immediately. She washed her face and secured her hair with several ivory combs. She was a woman again. Well, almost. A bath would complete the transformation. An unquestionable whiff of horse manure brought back the awkward memory of the man in Billings and reminded her of the pain in her arm. The boyish disguise she'd thought necessary before was no longer needed. Surely, Eli Sands hadn't followed her this far.

Straightening her mother's locket, she set her shoulders. *You can do this.*

There were a thousand things she'd rather be doing than facing the unknown. More nervous and afraid than she wanted to be, Beth reminded herself not to let it show. Michael and Maggie needed her to be strong.

"Second call. Passage to Hamilton…"

Beth grabbed her case and tried to imagine the Ravalli Hotel and Mr. Riley. A handsome tall man with distinguished silver hair, neatly trimmed. *Yes, he would have to be.* Wearing a tailored suit and a bright white collar, she added to the pleasing mental picture, *much like the older Mr. Tilny in Dickens' Northanger Abbey, only not as terrifying.* She hoped.

"You look pretty," Maggie said as they found their seats, "for a girl."

Beth squeezed Maggie's hand. Maggie hated ribbons and bows as much as she disliked peas and beans but always admired the adornments on others.

Michael tucked a hand inside his jacket. "I say, what is the price of tea in China?" Michael attempted a British accent. Beth and Maggie giggled like little girls, but Beth quickly regained her composure. As a little girl, she'd never carried such a heavy burden.

Michael seemed lost as they departed the station, and Maggie fidgeted with excitement. Even though they'd been in Montana for nearly two days, it wasn't real until now. The sight of the Bitterroot Mountains to the west took Beth's breath away. Every windowpane captured something picturesque.

"Told you they'd be magnificent." Michael gazed across the valley that separated the Bitterroot Mountains from the long rolling hills to the east.

Maggie chattered on about things only seven-year-olds could. "I see a horse, no, two horses, three, four." Maggie moved from one side of the train to the other, afraid to miss a thing. "I see bluffalo. Look," she pointed.

Michael roughed her hair. "Maggie, it's buff-a-lo." Michael pronounced each syllable.

"That's what I said." Maggie put a fist on her hip. "Bluff-a-lo."

Beth smirked and decided to give Maggie a break.

"I think Father and Mother would have loved Montana," Michael said as Maggie pulled him to the other side to search for bears.

Beth pictured her mother, letting herself surrender to the significance of their journey. "I *know* they would have." With her face pressed against the glass, she gazed at the backdrop and held her breath. For one perfect moment, everything seemed uncharacteristically calm. She wasn't running, wasn't anxious or afraid. She was light and unburdened, and somehow, it seemed as if the train would lift right off the track and ascend into heaven.

Muffled sounds surrounded her, but nothing broke the thought. Her nose tickled as it vibrated against the window, but she refused to bid this moment farewell. An imaginary orchestra began to play something beautiful in the background as she surveyed one mountaintop after another, her finger sketching the canyons on the glass.

Maggie tugged on her sleeve, legs dancing. "I've got to go bad," Maggie said, stealing her reverie. Maggie wiggled, confirming the dire situation.

"I told you to go at the station," Beth scolded more harshly than she should have, mourning the distraction.

"I didn't have to go then."

"Hamilton. Next stop." the porter called out.

Beth stared at the only family she had and smiled. "We're here." A cloud of dust kept the town from view as the train arrived at the station.

Someone opened the door, and the car filled with dust. They coughed and sputtered, unlike everyone else. The Hamilton station was a small wooden structure with a narrow platform. Nothing compared to the union station in Chicago. The arrival of the train was still a novelty for a crowd gathered to meet it. People waved and cheered like the train had arrived for the very first time.

As the dust began to settle, she made out buildings. Main Street came into view. Hotel Hamilton sat across the way but didn't fit the description of the Ravalli Hotel. Michael began to unload their belongings.

"Wait here. I'll get things settled at the hotel. I shouldn't be long—"

A loud thud drew her attention to the north end of the platform where the crowd had gathered. "Where's Maggie?" She panicked, heart pounding.

Michael dropped his cases. "She was right here a second ago."

Pushing her way through the people, to her relief, she saw Maggie beyond what held the crowd's attention. A dark mahogany horse stood like a magnificent statue at the center of the group. Maggie stared, wide-eyed. No doubt thrilled.

Beth sought her chance to circumvent the crowd and retrieve her sidetracked sister when the horse reared its front legs, bucking and kicking. An older man yelled and yanked hard at the rope. The crowd shrank back, nearly pushing her off the platform as another man grabbed her hand and pulled her from the edge. He stared for a second, and then with a hurried apology, pushed through the crowd to help gain control of the wild horse. He seemed oddly familiar and she wondered if he'd thought the same thing about her. She shook the thought. It didn't matter. He was a man. When it came to men and horses, she wasn't safe. Best to stay as far away as possible. She found her wayward sister and pulled her out of the crowd. "Don't ever do that again." Beth knelt in front of her, scolding her, not once but twice.

Maggie was still distracted by the horse. "I want one."

"Maggie." Beth shook her.

"All right." Maggie finally looked at her, but her eyes slowly found another object, forcing Beth to turn. She could see the top of a large structure above the treetops and knew that had to be the Ravalli Hotel. Retrieving the advertisement from her satchel, she memorized the address and rehearsed his name, "Mr. Thomas C. Riley."

Michael motioned to her, pointing to their trunks being pulled from a car.

With their belongings and bodies intact, Beth sighed, eyeing the hotel. "Stay here. I am going to meet with the hotel manager. Don't move a muscle." She made sure she'd been heard. Michael shrugged, and Maggie took a step toward the horse. Beth grabbed her. "I mean it. Stay put."

Michael sat with his back against the building. Maggie climbed atop their largest case saddle-style. The crowd dissipated as the wild beast was loaded into a wheeled carrier.

Beth shook her finger, reminding them to stay put and crossed the street—Bedford Street. It sounded so regal. The very name made her walk taller.

* * * * *

The photograph didn't do the Ravalli Hotel justice. It was grander than she imagined. The trees were taller, the entrance inviting. A white fence surrounded the brick establishment. Stepping onto the veranda lined with cushioned seats, she paused. A group of women stared. They sat drinking tea in their gowns and sunbonnets. Several whispered behind gloved hands.

She tugged at her jacket, swallowed, and reached for the door. A doorman greeted her and quickly motioned her inside. The lobby was lush with plants and soft carpet. A large chandelier hung overhead. It was everything she'd hope for and more. Moving to the front desk, Beth placed her satchel on the mahogany counter. "I'm here to see Mr. Thomas C. Riley."

The woman behind the desk lifted Beth's purse, still attached to her hand, and pulled her around the desk. A foot taller than Beth would ever be, the woman towered and stared down her skinny nose. "Name?" she barked in a masculine voice.

"Bet...Elizabeth Yates." Her confidence faltered. "I wrote to Mr. Riley—"

With a quick motion to follow her, the woman led Beth down a narrow hall to a large glass door etched with the words "Hotel Manager." She knocked.

"Come in." The man's voice was soft.

"A Miss Yates to see you, Mr. Riley." She scowled at Beth, pushed her inside, and remained like a sentry on guard at the closed door.

"Thank you, Tiny," Riley replied.

Beth glanced back at Tiny. Her name was Tiny? Mr. Riley didn't acknowledge her right away. Tiny nudged her closer to the desk and then resumed a militant position. The chair behind the desk slowly turned. Beth swallowed hard.

A little man overpowered by the large leather throne peeked over the top of his spectacles. First, glancing at her, then to Tiny, and back again. "Ah, Miss Yates. We didn't expect you to arrive today." He searched for something on his desk.

Beth started to explain, but Riley silenced her with a flick of his wrist.

"In fact, in your letter, you were..." he shook the letter in the air, "you were unclear as to your arrival date."

Her hands began to tremble. Scanning the letter in her mind, she shrugged. He raised his brows, making the long wrinkle across his forehead more pronounced.

She cleared her throat. "Yes, well...you see our train—"

"Our?" Riley said.

Clearly, he was the interrupting type. Beth briefly described her family situation, hoping to get back to the subject of her employment.

"Miss Yates, you did not mention anything about having family. We employ women and men of singularity. This is no place for children." He adjusted his glasses and folded his hands. "I regret to say that all of the available positions have been filled."

His words stung. Her heart thumped, and the room grew small. "Sir, I have come all the way from Chicago, halfway across the world, to work at the Ravalli Hotel. I've sold everything I have, and my parents are...." She couldn't say the words, not to a perfect stranger. She sighed instead. "We have nowhere else to go."

"I am sorry, Miss Yates." His nod to the sentry told her she'd been dismissed.

The wind of the side entrance door pushed at her back as Tiny shut it behind her. Wanting to sit down and cry, she grabbed at the post to calm herself. This must be a terrible, horrible nightmare, one she'd wake up from at any moment.

But the reality of that didn't come. Slumping to the step, she leaned her head against the post. What was she going to do now? Where would they live? Were they to starve? They were lost and alone in a new town without relations or connections.

The side door flew open, and several girls dressed in gray and white uniforms emerged. They worked for the hotel, as she should have. They giggled as they meandered down the path. A bitter taste bit her tongue.

Gathering what courage she had left, she pulled herself to her feet. *I can't give up this easy.* Michael and Maggie were depending on her. Surely there were other jobs in this town. She wasn't a snob. She'd do just about anything.

Well, almost anything.

She thought of Kitty's place. There was one place she would never go, one thing she would never do.

She fluffed her skirt, strengthened her resolve, and headed toward Main Street. Her best hope of finding a job, be

119

it temporary or not, would be there. Pinching her cheeks, she rounded the corner to Main Street. Her heart and smile lifted.

Could it be providence or had luck finally come her way? There, three or four buildings down, stood a woman—at least she thought it was a woman—on a short ladder posting a "Help Wanted" sign. Beth scoured the street for competition and then ran down the boardwalk as fast as her weary legs could carry her. Arriving winded and unable to speak, she pointed to the sign.

The woman dressed as a man stared down at her. "You ain't a mute now, are you? You got something to say, missy, just spit it out."

"I, huh—" Beth tried to catch her breath. "I would like to inquire about your available position." She stole a quick glance at the shopwindow, hoping she hadn't applied to be a saloon dancer. To her relief, the word "cafe" was stuck on the front door.

"How old are you? Got anybody lookin' for you?" The woman's voice was harsh, but there was an ounce of kindness in it.

Beth shook her head, ignoring the second question.

"Well, if you can work as hard and fast as you run, you're hired." She yanked the small wooden sign down from the post and descended the ladder. "Name's Jane. My husband and I run this here café." Jane pointed toward the back of the café to a man bent over a table, whistling a song off tune.

Beth nodded.

"If'n I catch you misbehavin', I'll box you right here." Jane stabbed her finger right between Beth's eyes. "And if'n I catch you stealin', you'd be wishin' you was already dead. Can you cook?"

"Yes, ma'am." She finally caught her breath. "I've cooked for more than fifty," Beth added in case there was any doubt about her qualifications, but didn't mention that those fifty were all under the age of ten.

Suddenly, two men stepped up to the post behind them to secure their horses. Men and horses—apparently, two things she'd have to put up with.

Jane pushed Beth out of her way. "Why you two good for nothin'…" A long string of colorful words followed. "I said I'd whip you both if'n you showed your two ugly faces 'round here again." Jane narrowed her eyes.

Beth sought a place to hide. She'd heard of gunfights and saloon brawls from the newspaper and had no intention of finding out how real they were from personal experience. The taller of the two men, who wasn't tall at all, fumbled for something in his pocket, but before he found it, Jane kicked him square in the backside, sending him face first into the dirt. After dusting himself off and making threats, the two men mounted and rode off, leaving dust in their wake.

"Fifty, you say? Good enough for me," Jane replied as if nothing had happened. "Sunday mornin'. Be here five o'clock sharp."

Beth nodded. "Five o'clock on Sunday. Yes, ma'am."

"Jane, just Jane." Jane leaned over the hitching post and spat into the street, revealing something shiny at her side.

Beth tried not to react, but how could she not? The woman carried a gun. *A gun.* Suddenly, Jane hurled the "help wanted" high into the air. A gunshot rang out, shattering the sign to pieces.

Beth gulped as Jane slipped her gun into is holster. "Yes, ma'am," Beth stuttered. "I mean, Jane."

* * * * *

"Your room keys, Ethan. Room 11 and 13." The hotel clerk slid the keys across the counter. "Billed to Daly's account."

Ethan nodded. This wasn't the grand Ravalli Hotel. Didn't have the need or the funds to frequent such a fine establishment. The Hotel Hamilton was simple and small. It had its charm. A tall, thin man leaned over the counter, tilting his head to avoid hitting the beam protruding from the ceiling. The permanent indent on his forehead said he'd hit a great many things in his time.

"I don't want no trouble this time." The clerk raised a whiskery brow. "Our man will board that beast of yours out back for the night—one night." He eyed Ethan, wobbling a pen between his fingers, tapping it on the counter.

"No, sir," Ethan replied apologetically. "And yes, sir." Ethan didn't want any trouble either. All he wanted was a comfortable bed and something to fill the hole in his stomach.

The Hotel Hamilton sat directly across from the train station with the second story giving perfect eastern views of the Sapphire Mountains. And except for the roar and tremor of the train leaving town, it was relatively quiet, far enough away from the nightlife to give a man some peace.

The front door swung open, hinges screamed, letting the distant sounds of town barrel in. Someone plunked on a piano desperately out of tune, men shouted, and women laughed. Ethan sighed, thankful that he had no desire to join the scene—never had.

Stepping onto the boardwalk, he unlatched his saddlebag from Jax. "I took the liberty of promising you'd be on your best behavior." Ethan patted Jax's neck, and she whinnied and then snubbed him. He'd known two stubborn women in his time—no, three, if he counted his mother.

Putting an extra knot at the post, he made eye contact with his constant but wayward companion. "You've got to stop getting me into trouble. You're getting a bad reputation around town and costing me a fortune." Jax nudged Ethan's jacket with her nose.

Ethan looked up and saw Russ Miles in the distance. Russ had settled Daly's horse for the night at Sam's livery on the corner of Main and Fourth, several blocks away. Took him long enough. Russ' quick heavy stride shortened the gap as Ethan surveyed Main Street. The south side of town displayed large, stately homes with manicured lawns and nicely trimmed trees. A buggy passed by, and he predicted the direction it was headed by its fine lines and well-trained thoroughbred. The Ravalli Hotel sat to the south, a hotel newly built by Marcus Daly to accommodate his important guests and relatives in grand colonial fashion, very unlike anything else in town—unlike anything west of the Mississippi for that matter.

A ruckus caught his attention as a fight broke out at one of the saloons. The music stopped. Two men crashed through a window, tumbled across the boardwalk and into the street. Wagons kept rolling, and people returned to their conversations. The music started up again. A man driving a large wooden wagon, wobbling in disrepair, passed the hotel and headed north onto First Street.

Two different worlds. The north side of town was rough and rowdy. It housed hundreds of mill workers, sawyers, and miners who worked the local industry, men unacquainted with good manners and a life of luxury. Folks who, for one reason or another, found themselves in Hamilton, living paycheck to paycheck, and some living on less than that. The houses were small and simple, except for a few particularly large homes owned by prominent townspeople. All the entertainment a man wanted after a long hard day's work could be found in one of the town's many saloons or in one of the numerous women's boardinghouses located in the "red light" district.

He gave Jax a hard pat and threw Russ his room key.

Ethan plunked his tired body onto the bed—boots, hat, and all. A knock on the door told him Russ was ready to go. "Warning. I'm moping."

"Let's eat," Russ said, kicking Ethan's boot that hung off the edge of the bed. Ethan didn't move. "Don't be so hard on yourself. If your offer is at the land office, it will still be there in the morning. Have some patience, my boy."

The title office closed before he could get there. They'd finished up at the Company Store later than expected, with it being payday and all. Ethan sat up and stroked his clean-shaven chin. "Well as you know, Russ, patience is not one of my finer qualities."

Russ slapped Ethan on the back and chuckled. "Come on. Bella will have supper on by the time we get there. Patience won't be required."

Ethan and Russ mounted their horses. The hope of a home-cooked meal reeled them in like fish—hook, line, and sinker. The thought brought back so many memories. His family sitting around the supper table. Father saying grace. Mother reminding him of his manners. "I was so close," Ethan said with a shake of his head. "Just seventy-five or so miles from home. Sure wish I could've seen my folks."

Russ gave an understanding nod.

"Knowing Mother, corn bread would've been hot out of the oven." Ethan closed his eyes and licked his lips. "You've never lived until you've tasted my mama's corn bread."

"You're a sentimental fool." Russ scratched his chin. "Never thought so when I met you, but you are."

Ethan smirked, ignoring the direction of the conversation and turned the tide. "I'm a fool? I've seen the way you look at Bella..."

Russ protested. "Why, I never." Shock lit his face as if it were the first time he'd realized it.

Ethan smiled, knowing Russ and Bella had feelings. It was love, but those two were too stubborn to admit it. "You can't fool a fool," Ethan added.

Chapter Eleven

Beth hurried from one boardinghouse to the next. With every "sorry, we're full up," her hope diminished a little more, and the sun sank deeper behind the mountains. She searched along the side streets for any sign of vacancy—permanent or temporary. She'd take anything. Lifting her father's watch from her pocket, she checked the time. Where had time gone? She imagined the look on Michael's face.

Second and Third Streets left a pit in her stomach. If she didn't find something soon, they'd be sleeping under the stars tonight. Turning onto Fourth Street, she slowed. Something didn't seem right. She dismissed the odd feeling, calling it exhaustion or hunger. The growl in her stomach agreed.

A man and woman laughed aloud as they disappeared between two buildings, and another man staggered toward her, fixing his eyes where they didn't belong. She tensed and quickly crossed the street.

Sensing his lingering stare as he passed, she felt her neck tingle. Looking back, she discovered, much to her relief, that he'd turned down another side street. With renewed determination, Beth continued.

Then she saw it.

In the middle of the block swayed a wooden vacancy sign. She quickened her pace to the two-story building. Though its white paint was worn with age and more than one slat was missing on the railing, it was a mansion to her.

She climbed the stairs and discovered two separate doors, one marked 1 through 8, and the other unmarked with a mat beneath the frame. She knocked on the unmarked door, but no one answered. A loud thud and the sound of broken glass told her someone must be home. Beth prepared to knock a second time when the door opened a couple of inches. A disheveled old man stood in the crack. Struggling to open it wider, he kicked and cursed at the dog that barred his way. "Git dog." He was half bald, half shaven, and what hair he did have stood straight out to one side. Thin and wrinkled, he hunched over with age.

"What do you want?" He said, annoyed.

Perhaps she'd interrupted dinner or maybe he was already asleep. Taking several steps back, she sought fresh air, for his breath was heavy with whiskey. Beth cleared her throat. "I am here to inquire about your room."

"Twenty dollars a month and twenty dollars deposit upfront or no deal." he shouted, making the slur in his words even more pronounced. "Don't wanna know yer business long as I git paid."

Mentally adding the figures in her head, she tried to factor in living expenses.

He cursed. "I ain't got all night, lady."

She nodded, still adding. He was impatient, rude, ill kept, and a drunk, the type of man so familiar to her now that she second-guessed her decision. Maybe sleeping underneath the stars wasn't such a bad idea. He started to close the door, and she wedged her tiny boot to block it. What if this room was all that was available, and she let it go? "The month is half over, sir. I will pay you the deposit and a half month's rent now and the full rent on the first."

His foul breath told her to run, but she stood her ground. Grunting, he shook his head, cursing.

Better not rile him. He might have a gun, she warned herself. If Jane needed a gun at her side, surely a man had two. Seeing rejection on his face, she had to think of something. "Sir, I can see that you are an important man." An unsettling sweetness tinted her voice. "You won't be disappointed—"

He interrupted with more colorful words and shot out his hand for payment. Hesitantly, she counted the bills. She paused as she laid the last bill in his hand.

"Second floor. Number 5," he shouted and closed the door abruptly, leaving her startled and confused. The word "thief" came to mind.

Dare she knock again? Common sense told her she would need a key to the room, but what if he did have a gun?

All of a sudden, the door flew open, and a solitary key came flying out. She scrambled to catch it, but the key flipped and flopped, landing on the porch in several bounces. The door slammed, making her jump. *Welcome to Montana.* She bent down, noting how close the key was to falling through the slats in the porch.

Suddenly, the numbered door opened, and a man stepped onto the porch with his boot on top of her key. She held her breath. Sunset kept her shadowed. He straightened his jacket and jumped the steps, heading toward Main Street, giving her no notice whatsoever.

Exhaling, she reached for the key, but it was gone. It had slipped through the crack to the ground below. Beth growled under her breath, aggravated at the situation and sighed.

Crawling on her hands and knees under the dark porch in her mother's finest suit, Beth imagined all sorts of awful things, things that made her skin crawl. She scoured the dirt and rocks beneath them, feeling the ground for the key, hoping the red light from across the street would shine at just the right spot.

Cobwebs touched her face and hair, sending chills down her spine. Finally, she felt something cold. She grabbed it and scurried out from underneath the porch, her skin itching all over but satisfied that what she held in her hand was indeed the key.

Swatting dirt from her skirt, she hoped she hadn't permanently damaged her suit. She scratched her legs and head and pulled cobwebs from her hair. But it didn't help. She still imagined spiders crawling on her. "Ooh whee," she squealed and stomped her feet at the thought.

Knowing Michael was waiting and Maggie probably starving, Beth opened the numbered door and climbed the stairs nervously until she stood in front of her door. Running her fingers over the number 5, she removed a thin layer of accumulated dust and turned the key. The door swung open easily and hit something behind. She smoothed her hands along the medium-sized bed and sat down, looking around the room. It was dusk, but she made out a dresser, a cupboard on the right, and a nightstand beside the bed. In the corner was a small stove and next to it, a table with two chairs and an ice chest by the window. "Perfect," she concluded. If the amount of dust on the door number was any indication, the whole room needed a good cleaning.

Beth stepped into the hall. The facilities were down a couple of doors to the left. Voices echoed up the stairs. She saw the man she'd seen at the station trying to control his horse. He'd shaved, but it was him. Two backward jumps and she was in her room with the door closed—mostly closed. She heard two voices—no, three—and one of them belonged to a woman. She put her ear to the door.

"Well, if you ain't a sight for sore eyes. And good evenin' to you, handsome," a woman said.

The voices trailed off as a door in the hall closed. She waited. After a few moments of quiet, Beth stole a look down the hall. She locked her door and took to the stairs. She rolled the small key between her fingers and slid it into her pocket as she rounded the corner to Main Street. It was dark, but the red lights from numerous windows lit her way. Beth could see the station at the end of Main Street, a small silhouette danced about while the taller one stood like a statue with his hands on his hips. Beth hurried.

Beth imagined right. Michael was very upset at the time. He grabbed a case. "Well, it's about time. Where have you been?" He said, understandably tired and grouchy.

"I'm sorry it took so long," She said, out of breath with the haste of her return. "Are you both all right?" She knelt down and fastened Maggie's coat. "It's a long story, but I have a job, and I found us a room." She smiled at her success and looked up at Michael, who hadn't wiped the scowl off his face.

"I'm hungry," Maggie said.

"I know. Let's get settled, and then we'll see about something to eat, huh?" Without a word, Michael gathered their trunks, dragging them from the platform. Beth gathered her bags and urged Maggie to do the same. "Home isn't far."

* * * * *

The boardwalk led them down Main Street past the Hotel Hamilton, a drugstore, Paisley's General, The Company Store, and various other merchants. She pointed out the café, conveying enough information to satisfy Micheal. The shops across the street were hard to make out in the dark, except for the local saloons, whose clanging of glass and loud music could be heard for blocks. Anticipating each saloon, she motioned them into the street, hoping to avoid a confrontation with the unsavory men and scantily dressed women standing at the entrances. Men slammed their fists on tables, yelling, "Another round for the boys, Mac," and "Give us another tune." The laughter of crass women brought Kitty to mind. Kitty and Donovan.

Maggie stared at the men and women as they passed. Michael cleared his throat. "Maggie, don't stare."

Beth knew all too well what kind of business went on in there. She glanced at each second-story window and could easily imagine the scene. She shook her head, disappointed in what she discovered about this new town and then reprimanded herself for being so idealistic. "Hurry up, Maggie," Beth called to her. "Catch up."

Looking at Michael, she saw the seriousness of their situation and the arduous journey displayed on his face. A thud and a diminished number of footsteps made Beth and Michael look back. "Maggie." Beth let her bags fall to the ground and ran.

Maggie lay facedown on the boardwalk. Bags, too heavy for one so young, piled on both sides of her. She whimpered but didn't cry as she struggled to get up.

"Are you all right?" Beth gasped at Maggie's red mouth and looked at Michael.

Maggie tried to talk, but bubbles of blood formed on her lips. Maggie wiped her nose with her sleeve and saw the blood. She panicked. "I've been shot!" A series of spits and coughs ensued, sending Maggie's front tooth flying.

With Maggie hysterical, Michael dropped his bags and reached for his handkerchief. "You've lost a tooth, Maggie. It was coming out anyway."

Beth examined Maggie, dabbing the blood away with the cloth. Sure enough, her lip was cut, and her front tooth gone. "Am I going to die?" Maggie said, grasping Beth's hand.

Beth helped Maggie to her feet. "Don't be ridiculous. No one ever died from losing a tooth."

"But how will I eat?"

Beth and Michael looked at each other and gathered their bags. "Knowing you, Maggie, you'll find a way," Michael added.

"We won't let you starve. Now, come on. We're almost there." Beth motioned to a nearby side street. "This is our street."

They turned onto Fourth Street, and Beth noticed how busy it was compared to the other streets. It was noisy. People were scattered everywhere. A strange red glow illuminated the street for several blocks. Beth looked up into a second-story window of a nearby building and saw a woman snuff out a single candle covered with a red shade. "Ah, here we are." She pointed to the house in a "ta-da" fashion. Michael rewarded her with a small grin.

"My mouth tastes like blood." Maggie was herself again.

Beth opened the door. "Up the stairs. First door on the left. Number 5."

Michael struggled and faltered with the weight and bulk on his shoulders. The racket of the cases and trunks hitting the wall and steps was sure to anger neighbors. They all froze midstair when they heard voices coming to the top of the landing. "The pleasure was all mine, ma'am," a man said.

"Good night, boys," a woman replied.

Beth panicked, wanting to drop everything and run, but it was too late. The man with the wild horse stood at the top of the stairs, soon joined by his older friend. The older man motioned to let them pass. Michael and Maggie scooted by, and Beth clung to the wall, trying to make herself invisible, avoiding eye contact.

"Miss, let me help with that." He tipped his hat and reached for her bags.

She stared at his face. His eyes confirmed what she hoped wasn't true. "I can manage." Pushing past him, she climbed the remaining stairs, dropped her bags, and fumbled with the key. Thankfully, the key slid into place, and she opened the door. The room was dark. Michael and Maggie followed her in. She heard the two men descend the stairs and close the door. This was his town. It was too much to hope that he was just passing through.

As her eyes adjusted to the darkness, moonlight made its way across the floor, beyond the table, and over the much smaller bed. Michael collapsed, the bed creaking and groaning under his weight, as did the floor. She hadn't noticed the noise before—doors slamming, people coming and going. She wanted to slap herself. She shouldn't be complaining. Not now.

They ate what remained of the cheese and salami, enough to satisfy the rumble in their stomachs. Maggie and Beth crawled into bed at the top, while Michael crawled in from the bottom. They'd have to make do. The three found the bed a welcome companion.

They'd sleep. Late night conversations could not prevent it. Even the steady flow of footsteps in the hall and the intermittent knocking on doors couldn't keep it from coming.

However small, it was home.

* * * * *

Ethan breathed in the hot steam surrounding him. A trip to the bathhouse was absolutely necessary, according to Bella. He'd settled Jax with a stable boy. *Lord, keep her out of trouble this time.* Last time he'd stayed at the hotel, Jax cost him a month's wages with the damage she'd done. He wasn't about to repeat that again, not with his ranch needing all of his available funds.

Getting into bed after a hot bath, Ethan could still taste Bella's fried chicken and biscuits, thrilled to have missed a camp meal. The men all knew the rules: "He who complains, volunteers." If a cowboy wanted to stay out of the kitchen, best to eat with his mouth shut.

Turning over, he watched the white curtains move gently with a breeze from the open window. It was her at the station. He'd wondered. She'd changed her clothes but little else.

Ethan remembered something his father told Peter on his wedding day. He said, "Build yourself a home, not just a ranch. There's no substitute." Why he remembered that now made no sense. Having a family was the furthest thing from his mind. Ranch first. Family, much, much later.

Someone knocked at the door. Ethan threw back the covers and dressed. "Just a second."

Another knock hurried him to the door. The hall shot a thin line of light into his room as he opened the door, but no one was there. He looked to the right, then to the left and frowned. *Molly.* Molly Singleton stood against the wall, crying... *or pretending to cry.* "Molly, what do you—"

Molly blew her nose and looked up at him. "I didn't know who to go to."

He rolled his eyes. *I'll bet.*

"I desperately need your help." Determination lit her eyes.

Ethan ran his fingers through his hair. "What is it this time? Someone's house on fire?"

Molly flipped around and grabbed at his shirt. "Not yet, but it could—"

Ethan ripped her fingers from his shirt. "Molly, please." The hall was empty but for them. *Lord, save me.*

"I see the way you look at me, Ethan." She tried to kiss him.

He uncurled her grip and pushed her away. She hit the opposite wall dramatically. "I look at everyone that way." Ethan hung his head. *That's not what I meant to say.* "What I mean is, I don't look at you in *any specific* way."

Pushing herself from the wall, she came at him again. *Vulture.* His hand stopped her. "Go home, Molly. Your father will be worried."

"He knows I'm with you—"

"Go home, Molly." Holding her out, he shut the door and watched the crack of light. Her shadow didn't move. He locked the door and fixed his shirt. Would she ever leave him alone? Her shadow finally shifted and disappeared. He exhaled. Didn't realize he'd been holding his breath.

Another knock at the door made him jump. He turned and whispered near the door. "Go home, Molly."

"You all right?"

Russ. Ethan unlocked the door and opened it. Russ stood, donning only his trousers.

"I heard voices," Russ said, scratching his head.

"Molly Singleton."

Russ nodded. "It must be hard being so de…si…red."

Ethan gave up. "That's what I keep telling everyone." He crawled into bed as Russ left. So much for a relaxing evening.

He shook his face in his pillow. If Mr. Singleton finds out Molly was here, he'd have them married by sunup. Marry Molly Singleton? What a nightmare that would be. First, Clarese Wright. Now, Molly Singleton. The only modest young woman he could think of just arrived in town, and she wanted nothing to do with him. And that was fine by him.

Chapter Twelve

Beth woke to a bloodcurdling scream. Michael heard it too and was at the window in seconds. "What is it?" Beth sat up, reached for her watch, and held it up to the window's light. "It's two o'clock in the morning."

The bed squeaked and tipped as Michael sat down and forced on his boots. The door closed behind him before Beth had time to comprehend the situation. "No, Michael." Beth called out, trying not to wake Maggie, but Michael was gone.

Frightened and tense, Beth jumped out of bed, trembling to lace her boots. Her hands stroked the wall in search of her coat. Confirming Maggie was still sound asleep, she ran down the stairs after him. She heard voices, shouting, and profanity. The sound of broken glass sent chills down her spine. "Michael." Beth pushed through the small crowd in the dark street but couldn't find him. Michael was going to get himself hurt or worse.

"You're a drunk, Jacob Skinner," a man shouted, charging into the crowd.

Beth's eyes finally adjusted, and red shadows danced in the street. Another scream rang out. Beth covered her ears. This can't be happening. She rubbed her eyes, but the horrifying reality remained. Jacob had cornered a young girl between two buildings.

"Hawk, stay back, you hear? Sadie's gonna give me what I paid for or I'll"—Jacob thrust his knife in the air.

"Or you'll what?" Hawk ordered and took a step closer.

Sadie tried to skirt the pair, but Jacob blocked her. "I say who. I say when—"

"Someone go for the sheriff." An older woman pushed through the crowd. "Jacob, don't be a fool. Put down that knife." Beth couldn't make out the woman's face. "Sugar, you don't want to do this. Now, put the knife away. Let's talk about it."

"Bella, you stay out of this. She's my girl."

Hawk cut in while Jacob swung around, displaying the point of his knife, pushing the crowd back.

"He'll kill me, Hawk." Sadie cried out.

Jacob took another swing. Sadie screamed and jumped, suddenly aware that he'd cut her leg. Two men lunged at Jacob from the crowd as he swung his knife at the onlookers. Beth gasped. The two men wrestled Jacob to the ground, trying to get control of the crazed man. The crowd closed in. Beth searched frantically through the crowd for Michael, but darkness distorted figures, and the dust hid faces. Beth heard the sound of horses, and then a figure split the crowd down the middle. She hoped that the figure wore a shiny gold star.

"Jacob Skinner, you've been more trouble than your worth. I have been waiting a long time for this." The opening in the crowd proved that it was the sheriff. "Show's over, folks. Go on home now. Nothin' more to see here." The sheriff hoisted the deranged man to his feet with the aid of his deputy.

"Michael!" Beth found him.

The sheriff shook Michael's hand. "Son, that was a mighty brave thing you did. We've been trying to catch up with Jacob Skinner for some time now. He would've killed that girl. He's done it before." The sheriff turned to the man holding Jacob. "Take him in, Dale."

Beth pushed past several people to reach Michael, who was dusting off his trousers, his eyes intent on Hawk as the man spoke in the girl's ear. "Michael." Beth embraced him, tears streaming down her cheeks.

"Hawk," the sheriff called out, "keep your girl outta trouble."

Beth and Michael watched the exchange. The girl couldn't have been more than sixteen years old.

"Oh, she won't be no more trouble to you, Sheriff Irvine. I promise you that." Hawk grabbed Sadie by the neck and led her away. "You worthless weed. We'll see how you like stayin' with me for a while."

Beth looked Michael over. "What were you thinking? You could have been…" The tremor in her voice gave way to a violent sob.

* * * * *

Ethan took his real estate papers from one of the Johnston brothers after hearing a lengthy tale of presenting his offer to Buck Reardon. "That man is crazy. Out of his mind." He yanked a briefcase from his desk. "Nearly shot me." He pushed a finger through the hole in his case, as if Ethan needed confirmation.

Reardon had a reputation. "I'm sorry for the trouble," Ethan apologized but figured that the Johnston Bros. Real Estate Company would be accustomed to dealing with such excitable folks. Water rights alone brought out the beast in a man and one specific woman, he recalled.

"You're on your own, Mr. Dawson, but mind your hat and your backside." The short, stocky man turned to reveal a patch sewn to his trousers, telling Ethan this wasn't Johnston's first trip down the river. "Mind all your sides." He returned Ethan's down payment. "If'n you're smart, you'd choose another piece of land altogether. There's plenty to be had." He tapped his temples. "Give it a couple of years, and ol' Reardon will keel over dead or gamble it away, sure as anything. It'll be ten cents on a dollar at auction."

Ethan tucked the papers away, thankful for the warning, but a couple of years, he did not have. And to profit from another man's misfortune or mistakes didn't sit well. He'd speak to Reardon himself, reason with him. Assured himself of all the reasons why this would work.

Besides, the Johnston Brothers charged too much to facilitate their land deals. The door to the land office closed behind him fast. He gathered his thoughts and considered the hole in Johnston's briefcase. Maybe the Johnston Bros. didn't charge nearly enough.

* * * * *

"What time is it?" Beth opened her eyes to the morning light and squinted. They stung.

"Time to eat." Maggie jumped onto the bed.

"It's nine in the morning." Michael was up, dressed, and his nose already in a book.

"Are you all right?" Beth asked as she threw back the covers and put her bare feet on the cold floor. How she longed for a rug.

"He's hungry," Maggie interrupted and pounced on the bed next to Beth.

Beth pulled her into her arms like a baby as she said, "all you think about his food." Beth looked up at Michael, who hadn't answered her question. "Well?" Beth smiled, and he joined her.

"I'm fine. Didn't sleep very well." He rubbed Maggie's head. "I didn't know Maggie was a bed hog."

Beth hugged her. "I should've warned you."

"I am not."

"You are," Michael and Beth said in unison.

Beth rose to check the stove. It still had some wood. They'd gather more this afternoon. They finished off the small round of cheese and last nub of salami. Today, Beth hoped to transform their little apartment into a real home. She twisted her hair on top her head with a pin and looked around the room. "It needs a good cleaning, and we'll move the bed over there," Beth pointed.

Beth set the order for the day, assigning each one a different task. A thorough cleaning was first on the agenda, and then the rearranging of furniture would commence. Michael's facial expressions made it even more fun, and Maggie laughed at his frustration.

"No wonder that suitcase was so heavy," Michael scowled as he surveyed the items she carefully pulled from the case. "Now I know why you wanted me to carry that one."

Beth smiled and continued to unpack. "I guess you're not the only one with brains in this family, isn't that right, Maggie?"

Maggie stuffed a slice of salami in her mouth and nodded.

Michael suddenly stood beside her, rubbing his forehead. "A rug. You brought a rug?" It was a question not a statement. "And curtains. Matching curtains." Michael rolled his eyes and exhaled has he stared at the open trunk.

"Yes, and beautiful matching curtains." Beth laid them out to remove the wrinkles then lifted several pillows out as well.

Michael sat down and put his head on the table. "This is my worst nightmare."

Beth and Maggie smiled at each other.

The bed needed to be centered on a different wall, and the dresser would never do where it was, but after several attempted relocations, the bed landed right back where it started, as did the dresser. She hung several framed family portraits on nails left by previous tenants, while Michael arranged the cases under the bed like drawers. A long, narrow shelf ran along the wall behind the wood stove and stopped at the window. Beth cleaned its surface with one long swipe and decorated it with a few memories of home.

Dusting the family Bible, she placed it on the shelf. The gilded pages still clumped together like new. It had been a wedding gift from her great grandfather. Inside, Mother had meticulously written down all the names of their relatives and the towns in which they were born, the only testament of who they were and where they'd come from.

She lifted Mother's jewelry box, and her throat began to tighten as her eyes started to water. Clearing her throat, she managed to hold back the tears. The time for crying was over. Her parents were gone. Their home was gone. A portion of her dignity was gone.

Mother's quilt, spread across the bed, made their tiny home as cozy as it could possibly be. Michael stacked what few books he'd brought on the nightstand, which he'd claimed for himself. His only sign of manhood, he complained. The nightstand had one small drawer for a few possessions. Beth watched as he held each treasure and placed the item in the drawer. When he pulled out a pocketknife and twisted it in the light, she gasped. "Where did you get that?" Beth said with a face that told him to put it away before Maggie saw it. She'd want one for sure.

Michael returned the knife to its case and shoved it to the back of the drawer. "Father."

Beth narrowed her eyes. She really didn't care where he got it. What really concerned her is that he had it in the first place. "Well—"

"I won't use it," Michael narrowed on her, "unless I have to."

After last night, Beth decided to drop the subject. Michael was sixteen and more than capable of handling such a weapon. Michael wasn't a boy anymore. He was the man of the house, and he'd be the *only man* of this house.

Chapter Thirteen

"Pa-is-le-yas," Maggie sounded out the letters to the best of her ability.

"Paisley's General Store," Beth read, correcting Maggie's errors as Michael pushed the door open, and a bell rang out. Both walls were lined with shelves with one lower shelf cut down the middle of the store, creating two aisles. A counter sat near the front.

"Canned meats on sale," she heard someone shout from the back. The store owner was a short, stocky man with gray wiry hair, his jaw defined by long bushy sideburns. The sign in the window identified the owners as Mr. and Mrs. Paisley.

"Candy!" Maggie ran like a locomotive toward the counter lined with glass jars. Beth's eyes followed around the corner past a display of small flat shovels and a sign that read, "The All New Dustpan." Maggie pressed her nose against the case that separated her world from the colorful one within, fogging the glass. Michael found something of interest at the back of the store.

Beth approached the counter and dictated the list of necessities she'd written down in her mind. "And if you have it—"

Maggie yanked at her sleeve but never actually made eye contact. "And three sweet sticks too," Beth added to the list. Maggie grinned, and she ran to make her candy selection.

Beth and the man shared a smile. He wrapped the goods in loud brown paper, tied it with string, and quoted the price.

Beth laid out exact change. "Is there a park in town, sir?" She nodded toward her purchase. "For a picnic."

"You must be new 'round here?" he replied. "The Bitterroot River is not far from here."

He walked into the back room without another word. A moment later, he returned with another piece of brown paper and a woman twice his size in height and weight waltzing behind. He spread out the paper on the counter, leaned down on his elbow, and started to draw a map.

"I'm Chaz Paisley, and this strange looking fella is my husband," she said with laughter in her voice. She nudged her husband with her elbow, forcing his pen off the edge of the paper, receiving a scowl in return. "Where'd you come from?"

Beth grimaced. Such a direct question required an honest answer. "Chicago."

"Chicago? Well, I'll be sidesaddled." Chaz slapped the counter, getting Michael's attention at the front of the store and calling Maggie to her side. "We had us a family come through just last week from Illinois." She emphasized the lacking "S" sound at the end as if she had been informed of the correct pronunciation recently. "Family had sick babies that needed Doc's medicine—twins, to be sure. Sad tale. The twins didn't make it. The ma and pa stopped in just as they was leavin' town," Chaz continued and shook her head.

"I said to that ugly man o'mine, 'The kindest thing we could ever do is feed their stomachs 'cause there ain't much we can do to feed their sad souls.'" Chaz closed her eyes as if she were going to pray then opened them wide. "I gave them three cans of beans and four cans of tomatoes. We had 'em on sale last week." She slapped the counter again and scrunched her lips like she'd eaten a lemon.

Maggie giggled. The woman hadn't breathed for a whole minute. Beth narrowed her eyes, reminding Maggie to be polite.

"This little one must be your daughter."

Michael stepped up to the counter and leaned toward Mr. Paisley's artistic rendition of the road to the river. Chaz stared between the two, confused.

"This is Maggie, my sister, and this"—Beth gestured—"is my brother, Michael."

"Oh heavens and all the stars in it," Chaz reacted as if she should have seen it all along. "Good-lookin' kids, all of you, that's for sure. Why, your folks must be mighty proud to have such fine offspring." She widened her eyes.

Beth tried to hear bits and pieces of Mr. Paisley's narrative in the background but didn't want to be rude. The pause in conversation left an opening, and Maggie jumped right in. Mouth first, brain second. "Our parents are dead. They live in heaven now." Acting as if she'd grown a whole inch, Maggie beamed.

Beth squeezed her hand in a brief scold.

"What? That's what you said."

Chaz appeared stunned, speechless. Probably for the first time in her life, Beth guessed.

Mr. Paisley slid his drawing across the counter to Michael. "River's 'bout a mile down, near the Big Mill. Can't miss it."

Beth thanked Mr. Paisley as the bell above the door rang. "Canned meats on sale," Mr. Paisley made the rehearsed announcement.

Beth blew at a stubborn strand of hair, annoyed that complete strangers now knew their story but offered a polite, "Thank you." Michael gathered the sketch and packages. As Beth turned, she froze. *Him again.* Was she to see him every day for the rest of her life?

143

"Ah, just the man I've been lookin' for." Chaz lifted the hinged counter. "I hear you've been meddling with the Singleton girl." She cupped her ear. "I hear wedding bells."

Beth studied him and then cocked her head when he didn't respond. He stiffened and offered a coy smile. She raised a brow. Men must be held accountable for their actions. Still, he said nothing. Beth smirked and hurried her family toward the front door. He tipped his hat and rushed back to open the door for her. "Miss."

Maggie pulled her stick of candy free. "I like your horse, mister." Beth ignored him and yanked her through the door in rebuke. "Well, I do."

Beth glanced back as he slapped his hat against his leg. "Chaz, you know I'm not the marrying type. Neither am I the meddling type."

The doorbell rang upon their departure. Beth shook her head. What that man was or wasn't didn't matter. She did, however, caution herself to avoid establishments he frequented. The less she saw of him, the better.

It was a beautiful day. A recent rain was evident, for the streets revealed deep dry ruts. With the sun shining and no cloud in sight, Beth knew a trip to the river was a good idea. The Bitterroot Mountains stretched out in front of them, north to south, like a painting. The mountains towered high above the rooftops of even the tallest buildings in town. Snow still capped the peaks, and the gorgeous haze of green outlined the different peaks and valleys. The backdrop echoed the bluest blue Beth had ever seen, rich and clear like a sapphire—breathtaking.

* * * * *

"You're mistaken." Ethan tried to explain the truth about Molly Singleton without ruining Molly's reputation completely and loud enough for the new girl in town to hear, but the girl left in a hurry, and Chaz wouldn't buy it. Ever since Ethan had come to Hamilton, Chaz had made it her mission to see him married. "Think what you like, but I've no intention of meddling with anyone's daughter or marrying one for that matter."

Ethan slammed the door against the wall as he left. *That woman cannot be reasoned with.* His list of stubborn women was growing longer. "You try talking some sense into her," Ethan told Jax, who was tied at the post in front of Paisley's General.

He scoured Main Street. There she was, walking toward the Big Mill. He supposed the other two to be her siblings. Now she thought he wasn't respectable. He slammed his hat against his trousers. He'd forgotten why he'd come to Paisley's General in the first place.

* * * * *

Beth heard the Paisley's door slam in the distance behind her. She kept walking. *Don't look.* The temptation got the best of her, and she finally gave in. He was riding in the opposite direction. Maggie's mumbling drew Beth back. "Someday, I'm going to climb that mountain all the way to the top all by myself."

"That's Downing Mountain. Climbing a mountain is dangerous, Maggie," Michael replied. "You have to have special tools and more equipment than one man can carry alone." He told of a climber who met their death after falling thousands of feet, smashing their head on the rocks. "It was a lady climber in that case—"

Interrupting, Beth gasped. "Michael!" Maggie didn't need to hear the details.

"Well, I won't fall," Maggie promised, "or die."

145

Beth frowned at the topic that Maggie felt so free to discuss. Maybe Maggie didn't comprehend their loss as Beth did. Michael rolled his eyes, and Maggie ate her candy.

The stroll through town was invigorating. Narrow two-story structures lined Main Street, each building with a character and design uniquely its own. Many were made of brick, but there were still a few wood buildings. Several of the largest brick buildings overshadowed the rest, creating an urban replica of the mountain range in the distance. The Company Store was the largest of all. Only a few plots of land remained vacant.

"Marcus Daly runs this town," Michael said. He really was a walking history book. "A giant in the mining business. Copper, I believe."

Beth smiled. After all, Maggie had her candy, and Michael's candy fed the brain, not the stomach. "How interesting," Beth baited him.

"Owns the Big Mill." He pointed through the trees. A long red building stretched out beyond the trees. "He's a giant in the timber industry too."

She'd give him this—he certainly was a man of information.

* * * * *

Their picnic ended abruptly when dark thunderclouds crept over the mountains without warning. Beth felt the drops of rain before she saw the threat. They hurried home, hoping to beat the storm, but the downpour had come and gone by the time her foot hit the porch. Soaked, she reached for the door when she heard voices in the stairwell.

"See you next week, handsome." The heavy sweetness in the woman's voice gave Beth a chill. She'd heard that tone before.

Footsteps descended the stairs. The door swung open, and a man stared at her for too long before leaving. Her muddy boot hit the middle landing, and floorboards creaked above, drawing her attention. She saw the back of a woman. A woman dressed in a long red silky nightgown trimmed with black and gold feathers, a puff of cigarette smoke trailing behind, disappeared beyond a closed door.

"Hurry up, Maggie," Michael urged.

Beth climbed the stairs, but all of her senses numbed. Her feet touched the ground, but she didn't feel them. The surrounding walls and doors blurred. The colors ran and bled together. Her heartbeat pounded inside her head and in her fingertips. Her thoughts went blank. She felt hot and cold, then dizzy when the darkness closed in despite her best effort to push it away.

"Beth, can you hear me? Do you think she can hear me?" Michael's voice seemed so far away.

"I think she's dead," Maggie said.

"Wake up, honey."

An unfamiliar voice was so close. A burst of red-hot flames hit one cheek and then the other. "She's coming to. Come on, sugar. Come back to us now."

Hearing a woman's voice again, Beth opened her eyes, still disoriented. "What"—she tried to get up—"happened?"

"You fainted, honey." The woman's face came into focus. Beth motioned Michael and Maggie to help her sit up.

"Slowly now," he said.

She could see clearly now. An older woman with a nice smile knelt beside her. Her fading blonde hair sat loosely on top her head, her eyes bright.

"Do you think you can get up?" the woman said.

"Yes. Thank you. I think I can." With Michael's assistance, Beth stood up, shaking her skirt, but it stuck to her legs. The woman wore a bright yellow dress accented with lace and a black corset, emphasizing her cleavage.

Bella assisted with the mud. "You look just fine, sugar. The heat gets the best of us at one time or another."

"I fell and lost my tooth, see?" Maggie grinned, displaying the missing treasure.

Beth managed a smile. It wasn't the heat.

Bella squeezed Maggie's cheek. "Name's Annabelle, but folks 'round here call me Bella."

"Beth Yates. I guess you've met Michael and Maggie."

Bella nodded. "You must be new in town." She pointed to the nearest door. "You live here?"

"Yes. Just moved in."

"I live in number 7." Concern creased her face. "You be careful 'round here, especially at night. Folks do some mighty strange things after supper."

Beth knew what Bella meant but hoped she wouldn't take the subject further.

Bella squeezed her hand and smiled. "You need anything, you let me know." She strolled down the hall to her room.

Michael put his arm around Beth. "Maybe you should lie down for—"

"I agree." Beth stiffened. Beth did lie down but didn't dare sleep. *Why? After all we've been through.* How could she have been so naive? Working for a woman who spits and carries a gun was one thing, but this? She couldn't leave Michael and Maggie here alone. Beth curled up and tucked her mother's quilt around her neck. This wasn't a boardinghouse. It was another brothel.

Chapter Fourteen

Beth wore her best gray skirt and white blouse. She adjusted the waist, tucked in her blouse to smooth the wrinkle, and frowned. The small oval-shaped mirror on the back of the door distorted her figure. Her hand trembled as she lifted a hairpin from the jar to secure her hair. *Stop it.* She tightened her fists, massaging the muscles to stop them from shaking. She expected to be working at the grand Ravalli Hotel today, not a local café. A local café would cater, no doubt, to a rougher crowd.

The reality reminded her of where she had come from and what she had lost. At one time, Father held a position of respect as a professor and leader in the study of science and medicine. They owned a stately home, and she had an easy childhood, but it was all a distant memory. In the reflection, morning shone through the window to greet her. She approved of her appearance and checked her watch. She scanned the room to make sure things were in order.

Michael and Maggie were not to leave for any reason. She'd made it clear. Except for the facilities, they were to stay put. She delivered the royal decree like a dictator. The reality of their situation scared her to death. Michael and Maggie didn't know what this place was, and she meant to keep it that way. *Out of the fire, into the fire.* Her mother's words resounded in her mind. The words were too true and more painful than ever.

Smoothing a small curl from Maggie's forehead, she tucked the covers around her face. Was this to be their lot in life? She shivered, for a chill still hung in the early morning air. She shook Michael to wake him. "I'm leaving for work," she whispered. "Lock the door after I leave."

Michael nodded.

"There are leftovers on the stove. I'll try to bring something home for dinner."

He mumbled something. Beth shut the door behind her and waited. When she didn't hear the lock, she opened the door again. "Michael."

He moaned and threw off the covers. She heard the door lock and took a deep breath. The crisp mountain air cooled her skin. She glanced at the place she called home before heading toward Main Street. It didn't look like a brothel. It was a simple two-story house. *I'll make good on my promise, Mother. I promise I will.*

Beth knocked on the window of the café and peered inside, one hand over her eyes, but no one came. The front door was locked. She didn't want to be late on her first day of work. She knocked again. Relief came when Jane hurried through the dining room and unlocked the door.

"You're here. Get an apron, girl, and get on into the kitchen. We got a lot to do this mornin'."

Grabbing an apron, Beth did exactly as Jane ordered, remembering the shiny pistol she carried. Jane's husband stood at the stove. Suddenly, the back door to the kitchen flew open. A girl, younger than Beth, rushed to remove her coat and wrap a half apron around her tiny waist.

Jane came into the kitchen like a police wagon, cursing. "I ain't gonna have none of your shenanigans this mornin', Millie," Jane warned, "'cause this here's a regular establishment. I'll put my boot in your backside if I have to."

The pompous smile on the girl's face made Beth cringe.

Jane huffed as she exited the kitchen. "Where's Anne-Marie?" She spit into an empty pot. "That girl needs to be horsewhipped. Late as usual. If I was her pa, I'd be tannin' her hide twice a week, just for good measure."

Beth gulped. Jane was a workhorse, a wild and crazy workhorse. When Jane made for the back room, ranting, Beth stuck close behind, following her through the back door and into the yard. Jane forced a large butcher knife into Beth's hand. Beth stared at the knife, confused. "Well, don't just stand there like a stuffed pig. Haven't you ever butchered chickens before?"

"Yes, ma'am. I mean, no, ma'am. Forgive me, but I…" Beth tightened her grip on the enormous knife as Jane leaned up against the wooden crate filled with lively chickens. Beth's stomach churned, and the horrible truth hit her right between the eyes when Jane opened the top of the crate and pulled out a chicken. The chicken squawked wildly, but with one swift snap of its neck, all was quiet.

Beth gasped and jumped. Bile warmed her throat before her self-control took over and prevented humiliation from coming up. Yes, she had eaten chicken before, and no, she had never butchered one. Mother purchased chicken at the market. It never occurred to Beth how it came to be at the market, but it occurred to her now.

Jane stripped the chicken of its feathers and its extremities. Beth watched in horror. The smile on Jane's face said she enjoyed her job. "Pluck 'em all." Jane walked inside with a naked chicken dangling at her side.

I can do this. I know I can. Beth set the knife down, tightened her apron, and rolled up her sleeves. With the knife in her right hand, she opened the cage. "I am so sorry. Please forgive me."

* * * * *

With every mile, Ethan rehearsed the land offer he'd prepared to give Buck Reardon. His negotiating skills didn't amount to much, but the basic terms of the purchase, he could manage. And if Reardon agreed, an attorney could make it legal. Wisdom told him not to hand over money until the deal was signed and recorded at the county office. The fact that Reardon had a gambling problem pitted Ethan's stomach. What if things worked out, and Reardon sold the place, only to gamble the money away?

He slowed Jax and his thoughts. He was getting ahead of himself. Reardon's rickety old barn came into view, and Ethan searched the landscape. Reardon had let the place go. Fences sat in disrepair. The barn and lean-to would need structural work. Reardon's house, nothing but a wrangled shack, and the water well leaned to the left. Ethan blamed the man's health.

He quieted Jax's gait. Startling the man wouldn't bode well for first impressions. Groves of low-growing trees hid his arrival, but the upcoming gap through the branches would expose him. He pulled Jax to a stop and dismounted. "Hello, there," he announced. He called out again, but no one answered. He scanned the barnyard. An old mare stood atop a mound of dirt. "Hello? Buck?" Still nothing. He secured Jax to a tree instead of the fence, given its present condition. Ethan didn't want any trouble.

As he neared the corral, Reardon's horse joined him at the fence. A stout Arabian, but years of hard work sagged her fine lines. She wasn't bred for farm work. "Hey, girl." He stroked her when she snorted and nudged him. "Got yourself quite a place here."

A gun cocked behind him. "Hold…it…right…there… mister." Reardon slurred the words. "Turn around…nice and easy."

Ethan slowly turned around to face the man. "I'm unarmed." He carefully lifted his jacket as proof.

Reardon motioned the barrel of his rifle toward Jax. "Can't you read. Sign says, 'Stay out.' Now, get…off…my land." He muttered something about trespassing.

Ethan swallowed hard and slowly removed his Stetson. "Well, Mr. Reardon, that's exactly what I'd like to talk with you about, sir."

"I 'spose one of the fancy city fellers sent you." Reardon huffed, mumbling about lowballs.

"No." Ethan steadied his gaze, his head calculating his next step.

"One of them Johnston boys then?"

"You mean the one who's briefcase now bears a bullet hole?" The second he'd said it, he was staring down the barrel of Reardon's gun.

"Ah." Reardon readied his aim. "Knew it."

Ethan rushed to correct him. "I'm not here on behalf of the Johnston Brothers."

Reardon shook his rifle in Ethan's nose. "Who sent you then?"

"Me. I sent myself."

Reardon slowly lowered his rifle until it targeted the dirt instead of Ethan's face.

"Name's Ethan…Ethan Dawson." He eyed the man's horse. "What's her name?"

Reardon still didn't take his eyes off him. "Horse."

Ethan didn't know if he'd heard the man right but offered a grin. "The horse's name is Horse?"

* * * * *

"Daggit. Aren't you done yet, girl?" Jane stood on the back porch, staring at two dead chickens hanging on the hook. "Good grief. Git yourself inside and cleaned up. I'll do it myself."

Beth dropped the knife but adjusted her grip on the wild chicken. This one had escaped several times already. Jane freed the chicken, letting it once again run free. "Git," Jane barked.

Would she lose her job before it even started? Beth hurried into the kitchen, preparing herself for what was to come. She would beg—and cry if necessary—as Maggie suggested once before.

Beth lowered her head and closed her eyes, wishing this moment miles away. "Git your apron off." Jane yanked at the fabric. "Hurry up, girl. I ain't got all day. You're gonna take orders this mornin'."

She struggled to untie her apron.

"Millie's attitude got me all riled, and you know what happens when I get riled up?" Jane swatted the air. "Well, no, you don't. I done fired her, and that's that. Anne-Marie can't handle them by herself."

Hanging her apron on the wall hook, Beth let the happy truth sink in. She wasn't fired. She hadn't lost her job. Take orders? *How hard can it be?*

Thrilled at the possibility, Beth swung around and caught her reflection in the window. "Oh, dear." She rushed to the sink and vigorously scrubbed and scrubbed until nothing more could be done. Nothing could remove the bloodstains from her skin and fingernails. Her hair had fallen out in several places. She pushed and tucked each fallen strand, trying to salvage it, plucking out the tiny feathers. "This is hopeless." She threw her hands in the air. "Just look at yourself."

"Quit your fussin'," Jane said rather harshly, in Beth's opinion, and pushed her into a room filled with strange, disgruntled faces.

Anne-Marie rushed by. A man in the front corner pounded his fist on the table. "I ain't got all day?"

"I've been waitin' over an hour," and yet another near the door.

Beth stood there in a panic. The counter with eight connected barstools wasn't completely full yet.

"You got yourself a hungry mob this mornin'. Nothing Calamity Jane can't handle, I 'spect," an older man at the counter said. "She's sure got a way with words."

Beth froze. *Calamity Jane.* As in Wild Bill Hickok's Calamity Jane? "Do you mean *the* Calamity Jane? The notorious—"

"That'd be the one."

Beth's heart sank. She worked for Calamity Jane? The wild rider. The sharpshooter. She'd seen the newspapers. Heard the terrifying tales of Calamity Jane's adventures. Beth rubbed her temples. What had she done? Working for Calamity Jane couldn't be worse than working for Kitty, could it? She stiffened. Told herself to be strong and brave. One misstep and she'd be out of a job. Or worse.

After glancing toward the back door window and seeing feathers flying, Beth quickly turned to take the older gentleman's order and recognized him. You. A bead of perspiration trickled down her back as she studied the room. Thankfully his young friend was not in attendance.

Anne-Maria pushed past her. "I've got the front half. You take the rear." Anne-Marie, with her bouncing blonde hair, disappeared into the kitchen.

Confused and trying to assess the situation, Beth exhaled and took a step. "Can you please repeat your order?"

At the statement, an angry man two tables over walked out, followed by several other customers. Beth glanced back to the kitchen, expecting to be looking down the barrel of Jane's gun but received only a simple nod.

If I can kill a chicken, I can take a simple order. Beth gathered her thoughts and steadied herself. "I apologize for the delay, sir. What would you like?"

"Call me Russ. Lord knows you'll be seein' me often enough."

Please, just you and not your friend. Russ ordered two plates of the same, saying he was mighty hungry. Beth worked the next few minutes methodically—taking orders, placing orders, checking orders, and pouring coffee—mimicking Anne-Marie as best as she could. The bell rang above the door. She stayed focused, balancing plates in her hands before retreating to the kitchen.

"Your doin' fine," Clinton called from the back room. Jane's husband was a quiet man—hadn't said two words to her since she arrived. She was happy he wasn't much for words.

"Sure you are. You're a natural, girly," Anne-Marie smiled. "Besides, Millie's a cat, and you have a prettier face."

"Clinton." Jane barked from where she stood, religiously stirring a large pot and mumbling. Beth and Anne-Marie jumped.

He raised a brow. "Coming, Martha," he answered with a slow Texan accent.

"Don't you be callin' me that, you old cow."

Why Clinton called her Martha, Beth didn't know, but knowing that Jane had a gun killed any curiosity she might've had concerning the matter.

"Good morning, son. 'Bout time. Your eggs are cold. Jane will warm them up for you," Russ said loud enough to be heard in the kitchen.

Beth heard the voices, peaked out through the crack in the door, and hoped it wasn't true.

Russ gave his young friend a pat. "Thought you was a mornin' person."

"I am…when I've had my coffee," he replied, holding his empty cup high in the air. "And the cup of coffee I had early this morning about killed me."

Beth put her back against the wall. His very presence made her furious.

"Anne-Marie, please take *that man's* order for me, I beg you. I'll trade you a table. Anything." She pointed, underhanded.

Anne-Marie identified the man and smiled. "Sorry. I would, but I'm out of here. I'm the morning girl. You're the 'all-day' girl. Besides, I've got a date. Although," she hesitated, "don't you think Ethan is the cutest?"

Beth refused to answer. *Ethan?* She turned to Anne-Marie but found a vacancy instead. Anne-Marie left the back door open to an eruption of giggles that echoed in the alley.

Beth sighed. She'd feed him, but she didn't have to talk to him. Grabbing the coffee pot, she proceeded to fill a woman's cup near the window. Ethan would have to wait.

"Watch out." a woman cried out and jumped back in her chair to avoid the spill.

"Oh, dear. I am so sorry, ma'am." Beth cleaned up the coffee, now running off the edge of the table. Thankfully, the woman bore the accident with grace.

As Beth wiped the table and floor, she glanced in Ethan's direction and growled under her breath at his grin. He obviously enjoyed her misdeed. *Please leave.* Russ seemed nice enough, though she didn't approve of his nighttime activities or the company he kept.

Continuing her rounds, she successfully ignored Ethan and even caught him sneaking around the counter once to pour himself a cup of coffee. *Suit yourself.*

"See, what did I tell you?" Russ exclaimed as Jane plunked a plate of steak and eggs in front of Ethan. "Eat up."

As Beth slipped by him, as she'd had to do several times to avoid his boot stuck out in the aisle, he asked her for sauce. She stared at him and wondered how she would be able to avoid him this time. "What kind of sauce?" Beth parked a fist on her hip, silently reprimanded herself for speaking to him at all.

"Steak sauce, you know, for the steak." Ethan motioned to his plate.

She relented as he pointed to her hair.

"You've got a feather in your hair."

She fiddled with her hair in search but didn't find it.

He reached to pluck it free without her permission. Beth slapped his hand. With a flick of her head, she retreated to the kitchen and heard Russ whistle the tune to "Yankee Doodle." Mad, she scoured the pantry, pushing jars of this and that aside. She found the steak sauce, and then a jar marked "hot sauce" caught her eye. Oddly, similar in color. Dare she? She checked around the corner and eyed him.

She placed a bowl of sauce on the counter, followed by a glass of milk for Russ. She made her rounds and watched as Ethan lathered his steak and eggs. His first bite brought disappointment. He seemed unaffected. She bit her lip. She had to get rid of him. A second bite, and it hit him. He begged for water, rushing for Russ' milk when he'd emptied his coffee cup.

She smiled. He wouldn't be coming in here anymore. Between his coughing and gasping, Ethan managed to say, "She did that on purpose." Russ held his laugh until he couldn't hold it any longer. Ethan threw his knife and fork onto the plate.

"Will there be anything else?" Beth smirked.

Russ winked. "We best be goin'. Don't want to be late."

Ethan swung out of his chair and dropped some change on the counter. "I'm still hungry," he scowled at her, and then smirked. "You haven't seen the last of me."

Beth whirled around and huffed, but then smiled triumphantly. She hadn't had that much fun in a long time.

Chapter Fifteen

Chicago, Illinois

Annie Parker sat at the counter of a corner café on Michigan Avenue, drinking coffee and picking at the eggs on her plate. Another day of job hunting. Her future as a businesswoman dwindled as fast as her savings. She scooted her cold eggs to the edge, remembering that cold eggs hadn't settled well with her last time, and slumped down on her elbow, disappointed. The monotonous job of sorting through dead people's papers gave her the creeps, and her curiosity seemed to get her into trouble on a regular basis. In the end, she was happy to quit the auction house. She sipped on her coffee and motioned for the waitress.

Here she sat, alone and without a job, her parents' endless hounding about marriage about to drive her over the edge. Did they not understand her at all? Marriage was the last thing she wanted. She looked up and smiled as the waitress appeared. "Can I have more coffee?" She didn't really like coffee, but it made her feel independent.

The fact that she wanted a career slid tiny slivers under her mother's fingernails. Annie dreamed of owning a dress shop, had since she was a girl. She sipped the last of her lukewarm coffee and pictured a simple brick storefront with tall windows displaying headless forms adorned in the latest fashion, most of her own design.

The mention of something familiar at the end of the counter brought her back to reality. *The fire at the sausage factory.* Annie remembered it like it was yesterday, a tragedy unfolding yet today. Poor Beth and the others. A dark cloud of sadness still hung in the air. At least Beth had moved on with her life. Montana? That's what her letter read. Of all places.

Mr. Clemens said they never found those two men who broke into the orphanage. Annie leaned closer, trying to hear what the officers were saying. If only the two women next to her would stop talking. Only bits and pieces were distinguishable between the women's constant complaining about the way their knees creaked when they got out of bed in the morning. *Please, I beg you. No more about your knees. I am trying to listen.* Something about the fire at the factory and new evidence pointing to arson.

"Arson?" Annie blurted, all attention on her. One of the officers glanced her way as she lifted the cup of coffee to her lips, acting disinterested. She sputtered and coughed after gulping hot coffee recently refilled by the ever-so-efficient waitress. Annie dropped the cup to the counter, spilling coffee down her newest design, a dark burgundy skirt with an ivory lace bodice.

"Are you all right?" The officer surveyed the damage, making her aware of the direction of his eyes. The two women next to her seemed annoyed at the distraction, and the other dark suit snickered to himself and ate his pastry.

She smiled. "I'm fine."

"Charlie Deneen, miss. Surely, I can be of some assistance," he introduced himself when the waitress finally came to her rescue.

"I said I'm fine," Annie snapped at both of them, embarrassed that the ivory lace, now translucent, clung to her body much too tightly. "Actually," Annie reached out as he turned, "I do have one question."

He nodded. "I'll answer any question you have if you'll let me take you to dinner."

She bit her lip. She actually had several questions. If she was to get any information out of him, dinner was a small price to pay. She smirked somewhat sinister. "That would be nice. I'd like that."

* * * * *

"Is Mr. Elias Sands available?"

Eli cracked the door to his office to listen. A police officer stood in front of Caroline's desk. Eli had seen the two men approach his office. What could they want with him?

"I regret to say that Mr. Sands has a very busy schedule today, but perhaps if you would like to make an appointment for next week," Caroline said rigidly and opened her appointment book.

I don't pay her enough.

"This is a police matter, ma'am, and we would appreciate if you could let Mr. Sands know we are here." The younger of the two had a chip on his shoulder apparently.

Eli's jaw tensed as he opened the door. "Caroline, busy or not, I always make time for our fine men in uniform." Eli waved the men inside his office, and Caroline returned to her task, face flushed.

"Sgt. Thomas Wells and Attorney Charles Deneen," Wells introduced and sat down. Deneen refused a seat and stood in the background.

Sgt. Wells made easy conversation, then got to the purpose of the visit. "Mr. Sands, you're a man of reputation and position around here. Might I ask you a few questions about the Sausage Works?"

Eli nodded. "I read about the fire in the newspaper. I'm not sure how much help I can be." He forced a smile and leaned back in his chair.

The sergeant casually inquired about Eli's relationship with the owners of the factory. "I've never done business with the family, though I've always wanted to. They seem like a nice family." That was true.

Wells wrote something in his notebook. "Have you had dealings with any of the deceased? Pardon me, relatives of the deceased?"

Eli leaned back in his chair farther and paused, calculating his response carefully. "Chicago Savings and Loan Company mortgages a great many homes in the area, and I would imagine that many of the mortgagees are...were employed at the factory." Eli tried to use general terms and not name anyone specifically. When pressed as to whether any of the deceased had fallen behind in mortgage payments, Eli was quick to answer. "I'm sorry, but that information is confidential. We must protect the privacy of our clients, you understand."

Sgt. Wells stood and offered a handshake. "Well, Deneen, it seems this too is a dead end. Sorry to have wasted your time, Mr. Sands."

The men reached for the door, and Wells turned. "Oh, one more question and we'll be out of here. We know you are a busy man. Do you know a man by the name of Donovan?"

"Donovan?" Eli scratched his chin nervously, thinking. "No, I can't say that I do. Sorry I couldn't have been more help."

The officers accepted his answer and left. Eli watched from his second-story window as the two men stood at the bottom of the steps. Eli tried to unlatch the window lock and push it open without being heard. The men appeared secretive. The window cracked. Eli strained to listen.

"It appears your source might be on to something," said Wells before he stepped into the street to hail a carriage.

Chapter Sixteen

Beth closed her eyes as she dried the dishes, pretending to be somewhere else other than the café. Jane was at it again. Calamity Jane, Beth reminded herself. A day didn't go by when Jane didn't shout or throw something, like the tantrums of a child. Even the smallest things set her on a rampage. Yet she had a heart of gold. People couldn't always see it, but it was there. On more than one occasion, Jane excused herself to run an errand, leaving with an armload of food and returning empty-handed.

Beth thought of Michael and Maggie stuck in that room all day while she worked. What else could she do? They didn't know anyone—anyone she could trust. How Michael and Maggie managed to get along, she didn't know. Michael loved to read, but Maggie...

At least they had a roof over their heads and food to eat.

Beth winced as a long string of offensive words came flying through the kitchen door. "Clinton!"

"What do you want now, woman?" He wiped his big hands on sackcloth and tossed it onto the chopping table. Beth placed the wet plates on the rack and glanced at the few remaining customers. Clinton paused as he passed by. "I've really done it this time." He pushed the kitchen door open so fast that it swung several times before finding its final resting place.

Clinton and Jane had a strange marriage. They fought like cats and dogs, yet neither threatened to leave. They drank too much. As if Beth didn't have enough crisis in her life, she had to experience a new one every time she came to work. Never a dull moment, that was for sure.

Kitty came to mind, followed by the face of the man who tried to rob her of the one thing she had left. When she pictured him, she felt dirty. How she wished a hot bath could forever wash away the memory of him.

She scrubbed several plates harder and blamed herself. Should have known better than to trust Eli Sands.

If God was so good, why hadn't He warned her? Helped her?

God wasn't there then. He wasn't here now.

Donovan's face and voice still haunted her.

She could smell the stench of liquor from a block away. The darkness in his eyes revealed his intent. His touch left permanent handprints on her body, like severe burns ravaged by fire. She tried to shake the thought, but she'd seen the damaging effects on bare flesh and would never be able to unsee it. Kitty's last words put a lump in her throat.

Beth was damaged, but her scars were on the inside.

Emotion took over, but she pushed it back. A glass slipped through her soapy fingers, crashing to the floor. She stared at the shattered glass, thinking of Mother's precious china. This wasn't the place nor the time to let emotions run wild. She bent down to gather the broken pieces. Tears fell down her cheek. Hearing footsteps, she dried her eyes.

Jane burst through the kitchen door, stepping on chards of glass. "What in tarnation?" Jane parked a fist at her hip, the one saddled with a gun. "Oh, quit your blubbering, girl."

* * * * *

The morning rush at the café wasn't a rush at all. In fact, Beth could count the number of customers on one hand. Jane and Clinton had left early, leaving her to clean and lock up. Business had slowed. She cleared dirty dishes from an empty table as the bell rang out above the door, followed by ruckus. "Sorry, but we're closed—" She stood face to face with a large horse. Chairs and tables scattered as the horse backed her against the counter.

"Jane…Clinton?" Beth's feet refused to move. She knew no one would come. Even so, she called out again. The creature side-stepped and came closer, snorting and sniffing the dirty plates in her hands. Nervously, she lifted the plate as she mounted a barstool, single-handed, in an attempt to climb over the counter. The horse tipped its head and devoured leftover eggs and toast. So close, she marveled at the beauty and dark eyes.

The horse nudged at the now empty plate she held. Frantic, she reached for another plate of leftovers on the counter. The horse reared and stomped, knocking over chairs, sending a table clear across the room to the other side. The bell above the door rang.

"Jax!" Ethan shouted as he grabbed control of the reins. He issued a string of apologies. Jax refused to budge. "You are as stubborn as a mule," Ethan scolded. "And you are embarrassing me in front of the lady," he whispered in Jax's ear but loud enough to be heard. Turning to Beth, he smiled. "Don't be afraid. She won't hurt you."

"She?" More terrified of Ethan than the horse, Beth lifted the second plate of half-eaten eggs toward Jax.

"You'll spoil her."

Beth reached out to touch the smooth, structured snout and hesitated. "She's beautiful."

"Yes, she is." Ethan looked at Beth.

All of a sudden, Jane burst in the front door, shouting. "Get that varmint outta here."

The horse spooked and jumped back into several tables, sending a chair through the front window. Broken glass exploded into the street. Ethan stepped between Beth and the horse, his full frame against her. Breathing became impossible as Beth panicked at his closeness. "Please." She pushed at his back until she'd freed herself to climb over the counter.

"Jax. Whoa, girl." Ethan tightened his grip on his horse. "I've got her now. I've got her." He pulled at the reins in an attempt to turn Jax toward the front door. Jane followed them out, hollering profanities.

Beth regained her composure and made a promise she'd never break again. She squelched the feeling of Ethan's body against hers and rushed toward the broken window, hoping. For sure, this would be the last time she'd have to see Ethan at the café. *Let him have it, Jane.* Jane wouldn't be dazzled by Ethan's good looks, handsome smile, and light blue eyes.

Suddenly shocked at the realization that she'd noticed his features, Beth scolded herself and blamed him. He'd pay for it. She'd enjoy this moment.

"Jane, I'm sorry as usual." Ethan lowered his head as he stepped onto the boardwalk, gathering shards of broken glass outside the café. "I'll make things right. I don't know what came over Jax this time."

That beautiful beast had done this before. Jane would make sure there wouldn't be a third time. She watched for the expected slew of choice words. Jane would run him out of town with a kick in the pants and the barrel of her shotgun.

Jane fisted a hip and surveyed the damage. "Well, Ethan, guess we'll be seein' a lot more of you and your hammer again."

What? That's it? Beth shrugged. *No staring down the barrel of a gun? No kick in the backside?* Where is the Jane that Beth knew and loved?

* * * * *

Ethan flattened against the wall of Calamity Jane's café. "Excuse me, miss, I didn't catch your name." Ethan let her pass. She smelled like fried chicken. The narrow hall of the café was impractical, but right now, it served its purpose.

She shot him a searing look while balancing several dirty plates in her arms. She hesitated, and Ethan smiled. Finally, he'd have a name. He waited. "That's because I didn't give you my name." She marched into the kitchen.

Well, there it was, like the Saturday before.

He mentally checked his calendar. He'd given Reardon enough time to accept his offer. But yes or no, he needed to know now.

Putting Jane's café back together had taken two full Saturdays. Finding out the name of the new girl in town would take an eternity.

Anne-Marie called her "girly." He knew that wasn't her name. Jane called her…well, names mother would never approve of. Why she wouldn't say her name, he couldn't figure out. Jane came flying out of the kitchen like a bull out of the pen. "Her name is Beth Yates. She's from Chicago. Don't know how old she is, but she's got a kid brother and sister. There, you happy?"

Fixing a broken chair in the back alley of the café, Ethan heard thunder in the distance. The storm could arrive any minute, bringing a quick downpour. The fields—his fields, hopefully—needed the rain, so he welcomed the dark clouds. Joining the leg of the chair to the seat, Ethan readied his hammer. He'd wasted two weekends repairing the damage Jax had done. In the end, one wall was damaged, tables and chairs were broken, and the front window shattered. "There, all done," he said aloud as the back door flew open. "Miss Yates." Ethan flipped the last broken chair onto its legs. He wanted to call her Beth, for it seemed natural.

She ignored him as usual.

"I'll be out of your hair shortly," Ethan said when Beth didn't acknowledge him. Never in his life had he met such a cold woman. Clearly, she couldn't stand the sight of him. He admitted he couldn't say the same, and that bothered him. She was the one fortune to his misfortune.

Ethan wasn't in need of attention. Anne-Marie made sure of that. He always had his share where women were concerned, but something about Beth's countenance irked him. The way her eyes flashed when she wouldn't speak to him intrigued him. To call her eyes blue would be a miscalculation. Green didn't do them justice either. They held confusion, even in their color. She had avoided him at every turn.

Ethan couldn't stand it any longer. "Do you dislike all men, or is it just me, Miss Yates?" She raised the bucket filled with dirty water then let it down slowly. There was a long pause, and he wondered if she might respond.

Suddenly, she emptied the contents of the bucket into the alley, missing him by a couple of inches. "Just you."

She turned to go inside, but the door was locked. She shook the knob and dropped the bucket to use both hands to pound on the door, but it was no use. Ethan knew Jane and Clinton had already left for the saloon. He heard her huff, and thunder cracked overhead.

Beth looked up and blinked as the first raindrop hit her face. The heavens opened. Ethan scanned the alley for shelter. He identified a solution and kicked several heavy crates out of the way, then grabbed her hand and pulled her under the small overhang as the storm arrived. She tried to free herself from his grip, but he only tightened it. She eyed the alley. "I have to go."

"No. You want to go."

A side rain poured in from the west. Ethan drew her closer. She stiffened as their arms touched. She shrank away until he couldn't feel her skin. She stared in the opposite direction. Rain molded several loose strands of her dark hair to her neck. Her features were so striking. He couldn't help but trace them.

"Both," she added, covered her head, and stepped into the rain. "I have to go, and I want to go." Her voice cracked, and she ran into the alley.

He started to go after her but stopped. He wasn't going to chase her. He had to tell himself several times.

* * * * *

Safe inside the café and relieved that she hadn't locked the front door, Beth collapsed against the wall and slid to the floor, burying her face in her hands. Water ran down her cheeks as she tried desperately to still the beating in her chest. She couldn't deny Ethan had rattled her again, but it had to stop. Other women might succumb to his charm, but she understood men, what they really wanted and what they'd do to get it. Ethan was like all the rest. She paired him with Donovan in her mind but had to relent. There was a big difference.

She rose, wiped her eyes, and blamed the rain for her tears. Pulling a kitchen towel from the hook, she dried her face and hair. She stared at the brass doorknob on the back door. He's probably drenched. She couldn't just leave him out there. That would be unkind. If he were a child, she'd not hesitate to let him in. A woman, an older couple, a family, a much older man—all categories of human beings—she'd not hesitate to help. Ethan was in the wrong category.

Unlock or don't unlock. The mental battle raged.

She pushed the small curtain to the side and stood on her tiptoes in search of him. He wasn't under the overhang. Suddenly, he appeared in the alley, soaked. He saw her. Her feet fell to the floor. The decision had been made. As she unlocked the door, she wanted to change her mind. Pooled water on the hallway floor told her it was too late. She stepped back and handed him a towel. "The coffee's still warm."

Beth busied herself in the kitchen, washing the last of the dishes and soaking the soiled pans. Ethan drank coffee at a table near the front window, still boarded up, for the first replacement window arrived broken in the crate and the second piece of glass hadn't arrived. *Maybe things didn't go as planned for other people too*, she thought.

Although she appreciated Ethan's distance, she'd unlocked both front and back doors for a quick escape, if one became necessary, but he hadn't made a single wrong move. Main Street was abandoned. Only one horse and cart challenged the storm and the mud in the street, the loud storm outside such a contrast to the silence inside the tiny café.

"I can dry."

Beth turned. How long had he been standing there? He flipped his coffee cup upside down, indicating he'd emptied the last of the coffee. She shook her head. "No need. I'm almost finished."

He stepped into the kitchen, and she tensed. She glanced over her shoulder as she scrubbed a large pot, eyeing the heavy rolling pin for protection. He lifted an apron from the hook and held it in the air before attempting to put it on. He appeared beside her, and she scooted away, dripping soapy water all over the floor. "I said I'm almost done."

He lifted a pan from the sink with a shake and started to dry it. "I heard you."

Mother's voice rang in her ears. *Two are better than one. Many hands make light the task.* Gritting her teeth, she wiped the floor clean, silencing the wisdom of a woman she loved and missed. Beth scrubbed faster. Ethan dried slower—on purpose, Beth decided.

The heavy rain began to let up. With the dishes done and the café closed up for the night, Ethan shut the front door, and Beth turned the key. He went to the right, and she walked home as fast as she could.

Chapter Seventeen

Beth's muddy feet hit the stairs to her room at a slow, heavy pace and stopped halfway when she heard familiar voices shouting. Beth jumped the next few steps then paused to listen at the door. "I hate you, Michael Samuel Yates," Maggie cried.

"Quit acting like a baby. If you say—" Michael stopped when the door opened.

Maggie crawled out from under the bed and flung herself into Beth's arms, trying to communicate the severity of the situation. A quick inquisitive glance in Michael's direction said it all. Beth saw his jaw tighten and braced herself. Michael did exactly what Father did. He held it all inside. He had been doing it for days, even weeks, and she was about to feel the effects of it.

Tired from working long hours, Beth forced compassion and understanding. It was to be expected. Two strong, very different, personalities in the same room for days on end. It had to come to a head. "All he does is read, read, read. I have nothing to do. I'm so flustrated, I could spit. I hate it here. I want to go home." Maggie sobbed as Beth pulled out a handkerchief to wipe her nose.

A book sailed across the bed, knocking over the candle on the nightstand. "If I hear, 'I'm hungry,' or 'I'm bored' one more time, I am going to…I hate it here too, Beth." He glared. "You aren't stuck in this oven all day, every day." He shook his head as if wanting to say more. "Forget it." He grabbed his hat, headed for the door, and slammed it behind him, shaking a picture from the wall to the floor.

Maggie started to cry all over again. Beth sat down on the chair and pulled her close. Mother would have known what to do. Beth didn't.

* * * * *

Michael walked away from the boardinghouse in a frustrated march, letting out a heavy sigh with every muddy step. He deserved every bit of this. That room was a prison, consequences of his actions.

"I know you," a girl voiced behind him.

He turned on his heel to correct her mistake. "I don't think so, miss." He forced his gaze elsewhere. Her fancy thin dress soaked against her frame and bright cherry-colored lips reminded him of what Beth didn't want to discuss.

She lowered her chin and pivoted, giving in to a slight limp on her right leg.

He did recognize her. "Sadie?" He thought that was the girl's name.

She turned, lit up with a smile. "Sadie Simone."

Michael panicked when she came closer. He looked up at the window, half expecting Beth to be watching him. Sadie stopped a few feet from him, following his gaze.

"Thank you for helping me the other night…with Jacob Skinner." There was apology in her voice, but what she was apologizing for, he didn't know or want to know.

Michael removed his hat out of politeness, fully aware of who she was—what she was. "It was my pleasure." He slapped his hat against his thigh, frustrated and embarrassed. Of all the things to say. Heat rose to his face and burned the tips of his ears. Sadie was a prostitute. Perhaps she was working right now. He panicked at the thought and took a step back. "I shouldn't."

Sadie frowned and started to turn away.

He reached out to her. "What I mean to say is, people might think I…" He pulled his hand back and folded his arms to his chest. Beth would have a fit if she knew he was talking to this girl. He knew what was going on here. A person would have to be blind not to. He knew about the red candles in the windows.

"Do you live around here?" Michael said, trying to cover up his rudeness.

"Why would you care?" Sadie squinted to shade her eyes from the sun that suddenly broke through the dark clouds. "Don't you think you should go? Someone might see you?"

An awkward moment passed. Michael mumbled something. Sadie fiddled with her dress. He stared at his mud-clumped boots. Finally, she turned and stormed off. He put his hat on his head without another word and headed toward the river.

Sitting atop a giant boulder at the edge of the Bitterroot River, Michael scrunched his knees and lowered his head, toying with pebbles in his hands. He needed to be a different version of himself. He'd fought flames alongside Carney and his men. Father thought him man enough to work at the sausage factory.

Guilt stung for a moment before he pushed it aside. He'd been clever enough to lock Eli's men in the cellar. He thought of those huge men standing at the union station platform. He and his sisters had escaped unscathed. He guessed that it might not be entirely true for Beth, but she refused to elaborate. At least, they'd made it to Montana safe. He remembered Beth's accident in Billings. Whatever happened there wouldn't happen again, he promised himself.

He hucked a stone into the rushing waters. He'd wrestled down Jacob Skinner. Sadie was free. He shrugged. Well, alive. He pictured her limping down the street.

He'd tried to be the man Father thought him to be and failed, couldn't even manage his little sister while Beth worked at the café. She despised working there, he could tell. She should be working at the grand Ravalli Hotel. "A beautiful end to their tragedy," he remembered her saying. She shouldn't be working at all. Mother and Father wished she'd chosen marriage instead of following them to open the orphanage.

He regretted what he'd said to Beth. Maggie too. He deserved whatever he got. They didn't. Something needed to change.

He stared at the running waters. Across the river, ponderosa pines and cottonwoods led up the hill to the mountain backdrop. He kicked the mud from his boots. They could be happy in Montana. Make a home here. A beautiful end to their tragedy? He'd make sure of it.

Suddenly, the sound of horse hooves drew his attention. Two men on horseback crossed the bridge about a stone's throw away. He could hear them but couldn't make out their faces.

"Been dead for at least a week. Ben Hammen says he'd been gone for two weeks is all, came back to find his wife on the floor dead. Seemed pretty broken up about it."

"No sign of a struggle?" Michael recognized the low voice of Sheriff Irvine.

"Makes no sense at all, Sheriff. No knife or bullet wound. You thinking ol' Skinner?"

Jacob Skinner? He's supposed to be locked up in Missoula. Couldn't be. Michael honed in like a lion stalking its prey, strained to listen as they drifted out of range.

No sign of a struggle, but the woman's body was covered with purple blisters. If only he had the second half of Father's medical library. Beth teased that she'd toss the first half if he mentioned the weight of her precious rug again.

Throwing the last stones into the river, he prepared himself for a lecture the size of Montana. He imagined Beth's words and rehearsed his apology. Perhaps he was a lot like his father, but Beth was exactly like Mother when it came to discussing a person's behavior.

Back at the boardinghouse, his boot hit the landing as he watched Bella welcome Sadie into her room. Ashamed at how he'd treated her, he promised an apology.

He turned the knob. Maggie jumped from the bed and into his arms. "I'm sorry. I am," she eyed Beth and then rushed, "but I was hungry and bored."

"Me too." He let her down.

"Me three." Beth stood up from her sewing, tears in her eyes, and embraced him without the slightest prelude to a lecture.

* * * * *

With his stomach full thanks to Jane and Beth, and Maggie fast asleep, Michael turned the page. Beth's day at work seemed better than normal, by the way she spoke. First, no lecture, and now she likes her job at the café. At the moment, he wondered if he knew his sister at all.

He read several paragraphs, but words blurred into the margins. He couldn't stop thinking about Sadie. His cruel behavior written on her face like a mirror staring back at him. She needed a friend and found a judge instead.

Over the years, children came to the orphanage from horrible situations like Sadie's, children forced to suffer moral deficiency or depravity, desperate for food and shelter and someone to love them. Mother would have embraced Sadie without hesitation. He pictured the scene and missed

Mother more. His parents changed when they left the university to open the orphanage. He remembered that. "That was their old life," Father always said and loved the children until the day he.... His chest tightened.

He wasn't Father nor did he have the means to help Sadie, but he could do something. He could be a friend, at the very least. Beth wouldn't sleep for a month if she knew what he planned to do. Resolved and worn out, he closed his eyes and fought for covers.

* * * * *

Michael's hands shook as he rehearsed the words. He didn't want Bella to get the wrong impression. He promised himself he'd apologize to Sadie, and as the days passed, the guilt intensified. He waited until Beth left for work before setting himself to the task. Maggie would be occupied for a little while, thanks to his new daily plan, and he would be right down the hall.

A few steps and he stood at Bella's door, his palms sweaty, his mouth dry. *Beth is going to kill me.* He took a deep breath and knocked.

Bella opened the door and smiled. "Michael, isn't that right?"

"Yes, ma'am," was all he could manage with the sizable lump in his throat.

She leaned against the doorpost, putting her hand on her hip. "And to what do I owe this pleasure?"

He cleared his throat and hesitated. Bella tipped her head.

"I am looking for Sadie," he said.

She lifted a brow that seemed painted. "I see."

He panicked. "Oh, no. It's nothing like that. It's just that I said something the other day, and...well, I need to make it right."

Her eyes widened. "Why that sounds like something right out of the Good Book itself," she said.

Michael scrunched his face. "The good book?"

"The Bible, you know. People call it the Good Book," she said. "Haven't you read it?"

He shifted. This wasn't the conversation he expected. "The Bible?" He rubbed his cheek.

"That's what we're talking about, sugar."

"No." Michael checked the hall. This made no logical sense.

"Why, I guessed you had, being's every time I see you, you're reading a book of some kind."

He shook his head, thinking what few books he had were the last of a dream never to come true. "Never saw the sense in it." He didn't like this conversation. The Bible was for…. The word "weak" came to mind but couldn't voice it, so he lied. "I'm preparing to go to the university." He *was*. He corrected the mistruth in his head. Educated men didn't need the Bible. Father never read it. Not that he knew of.

Bella reached behind the door and presented a small glass jar filled with candy, the red-striped variety. "Sadie lives on Third and Cherry Street, number 13." Bella held out two sticks.

Michael took them, confused. "Thank you."

"Maggie's a sweet little one."

You don't live with her. "Yes, she is. Good day, ma'am. I hope I didn't interrupt…your work."

He turned, but Bella touched his arm. "Michael, sounds to me like you're a man of information, an educated fella. That true?"

Michael nodded then shrugged.

"Read the Bible. There's more information in that book than any one man can handle." She patted his arm.

Michael walked away, stunned at what had happened. A prostitute telling him to read the Bible. He opened the door, still unable to make sense of it all.

"Candy. For me? Where did you get it?" Maggie exclaimed, reaching up for a piece.

"Bella." Michael held it high in the air, Maggie jumping in the game. He released a piece.

Maggie climbed onto the bed to eat her sweet stick. "Yum." She licked. "Yum." She licked again. "Yum."

Michael mentally added treats to the daily schedule. He tried to shake Bella's final words. He squinted at the family Bible sitting on the shelf and finally pulled it down. A layer of dust made it appear older. He pushed his sweet stick to the other side of his mouth and blew away the dust across the markings. "The Holy Bible," it read. What had Bella said? *More information than any one man can handle?* Michael pounced on the bed next to Maggie and propped himself up against the wall then opened the big book to the first chapter.

We'll see about that.

Chapter Eighteen

Beth leaned on the counter of Paisley's General Store, a box of eggs in hand, still processing what Chaz Paisley had said to the two young girls at the end of the counter. Giggles erupted. "Ethan's a man of faith, born and raised...and he's rich, or so Mrs. Fratt tells me," Chaz said.

Beth tried to ignore the conversation, yet she was drawn to it. Surely, it was no more than local gossip. Recalling her childhood memories of attending church, she made a quick mental list of qualities associated with such a term. *Ethan Dawson—a man of faith*, but that would mean.... "No, that can't be right," Beth realized her vocal mistake too late. A lengthy conversation with Chaz Paisley was an impossible waste of time.

"Goes to the church with Russ Miles every Sunday"— Chaz leaned on the counter, sliding closer to Beth— "according to Mira Tilts."

That's why Russ and Ethan came in earlier on Sunday mornings.

"Mrs. Tilts has been a longtime member of the Ladies' Worker's Society. Says he's stringin' along every girl in town, and that's a fact." Chaz tapped her knuckles on the wood.

Well that sounds more believable. He's a charmer all right. Chaz's eyes diverted as new customers walked in the door. "Peas and corn on sale this week, ladies. Oh, Mrs. Clarno, I have such news." Chaz chased her husband out of the way and lifted the hinged counter to huddle with Mrs. Clarno. Beth breathed a sigh of relief. She'd escaped Chaz. She gathered the eggs in her arms and waved Mr. Paisley goodbye.

"Ethan Dawson a man of faith? In church on Sundays and otherwise engaged the rest of the week?" Beth mumbled to herself as she stepped off the boardwalk at Fourth Street. She knew Ethan possessed enough charm to pull the wool over anyone's eyes. Beth looked at the big Montana sky. Admittedly, he did have a certain charm. Apparently, he had God fooled too.

Coming home from work, Beth hammered up each step, her mind firm. She didn't need a man who attended church on Sunday and visited brothels the rest of the week. She didn't need a man at all for that matter. Her foot hit the middle landing, and she paused. What if she was wrong? What if Ethan wasn't—

She heard voices in the hall, a man and a woman's. She took a couple of easy steps and identified the man's voice. Ethan. As she climbed the stairs, the voices grew louder.

"Honey, every man in town's got time for me." Ethan saw Beth and awkwardly distanced himself from the woman. "Miss Yates." He removed his hat.

The woman whose name Beth refused to know grabbed Ethan by the collar and pulled him toward her room. Beth looked away and pushed her key into the knob, but the door was unlocked. Ethan jerked away and started toward Beth. "Miss Yates, wait."

She slipped in, quickly closed the door, and turned the lock.

"Oh, Beth, I've always wanted to go to a county fair," Maggie burst out as Beth turned her back against the door.

Beth unpinned her hair and sighed. Ethan knocked at the door. She whispered to Michael, "Don't answer that."

Michael hesitated, and Beth shook her head and shushed them.

"Miss Yates, we have to talk." Again, he knocked.

Beth lifted a finger to her lips. Ethan murmured beyond the door, but she couldn't make out his words.

"Is he bothering you? I'll take care—" Michael stated, and she shushed him and held him back. A second later, descending footsteps told her Ethan was leaving. "A man with two faces."

Maggie hurried to the door. "This, I have to see."

Beth grabbed her. "It's just an expression."

Maggie smirked. "I know that. I'm almost eight, Beth."

Michael took the eggs from Beth's arms and set them on the table. "The Ravalli County fair is at the end of the month. We should go."

Maggie jumped up and down, waving a flyer announcing the festivities. "Please, can we go, Beth? Please? I get to wear trousers and everything," Maggie declared.

"You are not going to wear trousers ever again," Beth stated, still listening for footsteps.

Maggie wrinkled her nose at the statement.

A quick check at the window confirmed Ethan was gone. She faced Michael and Maggie. "Why do you want to wear trousers so bad?"

Maggie rushed to her. "It's a need, not a want."

Collapsing onto the bed, Beth kicked off her shoes. How her feet ached. She congratulated herself. She had been right about Ethan.

"I can't enter the 'catch a piglet' contest in a dress. You have to be a boy." Maggie collapsed on the bed beside her. "And what about the rat races?"

Beth widened her eyes, communicating the impossibility of both. "It's not proper."

Maggie threw herself onto the bed in a dramatic fashion. "Boys don't have to be proper."

Beth wholeheartedly agreed, hearing horse hooves in the distance.

* * * * *

Stopping by Paisley's General to pick up a few things for Jane, Beth hoped Chaz was out, for she had a unique way of unearthing the slightest amount of information from the most private individual.

"Good afternoon, Beth."

"Good afternoon, Mrs. Paisley." Beth tried not to make eye contact. Everyone knew if Chaz Paisley caught your eye, she'd talk your ear off. A crude phrase to be sure. Maggie repeated it incessantly, and Beth decided she liked it.

"You must be off early today."

Beth wanted to explain her errand.

"Why Mrs. Lovely was telling me just the other day how business in town is bad. Not for Mr. Paisley and me, though. Busy as beavers, we are. So, where are you off to today?"

Beth chose her words carefully as not to invite further inquiry. "Work."

Chaz scrunched her face, lips puckered as she eyed Beth. "I dare say that brother of yours will be heading off to work at the mill soon. Most young men his age do, you know," Chaz stated as fact, but implied a question. This was Chaz's way. Beth kept nodding, focusing on some unimportant item on the shelf while figuring out how to respond or how to avoid the subject altogether.

"Mrs. Miller tells me the Big Mill starts hirin' next week. Michael sure is a fine young man. Needs to be doin' a man's job. The mill's a fine job. Just mind he stays clear of that confounded machine. Chopped Mica Nelson's hand clear off—"

The door to the store burst open, and a young boy smaller than Maggie rushed to Beth's side. "Help. Please. It's my ma." He tugged at her, causing two potatoes to roll onto the floor.

Beth dropped her things on the counter. "Calm down, now. What's the matter?" The bell rang above the door, and a pair of boots stepped in.

"My mama is sick. She's real bad sick."

Ethan knelt beside the boy. "I'll go for the doctor, Andy." Beth rose, uncomfortable at his closeness.

"Take Miss Yates to your mama. I'll get Doc." Ethan stood, leaned in, and whispered in Beth's ear, "Mrs. Williams has been sick for quite a while." Beth stepped back, his warm breath sent shivers down her spine. She managed a simple nod.

"Yes, sir." Andy grabbed Beth's hand.

Ethan swung Paisley's door open, slamming it against the wall.

"Come on." Andy tugged.

Chaz mumbled to herself. "Oh, this is a real fine to do. First Nelda Jones, then Ada Smith, and now Mrs. Williams."

Beth scowled at Chaz for scaring the boy. Chaz yelled something back to Mr. Paisley and followed them out the door. "Oh dear me. All this excitement," she said, fanning her face. "Mira Tilts simply must know."

Beth tightened her grip on Andy's hand. At the house, Andy pushed the door open and ran to his mother, who lay on the kitchen floor. Beth untied her bonnet and brought herself to the floor beside his mother. "Don't try to move, Mrs. Williams."

Despite Beth's orders, the woman tried to get up. "I have to get supper on."

Beth held her shoulders to the floor. "Andy, get me a blanket." She pointed to the one on the rocking chair in the corner. "Ma'am, my name is Beth Yates. You don't know me, but I need you to trust me. You hit your head pretty hard, so I want you to be very still. The doctor is on his way."

"Your papa…" She reached for Andy, and he took hold of her hand.

"What is it, Mama?"

Mrs. Williams mumbled something. Confused, Andy stared at Beth with fear in his eyes, a fear she knew too well. "Do you know how to find your father?"

Andy wiped his nose with his shirtsleeve. "At the mill."

"Can you go for him? Do you know the way?"

He rose and nodded.

"I'll stay with her until the doctor arrives."

Andy leaned down and kissed his mother's forehead then disappeared into the street. Beth squeezed out the cold water from the kitchen rag into the bowl and wiped the woman's face. She must have broken her nose in the fall, given the blood drying on her cheeks and neck. She hoped that was a good sign. The woman's nose was puffy on one side and cut on the other.

Gently cleaning her skin, she removed all but the dried blood cemented in the creases. *Oh, where is the doctor?* "There, I'll bet that feels better."

In response, the woman reached out and touched her hand, grabbing hold like she would never to let go. "Am I going to die?" the woman's voice shook.

"No, no. Hush now," Beth assured her. She didn't have any idea if that was true. "You are going to be just fine. Had a little tumble, that's all." The woman could have internal bleeding. Beth couldn't tell but knew if she had passed out because of hitting her head earlier, more could be happening on the inside than was visible.

"I made my peace with God a long time ago." The woman breathed deep between each word and then closed her eyes.

Beth covered her lips with her other hand, wanting to cry. *God, if you are there, please don't let this woman die. She has a family to take care of.* The sound of horses drew her attention.

"Doc's here." Ethan came through the door, out of breath, with sweat running down his face. Beth wiped her eyes with her sleeve as the doctor rushed in.

Ethan reached down and lifted Beth to her feet, his touch chilling but kind, his eyes soft, threatening to break her guard. She broke free of him. They stepped back in perfect rhythm as Andy ran inside, his father not far behind.

Beth cleared her throat to clear her mind. She was reliving her mother's death all over again. She glanced heavenward. *Do something.*

* * * * *

"You were right not to move her," the doctor said as he closed the door to Mrs. William's bedroom. "Probably saved her life. I'll be watching her for the next forty-eight hours until she is out of danger."

Relief gave way to a deep sigh, a sigh that emptied her lungs. "You can't imagine my relief, doctor." Beth took his hand.

Mr. William's eyes were wet, and Andy was at his side. "I ain't much for words, but thank you both for all you done."

Ethan shook his hand and reached for the doctor's hand. "Ethan, thanks for not giving up. God knows it might've been too late if you had."

Ethan nodded. "It's the Dawson in me." Beth wondered what had happened and what Ethan meant by "Dawson in me." He touched the curve of her back as he led her out the door. A tingling sensation crawled up her spine until he

185

pulled his hand away. She swallowed as inconspicuously as she could. She had no intention of letting him know he had that affect on her.

"May I walk you home, Miss Yates?"

Shaken and numb and a little embarrassed at her tear-stained appearance, she put some distance between them. A moment of silence passed. She stared at him and hesitated. How she wanted to give in, let down her guard. She even imagined it for a second. No, she couldn't. "I have to go back to work." The excuse would save her this time. Avoiding him had become an impossibility.

"I'll walk you back to the café, then."

She panicked. "No." The guard she'd considered letting down only moments ago stiffened, and mistrust took its ugly hold. "I am fully capable of seeing myself home or anywhere else for that mat—"

Ethan narrowed the gap between them. Beth gulped. His action was unexpected, yet not. "Miss Yates, *indeed*, you are a capable and experienced walker. Just being polite. I'm sure you are exhausted. I am a gentleman, which compels me to offer assistance whenever needed." His jaw twitched, and his eyes sparkled.

Beth felt his warm breath on her cheeks. His working-man's scent was overwhelming. "A gentleman?" She lifted a brow.

"You doubt me?" He stepped back, brows knit firm.

She heard the question, but stubborn resolve and seeing another man's face, forced the question to remain unanswered.

"I see." Ethan mounted his horse.

He tipped his hat. "Good afternoon, Miss Yates."

Beth turned away, thankful Ethan was heading in the opposite direction. Her face was warm, her eyes were wet, and her heart was beating so fast, she could hardly breathe.

Chapter Nineteen

Michael knocked on Sadie's door, his courage higher the day before. "Just a minute," she said.

He gulped, and he wiped his sweaty palms down his trousers. *I don't even know what to say.* Strange noises penetrated the hall of Sadie's two-story building. A man with his arm around a tall brunette entered the hall. Michael moved to let them pass. He tapped his foot on the floor.

Exhaling, he stared at the still-closed door in front of him. *Don't back out now. Just say you're sorry and leave.* He tightened a fist as he approached Sadie's door again. He knocked as the door cracked.

Sadie peeked through the thin opening, as if hiding something. "Yes...oh, it's you."

Thankfully, she was fully dressed. He hadn't considered the alternative until now. She fidgeted with the buttons on her bodice, then he saw her face. He pushed the door open, but Sadie resisted.

"You're hurt." Michael forced the door open, revealing Sadie's swollen cheek and black eye. He pushed back her hair to get a closer look.

"It's nothing. I'll be fine." She turned away and began smoothing out the sheets and arranging pillows on the bed. "What are you doing here?"

Watching her, Michael tried to swallow. "I'm not here for...that." He pointed to the bed. "I came to apologize." She wouldn't look at him. He circled her until they were face to face. "I came to say I'm sorry for the other day. I'm sorry I treated you that way. I shouldn't have—"

She shrugged. "I'm used to it. It doesn't bother me anymore."

Michael examined her face. "Sit down. Let's have a look at this."

Sadie jerked away. "Don't—"

He placed a hand on her shoulder. "Sit." He gently urged her to a chair and went to the icebox. Chipping a small piece of ice, he wrapped it in his handkerchief and placed it on her cheek. She winced at the cold. Perhaps it was the pain. "Who…did this to you?"

Sadie bit her lip.

"Does…this happen often?"

She didn't answer. She didn't have to. A tear rolled down her cheek, landing in her hand. Michael sat beside her. Sadie needed a friend. "I'd like to be your friend."

Although stiff and guarded next to him, she didn't move away. Minutes passed, and they sat in silence. Suddenly, she sighed and put her head on his shoulder. "I hate my life," she whispered.

He nodded. "I know."

* * * * *

Michael braced himself. This was bound to end badly. Beth threw her bonnet on the bed and slammed the package from the general store on the table. Maggie pouted. "If I count, I think Bella's nice."

He scowled at her. Maggie's opinion wouldn't help matters.

Beth's look of shock, he would never forget. The hour of silence that followed was misery. Beth marched around the room cleaning, organizing, and grumbling.

Maggie seemed displaced, always in Beth's way. He opened a book but didn't read. He tried to help clean, but Beth scolded him. All he could do was wait, wait and prepare the words to say once the impenetrable queen of worry was ready to talk. He tensed every time she cleared her throat.

Finally, Beth stopped in the middle of the room, twirled around with her hands on her hips. "How could you, Michael? How could you leave Maggie with *that woman?*" She pointed across the hall.

Michael closed his book and stood. "I needed to," he started to lie but knew he'd regret that. "I had to get out for a while." He noticed the Bible peeking out from under his side of the bed and shoved it into hiding. Beth wouldn't understand. He didn't understand.

Beth sighed. "Bella is a"—she closed her eyes. "She is a prostitute."

He gripped the bedpost. "I don't think..." Tell her about the Bible. *No.*

Maggie jumped in. "I like her."

"Be quiet," Beth and Michael said in unison.

Maggie stomped and threw herself onto the bed.

His jaw twitched. "Beth, give me a chance to explain."

"No. I gave you strict instructions."

Michael attempted to argue, but she silenced him.

"Maggie, what did you do at Bella's?" The sudden sweetness in her voice obvious to him.

Maggie rolled over. "Cooked yellow cakes."

"You cooked? Was Bella alone? Did she have visitors?" Beth hovered over Maggie like she was interrogating a prisoner.

Maggie wrinkled her nose. "I don't know."

"Beth, please," Michael said.

Beth scowled at him. "Was Bella...working?"

Maggie shrugged. "She says, she's too old to work."

"You are not allowed go to Bella's anymore. You stay put." Beth pointed to the floor. "I don't care how nice she is. It's not proper."

Maggie buried her head in a pillow and started to cry. "I like her. I hate proper."

Michael sank into a chair. "Beth, you don't have all the facts." He hesitated. *Tell her about the Bible. No. Yes.* "Bella reads the Bible." There, he'd said it, as ridiculous as it sounded.

Beth sighed. Her hands dropped to her side. She tucked several strands of hair behind her ear and joined him at the table. "Well, she probably reads the Bible to comfort herself from a life of poor choices and self-indulgence."

Michael nodded. *Beth, you have no idea just how close that might be to the truth.*

* * * * *

Michael wedged the wooden flower box into place outside Sadie's bedroom window and secured it. "There."

Sadie squealed in delight. "Michael, it's beautiful. I've never had such a wonderful thing."

"Made one for Bella too. Maggie's helping her plant some flowers in it. Right now, I think." He dusted his knees and pushed from the floor. Sadie's room was still unfamiliar to him. It would stay that way.

Sadie leaned out her window, admiring the addition.

As the first weeks of August slipped away, Michael and Sadie visited Bella on a regular basis. Attending Bella's Bible reading wasn't the only secret he kept from Beth. Bella introduced he and Sadie to the Bible—to Jesus. Beth would never approve his friendship with Bella, never allow his friendship with Sadie.

Sadie needed a friend. He'd fixed that. She'd never been educated. He would fix that too. According to Bella, there was one thing he couldn't fix. Sadie was still a prostitute.

* * * * *

Ethan patted the deed in his pocket and pulled himself into the saddle. "I figured we'd get an early start." The sun greeted them as it peeked over the Sapphire Mountains, shining its light on the tallest peaks of the Bitterroots. His mountains. It hadn't seemed like home here, until today.

"Your definition of early is sorely different than mine, son." Russ adjusted his glove as he readied to mount his horse and rubbed his eyes. "Why, I'm not even sure God is up this early." Russ slapped himself. "A man needs his beauty rest."

Ethan chuckled, tapped the bulging map in his coat pocket, and then called to the slowpoke in the rear. "I can't say that sleep is gonna help you much, Russ."

"Ha." Russ faked laughter. "I must've left my funny bone back in my nice warm bed this morning." Russ urged his horse to join him.

"The sun's up. We should be too." Ethan pulled his watch from his vest. He'd been up for hours, couldn't think of anything else but his land, land he still couldn't believe he now owned.

"I thought for sure Reardon would never give it up, even after he kicked the bucket." Russ tugged his leather glove off with his teeth and lifted his hat to scratch his head.

"I offered a fair price is all." Ethan beamed. It was a fair price. He wouldn't have felt right about any other price.

"Fair price? That stubborn old mule flat out refused every other offer. Why all of a sudden?" Russ adjusted his hat.

"He had his reasons." Reardon's secret was safe with him. All was right with the world. Ethan had his land, and Reardon had his respectability back.

Heading south, several carriages traveled down the tree-lined lane and moved to the side. He tipped his hat politely as they passed.

"Well, I'd say the good Lord had a hand in it." Russ nodded. "Whether Buck will ever admit it is another story."

Ethan and Russ crossed over the railroad tracks toward the south end of town. Ethan surveyed the vast mountain range to the west—such unsurpassed grandeur. His gaze jumped from peak to peak for as far as he could see, naming each mountain. Blodgett, Downing, Ward...

"Buck's always been a hard man. Probably hasn't changed a bit. Same ol' Reardon," Russ said.

"Don't get your hopes up," Ethan said. "People change. Their plans change too."

Russ let out a hearty laugh. "Well, Mr. I-Ain't-Gonna-Let-Nothing-and-No-One-Stand-in-My-Way...I'll remind you of that someday."

They continued along the dirt road. Ethan became keenly aware of each house and side road, noting every tree, aligning it with a particular canyon in the background. A cool morning breeze hit his face, carrying the familiar scent of home, memories of fires burning and freshly tilled gardens. They passed the last house in town, and the smell of fried eggs and bacon hung in the air.

"Buck'll have coffee on by the time we get there," Russ said.

Ethan shook his head. "No, thank you. I've tasted mud I liked better."

The smoke from Reardon's cabin rose above a tree line of pine and aspen as they reached the small narrow drive leading toward the foothills. Ethan sighed and looked up to the sky, amazed that the Creator of all this saw fit to breathe his name across four hundred acres of the most beautiful countryside in Montana. Ethan dismounted and secured Jax near the front door.

"Jax," he whispered in her ear, "we're home."

Ethan smelled coffee brewing before he knocked on the door. He plugged his nose and glanced at Russ. "Pure poison."

The door opened. "Ethan, come on in. Ah, Russ Miles. Haven't seen you in years. Figured you died or something." Buck patted Russ on the back and yanked an extra chair to the table. "Just made a fresh pot of coffee three days ago."

* * * * *

Eli tried to untangle the telephone cord. "I'm leaving town for several weeks." *This is all Clemens' doing.* His finding of the mysterious Yates' will. If it weren't for that irritating old windbag, Eli would've broken ground on the development already. He needed to distance himself from the Sausage Works fire as soon as possible and get away from that annoying insect Charlie Deneen, some small-time attorney trying to make a name for himself.

There was a pause and a click on the line. Georgie Burns, a business associate from New York, had also installed the telephone and needed to play with the thing to get the hang of it, but this conversation was approaching a topic Eli couldn't talk about at the moment.

"Going to do some sporting in Montana," Eli smiled to himself, "with some of my business partners." It was a diversion. Schwab still hadn't signed the deal. Eli had finagled a way to get in good with Schwab and got the mighty Marcus Daly in the deal—might turn into a lucrative one. "Daly won't know what hit him." Eli chuckled. Static on the line interrupted the conversation.

"Hello? You still there, Burns?"

A slew of curses ensued and some fumbling noises then a thud. *Lost the line.*

"Sands, I'm still here."

Eli removed his spectacles and pinched the bridge of his nose. "Thought I'd lost you."

"Say, what's the status on the development? Has the little matter been taken care of?" Burns said.

Wish I had lost the line. Eli leaned back in his chair and stared at the ceiling. *Lie. Stall. Hang up the telephone.* "Yes, of course, that building is mine. Ours." *All mine.*

"Good, good. Say, did you hear about Sausage Works factory fire? They say it was arson."

Eli bent the telephone cord in half and imagined himself cutting the cord, severing the conversation. Eli didn't like the new telephone Eleanor assured him he needed. Made him nervous. With a letter, he could choose his words more carefully. "Yes, a terrible tragedy, wasn't it?" In person, Eli could read facial expressions and body language and know how to proceed, but not so with the telephone. He had to respond. Remembering that someone might be listening on the line, he determined to cut the conversation short.

"Read it in the New York Sun this morning," Burns said. "Sure wouldn't want to be the fellow responsible. He'd be running for his life, to be sure."

Arson? *I'm going to kill Donovan with my bare hands.* "Hello? Still there? Think I've lost—" Eli clicked the lever and returned the earpiece to its base. *So, it's arson now, is it?* "Roberta?" he called to his third new secretary this month. "Get me a copy of the Chicago Times—the morning's edition—the section about the fire at the sausage factory."

"Yes, sir." She appeared in his office. "And a Sergeant Wells and Attorney Deneen are here to see you."

* * * * *

Ethan wiped the sweat from his brow and then sent the shovel deep into the ground—his shovel, not Daly's shovel. Just another week and his Daly days were done.

He acknowledged God's hand in his working for Daly, even understood what he'd learned, but still wondered why it took so long. He'd been up since daybreak, splitting wood and digging holes. Another load of timber was ready at the Big Mill. After adjusting his Stetson, he gazed at the long line of posts rolling and swaying with the land. What a beautiful sight. After two long years.

Russ—God love him—was working on the barn. Three Saturdays in a row. Still a Daly's man. Ethan could see him in the distance. Smiling to himself, he watched Buck hobble from his cabin, offering to give Russ a hand. Russ and Buck got along fine, which only fueled Ethan's idea. Buck would stay where he belonged and have the friends he so desperately wanted, and Russ would marry Bella and build a place south of the barn. It would be nice to have a woman around the place. Hadn't mentioned it to Russ yet, and wouldn't until the man got the rocks out of his pockets and asked Bella to marry him. He smirked. Or maybe he would mention it.

With Russ and Buck's help, they'd flagged the ground for the barn and laid out the plans for two corrals, three pastures, a show track, and several growing fields.

Jax whinnied.

"I know, girl. You're not a workhorse, but you're doin' just fine. We all have to pull more than our weight around here."

Jax yanked her head in the opposite direction, trying to bite at her tether. Ethan lifted a post from the wagon and set it in the hole, twisting and turning to sink it. Wiping his brow again, he thought of Miss Yates, who undoubtedly would not easily settle.

He'd been avoiding her, he admitted. He kicked at the post with his boot, and it finally sunk. He questioned heaven. What had he done to give her such a bad opinion of him? The Dawsons had a reputation, one he wasn't willing to give up.

He straightened, more proud of his character than he ought to be. The blade of the shovel sunk into the ground with the force of his boot heel. He finished rounding out the hole and threw the shovel against the wagon. What did it matter? He narrowed his eyes as he forced in the next post.

It did matter, and he was going to settle things with Beth Yates once and for all. But right now, he needed to finish the north side. He stopped to check the time, but his pocket watch was gone. After checking several other pockets, he scanned the long line of posts then glanced at Jax. His heart sank, and he knew.

"Jax, you didn't."

* * * * *

Beth put the order on the wooden wheel and spun it around to Jane, who yanked the ticket off before it stopped spinning. Beth peered through the kitchen door into the dining room. The dining room had emptied. The bell above the door announced a customer. *Ethan Dawson.*

"It would have to be you," she whispered. He sat down, and she frowned.

Beth turned to Anne-Marie, who was applying lipstick in the back room. "You have to take Ethan's order. I'll pay you."

Anne-Marie glanced at Ethan sitting at a table, reading the newspaper. "I would, but I gotta' get out of here early. A bunch of us are going down to the river. Besides…he's your only customer, and he likes you best."

Poor excuse. "Please," she begged.

"Sorry, girly." Anne-Marie winked. "Guess you're gonna have to take him this time."

Anne-Marie normally would have jumped at the chance to take Ethan's order, but since a couple of young cowboys arrived in town, she'd been preoccupied. Beth always liked Anne-Marie, but at this specific moment, not so much.

Beth pushed through the door to the dining room. Ethan shifted in his chair to face her. "Good, you're here."

Beth readied the pencil and paper she held to jot down his order. "I'm always here."

"We need to talk."

She cocked her head. "I don't think so."

The bell above the door rang, and a young family with six children flooded the dining room. Children, Maggie's age and younger, zigzagged through the center and back again, alerting Jane.

"My brother tells me you got the best fried chicken west of the Rio Grande." His Texan accent brought Clinton from the kitchen.

Beth shoved her pad into her apron pocket. "Yes, we do." She attempted to slide two tables together to accommodate such a large group.

Ethan jumped up, leaving his newspaper open on the table to assist her. "We need to talk," he whispered as he easily pushed two tables together and helped arrange the chairs.

She grit her teeth. "No, we don't." Beth turned to the family and smiled. "I'll be right with you. Just let me take this gentleman's"—she froze and shot Ethan a look, realizing she'd called him a gentleman—"order."

Ethan raised a brow and smiled. "How was the county fair?"

She ignored the question and smirked. Poised with pencil in hand, she glared at him as he picked up the newspaper. "What would you like for breakfast?" She cleared her throat.

He flipped down the corner of his newspaper and leaned in. "You don't even know me."

She tapped the point of the pencil on the pad. "I know all I want to know."

"I'm not who you think I am. I'll prove it to you."

She lifted her chin. "You are a man with two faces."

He leaned in closer, and she bent down with a scowl on her face. "You are as stubborn as a mule," he said then ordered eggs and bacon without sauce.

Chapter Twenty

They were broke. Beth lay awake, hoping for once the sun wouldn't come up. They had a few dollars left. Mentally adding the money she'd put in the rent jar from the last payday and added her next. Still not enough.

Mr. Gurney wasn't a patient landlord. If she couldn't pay the rent, he'd kick them out for sure. "I have a list a mile long of folks dying to rent this place, so if you can't pay your rent, you're out," she recalled Gurney's words exactly.

Rolling over in bed, she pushed the covers aside, fanning a sheet to cool herself. She looked out the once-cracked window. If it weren't for Michael's ability to fix things, she didn't know what she would've done. He'd fixed the stove, the broken window, the rusted door hinges, and the broken lock. The list went on.

Without a word of complaint, Michael saw that things got done. He took care of Maggie without protest. He kept up with his studies. Maybe her little brother had grown up, and he seemed happy despite the tight living quarters and the tiny bed. Maggie was happy too.

Beth shrugged. Now, they were in trouble because she couldn't pay the rent. She adjusted her pillow. Would this ever end? Water filled her eyes.

She'd beg Jane for more hours. Find a second job, perhaps. Sell Father's watch…or mother's jewelry box. Shaking her head, she silenced the sob. No, she would never sell the precious box. How could she even consider it? They'd starve before…She pinched her nose to keep from sniffling. She'd sell the box if she had to. But even if she did sell Father's watch or the box, what would that get them? Another month?

Maybe.

She glanced over to the table and then to the icebox. They had very little food. Would it really come to starvation? She sat up, throwing the covers off and landing her feet on the floor with a thud.

Maggie stirred, and Michael rolled over. "What's wrong?" he mumbled, half asleep.

Beth shook her head, assuring him everything was fine. "Go back to sleep."

He groaned as he checked the clock, angling it for moonlight. "For goodness' sake, Beth, it's four o'clock in the morning."

Beth stood at the window. A faint skyline of mountain-tops would soon welcome the sun.

"Beth."

She turned to him. "Michael, we're broke. We"—she shouldn't have said it like that. "We don't have enough to pay the rent." She returned to the mountain view. "My hours have been cut at the café. Jane says business is bad."

He sat up. "I'm sure it's temporary. Business is bound to pick up."

Beth dipped her chin, conveying doubt.

"It will be all right, Beth. I know it will." His smile gave her hope. "Try to get some sleep."

She nodded and opened the window, letting a warm breeze ripple the curtains and her nightgown. Michael rolled over in bed. She sighed and heard him whisper, "Lord, we need your help…"

* * * * *

Michael held the door open to Paisley's General. "Good morning, Michael and little miss Maggie," Chaz greeted as she oiled the wooden display cases. She rose and put her fist on her hip. "Well, I do declare, I believe you have grown a whole inch since yesterday, Lil' Missy." Maggie smiled. "Ah, and I see that new tooth's coming in." Maggie beamed. "Hank's out in the store room."

Michael nodded. "I'll see if he needs some help."

This was their daily outing if weather permitted. He helped Hank around the store, and Maggie assisted Chaz.

Chaz grabbed Maggie's hand, requesting her help at the candy counter as Michael headed to the back room. He paused, seeing an advertisement posted on the wallboard. "Mill workers wanted." He glanced at Chaz and Maggie and then reached up, yanked the piece of paper from its pin, and stuffed it in his pocket.

"Wish I was thirty years old again, son." Hank stood high on a ladder, stacking cans of tomatoes on a shelf. "Hand me that box, would you?"

Michael lifted the box. It felt good to be useful. Hours in their room made him want to throw something.

After a shorter-than-normal visit to the general store, they headed home. He had a new plan for the day, and it was something he had to do by himself.

* * * * *

Michael stared at the floor. Sadie shortened the gap. "You did what?"

Bella looked up from making cold tea but didn't say a word.

Sadie folded her arms. "You won't have time to study for the entrance exam. Tell him, Bella." She motioned for help.

"Leave him alone, Sadie." Bella stirred a pitcher of iced tea.

Michael straightened. "I prayed for help." He watched for Bella's reaction. Her eyes softened. "I prayed for help, and then I saw this advertisement on the board at Paisley's General."

"You won't have enough time to study *and* work at the mill," Sadie repeated.

"I'll have enough."

Bella brought several glasses to the table. "What about Maggie?"

Michael shifted. *What's the use of having brains?* "Beth is going to kill me."

"Bella can keep her," Sadie shot out as if the idea had come from heaven itself. "Besides, Maggie starts school soon."

He squinted at her.

"Sure I can," Bella added.

Michael nodded. He hadn't told Beth about his attending Bella's Bible reading. "Beth is not going to be happy about this."

The foreman at the mill hired him on the spot. He was to report for work at six o'clock on Wednesday morning. He would study at night and attend Bella's Bible reading on Saturday mornings. It was a rough plan, but it was a plan at least.

* * * * *

"Sir, I can work weekends or evenings to pay for these." Michael leaned down to lace up the other black boot.

"Don't be daft. Why, it's the least we can do," Hank Paisley replied. "They're a good fit."

Maggie hugged his arm. "You look like Father."

Michael offered Hank a handshake. "I can't thank you enough, sir."

Chaz had gone on an errand, leaving Hank to man the store. Hank reached over the counter and handed Maggie a stick of candy. "You let me know if you need anything else. Anything, you hear?" Hank shook the stick at Maggie. His sideburns bobbed as he spoke.

"We don't have any food."

"Maggie!" Michael scolding with a frown. "Hank, we're fine."

Hank shook a finger in the air and retreated to the back room.

"Maggie, you shouldn't say things like that."

"Well, it's true, isn't it?" She licked her stick. "Beth's starvated. I can see it in her eyes."

Hank returned with a sack full of food and ignored Michael's polite refusals, stuffing a pair of work gloves into the sack as they left.

"Sir, I don't know what to say," Michael lowered his head.

"Say nothing at all, son. Nothing at all." His face silenced the matter.

Chaz returned as they were leaving. "Michael. Maggie. Well, well, well. It looks like you've cleaned us out."

Michael started to reply, but Hank stepped in. "It appears, dear, there is a miscalculation on our inventory list."

Chaz panicked. "What? How can that be?"

* * * * *

Beth didn't know whether to scream or cry.

Michael had taken a job at the Big Mill and arranged for Bella to care for Maggie, and he had done so behind her back. Not only that, he hadn't honored her wishes. "How could you?"

But how could she be so upset? He had a job. A job meant money. She collapsed into the chair, shocked yet afraid of what might come of this. One thing after another. Relief was as far away as Chicago, and all she could imagine was awful. Trauma tends to shed a negative light on everything.

"I appreciate the fact that you found a job, but I will not"— her eyes narrowed on Maggie—"allow her to be raised by a woman of ill repute."

Michael straightened like a soldier. "My mind is settled. There is nothing more to be said."

Beth tried to argue, but Michael set his jaw. She knew if she stayed, she'd say something she'd regret. How could he? Her current frustration was not even the half of her problems. Michael wasn't to blame here. God was.

"Fine." She grabbed her bonnet and slammed the door as she left. She descended the stairs and reached for the door when it opened suddenly.

"Miss Yates?" Ethan jumped, holding the door open. Russ stepped out of the way too. Beth tensed as she moved past him.

"What is it?" He grabbed her hand. "Tell me."

She stared at his hand and then yanked hers away. Her feet hit the street at a heavy pace. The door didn't slam, and she knew he was still standing there.

Tell him.

She tightened her shoulders and kept walking. He had no idea what they had been through, but she planned to have words with the one who did.

* * * * *

Sadie Simone shielded her face, bracing herself.

"You stay away from Bella, you hear me?" Hawk shouted and slapped her again. "And you stay away from that boy." He crushed her against the wall with her wrists bound in his determined grip. "You doin' him and cheatin' me? Cheatin' me outta my money?"

"No. I swear, Hawk." She didn't want Michael mixed up in this. "He isn't like—"

"I take care of you, give you clothes, food…and this is how you repay me?" Hawk grabbed her chin. "Is that boy the father?" He pressed a hand against her stomach.

"No, Hawk. Please." She screamed at him for the first time. "Leave him out of this." She'd never had a friend before. "This is my fault." She'd never carried a baby before. She knew the rules.

"You're right it is." He slammed his knee into her abdomen. Pain surged through her body. He did it again and again. Like a hammer in her gut. She collapsed to the floor, shaking.

Hawk spit on her. "Maybe I should've let 'ol Jake have you when I had the chance. You're nothin' but trouble…"

His cold and heartless words trailed off as her head began to spin and pound so hard, she couldn't hear him anymore. Her eyelids fluttered beyond her control, and the pain was more than she could bear. *God, please help me.*

Hawk kicked her. Everything went black.

Sadie heard pounding footsteps and a man shouting, but she didn't feel anything. She couldn't speak. Her lips wouldn't move. Suddenly, she felt a breeze, like sheets waving in the wind over her.

My child.
I am here.

A voice so kind, she'd never heard it before. She struggled to open her eyes, to see the man's face. One eyelid refused. The other cracked open. Hawk stood over her, but it wasn't his voice. He was shouting at the doctor. "She fell is all, Doc. I swear."

I see every piece of your broken heart.
You are mine.

Doc's lips didn't move. She tried to blink and clear her vision.

You are precious to me.
My daughter.

She remembered the father who had abandoned her.

I knew you before you were born.
I will carry you.

She thought of the baby she'd lost.

I want to give you life.
I want to give you hope.
I want to give you a future.

A blanket as soft as a cloud cradled her, held her, loved her.

Chapter Twenty-One

Bella opened her door. "Boys."

"Something smells good," Ethan said. Russ took a big whiff.

Bella patted his cheek. "Russ tells me you've been mournin' your mama's corn bread."

"That I have." Ethan kissed her cheek.

Her smile always made him feel at home. "I fixed you up a batch." Long before he'd met Bella, she'd won his heart. She and Russ' story still amazed him.

He licked his lips. "Makes a man wish he was the marrying type, doesn't it, Russ?" Ethan jabbed Russ with his elbow. Russ scowled.

"Oh, stop it. Eat them while they're hot." She swatted at him, a hint of embarrassment in her eyes. Her response made him wonder if she'd considered the possibility of marrying Russ before.

Russ hotfooted it to the table. "No need to tempt me, woman. I'm a taste tester by profession." Ethan nipped at his heels. Leaning back in his chair, his head hit the wall, jolting his thoughts from Bella and Russ to someone much younger and prettier. Beth's dark curls were such a contrast to Bella's sweeping blonde hair.

"Miss Yates seemed upset, angry even." Ethan's thought verbalized before he realized it.

Bella and Russ turned, surprised at his comment.

Russ shrugged. "I suppose she did."

"Beth has got a lot on her shoulders." Bella described how she was acquainted with the family. "Michael's a smart young man. Starts work at the Big Mill next week." Placing a large blue-rimmed platter on the table, Bella continued, "That little Maggie, she is a lively one. I'll be lookin' after her till school starts up. I've never seen a child so determined yet so sweet."

Ethan shot his head up, words forming in his mind, but Russ beat him to the punch. "A lot like her older sister, is she?" Russ winked.

Ethan wrinkled his brow.

Bella caught the exchange. "Now, now. She's not as cold as you think. There's a real big heart in there. I'd say she's had a pretty hard go of it with losing her parents and all. And according to Michael, there's more to the story. A scary tale, some of it. And now, money's tight."

Bella shared their plight as she reached across the table and fingered a piece of fried chicken. "Eat up, boys." She held a corn muffin, dangling it like a carrot in front of a hungry horse.

Ethan grabbed it out of the air. "What about her job at the café?" He buttered his muffin.

"Business is bad. Michael took a job to help pay the rent, but I'm not sure they can wait for his paycheck. Gurney'll kick 'em out if they can't pay." Bella wiped a crumb at the corner of her mouth. "Beth's worried sick about it."

Ethan's chair hit the floor. "Gurney wouldn't dare."

"Bet me." Russ' eyes narrowed.

Ethan tensed, tapping the corner of the table. So that's why she was so upset. He recalled her cold greeting. It lacked its usual bite. Her shield was down. *She was angry. Running scared.*

Bella mumbled something.

Fear. Anger. He remembered the feelings like it was yesterday. Almost losing his father, Mother beside herself, and
then Peter's world fell apart. At the time, Ethan didn't think
they could handle one more setback. He took another bite
of his muffin. He became a man that year. He knew exactly
what was going through Beth's mind. It was all up to her
to hold things together. Knowing Beth's ability to speak her
mind, faith or no faith, she and God were about to have
words.

Russ coughed. Bella cleared her throat. "I don't think
he's heard a word I've said, Russ."

"Oh, the corn bread is delicious." Ethan smiled and
stuffed the remainder in his mouth. Russ and Bella grinned.

Ethan tried to participate in the conversation, but the
thought of Beth held him. He scratched his neck at what
Bella had said, about there being more to the story. His mind
began to reel, how Beth avoided him, hated his being close,
shrinking at his touch.

Bella cleared her throat. "Something's going on upstairs,
Russ. See that?"

Russ replied, "Light's begin' to dawn."

Someone had hurt her, done something unthinkable.
His blood began to boil. Light was beginning to dawn. Beth
didn't just despise him. He remembered her tense behavior
with some of the other men at the café. She detested all men
in general. The realization hit him right between the eyes,
like Russ' finger.

"Come back to the barn, son," Russ eyed. "Everything
all right?"

Beth needed a man to make her feel safe, someone to
protect her, carry her burdens, take care of her needs. "It is,
or at least it will be." He accepted the challenge as if sent
directly from heaven itself. He smiled and slapped the table

to divert the focus. "Let us see you to church on Sunday, Bella. Please say yes this time."

Ethan eyed Bella and glanced at Russ. Bella patted his cheek and rose to clean plate. "If it were only you, me, and God, I'd be there in a heartbeat. Church ain't a place for people like me." She busied herself in the kitchen.

Russ shushed him from saying more.

"Someday, perhaps?" Ethan reached for the last muffin as she cleared the table.

"Someday." Bella's weak smile promised the unlikeliness of that event.

* * * * *

Beth stormed toward the river, pounding the ground to the rhythm of a nearby saloon tune, more angry at God than ever. People said He was good, but He'd left them to fend for themselves like orphans. She sought solitude—a place to disappear—amongst the trees, putting town behind her.

If He was God, He was doing a terrible job. She'd held her resentment back for too long. He was to blame. She ran until the river's edge barred her way. With the happy tunes of town still able to be heard, she ran along the river banks. Any relation to joy annoyed her and only added to her outrage. She'd run all night. Up ahead, several downed trees crossed the river bank, their top branches being pulled by the current. She stared at the sky irritated.

Who was up there playing God? Did He even know where they were? "We live here now," she yelled to the sky. "I know you don't care about me, but what about Michael, his dreams of the university? Now he has to work at that...*death trap*." She meant those exact words. "He talks to you now. Do something."

"And Maggie, what about Maggie? She's just a little girl, an innocent child now in the hands of a prostitute." Beth grit her teeth at the thought. A prostitute. "That one's on you. I have done everything"—she was shaking—"everything humanly possible. Yet You have done nothing." She made God smaller in her mind. "If You really are God, big and tough, do something. Why do people even pray to You anymore?

"Father is dead. I could barely recognize his face. I'll never hear his voice again. He burned to death. Burned. Pain no Father should ever have to endure. Do you even understand what I'm saying?" She pictured her father's charred body. "Can you hear me?" she shouted.

I hear every word, Beth.
I am here.
You have never been alone.

"Mother was just taking Father dinner. You could've stopped her. You should've stopped her. Saved her. But no. You left her there to die. To die. To suffocate, gasping for every breath. You have no idea what it was like. How horrible it was to watch. To watch someone you love die. You did nothing. Nothing!" she screamed, trembling to the point of exhaustion. She fell to her knees, crying.

I knelt beside you that day.
I held your mother and father in my arms.
I know you are hurting.

Donovan. The devil himself. He had no right, no right to do what he did to me.

"Why didn't you stop him? You could've stopped him. You stood there and watched him defile me. You allowed it to

happen. He robbed me of…everything." She thought of the
endless nightmares. Hands all over her. She'd never be free.
"You don't care. You don't care…at all."

Trust me, Beth.
I still have plans for you.
I will keep you safe.
Your heart will heal.
And you will be stronger.

"This is all Your fault, and I will never…" She collapsed
against a nearby pine tree and sobbed as loud and long as she
could.

* * * * *

"Beth." Ethan removed his hat, seeing her at the bottom of the boardinghouse steps. Color had returned to her
cheeks. She'd been crying. He shouldn't have called her by
her first name, but it came so easy. He wanted to comfort
her, tell her everything would be fine, but braced himself for
a cold remark instead. Russ descended the stairs behind him
as Ethan held the door open for her.

She slipped inside and hesitated. "Thank you, Ethan."

He held his breath. "Are you all right?" She was inches
from him. He widened the gap and hoped she noticed.

"I don't know." She took to the stairs as Russ hit the
bottom step. "Good night, Miss Yates," Russ called up to her.

She rounded the landing and was gone.

Russ elbowed him. "It's a start, son. It's a start."

Ethan slugged his shoulder in return.

* * * * *

Eli Sands shook the hand of his esteemed host. "Mr. Marcus Daly, I presume. Elias Sands, Chicago."

"Mr. Sands, welcome to Montana. The rest of the men are to arrive tomorrow."

Eli's eyes widened. "I was sure it was the twentieth." He felt for the invitation amongst several of his pockets but knew the mistake played well into his hands. "Well, I hope my unexpected early arrival won't be an inconvenience."

"Not at all." Daly motioned his doorman to assist with his luggage and then walked them to the house.

A circular drive surrounded a rose garden in front of the house, a house of great expanse. Tall, Victorian rooflines jetted out in an unorganized fashion. Looked more like a church than an estate. An arched door adorned the entrance, and thin pillared porches overpowered the elevation of the structure, no thought to its design whatsoever.

"A remodel is already in the works."

Eli shot Daly a look. Had Daly read his mind?

"This is the first remodel. You know women." Daly smiled.

"Indeed, I do." Eli shifted his briefcase. He knew more women than he could count. Climbing the stairs to the large sturdy porch, Eli grinned, proud of his accomplishment. He'd cashed in several favors and pulled more than a few strings to secure his name on Marcus Daly's guest list to have another run at Schwab.

As they entered, a teenage boy crossed the hall, wearing swim trunks and a towel around his shoulders. Daly called him over. "This is my son, Mr. Sands. Marcus Daly II."

The boy dried his hair with the towel. "Nice to meet you, sir."

The heir to the copper throne. Eli shook the boy's hand. "Pleasure to meet you. I am looking forward to seeing this part of the country."

The boy nodded and then climbed the staircase, leaving tiny pools of water with each footstep.

Daly ushered Eli into a sitting room adorned with a marble fireplace and two sitting couches. Ornate crown molding and tall clustered windows defined the high ceilings. A young girl ran through the room, paying Eli no notice. "Do you have children, Mr. Sands?"

From his research, Eli knew Daly was a family man. "No, sir. Unfortunately." He lowered his head, preying on the Daly reputation. "I longed for a family, but my wife, Eleanor, is ill and has been for years."

Sympathy creased Daly's face. "I'm sorry to hear of your wife's illness. That must be a great burden." Daly offered Eli a drink.

Eli nodded and smiled inside, knowing he'd hit his mark. "At times."

"Well, we shall see that the fresh mountain air eases your mind." Daly patted him on the back. "And we might do a little business. I understand you know Schwab," Daly added as the doorman brought in his luggage and took to the stairs.

* * * * *

Beth took a deep breath before knocking. Bella opened her door. "Beth." She seemed surprised.

"Bella."

Concern grew on her face. "What is it? What's wrong?"

"No, nothing's wrong." Beth balled her fists, forcing herself to continue. "I need to speak with you, if that's all right."

"Sure, honey. Come on in," Bella invited her inside. "I'll make us a pot of tea."

Beth hesitated as she crossed the threshold, feeling as if she was breaking the promise. Her upbringing told her a "thank you" was in order, but she still questioned Michael's decision. What would Father and Mother say? She ignored the answer and took the chair offered. "It's a lovely room."

"I hope it doesn't make you uncomfortable. I've always loved fancy things." Bella's room was a dream, like something out of the Sears, Roebuck and Co. catalogue. Pink, calico flower curtains with a coordinating bed cover and lacy pillows. A tattered but still regal floral rug lay in the center of the room. A table beautifully set, as if Bella had been expecting guests. And four tapestry cushioned dining chairs. Two lovely velvet chairs by the fire—a real fireplace with a mantel adorned with clock—and then she saw it, a Bible.

"Bella." Beth's determination returned. "I wanted to thank you...for your assistance...with Maggie." She wrung her hands in her lap. *See that wasn't so difficult.* She tried to relax. "It won't be long. She starts school..." She couldn't remember the day, but wished it was tomorrow.

"We all need a little help now and then." Bella set a tea service on the table, and Beth held her breath. *It couldn't be.* Before her sat a full setting of her mother's strawberry patch china. Suddenly, she heard her mother's voice. Something about going to the market and not being home before lunch. "My mother loved this china." She tipped a teacup upside down to confirm the pattern then hugged it to her chest. "It was her favorite. My favorite."

"It is my favorite pattern too. It belonged to my mother." Bella heated the kettle on the stove, and it released steam immediately, a sign it had been heated recently. Bella pulled a plate of muffins from the oven, and a sweetness filled the room.

Beth couldn't make sense of her thoughts. This wasn't the home of a prostitute, not the ones she'd known. She

KIM TAYLOR

forced a smile as Bella poured her tea. The moment didn't seem real. Beth felt her fingers tremble as she lifted the cup to her lips, reliving a happy memory and then recalling her reason for coming in the first place. "I need to ask you a question, a few questions, actually? I don't mean to pry. It's just that…" She set her cup in its saucer. "I hope you can understand."

"Sure, honey. Ask away." Bella stirred her tea.

Beth's eyes shifted to the Bible on the table. "What is it that you do…exactly?"

Bella set her cup down. "For money?"

This was going to get very awkward very fast. "I suppose, yes." *The truth. Just tell me the truth.* She braced herself.

Bella lifted her brow and then sighed. "I see what you mean."

A long pause made Beth feel she'd overstepped.

Bella continued, "I don't do that anymore. I've changed since—"

Beth waved her hand to silence the matter, embarrassed and a little ashamed. "That's all right, you don't need to explain." She narrowed her eyes. "Can I ask you another question?"

Bella nodded.

Prefacing her question with a short narrative of how they came to be in Montana, she said, "Michael is different now."

Letting out a small chuckle, Bella replied, "You've changed too, I s'pose. Life has a way of doing that."

True. "But how is it that Michael trusts you? He hardly knows you." The question was awkward. Beth adjusted in her seat and sipped her tea.

"I'll tell you why, but do you mind if I tell you a story first?" Bella leaned close.

"All right," Beth replied.

"When I was a girl, all I wanted to do was sing," Bella said.

"Sing?" Beth scrunched her face.

"Yes, sing. Oh, I loved to sing. I was going to be famous, you see?" Bella offered her another muffin, and Beth took it. "But like I said, life has a way of changing us and our circumstances. I tried the stage, but they wanted dancers, not singers. The only establishments that wanted singers…were saloons."

Beth held her muffin in the air.

"Times were hard. The saloon burned down. I was jobless, homeless—I had no money. The fire took everything but my trunk." She held up her teacup. "Then a stranger came to town. He offered to whisk my troubles away. At the time, I thought I didn't have a choice. In my mind, it was a small price to pay for food and shelter."

"I see." Beth shifted, so uncomfortable that she wanted to run. Bella's tale was far too familiar.

"I didn't choose that life. No woman would choose that life if they had any hope of other options." A troubled silence followed the statement. Beth never considered that truth, always thought a woman chose that profession. Suddenly, she remembered the young girls in Chicago. She'd escaped, but they hadn't. If she had the means and a gun, she'd go back and set them free, all twenty-five of them.

Bella appeared lost in thought. "That was years ago now. I've changed. Russ too."

Beth winced. "Russ? I don't understand."

"He'll have to tell you himself." Bella stood. "Beth, it was *God* who changed me." She lifted the teapot. "More tea?"

Beth accepted.

Chapter Twenty-Two

Beth tied her bonnet and leaned over to kiss Maggie as she slept. She tapped Michael's shoulder to wake him. "Michael, I am leaving for work. You should get up. You don't want to be late on your first day of work." *Please keep him safe*, the thought more of a prayer than a demand. She paused, given the heated talk she'd had with God recently, and Bella's story gave her more to consider. *And please keep Michael away from the saw blades*, she added before her moment of faith faltered.

Michael sat up and started buttoning his shirt before she closed the door. She hesitated on the landing and heard a door open down the hall.

"Beth," a whispered greeting echoed down the empty hall.

Beth turned and saw Bella standing in her princess robe.

"Michael will be fine, and I'll take good care of Maggie. Don't you worry."

Beth nodded and waved. "Thank you." *It was God who changed me.* Bella's words she'd never forget, and God was changing Michael, apparently.

For the first time in her life, Beth put herself in another person's shoes. Bella's story could have been her own so easily. Sunrise burst through the window at the end of the hall and danced across Bella's face. Beth saw Bella in a whole new light.

The early morning sun shone in all of its glory. It warmed Beth's back, yet her skin felt the chill. Her footsteps reverberated on the hollow wooded slats of the boardwalk. She'd crossed the road to avoid the path she'd taken in anger, not liking where it took her.

Rounding the corner to Main Street, Clinton swept the boardwalk outside the café, and Mr. Paisley stretched beyond a ladder, hanging a banner. "Beans on sale," if she read it right.

Rubbing her right arm, she checked for scarring. It had healed completely. She recalled Ethan lifting her from the road back in Billings. He was kind. She was rude. Beth sighed. Who was the stubborn mule, now?

Gunfire rang out, jolting Beth from her moment of admission. Jane stood in the street outside the café, gun cocked ready for another blast. "Girl, you're late."

Beth picked up her skirt and jumped the boardwalk. *What have I done?* Her feet ran as fast as her mind. "I am so sorry, Jane. It won't happen again."

All of a sudden, Jane leaned against the post and spat across the dirt. "Just wanted to see you run like you did the first day I met you."

Beth's shoulders relaxed as she looked at Jane. Clinton joined her, leaning on the broom handle. Beth stared between them. Jane growled like a bear, jumping at her. Beth winced. "Girl, you need to stop living in fear. Have some fun." Jane said.

I can't afford to have fun.

Clinton slapped Jane on the back.

Beth grimaced. "It was a joke then. I'm not fired?"

Clinton and Jane had a hearty laugh at her expense. Far too expensive for her to join in.

* * * * *

Michael reported to the foreman at the Big Mill office at six o'clock sharp.

"Name's Ben Coultry. I'm the day foreman. The boys call me Colt. You will report to me directly."

Michael shifted. "Yes, sir."

Colt wasn't an old man. Looked older than he actually was, he figured. Colt's face and hands wore years of hard labor. Colt stood and shook Michael's hand across a large mahogany desk then pulled him to the back door. A quiet hum surrounded the small office. Colt opened the door to the warehouse, and noise blasted Micheal's ears.

Large saws operated at full throttle, spitting out lumber, making the ground vibrate beneath his feet. "What exactly am I to do?" Michael heard his own words echo in his head as if sound hadn't escaped his mouth at all. Colt leaned over, pointing and yelling instructions in Michael's ear and then motioned toward a large pile of lumber.

Michael watched his lips for hearing was impossible. "Check in with me at lunch." Colt left him standing there, joining a man hovering over a stalled machine.

Michael loaded scraps of lumber into a large cart and dumped them behind the mill near the river. The exact location he'd found wood to build shelves for their apartment and to build Sadie and Bella flower boxes. To him, the odd-shaped pieces were a luxury, but to the mill, they were nothing but scraps.

* * * * *

Beth tied Maggie's bonnet and tightened a grip on her emotions. Jane had sent her home early again. Father's pocket watch weighed heavy in her pocket and on her heart.

Maggie squirmed. "Why can't I stay with Bella? This hat makes me look like a girl," Maggie whined, tugging on its fringe.

"You are a girl, almost a young lady. Besides, we have an important meeting this afternoon."

"We used to go to Paisley's all the time. Michael never made me wear a stupid hat."

Maggie turned to face Beth. "Now if I had a cowboy hat, I'd wear it the whole time. Honest. Cross my heart and hope to—" She quieted her voice. "Bella says not to say that word 'cause it's important."

"Well, she's right." Beth shook her head at her misjudgment. Bella was right about a great many things. Beth rolled her eyes.

"So I can have a cowboy hat?" She untied her bonnet.

"That's not what I said." Beth tied a bow again.

"Well, it's what I heard."

She and Maggie were different in so many ways. "Be who you were meant to be," she repeated Mother's words.

Maggie frowned. "Bella says to be who God meant me to be."

"Well, yes. I suppose that is true." In a way, that is what Mother meant.

Maggie yanked at the tie and flung the bonnet halfway across the room. "God meant me not to wear hats."

Frustrated and wishing she'd left Maggie with Bella for a little while longer, she searched out the bonnet and secured it around Maggie's dark girls. "He made you to obey those in charge. You will wear a bonnet."

Maggie relented with a pout. "When I get big"—she looked to the ceiling—"I'm going to be *exactly* what God meant me to be."

Beth locked the door behind them, determined not to cry. This was not a day for tears.

Pushing through the door to Paisley's General, Beth searched for Chaz. Hank popped his head up from behind the counter. "Peas and beans, oh. Good day, fine ladies."

Thankfully, Chaz was out on errand, giving Beth the opportunity to convey her gratitude to Hank. "Sir, we can't thank you enough. Michael told me—"

He stopped her. "Let's just keep that between us, shall we?" His stiff eyebrows raised, and his eyes glanced over at the cash register.

Beth nodded. "Can I ask you a question?" Hank nodded, digging deep into an almost empty candy jar. "If a person needed to sell something, you know, of value, where would that person go?"

He slapped the counter. "Henry George is the man you wanna see, the man with two first names."

"Oh, I didn't say I needed to sell something," Beth tried to explain.

Maggie stared at her, puzzled. "Yes, you did."

Hank grinned. "Check George's saddle shop behind the post office."

"Is it Henry or George?" Beth said.

"Depends on the mood he's in."

She bit her lip. "I see. Let's hope he's in a good mood then."

"Then you'll be looking for Henry today," Hank said.

Beth found George's Saddle shop and rang the bell on the counter several times before a man appeared. "Yes?" A tall man with messy hair and goggles on top his head stepped into the room.

Beth squeezed her satchel tight. "Are you Henry?"

"George."

She panicked. "We'll come back tomorrow. Maggie lets go."

He leaned over the counter and grabbed her sleeve. "Hold on now. You got something to sell?"

Beth hesitated. Rent was due in a few days. "I have a pocket watch. It's solid gold." She lifted the treasure from her satchel, staring momentarily, then stiffened and slid it across the counter.

He examined it for a moment, squinting. "You mean… gold-plated."

Beth motioned Maggie to a bench by the door. "Sit here and don't interrupt."

"Don't forget to cry," Maggie whispered in her ear.

Beth waited at the tall counter as George examined her father's watch. "It's got writing on it…ain't worth as much."

Beth frowned.

He lifted the piece to his ear. "Timing is spot on."

Beth smiled.

He used tiny tools to open its casing. "Coils are worn. That'll cost me to fix."

Beth sank beside Maggie on the bench, wishing Henry had been in today and not George.

When the deal was done, George slammed the door behind them. After a quick calculation of how little he'd paid, she turned to face a locked door. It was still not enough to pay the rent. The "closed" sign swayed like a pendulum behind the window. Through the window, George huddled close, fiddling with Father's watch—her watch. She exhaled and looked down at Maggie, feeling swindled.

"That was our only watch." Maggie frowned. "How will I know when it's time to eat?"

* * * * *

A loud whistle sounded the noontime lunch break as Michael knocked on Colt's door. Men had gathered to eat lunch, something he'd neglected to bring. Colt rose from the group and offered half of his sandwich, detailing Michael's next task. "Into the wheelbarrow, up the hill, and into the pit."

Another endless job.

Hearty laughter filled the tiny shack of an office as men reminisced their first day working at the mill. A blond Norwegian fella poked Michael's chest. "You've never done a hard day's work in your life, have you?"

Ouch. Michael remained calm. "That depends on how you define a hard day's work." The scowl on the fella's face told Michael he shouldn't have said that. Trouble wouldn't look good on his record. Beth wouldn't be happy about it either.

Colt raised his hand, his mouth full of food. "Leave him be."

The other boys jeered and poked at him all day. Mocking clean hands and ingenuity.

"Don't let it get to you. You're the new kid." Colt's words meant to be an encouragement, but they didn't have the desired effect. He did let it get to him.

First, there was the oil spill on the floor and then the water above a door. His trousers crinkled against his leg. Oil was stronger than starch. No doubt, his hair stuck to his head thanks to the bucket of water, and he had a headache. And last but not least, there was the stick of black tar in the soap bucket. *They'll pay for that one.*

By the end of the day, Michael was more worn out from the pranks than the work. The six o'clock whistle blew, and Michael hung the hand saw on the wall. Men scrambled and disappeared. Machines quieted, and shouting ceased. The mill emptied out in minutes.

"You done real good, kid." Colt wiped his forehead with his sleeve and gave the orders for the rest of the week. Michael kicked at the dirt as he walked home, had no idea that he'd have to work so late. His stomach growled. When would he study? Ignoring the question, he turned onto Fourth Street. He didn't have the answer. Right now, all he wanted was food and a bed.

"Michael," Sadie called out from between two buildings. She waved him closer, checking the street.

Someone had roughed her up again. He lifted fallen curls to survey a swollen cheek and cut lip. "What happened? Where have you been?"

She stared at him. "I could ask you the same thing." She tipped his chin.

He ignored her. "Are you...all right?" He expected a "Yes, I'm fine."

"No." Her lip quivered, but she gained control.

He offered his handkerchief and dabbed blood from her lip. "This has got to stop. You have to quit," he whispered.

She nodded, but he knew she wouldn't. She was too afraid.

"Well, how was it?" she said. She'd learned to harness her emotions by changing the subject.

Michael wiped his forehead. "How was what?"

"Your first day at work?" Sadie adjusted her bodice. "Silly."

"Fine."

"Just fine?" A noise drew her attention. "I have to go before Hawk sees me with—"

Michael grabbed her hand. If he refused to let go, Sadie wouldn't get hurt anymore.

She pulled from him. "Michael, go home. You need a bath."

Chapter Twenty-Three

Beth shook her finger in Maggie's face. "Don't you dare say a word, Maggie Yates. I mean it. He's had a long day." Maggie made an excuse. Beth shushed her again. "Not. One. Single. Word."

"I'll try, but I can't make any promises," Maggie replied. Beth narrowed her gaze. Maggie sounded so grown up. First Michael, and now Maggie. She opened the door to check the hall. Michael was still in the facilities.

Michael came home from work exhausted, his face and hands stained yellow-black. Footsteps echoed in the hall. Beth pushed Maggie onto the bed and shoved "Disorderly Girl" into her hands. "Look busy." Rushing to the stove, Beth stirred a pot of beans and reminded herself not to ask a thousand questions.

Michael shuffled in, sat, untied his boots, and kicked them off, rubbing his heels. "I'm hungry...I'm sore...I'm tired." He cleared his throat. "And was anyone going to tell me?"

Beth turned. He pointed to his face. She'd never seen a man with a hard day's work so evident on his face. She thought of her first day at the café, live chickens and feathers.

Maggie snickered first, and then she did. She apologized but couldn't hold it in. She snickered again. Michael smirked as Beth and Maggie burst into laughter. "Think its funny, do you?" He made a scary face. "It will take days to wipe this tar off my hands, let alone my face."

"Between the two of us, we've officially been tarred and feathered," Beth added. More laughter, the kind of laughter Beth hadn't known for years.

"The boys at the mill got me real good. Real pranksters, all of them." He tapped the side of his forehead. "But they've not got the better of me."

Don't ask, Beth told herself. *You don't want to know*. Beth dished up the plates and joined them at the table. "Sorry, it's beans again."

"I miss meat." Maggie frowned but then forced a smile. "I love beans."

Michael eyed Beth. "I love beans too."

Beth recalled Jane's words, "You need to have more fun." Beth drew a deep breath and lifted a spoonful in the air. "They're my favorite." She ate them with an added, "Yum."

"Do you mind if I say grace?" Michael interrupted, folding his hands together with elbows on the table.

Laughter ceased. Beth cleared her throat. To pray meant to depend on someone else, someone other than herself. She bit her lip.

"Beth?" Michael raised his brows.

She held up her hand, buying some time. *If I say yes, there's no going back. And if I say no….* She pictured herself at the edge of a great cliff.

"It's just a prayer, Beth," Michael said.

"Yes, yes. Of course." Beth nervously folded her hands and closed her eyes. It wasn't just a prayer, not to her. It was much more than that.

Maggie joined them. "Pray for meat."

* * * * *

228

Beth laid out several of Michael's shirts. How did they get so many tears? Poking two fingers through the largest hole, she estimated the length of thread and lifted the small makeshift sewing basket to her side. Beth's eyes filled with tears as she threaded the needle to do the task Mother had done so many times.

The door opened, and she pricked her finger with the needle. "Ouch." Michael and Maggie had returned from Bella's carrying a hot pan.

"It's a miracle." Maggie lifted the lid with a mitt. "Smell that, Beth?" She put her face in it's steam.

Beth scrunched her face in confusion.

"It's roasted chicken. Hot off the stove." Michael placed it on the tiny stove and lit the fire inside.

"It's meat. We prayed for meat, and here it is." Maggie offered in "ta-da" fashion.

Beth wiped her tears. "It's not a magic trick, Maggie." Although it did seem strange, the timing of it. She'd thank Bella in the morning.

Michael seemed satisfied with his fire. "That should do it. Anyone still hungry?"

"Me. And me. And me."

"I'm fine." More for them. It could last them for a couple of days.

"Beth, what's wrong?" Michael joined, voice low so Maggie didn't hear.

"I sold Father's pocket watch today," Her voice cracked, and she covered her mouth to gain her composure.

Maggie joined them suddenly. "I know all about it. You don't have to whisper about everything. I'm not a little kid anymore."

He sat down beside her, pulling Maggie close. "It will be all right. Beth, trust me."

She wiped a fallen tear, nodding. *Yes, everything would be all right.* She'd know for sure tomorrow.

* * * * *

Just a few more days and Ethan would be sleeping in his own bed in his own barn. The simple amenities wouldn't bother him.

Ethan rolled over in his bunk and heard Cook whistling off tune in the camp kitchen, clanging pots to his rhythm. The ranch hands at the Daly ranch bunked at a camp house. Each room had several bunks with a washbasin in the corner. The smell of burnt coffee seeped through the crack under the door and burned his nose. Ethan tapped Russ' shoulder across the floor space between them. "Russ, get up."

Russ turned over and threw off his covers, begrudging the hour. "Can't a man get his beauty sleep?"

"Shhh." Ethan held up his hand. "Smell that?" He thumbed the direction of the kitchen.

Russ took it in and frowned. "I'm startin' to like ol' Readron's brew."

Ethan grabbed his Stetson. "Come on. We'll stop in at the café."

The horses were more than ready to ride. Their hindquarters twitched with anticipation. Autumn was coming. Ethan could smell it in the air. Nights had cooled off, and the days were a perfect temperature. The ride cleared his head.

Beth had occupied much of his thinking lately. Today was the day. He'd tried yesterday, but Jane had sent her home early. He couldn't just show up at her door and say, 'here's some money.' It had to be in secret. She wouldn't accept the help, especially from him. Slapping his gloves against his thigh, he adjusted in the saddle. *Mr. Gurney, I guess you've met your match.*

"You know what you need, Ethan?" Russ called out from the rear.

Ethan didn't turn. "I can't imagine."

"A good woman."

Russ wanted for him what he wouldn't admit he needed himself. "I've got you and Buck? What else could a man want?"

Russ joined him, scratching his head. "Well…"

"Don't answer that."

Russ chuckled.

"Besides, she'd find herself sleeping in a barn. I couldn't ask a woman to do that." Russ slapped him on the back. "We best be stakin' out a house if that be the case." Russ urged his horse to avoid a punch in the shoulder.

Ethan smirked and reached for his watch but found an empty pocket instead. Without a watch, how could he stay on schedule? He urged Jax to a faster pace, leaving Russ in a cloud of dust. Time to buy a watch.

* * * * *

The bell jingled above the café door. *Thank goodness. Another customer.*

Anne-Marie's hours had been cut too, but she didn't mind. *I mind.* She added every tip like a cash register in her head. Even with payday, she was still eight dollars short.

"Good morning, Ethan," Beth heard a man in the street call out before the door closed. Her stomach fluttered as she caught her reflection in the kitchen window. Why did she always wear her hair tightly pinned back? She unpinned it and pinched her cheeks. Be nice. Be sweet. He may not be the biggest tipper, but she needed all the help she could get today. She rolled her shoulders and stepped into the dining room.

"Good morning, Ethan," she greeted, forcing herself to stare at his lips. To look in his eyes would give her away. That, she couldn't afford.

* * * * *

"Good morning, Beth." Her confused blue-green eyes threatened his plan altogether. He took in the moment. Could it be? Had the wall finally crumbled?

"Will you be having your usual this morning?" She smiled and cleared her throat.

What is she doing? "My usual?" He picked a speck of mud off his Stetson and placed his hat on the table. "Without sauce."

She read off his order, eyeing the window and clearing her throat again.

"Two plates. Russ will be along shortly." Ethan raised a brow, bewildered. He leaned back as she poured his morning coffee, watching her. She could take as long as she wanted. Her presence was just the thing he needed this morning. He liked her hair worn down. What a man wouldn't give to wake up to her. She was mesmerizing and sweet. Her standing at the stove in his kitchen… He shook the thought, terrified at the direction he was heading.

"I can call you Beth, then?"

Her hands shook as she added another plate to his order.

He held his breath when she didn't answer. This sweet moment had come and gone in a matter of seconds.

"Of course, yes. Of course." She poured him coffee and missed his coffee cup, splashing his hand. "Sorry." She dapped the hot coffee with her apron.

The hot coffee didn't bother him, but her touch did. Time slowed. The café was half full, conversations continuing in the background. Dishes clanged, but to him, they were all alone. They both cleared their throats. He hadn't counted on her being…like this. His plan threatened to verbalize, but he refocused. The plan was to get in, eat, do what he wanted to do, and then get out unnoticed.

"Honey?" He stared on the honey jar she held out to him. He thought of all the other women who'd called him "honey," and nothing compared to how it sounded coming from Beth. She could call him "honey" the rest of his days.

This wasn't going according to his plan one bit. He got it together, knowing if his thoughts were written on the wall, she'd run for the hills. "You seem chipper this morning," he said. The sparkle in her eyes dimmed.

"I…am chipper." Her voice cracked. "I'll get your order in right away," she added and hurried away, knocking over the salt and pepper shakers on the next table.

* * * * *

Beth fled to the kitchen, put her back against the wall with heart pounding. She couldn't do it. He rattled her. Somehow, it was much easier to be mean and cold. Talking to him felt too comfortable. He had a way of disarming her, even on a day like today. He hadn't been into the café for several days, and for some reason, that bothered her. And now, she'd give him permission to call her by her first name. She'd let down her guard. Maybe he wasn't the man she thought at first, but he was a man.

She tucked his order onto the rounder and swung it toward Clinton and then glanced back at Ethan. He had been watching her. She smiled and whirled around to hide the fact that she liked it too much.

* * * * *

Ethan adjusted in his chair and shoved his hand into his pocket, pulling out a thin roll of bills. The bell rang above the door, and several young cowpokes waltzed in, taking a seat at the counter. *Don't even think about it, fellas*, he warned in his head.

When Beth pushed through the kitchen door holding his order, she paused and looked at the men. "I'll be right with you," then glanced at Ethan.

"Dumplin', I'll wait all day if takin' you home is the prize." The idiot whistled, followed by a slap on the back from the other. If they so much as touch her, there would be…well, they'd pay. Ethan grit his teeth, hoping they'd look in his direction. He had a scowl fully prepared.

Beth sat the plate in front of him, giving the men a quick glance.

He grabbed her hand and pulled her closer. Her eyes darted and then fell to his hand over hers. "If those boys give you any trouble, I'm right here."

She glanced at the men as Ethan slipped the roll of bills into her apron pocket and leaned back quickly, fork already in his other hand.

"I think I can take care of myself." Beth slid her hand away, and he wanted to take it back.

"I'm late." Anne-Marie came flying through the kitchen door, the normal squeal in her voice turning sweet. "Well, what do we have here?" She leaned on the counter in a way he knew Beth would never. "Good morning, boys."

Ethan shoved several quick bites into his mouth. Anne-Marie shot Beth a look as she tied on her apron in front of the men. Beth turned to Ethan and rolled her sparkling eyes. "It looks like I won't have to take care of myself…this time."

He nodded. "No, not this time." He gulped down his coffee and rose. After plunking several coins on the table, he grabbed his Stetson. "Good day, *Beth*."

"But you've hardly eaten a thing. And what about Russ' breakfast." Her voice trailed off as he left the café. *His loss, my gain.*

His heart about beat its way out of his chest. He hit the boardwalk, looked both ways, and went left. Who knows why he turned left. He had to get out of there—and fast. Once he'd passed the café window, he flattened against the wall. *Should've gone right.* What business did he have in this direction? Now, he'd have to circle all the way around the block to avoid being seen.

And there, Jax stood tied up on the other side of the café. He whistled as quietly as he could. Jax lifted her head and sidestepped. Using all his body language, he tried to coax her into doing what she always did, but she ignored him.

* * * * *

Beth stood there, full plate of food on the table, stunned. Was it something she'd said? She tried to be sweet, especially today. *Who's two-faced now?* She bit her tongue, wishing she'd never said those words to him.

"Isn't the blond a dream?" Anne-Marie whispered in her ear as she stood by the window.

"Not interested," Beth scowled.

"So, you like the dark-haired fellows," Anne-Marie joked, prying mostly. "Is that it?"

Beth shooed her off.

"Bet I know the kind of fellows you like." Anne-Marie winked at the boys at the counter. "The Ethan variety."

"That's not true, and you know it. Stop pestering me." Beth snapped a towel at her. Well, it was sort of true, but she would never admit it to Anne-Marie. She'd never hear the last of it.

"Lighten up. I'm just teasing." Anne-Marie leaned in. "Besides you don't need to worry about Ethan. He's snubbed every girl in town. Trust me."

The kitchen door swung open, and Jane hollered, "Where's Clinton?"

Beth and Anne-Marie shook their heads. *Probably at the saloon.* But Beth didn't dare say it.

Jane retreated to the kitchen, carrying on as usual, and Anne-Marie paid particular attention to the young blond-haired man at the counter. Beth peered through the window. Jax was still tied up outside, but Ethan was nowhere in sight.

Just then, movement caught her eye below the front window outside of the café. A head bobbed up and down. She pressed in. It was Ethan crawling on his hands and knees past the window. He untied Jax's knot, mounted, and stole away as if he'd just robbed the bank. *What's he up to?* She folded her arms.

The bell rang as a customer walked in. "Good morning, darlin'," the old man greeted.

Beth helped him to a table, placing his cane against the wall.

Jane squealed from the back. "Buck Reardon, ol' Buck-eye. Aren't you a sight for sore eyes?" Jane appeared in the dining room, wiped her hands on the towel around her waist, and slapped the man on his back.

"Little missy Martha Jane, you ain't changed one iota."

Beth poured him a cup of coffee and grabbed sugar from a neighboring table.

"Just black," he said, covering his cup. "And I like it strong."

"I heard you done sold your place. Too much pressure from them big shots from the city, eh?" Jane nudged his shoulder.

"Nope, a local fellow."

"Daly himself?"

"Nope. Fella by the name of Ethan Dawson, one of the finest young fellows I ever met."

Beth dropped Ethan's plate. Steak and eggs scattered across the floor. "Ethan bought your ranch? I thought he worked for Mr. Daly." No time to remind herself not to speak her mind.

Jane grimaced and motioned for her to clean it up.

"Won't be workin' for Daly much longer." He leaned past Jane. "So, you know him, do ya? A real gent, ain't he?"

Beth cleared her throat and stared at the downturned plate on the floor. "Yes, as real as they come."

Chapter Twenty-Four

Beth emptied the contents of her pocket, hung the work apron on the wall peg, and gathered her bonnet and purse. "Jane, I'm leaving. Is there anything else? Clinton?" No answer. They must have left early, probably already at the saloon.

As she reached across the back kitchen table to sweep the change into her satchel, she paused. Her eyes widened. A perfect roll of bills sat amongst the coins. She checked the hall, suddenly aware that someone might be watching. Trembling, she reached for the treasure.

The back door swung open, its squeal announced an intruder. Beth quickly concealed the roll.

Anne-Marie appeared in the doorway. "You look like you just seen a ghost." Anne-Marie lifted her paycheck from the wall box. "Payday, girly." She waved the envelope in the air. "My last one, most likely. I'll be far too busy being married."

"Anne-Marie, git in here, girl," Jane shouted from the dining room.

So, Jane and Clinton are still here.

Anne-Marie rolled her eyes and flipped her ever-so-blonde hair. "Coming, Jane," she smirked. "Wait for me. I will tell you all the news."

When she was gone, Beth uncurled her fingers to reveal what she hoped wasn't a dream. She unrolled the bills. Five twenty-dollar bills. Lady Liberty never looked so beautiful. Heart pounding, she dumped the bills into her satchel. Could she be dreaming? Where had it come from? And how…did it get into her apron?

Footsteps made her jump. What if someone was searching for it? Would they think she stole the money? She swung around to meet a flushed Anne-Marie.

"No harm done. Just the usual 'we're not gonna have none of your shenanigans' talk." Anne-Marie grabbed Beth's hand. "The summer dance is tonight. You simply have to come. I won't take no for an answer. Well, I might if you're gonna be all boo-hoo about it." She stood there, arms folded, a paycheck dangling in one hand.

"I can't." A summer dance was for girls in want of a husband and needing the chance to show off.

"All the boys will be there. Sarah Lee met Arnoldson What's-his-name last year, and now they're going steady. Horrid name, isn't it? *Arnoldson.* Please say you'll go. I'm sure I can find you a man. Not Ethan, of course, but another for sure."

Beth straightened, hoping the owner of those bills wasn't looking for them right now. "I have responsibilities."

"And Mrs. Paisley lent out the store's front window string lights. They're red, but Mrs. Sadler hung them with rose-colored chiffon. It'll be pink heaven. I'm gonna wear last year's dress, but so what? It's a dance. I've altered my dress. I look absolutely divine in pink. It's the loveliest thing…"

Anne-Marie's description of her gown faded into the back of Beth's mind. She nodded once or twice. Where had the money come from? She exhaled and wished Anne-Marie would take a breath.

It wouldn't be right to keep the money. Beth had to tell someone. "I'm sorry. I just can't go." She left Anne-Marie mid-sentence and pressed through to the dining room.

Clinton and Jane sat at a table near the window, money spread out and receipts stacked in piles, two bottles of whiskey between them. Jane counted money, while Clinton stared out the window. Tiptoeing toward them, she chose her words.

"What?" Jane yelled.

Beth jumped, fidgeting with her satchel and formulating her question. "Is all the money accounted for today?" She knew it sounded strange the minute she said it. The pecuniary standings of Calamity Jane's café weren't any of her business. As awkward as it came out, she needed to know if money was missing.

Jane thumbed the stack of bills in front of her. "Appears to be."

"It's all here." Clinton added in his Texan drawl. "What there is of it."

Beth hesitated. She couldn't live with herself if she took the money only to find out later it belonged to someone else. "It's just that I found some money today," she explained. "Well, actually, I found it in my apron pocket."

Clinton leaned in. Jane stopped counting. They shared a look. "Finders keepers. Must be your lucky day. Now git." Jane swatted Beth's behind and took a swig of whiskey.

Beth turned, a smile as big as the sun on her face. She ran out the back door, her heart about to explode. She knocked on Mr. Gurney's door and placed the bills in his hands. He never drank the night before rent was due. He licked his fingers like his lazy dog licked his paws and thumbed through the money. No "thank you" came, just a quick nod and a closed door.

"Good day," she called to the closed door. Today was a good day indeed. A miracle had happened, as Maggie would say. Did she believe in miracles?

Of course, she believed. A thrill rose within her. They could survive for two more months at least. Maybe three.

After arriving home, she dumped her things on the bed and lifted the remaining bills from her satchel. "Thank you," she said, looking heavenward, her reaction so shocking yet so…natural.

* * * * *

"I can't believe you got yourself horsewhipped into this." Ethan stood at the blackened oval mirror at camp. He washed his face and hands, sweeping his hair from one side to the other. *You shouldn't have taken that bet. You know better.* But when the boys at the ranch bet him he couldn't stay on that horse, he couldn't pass it up. *Fool.* He never could pass up a dare. *Pride comes before the fall.* His mother quoted the Bible in his head.

The summer dance was the last place on earth he wanted to be. He was ancient compared to these boys. *And I rarely dance.* Couldn't even remember the last time he'd tried. He'd much rather ride out to his ranch and get an early start in the morning. He was behind as it was, and now he was going to a dance. No doubt, it would be a night of humiliation, a night he'd never forget.

Perhaps there was still time to wriggle out of this. He could—

A knock at the door told him it was too late. One dance. That was the deal. *Then, I'm outta there.*

* * * * *

Beth stared at Bella in disbelief. "Well, you're going, aren't you?" Bella said.

Not the reaction Beth expected. "I have things to do."
Besides, she didn't have a dress. And to parade herself around?
She'd never learned the art of it. Probably never would, this
late in the game.

Bella raised a thin brow. "You don't have a dress."

"It's not just that—"

Bella silenced her and began sorting through her closet.
Beth tried every excuse imaginable.

Maggie cheered Bella's efforts. "You're going to the
dance!"

Beth hung her head. Something told her she was going
to that dance whether she wanted to or not.

"Aha!" Bella exclaimed, displaying the most beautiful
dress Beth had ever seen, an ivory evening gown with a laced
bodice and long flowing sleeves, not all puffed up like some
of those ridiculous gowns she'd seen advertised. Simple, yet
elegant. Bella smoothed out the lace at the neckline. "It's
been a long time, my old friend."

"It's glorious!" Maggie exclaimed.

And for once, Beth agreed. Beth tried to find an excuse
Bella would believe. "It's not about the dress, Bella. I have
a family—responsibilities." There. It was the best she could
do. But by the look on Bella's face and Maggie's giggle, Beth
knew she was in trouble. They weren't buying a word of it.

"Maggie and Michael can have dinner with Russ and
me tonight, and you, honey, are going to stop worrying about
everyone else for once and go to that dance." Bella held the
dress against Beth's front.

Beth was clearly outnumbered by age, by experience,
and by a great many things. "I suppose—" she touched the
fabric, "I suppose I could go for a little while." She lifted her
head to meet Bella's big smile.

Maggie gasped. "Beth, you don't know how to dance."

Beth fingered her mother's locket around her neck as she studied her reflection in the mirror, shocked by the transformation. She wasn't herself. And tonight, it would be nice to have a break from Beth Yates.

"You'll be the prettiest girl there. I know it. I can see it in your eyes." Maggie hugged her from the side.

A knock at the door drew their attention. Maggie ran to the door and reached up to cover Michael's eyes. As Maggie pulled her hands away, Michael sighed, smiling. He turned her around in an attempted dance move. "You look beautiful. Remember the parties at the university?"

Beth smiled at the memory. "They were lovely parties."

"Was this really your dress a long time ago?" Maggie said to Bella.

Bella put a fist on her hip. "Well, I used to be... younger." She sucked in her frame. "And thinner." The four erupted in laughter.

The door cracked, and Russ' eyes widened. "Sounds like a celebration goin' on in here." Russ was here, and Beth knew what that meant. There was no turning back now. But to her relief, Ethan wasn't with him. Russ apologized, for Ethan said he had business in town. "I'll walk you over now, and then fetch you around ten o'clock. How's that sound?" Russ said.

"Thank you, Russ, but I'll be fine to walk myself." Beth curtsied and hoped her response fit the dress and the evening.

"Not in that dress," Russ refused. Bella kissed her off, and Russ offered his arm as they waved goodbye.

"If I'd known I'd be escortin' you this evenin', I'd have hired a buggy. A girl needs a buggy for this sort of o...ccas... sion."

Beth smiled. "I'm afraid, I missed that opportunity a long time ago."

"That smile looks good on you." His cheeks turned pink. "You should wear it more often."

As they approached the hall, music and light seeped from the windows into the street. She slowed her pace, hesitating. "Maybe, I shouldn't—"

She stared at the bright windows on the second story. "I only know Anne-Marie."

Russ squeezed her arm. "Go on. Have yourself a good time. You might find that you know more folks than you think."

She nodded, picked up her dress, and climbed the stairs, Russ right beside her.

Beth tightened her grip as they entered the room. A small quartet sat in the corner, playing a lively piece. The music was loud, nearly drowned out voices completely. Such a lovely sight. It reminded her of the dance hall at the university. Beth had never actually danced before but watched the couples from afar. Father always told her, "You're too young. Maybe next year."

Russ said he'd return at ten o'clock and left her in the hands of a stranger. Ten o'clock seemed like an eternity.

"Let's see if we can't calm your jitters," an older woman whispered in her ear. The pink ribbon hanging from her corsage matched the rose-colored lights strung around the room in crisscross fashion.

The dance floor seemed crowded, and onlookers pressed in. By her estimation, the girls outnumbered the boys nearly two to one. She liked those odds.

Chapter Twenty-Five

Mrs. Sadler introduced Beth to several young girls huddled in a group near a row of chairs, all of them far younger than she. *Maggie would fit in better than I.* And she'd overdressed. This was a country dance. Mrs. Sadler left her, having been called to refill the punch bowl. She sighed and scanned the room. *Anne-Marie, where are you?* Stepping from the group, she found a place in a shadowed corner. Several young men noticed her. Others followed suit.

This was a bad idea. She didn't know how to dance. She didn't know how to fit in at social events. What a fool to think she belonged here. What would she say if someone asked her to dance? *"I don't dance"?* She couldn't say that. What girl comes to a dance to not dance?

I'm waiting for someone. That one might work. She would wait the entire evening if she had to. She was content to watch and listen to the music.

She searched the room for a familiar face, but except for the dance floor, lights shadowed faces. *What was I thinking?* In order to dance, one must have a partner—a man, in most cases. It was highly unlikely that Anne-Marie would stand up with her.

Across the room, a group parted. Ethan Dawson stood exposed by the opening in the crowd. She hid her face.

Not only was this a bad idea, it was a terrible one.

* * * * *

Ethan stared at Beth as she floated into the hall, hanging on the arm of Russ Miles, a friend until this moment. He'd hog-tie him later. How could Ethan not stare? Every man in the room was staring. She was the most beautiful girl in the room. Russ was going to get a piece of his mind. He hadn't said a word about escorting Beth to the dance.

He watched as Mrs. Sadler introduced Beth to a group of young girls. *They don't hold a candlestick to her.* Shifting his gaze, he focused on the group around him. They closed in, whispering something about Beth's dress and her perfect hair. The mix of perfume punched him in the nose. He wanted air. "It's hot in here, isn't it?"

"It is very hot in here." A younger-than-she-wanted-to-be hugged his arm.

He uncurled her fingers from his arm. "Thanks, but I'll be fine...alone." Hurrying away, he stiffened. He was free of her and them—girls so giddy and silly, his head ached. At least, Molly Singleton and Clarese Wright had found themselves different fellows to bother.

One of the boys grabbed his arm. "Remember, you lost the bet, Mr. I'll-show-you. We'll see you to the dance floor tonight, even if I have to dance with you myself." A billow of laughter followed him across the room. Without knowing it, Beth Yates would rescue him this time.

"Beth." He bowed, pulling his Stetson to his chest.

She curtsied and then straightened. "Ethan."

He wanted to add, "Your timing is perfect," but her reluctance to look at him kept his lips sealed. Of all the girls in the room, she would be his safest bet. She disliked men in general—and him specifically. He had no intention of dancing his one dance with Miss Trouble. He thought of several girls that fit that description. Standing beside Beth, he watched the dancers. Maybe—just maybe—she was relieved to see him too. Observing her, however, her face didn't show it. But she was here, and what girl comes to a dance…not to dance? "Do you dance?"

"Yes. No…no," she sighed. "What I mean is…I think I'll watch for a while. Thank you." Her words sputtered like water spewing from an artesian well.

"Good. Me either."

* * * * *

Horrified by her response, Beth frantically searched the room, hoping to find Anne-Marie. *She said she'd be here.* Nervously, she tapped her foot off-beat to the music.

In her pursuit, she caught the eye of two men walking toward her, each from a different direction. She bit her lip. Anne-Marie was nowhere to be found, and Ethan was inches away. Heat rose to her cheeks as she sought a rescue. The door was an option. Ethan shifted beside her. He was another option. The men drew near, both watching the other. "Ethan, I'd love to dance." She grabbed his hand before considering the consequences of her words and action.

* * * * *

Ethan flinched at her touch, for it caught him completely off guard, more off guard than he had been in years. He read her face and followed her gaze. Both men halted. He eyed each suitor, conveying something he couldn't put into words. One fella jumped into a conversation with a hearty laugh, as if someone had said something amusing. The other cowboy saw the exchange and simply turned away.

Beth relaxed her grip but didn't let go. "Thank you."

"You're welcome." He glanced at their hands. "Let's have some punch."

She nodded, her fingers trembling. "All right."

They weaved through the crowd, dodging would-be suitors and stares. She fussed with her necklace. "I feel overdressed."

"You look fine." *Better than fine.*

"Everyone is staring. I've never been such a spectacle." She closed her eyes. "Bella talked me into this."

"The boys forced me into this," he replied without thinking. "People are staring because you are—"

He caught himself. *Stunning.* "Because you're the new girl in town." If he'd said what he wanted to say, she'd have found a cliff and pushed him over the edge. He was sure of it.

She smiled. "We're years older than most of these... kids."

Her hand slipped from his, and he mourned its absence immediately. Mrs. Sadler poured them punch and winked at Ethan. "And you didn't think you'd find a friend."

Beth blushed. Ethan tried to distract her. "I was wondering if you'd be willing to do me a favor."

She glanced over the rim of her cup, smoothing her other hand down her dress. Never had such a small gesture captured his imagination. Beth cleared her throat. "A favor?"

* * * * *

"I don't dance," Beth finally admitted after agreeing to Ethan's plan.

Ethan grinned. "Me either."

She shrugged. "No. What I mean is...I can't dance." If she was a fool before, there wasn't a word in the English language to describe her now.

"Just follow my lead." He grabbed her hand and led her to the dance floor. His skin was warm, despite her gloves. The crowd opened up like the parting of the Red Sea. The music stopped, and they looked at each other. Then it started up again with a melancholy tempo and smooth strings. Ethan shrugged. Beth panicked.

It would have to be a slow song. Several couples spun around them, floating like clouds. Ethan held up a hand. *You can do this.* She put hers in his. His arm cradled the small of her back. She felt the placement of each finger.

He took the first step, bidding her to follow. *Please, don't let me trip and fall, not in front of all these people.* She looked down at her feet and started to get off beat.

"Beth, look at me."

She stared at his mouth, for his eyes would be more of a distraction than her feet. Ethan's plan included punch, one dance, and a quick getaway. It was a fine plan in the beginning, but now? Her heart was beating so fast, she feared she would lose time, her balance, and her dignity.

* * * * *

If he messed this up, she'd never speak to him again. He watched her but could only see the next dance steps in his mind. It had been years since he'd done this. Thinking back on it now, he remembered that girl didn't speak to him afterward.

He had to focus.

It all happened slowly and methodically, as if time itself relaxed just for him. He saw faces and heard the conversations of people as they passed by. Beth's gown swayed to the music, melting against his legs. The dance floor emptied out as the song played on. Pink lights made Beth's dress two-toned, much like her eyes. All of a sudden, the crowd spread out, and they found themselves alone on the dance floor.

Beth started to panic. He pulled her closer and whispered in her ear, "It's almost over." She offered a weary smile in return. The musicians hit the final note, and the room exploded in applause. He bowed slightly, and she curtsied, signifying the end of the dance. The look in her eye, he'd never forget. It may have been the end of the dance, but it was the beginning of something else entirely.

* * * * *

The crowd and congratulations flooded the dance floor, overwhelming them. "Beth, I knew you'd come." Anne-Marie hugged her. "I knew you'd hog-tie the most eligible man in town." She slapped Ethan's shoulder.

Beth blushed and was sure the color showed. "I looked for you."

Several men overtook them. "You've been holding out on us, Ethan. Who's your little dumpling?"

She and Ethan exchanged a smile. The mass of people began to force them apart. Ethan grabbed her hand and tightened his hold. Her heart jumped. The room seemed to spin around them. She tried to be polite and watched as Ethan tried to find a quick escape route.

Anne-Marie grabbed her arm and pulled her away from the crowd. "You don't fool me, missy. 'All duty and no play.' Isn't that what you said?"

Beth's hand slipped from his grasp. She glanced back as a crowd of girls surrounded him, heat no doubt coloring her cheeks. "I have to go."

Anne-Marie scowled. "You just got here."

"I really have to go." Beth searched for Ethan, but he was lost. She hurried down the stairs, holding her breath. She was living in a dream.

* * * * *

Ethan felt her let go of his hand, and then he couldn't find her. He peered over heads and in between shoulders. She had disappeared. He pushed through the crowd and found Anne-Marie talking with two other girls, but Beth was gone.

He grabbed his hat and thanked Mr. and Mrs. Sadler before descending the steps. Jax was still tied up out front, along with other horses. It was early yet, but the sun had disappeared behind the mountains. The sky was dark blue with strips of low white clouds still visible near the horizon.

After releasing Jax's tether, he walked around the corner to Main Street. Beth walked on the boardwalk at a fast pace. He was quick at her heels. "I thought you said you *couldn't* dance."

* * * * *

"I thought you said you *didn't* dance," Beth replied and regretted the tone in her voice.

Ethan matched her steady pace. They approached a rowdy bunch of men outside a saloon. Hoping to avoid an altercation with the men, she paused and checked the street.

"May I?" Ethan offered his arm.

Beth hesitated. She shouldn't, but she wanted to. Laughter drew her attention, and she accepted his assistance. Together, they walked straight through the crowd. The rowdy bunch grew louder. She released his arm once they had passed. "You don't have to do this," she said, knowing that within minutes, they'd be alone.

"Do what?" He glanced over his shoulder at the rowdy bunch.

"Walk me home." She tensed.

He stopped, gently taking her hand. "Let's get one thing straight. I am a gentleman, whether you believe me or not." He forced himself to let go of her hand.

A long and uncomfortable silence followed. Jax nudged Beth's shoulder from behind, encouraging a response. "Yes. I see that now." She stared at the ground and tugged at her gloves. "You danced beautifully, by the way."

"As did you." He urged Jax forward.

Except for Jax's occasional nudge or whinny, they just walked. "How much longer will you be at Mr. Daly's Ranch?"

"For a couple more days." He unbuttoned his vest.

"What kind of ranch are you building?" He looked at her, surprised. "I overheard Jane talking to Buck Reardon the other day." She put her hands behind her back.

"Oh. Horses, mostly. I'll have some cattle too." Jax nudged him from behind, and he shooed her.

Fourth Street displayed all its usual color. Red lights bright in the windows, loud laughing, drunk men, and loose women. She didn't seem to take much notice anymore. This was her street.

"I understand Michael works at the Big Mill," Ethan said.

Beth sighed. "I was against it at first."

"Your little sister couldn't be in better hands. Bella is a fine woman."

She smiled. "I know that now." She'd grown weary of being wrong. She stared at him as they walked. Traced the contour of his face for the first time. Never looked at him long enough before.

"I hope to finish the fence this weekend. After that, I'd like to get started on the farmhouse. It'll have four bedrooms and a nice-sized kitchen..."

He swallowed and didn't finish his sentence.

"I go to church on Sundays."

The transition jolted her. "Yes, I've heard."

"Do you go to—"

"No." Not since her parents opened the orphanage. *But Michael prays before our meals now.* How she wanted to tell him that.

"Perhaps you might consider—"

"Well, I have to work on Sundays," she said as they arrived home. He tied Jax to the post and helped Beth climb the stairs. It was after nine. Michael and Maggie would be in bed. Ethan knocked on Bella's door. Bella opened the door, concerned. Russ stepped behind her and checked his watch. "It's not ten yet."

Bella ushered them inside. "How was the dance?"

Ethan and Beth shrugged, smiled at each other, and chuckled. Ethan removed his hat. "Just fine."

"It was fine," Beth added. She fidgeted with her gloves. "Very fine."

"Better than fine." Ethan ran his fingers around the rim of his hat.

Russ lifted his brows, and Bella cocked her head. "Well, Ruston Miles. Apparently, the dance was just fine." Bella closed the door. "Let's have some tea."

Chapter Twenty-Six

It sure beat the oppression of the thick Chicago air, crowded streets, and tightly cramped houses. Eli looked around Daly's study. Some men smoked cigars, huddled in a group. Wright sipped a glass of wine in solitude. Schwab had his nose in the newspaper. Eli needed another run at him. Schwab had been avoiding him all week.

The room was adorned with Daly's trophy kills, local and abroad. A large bear stood eight feet tall, guarding the doorway. A full-bodied mountain lion loomed over a beautifully carved wooden liquor bar. Treasured and prized animals, the room's only decoration.

"Jello for you, sir?" the footman offered. Reddish-clear dessert wiggled as the man swung the silver tray in Eli's direction.

"No, thank you." Eli smoothed the cool leather of his chair and took another sip of his merlot. A man could get used to living here. This was Daly's summer home, and Mrs. Daly had plans to renovate the place entirely. Such a shame really. A marvelous house with a spectacular mountainous setting. *She'll make it too big, and it will overtake the view.*

Two men in the corner laughed. *Too much wine.* Most of these men knew each other. Previous dealings, most likely.

He took another sip and spilled wine down his best suit. A footman came to his aid, drawing too much attention. "Stop." Eli pushed the man away. "It's fine." Eli shooed him.

The men were staring. He smiled and nodded. As he surveyed the damage, the men returned to their conversations. *You fool. You are sitting with big names here.* Daly, Schwab—he added his name to the list. He'd worked his way to the top, and once his development plans in Chicago were final, he'd never have to climb another social ladder again.

Eli watched and listened as men whom he'd admired for years spoke of lucrative investments and future opportunities. He took notes in his head and wrote it all down after everyone went to bed. These were some of the most brilliant business minds of the times, and he was one of them. He aspired to join these men in their endeavors, if not to beat them to it.

"Good night," Ulysses Schwab bid and disappeared into the dining room.

He'd make sure to have a seat next to Schwab tomorrow. "Good night," Eli replied.

Tomorrow, Daly planned a fishing excursion. He patted his jacket pocket, finding hope inside. In town, he'd purchased C. C. Filson's Fishing guide at Paisley's General Store. Quaint as the store was, the woman annoyed him. *Asked too many questions.*

He'd study the guide in bed. He refused to play the fool. He glanced around the room. Several men gulped their drinks. Others concluded conversations. He stood, not wanting to be the last. "Good night, gentlemen."

No one replied.

Chapter Twenty-Seven

Beth awoke early even though she hadn't slept long. She knew she'd pay for a late night.

Buttoning the tiny pearls of her blouse, a horrible face seized her mind. *Donovan.* She stared down at several buttons and shot her head in the air. *No more. You'll have no more of me.*

Beth would've yelled it at the top of her lungs if the hour and location had allowed, but Michael and Maggie were still sound asleep.

She hated to wake Michael. He'd worked so hard. When he was a boy, she wished he'd grow up and show some responsibility. Now that he'd grown, she wished he'd stayed a little boy. Father would be proud.

"Michael, I'm leaving," she whispered and kissed Maggie's nose.

"I'm up," Michael covered his eyes from the morning light.

"Michael, it's Saturday. Go back to sleep."

She readied herself for work and slipped out the door, yawning as she stepped off the front porch. Her head was full of rosy lights, pink punch, and him. Her cheeks warmed at the thought. She woke this morning and had to tell herself it wasn't a dream. Last night, she and Ethan had tea with Russ and Bella—in her mother's china. Listening to their banter and lively conversation, she found it believable that they could make a home here. It was easy to smile and laugh. She was a better version of herself, and Ethan was—

She sighed. Great. *To have friends and family again.* She'd hold that picture in heart for a long time.

Standing in the back room of the café, Beth tied on her apron and turned as Anne-Marie pushed through the door, her eyes puffy and red. "You look tired."

"Aren't you?" They smiled in common.

"I thought you quit. Far to busy being married, remember?"

Anne-Marie shooed her. "I hate men. I don't want to talk about them or see one again."

That was impossible with the steady flow of customers to keep them busy. Beth was thankful for the rush. When business slowed, Anne-Marie clicked the order onto the wooden wheel and spun it around to the kitchen. "So, spill the beans."

Beth wrinkled her nose, confused.

Anne-Marie swatted at her. "Well, what happened last night, silly?"

"I thought you didn't want to talk about men ever again."

"Oh, I can't help myself."

Beth busied herself with a pot of coffee, and Anne-Marie pressed her.

"Nothing happened." *Nothing happened last night.*

Anne-Marie snuggled closer. "Did Ethan kiss you? Did he—"

Beth whirled around. "Of course not, don't be ridiculous."

Anne-Marie smirked with arms folded, doubt written on her face.

Shocked, that's what Beth was. "I have never. It's not like that at all. We're just…*friends.* It was one dance. One. Little. Dance." Beth shook her finger at Anne-Marie. "Period."

"Friends, huh? You weren't *acting* like friends last night or *dancing* like friends. You can't fool me, Beth Yates."

Beth pushed through the kitchen door, ignoring the direction the conversation was heading. Had she acted inappropriately? She hoped not. It was just one dance—one dance. Wiping down a table, she shook her head. *Unbelievable.* It was the gesture of a true gentleman—

Clearing dirty dishes away, she paused. Her opinion of Ethan Dawson changed so fast, she couldn't keep up. We are friends. *I think.* Friends and nothing more.

Ethan had his ranch and his priorities. She had her family and her priorities.

"I attend church on Sundays," she recalled Ethan's words. And he invited her, sort of. She had work, but Michael and Maggie should go. They could go with Bella. That decision was made right then and there.

Joy poked at her heart, but fear and bitterness had rooted deep. Ignored lately, they riled, reminding her of the pain within, pain from losing her parents and her home—everything. She yawned. She was tired of bitterness, tired of pain. Giving into joy, she allowed hope to enter.

Gathering a few coins from the now empty table, she dumped them into her apron pocket. The jingle, a reminder of the money she found in her pocket. She concluded that someone must have put it there. There was no other way.

She'd retraced her steps several times already. Trying to recall the handful of customers that had come that day, she ran down the list.

Jane. *She might've.*

Clinton.

Anne-Marie. *No, she came in late that day.*

The grouchy old man who always sat by the window.

The woman who complained about everything. What was her name?

261

Ethan. Russ. *No, Russ wasn't with him.*

Then Beth remembered the rowdy bunch that came in. Ethan took her hand. He seemed worried about those boys. How could she forget about that?

She jerked at the realization. That's when he did it. Ethan Dawson put that money in her pocket.

* * * * *

Hamilton was a lively little town. Eli counted the measly structures. False fronts. Made them seem taller than they were. He'd do the same thing. Already had.

Standing outside Daly's company store, the men corralled, anticipating the fishing trip. Eli tried to pull his sporting vest below his waist, but it was too small. He cursed the catalogue for sending the incorrect size. He'd tucked his guide in an inside pocket. Horses lined the boardwalk, and a young man readied them.

Joining Schwab and Wright, Eli interrupted a conversation already in progress. "I feel lucky today." The men ignored him. Morning sunlight pushed shadows west and lit Main Street from the train station to the river. The boardwalk shook beneath his feet. Daly and several men called to them.

"If there's anything you need, men, my company store will happily supply."

Schwab and Wright fell into step with Daly. Eli and the others trailed behind. Passing by Paisley's General, a little café caught his eye. He paused and adjusted his spectacles in the reflection of the window. He squinted—couldn't believe his eyes. It was her. Elizabeth Yates waiting tables.

"Sands. You're slower than molasses," Schwab called to him.

Eli held up his index finger. "I'm coming." He hurried his pace to join the leader. "Daly, is there a telephone in town?"

* * * * *

Beth smelled corn bread in the hall as she hit the landing. She knocked on Bella's door. Maggie opened the door with a mouth so full, she couldn't speak.

"Something smells so good." Beth wiped several crumbs from Maggie's cheek. "I wish I had your talent, Bella."

"Nothin' to it," Bella said.

"I know how to cook the basics pretty well, I think." Beth untied her bonnet.

"No. You. Don't." Maggie scratched her nose. A smudge of flour remained.

Beth scowled. "All right, I'm not the best cook."

"It'd take a miracle," Maggie replied.

Bella chuckled. "I can teach you how, if you like."

"Would you? Something more than eggs, beans, and potatoes?"

Bella pulled a cookbook from her shelf. "How 'bout we start with spiced corn bread."

"That would be a nice change." *And speaking of change.* "Bella, I want Michael and Maggie to go to church with you on Sunday, if you wouldn't mind."

Bella wiped her hands on a kitchen towel and ushered Maggie over to the table to lick batter from a wooden spoon. When Bella didn't respond, Beth added, "If it's too much trouble, I understand."

Bella patted her cheek. "It's no trouble at all, honey," Bella's voice cracked. "I think it's about time." She handed Beth an apron.

"Thank you. You know I work Sundays, but it will be good for Michael and Maggie," Beth said, putting on the apron.

Bella set a large jar of corn meal on the table, along with a canister of sugar and an onion, and then handed Beth a large knife. "It'll be good for me too, honey." Bella tossed her the onion. "Now, cry your eyes out."

Chapter Twenty-Eight

"Ouch." Ethan jumped up from his knees, bending over in pain. It was the third time this morning the hammer went head to head with his thumb. His heartbeat throbbed to the tip of his thumb. He surveyed the damage. No blood. He stared at the stack of posts piled high on the wagon, counting them by tens. Jax barely made a sound all morning. In fact, she'd been unusually well behaved. Not like her.

He imagined himself dancing with Beth last night. He could almost feel his arms around her, his face inches from hers. He'd dance a thousand dances with *her*. She was so at ease at Bella's—smiling, laughing. For the first time, he saw the real Beth Yates, and he liked what he saw.

Footsteps drew his attention. Buck's wobbling figure appeared in the distance, drawing near. He waved his hand. Ethan nodded and monitored his progress this morning. Sixty plus posts yet to go. The fence line had to be finished this weekend. Only a couple of weekends left before his cattle arrived. *Focus*, he told himself. A photographic timeline flashed before his eyes. Beth in Billings wearing boys' clothes. Beth outside the café, soaking wet. Beth washing dishes. Beth dancing with him. Beth smoothing her hand down her dress. *Whoa, boy!*

Ethan tipped his Stetson and wiped the sweat from his brow, clearing his mind at the same time. Buck crossed the field, carrying a liquid form of revival. *Buck's certainly earn-*

ing his keep. Not that he needed to by any means, but Ethan wasn't about to deny him now. Buck walked along the staked path, limping as usual.

"Something to wet your whistle?" Buck held out a mug of cold water. The water sloshed with the motion, splashing Ethan. Not an unwelcome incident. He needed to wake up. Buck didn't notice.

"Thanks." He sat the cup on top of a post.

Buck scratched his neck. "You're making good time. Don't let me stop you."

Ethan nodded as Buck leaned against a seated post and watched Ethan dig and bury the next two.

"Well, I best be gettin' on. I got britches needin' aired."

Ethan watched Buck meander across the field toward the Bitterroot River. In no hurry at all.

Ethan pulled several posts off the wagon, letting them fall to the ground. He dropped another post in a hole and slammed it down with a sledgehammer, consciously moving his swollen thumb before impact. Exhaustion was getting to him, though exhaustion was the least of his problems. He'd stayed out too long last night, slept in too late. *It's your own fault you're behind schedule.* He leaned against a post, slid to the ground, and slammed his hat against his leg.

He couldn't get Beth out of his head.

He buried his face into his arms, trying to refocus, even made a mental list of things left to do, scratching Beth off the list twice. *You've got to get this ranch off the ground.* He stood and placed his Stetson on the wagon bench. *Get your head on straight.* This ranch had been in the making for a long time, long before Beth Yates came to town. *Nothing was going to get in your way, remember? Nothing.*

Not even a thing with long dark hair and big blue-green eyes. Ethan shoved the blade deep into the ground, making way for another post and nicked his thumb with the hammer again.

* * * * *

Michael had forgotten what it felt like to sleep in. A knock at the door woke him. Maggie ran to the door and found Bella's bright smile and sweet greeting. "Good morning, sunshine." An apologetic look dawned on her face. "And you too, Michael. Did I wake you?" If he nodded, he didn't know it. "How about some breakfast?" Bella leaned against the doorframe.

"Ours is gross." Maggie gagged.

Michael swung his feet to the floor, pain shot from his heels to his thighs. "Give me a minute."

"It's biscuits and gravy." Bella started to leave.

Temptation indeed. "Give me a second then," he called out before the door closed.

Bella was a gracious host as always. Her contagious laugh could lighten any man's load. She didn't disappoint in the breakfast department either. The biscuits didn't last long. He had his fill.

Bella rose to fill the kettle with water when Maggie made an announcement. "I've decided to go to school."

Michael hid his smile.

Bella looked surprised for Maggie's benefit, Michael guessed. Bella gave her a squeeze. "That's right, sugar. Beth told me last night. You still have a couple of weeks, though."

Maggie beamed. "I'm eight now. I have to make my own decisions."

"You do?" Bella was great with Maggie.

"I have to make the bed and lace my boots too." She straightened. "It's hard getting old, isn't it, Bella?"

"Well, I…wouldn't know about that," Bella said, snapping a dish towel at Maggie.

Michael chuckled, and Bella snapped the towel at his leg. "Ouch."

Maggie cocked her head. "Bella, how old…are you?"

"Maggie." Michael frowned.

Bella put her fist on her hip. "How old do you think I am?"

Oh, no. Not good. This will only end badly.

"Ninety…no wait, a hundred?"

Bella squealed and hugged Maggie.

"Am I right?" Maggie glanced at Michael.

"You're close," Bella replied and then grabbed her Bible from the table and checked the time. "Sadie's late."

Michael checked the time. "She'll be here."

Sadie had been late before—consequences of her employment—but she'd never been this late. He thought of Hawk. "Maybe we should check on her."

Bella reached for her shawl. "I'll go."

"No. Let me," Michael said.

Bella's eyes narrowed. "All right," she said. "Maggie, how would you like to help me with the dishes?"

Maggie perked up and then sank. "Do eight-year-olds do dishes?"

"Most certainly, they do." Bella smiled at Michael and hurried him out the door. "She probably slept in, is all."

* * * * *

Michael knocked on Sadie's door, but she didn't answer. His fists tightened. He knocked again. Nothing.

He put his ear to the door. The sound was faint, but he knew her voice and her cry. "Sadie, I know you're in there. Please let me in."

A whimper followed a loud thud. *She's working.* He shouldn't have come.

"She ain't available." The man inside yelled. Michael heard a stifled scream.

He tried to open the door. He threw his shoulder hard against the door a number of times, shouting for her to unlock the door.

"Get yer own gal. This one's taken."

"Sadie!" There was a scream and another thud. Adrenaline soared through his body as he pounded against the door again until he jarred it loose.

One final blow broke the lock free. "Sadie!"

Jacob Skinner had her pinned on the bed, one hand over her mouth, the other clutched the gun on the side table.

"Get off of her." Michael lunged forward, but the man secured his pistol and waved it in the air. A bottle of whiskey fell from the side table, crashing to the floor.

Michael froze. Jacob was drunk. The man was capable of anything.

Jacob slid his hand from her mouth and yanked her robe open.

She turned away. "Michael, please go away."

Jacob grabbed her chin, forcing her to look at him and smothered her with his drunken lips.

"Let her go." Michael forced his words to slow down. "Please, put the gun down and let her go." His voice calm despite the inferno of rage that engulfed him.

Sadie squirmed until Jacob stopped. "Michael, go."

Jacob tore her blouse and pressed his mouth on her bare skin. Impaired though he was with alcohol, Jacob jerked the gun, demanding Michael leave.

"Please, just let her go, Jacob."

Jacob paused for moment, narrowing his eyes. He rose, holding his gun steady. "I know you." Michael stepped back.

"You almost got me hanged." The man's words spit and slurred.

"Just put the gun down." Michael watched Sadie.

She was injured, one eye swollen shut, blood on her cheek. She looked away. Her blouse hung at her side, revealing parts of a woman he had never seen. She struggled to free herself as Jacob stood. His fingers tangled in her hair.

"You made a mighty fine mess of things." Jacob spat across the pool of whiskey on the floor. "If it weren't for you, you little insect, I'd be halfway to California by now." He was babbling, and Michael sought a chance to take him down. "I always get what's coming to me, no matter what," Jacob promised.

When Jacob lowered his gun to reach for an empty bottle of whiskey. Sadie freed herself and rolled across the bed onto the floor. Michael launched like a catapult, striking Jacob's midsection. Jacob fumbled with his gun, and a shot rang out. He pushed Michael against the table, sending chairs flying. Michael knocked the gun loose and lifted himself up to deal Jacob another blow. Jacob leaped for the gun, but Michael slammed his fist into Jacob's lower jaw and landed another blow to his nose, dead center. Jacob crumpled onto the floor, still searching for his gun. Michael climbed over him and grabbed the pistol. He pulled himself to his feet and pointed the gun at the crazed man.

"Get out. Get out of here. Now." Michael shook the gun, but his voice was steady. "And don't ever come back." Fully prepared to pull the trigger, he cocked the hammer with his thumb.

Jacob picked himself off the floor and glared at Sadie curled up in the corner.

"Out." Michael demanded.

Jacob fumbled for his boots, grabbed them, and stepped over a broken table and chair into the hall. Even the slightest move and Michael wouldn't hesitate to shoot. Several girls gathered in the doorway. Jacob pushed past them. Michael heard the basement door slam. "Get the sheriff. Run!" A young girl took to the stairs behind the house. Her footsteps reverberated in the hall.

Michael slid to the floor beside Sadie curled into a ball in the corner. She winced when he reached for her. She gathered her shredded clothes to her neck. "He's gone, Sadie." He pulled her close. "Are you all right?"

She sobbed against his chest and then jerked away. "Michael…you're bleeding."

Chapter Twenty-Nine

Michael woke. A grizzly man hovered over him. He looked beyond the stranger. Everything was so blurry. *Where am I?*

"I'm Dr. Ownings, son."

Michael grimaced and tried to lift his head. *Sadie's room.* Sadie sat across the room, while a woman with red hair examined her. "Is she all right?" he asked, fighting to sit up. "Jacob Skinner. He—"

Dr. Ownings pushed him to the pillow. "She'll be fine. Now, stay still."

Cloth ripped and jolted Michael from his thoughts. He rose to see. Dr. Owning had torn his trousers wide open. He fell against the pillow. *The gunshot.* The gun sat on the bedside table. His body tensed.

"Calm down. You've taken a bullet to the leg."

Michael hadn't felt a thing until now. Shock helped with that. Now, every twitch of every nerve pulsed. Pain jabbed with every movement of the bed as Dr. Ownings attended him. He groaned as the doctor poured something cold on the wound—so cold, it burned.

"Ow." His body writhed in pain.

"You're doing just fine." Dr. Ownings put a cloth over his mouth and nose. The smell was intoxicating. He couldn't get a deep breath. The room began to spin. He wanted to cry out but couldn't make a sound. In all the books he'd read and stories he'd heard, never had he imagined the intensity of the pain associated with a gunshot wound.

I'll never be able to walk again or work again or go to the univers—

The last thought hung unfinished as his body relaxed. Familiar voices surrounded him. A light as bright as the noonday sun shone all around. His senses vibrated like a train traveling a hundred miles per hour on a track stretched out to forever. He was hot, then cold—very cold.

* * * * *

Beth scooted a chair closer to him. Her hands shook. She wanted Michael to know she was here, to hear her voice. He had been shot—her little brother. *Shot.* She squeezed his hand. *Cold.* Rubbing his fingers, Beth glanced at Dr. Owning. "Will he…recover completely?"

"Time will tell." Dr. Ownings swung his medical bag to his side.

Beth glanced at Sadie cowered in the corner. "What about his fever?" She refocused on the doctor.

He patted her shoulder. "Keep him warm. I'll be back in a little while to check on him."

Beth nodded. She stood and pushed a lock of Michael's hair away from his eyes. He shivered as if he was cold, but the sweat on his brow told another story. Sadie took several steps toward her.

Dr. Ownings reached for the door. "Send for me if he changes."

"All right," Beth and Sadie answered the doctor in unison. They looked at each other.

"The sheriff and his men caught up with Jacob Skinner," the doctor said before he left.

Turning to Michael, Beth heard the door shut. Dr. Ownings was gone. She wrung out a cold compress into a porcelain bowl and placed it on his forehead and then adjusted his blanket. She wondered at the need to keep him warm while trying to bring his fever down. Nothing made sense right now. What was he doing here…with her?

Sadie cleared her throat. "I'm sorry. It's all my fault." Sadie winced.

Beth shifted her gaze to the window. Horror filled the vacancy. *Sadie was a prostitute.* And Beth must leave Michael in *her* care. She tensed. Blaming Sadie wouldn't help. She had to accept. "Bella will be back after church. I'll be off work about three." Beth reached for her watch, only to mourn the emptiness in her pocket.

Sadie nodded. "I'll look after him."

Beth fussed with Michael's blanket, duty in her feet but loyalty in her heart. How could she possibly leave him like this? Her stomach tightened, but she couldn't afford to lose her job either, especially now.

"Send someone to find me…if he gets worse." Beth stepped away to allow Sadie in. "You know what to do?"

"Yes. I won't leave his side." Sadie grabbed her arm. "I promise."

Her profession made Beth question that promise, but Bella would be back soon. Taking Maggie to church was a perfect distraction. Maggie may be a tomboy, but the sight of blood threw her into a tizzy. Checking the wall clock, Beth gathered her things and reached for the door.

"Beth, wait,"

Beth looked at Sadie. *Just a girl.* The bruises—a reminder that things could have ended much worse if Michael had not been here.

"I never…I mean…Michael and I never"—Sadie's voice cracked. "He's my best friend."

275

Relieved, Beth nodded. "Yes. Thank you."

* * * * *

Sadie leaned against the door and sighed. Relief flushed her already hot cheeks. Pushing herself from the door, she stared at Michael, still alive but not all right, not at all. He could have been killed. She fingered the blanket and shuddered. *What if he hadn't come?*

She gathered Michael's hand. *Please, don't let him die.* Leaning down, she kissed his knuckles. "I'll do anything, Lord." Sadie buried her face in the covers. "Anything. Just please let him be all right."

Quit your job.

A voice surrounded her like a gentle breeze. She scanned the room. The window wasn't open, not even cracked. A chill ran up her spine. She glanced at the door, but no one was there. She'd heard this voice before, the night Hawk murdered her baby. There it was again, as if someone had whispered in her ear.

Don't be afraid.
I am with you.

It was Him. He was speaking to her. "I want to, but I'm afraid." She closed her eyes and quietly prayed the words she'd heard Bella pray so many times, prayer for forgiveness, for a new life—a new start with Jesus in her heart.

Michael's finger twitched in her grasp, jolting her from her prayer.

"Sadie?" His voice was dry and raspy.

"Michael." She rose and pressed a palm to his forehead.

She reached for a glass of water and put it to his lips. "I...am so sorry...this is my fault." He strained to lift his head then twisted in pain. "Don't move. Rest." She held him still. "I have something to tell you."

"I already know. I've...been...shot. Doc told me." His words slurred.

"No."

He winced. "No?"

"Better than that."

* * * * *

Michael couldn't stare at the ceiling for one more minute. He'd counted the slats too many times already. How long had it been? How long would it be?

"Rest," Doc says.

Rest? *I'd rather die.* He tried to push then pull himself into an upright position. His right hand gave way, and his elbow bumped the table, knocking the gun across the floor. He growled and shoved several books off the bed. *Won't be needing those anymore.*

Sadie emerged from her small closet-like kitchen. "Is it the fever?"

He shook his head. "I'm fine." He regretted his tone immediately.

She picked up the books like a mother would after a child's tantrum. The gun, however, remained on the floor. She hesitated and wouldn't go near it. Did he blame her?

His imagination couldn't help but recreate the horrible scene. Jacob Skinner stood over Sadie, gun aimed. Sadie screamed. A gunshot sounded. Michael jerked. A groan in the pit of his stomach crept into his throat. *I should've killed him when I had the chance. Everything is ruined now.*

Sadie stood at the mirror, examining her eye. *At least, she is safe.* Jacob could have killed her. She glanced at him in the reflection. Their eyes met. He blinked away his tears and turned away. *What if he'd lost her?* His chest tightened, sending shards of pain through his leg.

She came to his side, adjusted the pillows behind him, and pulled back the covers. "I need to change your bandage."

Michael yanked the covers from her. "It's fine."

"Don't be a prude, Michael. I've seen a man's leg before."

You've never seen my leg before. Her determined smile weakened his resolve. He stared at the horror before him. Blood had soaked the bandage. It was worse than he'd thought. "I won't be able to walk, will I?" *Don't lie to me.*

Sadie picked at the bandage. "Dr. Ownings seems hopeful."

"I want the truth."

She pulled the bandage off. The tape tore at the hair on his leg. "Ouch."

"Sorry."

"Will I be able to walk?" He grabbed her hand.

"Doc said, time will tell." She stared at the floor for too long.

My parents are dead, our house repossessed. And now, I can't work. Beth must be worried sick.

Time? His jaw twitched.

After Sadie tended the bandage, she walked into the kitchen. *Sadie wouldn't understand.* She'd gained something, but he'd lost everything.

Sadie returned with a bowl and spoon in her hand. "Here, have some. Bella made this broth." Sadie lifted the spoon to his mouth. "She'll skin me alive if I don't make you drink it."

A rumble in his stomach said he needed much more than broth. He watched her face each time she dipped for another spoonful, her smile more radiant than ever. Even the bruises and swelling couldn't hide it.

The sun brightened the window and crawled across the floor to the bed. Its glare burned his eyes, but he didn't shield them. He deserved it. His laziness forced Father to take that job at the factory. It should've been me in that fire.

"Michael?"

His strained gaze broke. Sadie held the spoon in mid-air. He leaned in and sipped the last of the broth. *God saved me.* Her words pierced his heart deeper than any bullet ever could. "What am I going to do?" he whispered. A confused answer came to him, but he ignored it.

She stood and smoothed his hair. "You're smart, Michael. You'll figure it out." She took his hand, and his heart leaped. "I need to send for Dr. Ownings. Beth will want to know you're awake too. I won't be long. I'll send one of the other girls."

The door shut behind her, and he closed his eyes. He was smart. At least, he thought he was. But right now, his mind couldn't comprehend what his heart begged him to do. It wasn't logical, didn't make sense. How could he trust God to save him when so many bad things had happened?

God, I know I was selfish. I know I should have taken the job so that Father didn't have to. If I had, they wouldn't be dead. You are supposed to be a loving God. You should have saved them in spite of me, made good from all of the wrong. Why? Why didn't You do something? If you didn't cause it, why did You allow it?

Pressure mounted within.

Why?

Michael pounded his fists on the bed, and pain seized him.

Why? Tell me. I need to know. I need answers.

Michael buried his face in his hands, hearing words he'd recently read in the Bible.

> *It's time for you to become a man.*
> *I have some questions for you, son.*
> *Were you there when I formed the earth?*
> *Who marked its dimensions?*
> *Surely, you know.*
> *Were you there when I fixed limits for*
> *the sea, and said 'only this far'?*
> *What is the way to the home of light?*
> *Where does darkness reside?*
> *Surely, your many years will enlighten you.*
> *You ask, why all the suffering and heartache?*
> *Why do bad things happen to good people?*
> *That only happened once, and He willingly gave His life.*

Michael tensed. Bella's challenge filled his head. Read the Bible. There's more information in there than any one man can handle.

All right. I don't know everything. It's beyond me.

Michael forced himself up, ignoring the intense pain. If he was going to do this, he was going to do it sitting up.

* * * * *

Beth tied on her apron around her waist. "Jane, thank you so much for understanding."

Jane wiped her hands on a towel and left bacon sizzling in the cast-iron pan. Two long strides and she embraced Beth. Stiff in the arms of Calamity Jane, Beth stared at a distant wall. Jane's hug was tight. "How is he?" Jane pulled away and cleared her throat.

Beth studied Jane's face. "We don't know for sure. Dr. Ownings seems optimistic."

"Good to hear it." The soft lines of her face hardened. "Anne-Marie's late. Clinton, git in here!"

Stunned, Beth pushed into the dining room. Michael was never far from her mind. She served her customers with great haste. *I should be with him.* She replayed Bella's words over and over. *Michael won't be able to work now.* She'd paid Dr. Ownings this morning. With Bella's help, she could manage, but they'd soon be right back where they started. Broke, with not enough money to pay the rent.

"Good morning, Beth." Russ always had a smile on his face.

"Good morning." She checked the doorway. Ethan wasn't with him.

Russ sat at the counter. "I'll have my usual."

Tapping the pencil on her pad, she hesitated. *Tell him about Michael.* "Did you hear about my brother?" Maybe, he'd seen Bella already.

Russ looked up, confused. "What happened?"

"Jacob Skinner shot him yesterday." She bit her lip, telling herself not to cry in the café.

"What?" Russ grabbed her hand.

"Sadie was hurt too but only cuts and bruises," Beth added.

"And Michael?"

"He had a rough night, but Dr. Ownings hopes he'll pull through." *Ask him.* "Russ, I don't normally bother people with private matters, but…would you mind praying for Michael?"

Russ leaped from his chair and threw his arms around her. "I will. All God's people will pray today."

"Thank you," she said, aware that people were staring.

"Ethan had some things to do before church this morning," he said as she turned to put in his order.

She nodded. Ethan's whereabouts were none of her business, yet she *liked* knowing. She returned with Russ' breakfast and couldn't help but glance at the empty chair next to him.

"Said he had some loose ends to tie up," Russ said with food in his mouth.

She lifted a pot of coffee. "More coffee?" Russ nodded after taking a big bite. "Tell Bella how much I appreciate her taking Maggie to church this morning. Maggie needed the distraction."

Russ threw manners aside. "Bella is taking Maggie to church...today?"

"Yes," she answered, a little surprised at his question.

Russ slammed his fork down and searched his pockets, laying enough coins on the counter to more than cover his bill. He grabbed his hat and disappeared.

Beth stared at his plate. Hardly ate a thing. She leaned toward the window. His horse was still tied up out front. Russ was running down the middle of Main Street. *Those two must have some story.*

* * * * *

"Mr. Sands, a telegram for you, sir." A young butler held out a piece of paper as Daly and the men prepared to depart on another fishing excursion. Another day in the saddle surrounded by mosquitoes.

Eli nodded and took the note. "It came about a half an hour ago."

His eyes scanned his colleagues busying themselves with gear and tackle. "Thank you." Turning away from the party, Eli unfolded the paper and smiled. He reread the words, crumpled it into a ball, and stuffed it in a nearby barrel. R. C.

Clemens won't be a problem anymore, and Donovan would take care of Miss Yates once he arrived.

Eli wasn't a sportsman—a skilled fisherman—not by any means. But today, he might as well have caught the biggest fish in Montana.

* * * * *

Ethan joined Russ in the church pew. The music had already begun. *I'm late.* And he was never late for church.

"'Bout time." Russ nudged him.

"I need a cup of coffee." Ethan's smile faded as Russ leaned back. Could he believe his eyes? The stubborn Miss Bella Johnnes had finally come to church. Nearly ten years of Sundays, and here she was. "What happened?" Ethan whispered to Russ, giving Bella a nod.

Bella shooed him with her skirt, a perfect response from Bella. Russ beamed, and rightly so. The little girl next to Bella smiled at him then wiggled a loose tooth. Beth's little sister, Maggie, he presumed.

Russ cleared his throat as the organist started to play "Blessed Assurance." "Beth's brother was shot yesterday. Jacob Skinner."

Ethan jerked. "What?" He glanced at the door then back to Russ. He needed to go to Beth. Run, in fact, but would she want him there? Would she want to be left alone? Unanswered questions kept him in his seat.

"He took a bullet to the leg. Doc Ownings saw to him yesterday, and again this mornin'." Russ glanced at Bella.

"Shhh." Bella shook her finger at them.

Ethan waved apologetically. With head bowed and his Stetson between his knees, all he could think about was Beth, how worried she must be, how scared she must be. Reverend

Burkhart spoke, but Ethan didn't follow. "Did you see Beth this morning?" Ethan asked Russ.

Russ kept his focus on the reverend and nodded.

"Was she all right? What did she say? Did she seem—"

Bella glared like his mother did when he and Peter were boys. You'd think she'd been raised in church. Ethan tapped his foot on the floor.

Reverend Burkhart called for the benediction. "And for the Yates family, Lord. Be with them in their hour of need and draw them closer to you," he added at the closing. The church service ended, and Ethan shot up from the pew.

People gathered around, much like they did at the dance. Only this time, they surrounded Bella and Maggie. Ethan found solace beneath one of the eight stained glass windows, right where the light brightened the multicolored glass. If it had been any other Sunday, he'd have gone to her already, but this was a memorable day for Bella.

He frowned. It was for Beth as well.

Russ introduced Bella to every outstretched hand. Reverend Burkhart and his wife lit up when Russ approached with Bella on his arm.

Standing near the door, Ethan fingered his hat. He couldn't think straight. Should he go to her? *No. Yes.* Would she even want him? *No. Maybe.*

"We're going to look in on Michael and Sadie," Russ said as Bella and Maggie joined them.

"I'll come with you." Ethan rushed out the door, mounting Jax and racing down the street before Russ even had time to respond.

Chapter Thirty

Footsteps echoed in the hall beyond Sadie's door. Michael searched for Skinner's pistol. It still remained on the floor. He motioned to Sadie and mouthed, "Get the gun." *Could be one of Hawk's men...or Hawk himself.*

Sadie shook her head. "No," she whispered, "I can't touch it." Sliding the kettle from the stove, Sadie tiptoed toward the bed.

A knock at the door made them jump. "The gun, Sadie." Pain soared.

"Sadie, honey, it's me."

"Bella," they said in unison.

He relaxed as Sadie ran to the door. "Thank goodness, it's you. Michael is awake."

Bella gasped. "I can see with my own two blues that he is...just fine." She engulfed Michael's hand in hers. "Sugar, you've got your color back." Behind her, the room seemed to fill with people. Russ and his friend Ethan, he recalled.

He felt the cut above his eye. The blood had dried but still stung. Russ stood beside the bed. "Son, you'll be back to your old self in no time."

I hope not. "The morphine will help, hopefully. Right now, everything hurts. Doc says it will be a while, but it will heal."

Maggie rushed to his side and then froze, seeing the pistol on the floor. "Is it real?"

Russ picked up the gun and stuck it through his belt. "Skinner won't be needin' this anymore."

Michael adjusted in the bed. "Is it true? Jacob Skinner is dead?"

"Dead as dead can be, honey." Bella patted his cheek.

Michael didn't know whether to congratulate himself or feel sorry for the man. Eternity had a whole new meaning.

Ethan removed his hat to greet him. "Ethan Dawson."

"I know who you are," Michael said, trying to sit up straight.

"We've met before?"

Michael tensed. "Not officially, but I've heard about you."

Bella grabbed Maggie before she jumped onto the bed.

Ethan grinned. "From Beth?"

"My sister?" Michael scrunched his face and then winced. "No. Chaz Paisley told me things, but don't worry. I don't believe everything I hear."

Ethan chuckled. "According to Chaz Paisley, I've been married six times and have eighteen children."

"You forgot the most outlandish one," Russ said. "You're awfully rich too."

"Well, I guess I'd have to be with eighteen children," Ethan said. Laughter filled the room.

Bella cleared her throat. "Sadie says that you both have some news."

Michael swallowed hard. *Makes it sound like we're getting married or something.* He ignored the thought. He and Sadie exchanged glances, and both started to speak. Sadie quieted, and Michael continued. "We accepted Christ today."

Bella embraced Sadie. Ethan congratulated him. Russ put his hand on his shoulder. "Welcome to the family, son."

"I just knew you would," Maggie squealed, "what with you having brains and all."

Michael searched beyond the small crowd around him. Sadie and Bella stood in the corner. Sadie was crying. He wanted to go to her, tell her everything would be all right, but every nerve reminded him of the impossibility.

"Sadie wants to quit the business," Bella announced with her arms around Sadie. "Right now."

The room fell quiet. Sadie's eyes locked on Michael. With an encouraging smile, he mouthed, "You can do it."

Russ grabbed his hat. "I'll get Sheriff Irvine and meet you at Hawk's place. Lord help us."

Ethan patted Maggie's head. "We'll hold down the fort here, won't we?"

Michael smiled. *I should go with her.*

Maggie tugged Ethan's arm. "Are you my sister's *favoritest* friend?"

The odd question stole Michael's attention as Bella, Russ, and Sadie left. Michael felt as though a piece of him left too. Ethan leaned in and whispered to Maggie, "I hope so." He sat Maggie onto his knee. "I understand you have a loose tooth."

"Two." She wiggled them. "Thsee?"

"Looks ripe for a good door pull—" Ethan winked at Michael "—if you ask me."

"That sounds dangerous. Does a door pull involve any...blood?" Maggie covered her mouth. "I'm not so good with blood. Tell him, Michael," her voice muffled.

Michael recoiled in pain. He grabbed his upper leg. Ethan rose, lifting Maggie from his lap. "Took a bullet in the leg, I hear. Let's have a look." Ethan removed the blanket to reveal a blood-soaked bandage.

Maggie turned white. "I think I'm going to be sick."

Ethan gave her a peppermint from his pocket. "Plug your nose." Maggie obeyed and smiled at the result. Ethan examined the bandage. "You'll be back on your feet before you know it. A fresh dressing will help."

"You think so?" Michael forced out. *It hurts so bad.*

"I do." Ethan removed the blood-soaked cloth. "Now, young man, we just have to convince your sister of that." He nudged Maggie and began to redress Michael's wound.

Michael studied Ethan. "You know my sister better than I thought."

* * * * *

Sheriff Irvine pounded on Hawk's door and continued until they heard footsteps. *I don't think I can do this.* Sadie stepped back, and Bella squeezed her, building her confidence. Nothing could have prepared her for this moment. "It will be all right, honey. God is with us," Bella said. Russ added an "amen."

"It helps to have the law on your side too." Irvine pounded on the door. "Hawk!"

The last three years flooded Sadie's memory. Hawk had beaten her, raped her, and nearly starved her to death on more than one occasion.

A slew of obscenities exploded inside the house. She winced. How would it be that Hawk would let her go? He didn't take bad news well. She knew that firsthand. Rubbing her stomach, she thought of her baby, the tiny life that once grew inside her.

Russ peeked around the end of the porch and shrugged. Bella tightened her embrace. "Be strong."

Irvine knocked again. "Hawk, I'm gonna count to three."

Some memories would never fade, Sadie told herself. She was twelve years old when Hawk came for her. She and her father were passing through town on their way to what Father called "a better life." He'd been gambling and drinking again, despite his promises—empty promises. Empty, like the whiskey bottles she'd found beneath his bedroll in the wagon.

"Hold yer horses," Hawk yelled from behind the still closed door.

Tensing, she watched the doorknob for movement.

"We ain't got all day," Irvine replied.

"You're gonna be a fine lady by the time I get through with you, a real fine lady," Hawk had promised as she watched her father roll their rickety old wagon out of town, never to be seen or heard from again. Hawk's real goal became abundantly clear in a short amount of time. Sadie tried to shake the thought.

Hawk cracked the door thin. "Yeah, what do you want?" His voice was hoarse, and Sadie knew from the bags under his eyes that they'd awakened him.

"Hawk, your girl wants out," Irvine stated. "Don't make this harder than it is."

Hawk slammed the door, spewing out a mouthful of profanities. Sheriff Irvine ignored him and pushed the door open. "You know the law, Hawk." Sadie would never forget the crazed look on Hawk's face as Irvine and Russ demanded her release. The truth of his name had never been more real than it was at that moment. *Help me, Lord.* His eyes darkened and glared at her with eternal contempt. Hawk preyed on her fear.

"She's nothin' but a worthless piece of—"

Sadie covered her ears, and Bella hugged her close. Russ threw the first punch. Hawk staggered to his feet, wiping blood from his lip. "Hundred dollars."

Russ tightened his fist. Irvine held him back. "Russ, let it go." Irvine poked at Hawk's chest. "A hundred, and you let her go."

"No, two hundred and you can have her." Hawk spit at her and cursed.

Russ searched his wallet and threw money at him. Sadie ran to Russ. "No, don't."

Hawk gathered the bills from the porch and slammed the door. His rage continued inside.

Russ embraced her. "You're worth far more."

Overwhelmed, she hugged him. "Thank you. Thank you. Thank—"

Bella joined them. "Sadie, you are free."

"Free?" A word so foreign to her.

* * * * *

Beth heard a ruckus and took to the stairs, two at a time, like Michael always did but would never do again. Sadie's tiny room sat at the end of the hall. Passing several doors, all seemed quiet. The noise hadn't come from Sadie's place after all. Then she heard a man's voice.

Without knocking, Beth swung the door open. Confusion greeted her, nearly shook her hand. Ethan stood. "Beth."

"Ethan." Her gaze shifted, resting on Michael. "Michael!" She ran to him, throwing down a basket of chicken.

"I'm here too," Maggie said, her voice smug.

"Yes, I know." Beth pulled back the blanket to inspect Michael's leg. She smoothed his hair and felt his forehead. She sighed, relief flooding her mind. She kissed his cheek and tucked the covers around him like a child.

"Well, Doctor Yates, what is the diagnosis?" Ethan joined her.

"He'll be fine." Beth stiffened. "Nothing some corn bread and fried chicken can't cure."

Ethan and Michael laughed. Though a little embarrassed at her humor, considering the situation, she smiled. "Who changed your bandage?" Beth expected the answer to be a man with a beard carrying a leather bag.

"I did," Ethan's voice sounded shaky.

Beth cocked her head. "You did?" She pointed her finger. "You shouldn't have."

Ethan shortened the gap and grabbed her finger and then her hand. "I wanted to."

"What I mean is, you have your ranch. You don't have time for this." Beth looked into his eyes and regretted the decision immediately. Any resolve she had fell flat on the floor.

He tucked her loose curl behind her ear. "I came because I wanted to."

She tried to swallow the lump in her throat.

Michael cleared his throat. "Did someone say something about fried chicken?"

"Yeah," Maggie said, "and corn bread."

Beth pulled her hand from his grip to open the basket of chicken Jane had sent. "Jane made us a feast, a miscount of chicken on her part," Beth said. *So like Jane.* Beth heard herself speak, but barely, the sound of her heart pounding nearly drowned it out completely.

Ethan nodded and turned to hear Maggie's rendition of Michael's heroic tale while she set out the food.

"Ethan likes you, Beth," Maggie said, standing on a chair and leaning over the table to view the feast. "I can see it in his eyes."

"Shhh." Beth shook her head. "That, my dear, is none of your business." Beth glanced at Ethan, who appeared unmoved, thankfully. "Where is everyone?"

Michael coughed. "I have something to tell you, Beth."

Beth wiped her hands on a towel. "I doubt anything you have to tell me could shock me now."

Ethan stepped away from Michael's bed. "Maggie, let's you and me go rock picking." Ethan helped her jump off the chair.

"Rock picking? How *tremendousness*! Beth, can I?"

Beth nodded, understanding now that a secret was about to be revealed. Beth tipped her chin when the door shut. Maggie's delight grew faint.

"I know about Sadie." She wanted to ease his mind. He'd suffered enough.

"Good," he swallowed, "but that's not all."

Biting her lip, she braced herself. *Sadie's pregnant.*

"Something's happened."

Yes. I know. Just say it.

"I asked…Jesus into my heart today." He lifted his cut brow and winced.

Surprised, yet relieved, Beth considered what she'd previously thought. "Today? I thought it happened weeks ago."

"I think God started working on me a while ago, but it wasn't until today that I realized how much I needed Him."

Beth stood beside him, fingering the covers. "Why didn't you tell me sooner. I'm not upset. How could I be?" God *had* changed him, had been changing him for a while. She stared at the floor, heart pounding. Was God trying to reach her too?

The door opened, and Russ, Bella, and Sadie walked in, gathering at Michael's side. Thundering steps sounded behind them, and Ethan appeared in the hall, carrying Maggie over one shoulder like a bag of flour. Maggie squealed. "I found a skipping stone and a…what's this one called?"

Ethan ducked to save Maggie's head from hitting the doorframe and caught Beth staring. "It's an agate."

Beth swiveled on her heels and pressed both hands to her chest. She'd been so wrong about Ethan.

His footsteps grew close. "Let's have some of Calamity Jane's fried chicken and corn bread." Ethan's warm breath tickled her neck.

Turning around, she stuttered. "Yes. Let's."

Chapter Thirty-One

Beth rose from the small table and cleared Maggie's plate. Sadie joined her near the kitchen. "I was wondering…if it might be possible…" Sadie cleared her throat. "I want to help Michael, only until he's back on his feet. If that is all right with you? I can read to him. And Doc says if he exercises his leg—"

"I can manage. Thank you. Your help is not needed." Caught off guard, Beth stung with her words. She hadn't given Michael's care a moment's thought. Sadie is, or was until today, a prostitute. It wouldn't be proper. *Father and Mother would never approve.*

"He saved my life…twice. You have to let me help."

Beth faced her. "I need you to understand something, Sadie. You are…or were a prost—"

Ethan grabbed her hand. "Let's go see about a wagon, shall we?" His stare didn't give her the opportunity to decline.

* * * * *

Ethan waited for Beth to grab her purse but didn't let go of her hand, and she was not going to let go, not if he had anything to say about it. "I wanna come too." Maggie swept a pile of rocks from the table into her pocket.

"No, honey. You stay here with me." Bella waved them on.

"Bella, do you know about rocks?"

The door shut, and Ethan tightened his hold. Beth watched him as they descended the stairs but said nothing. His jaw twitched. They reached the middle landing, and he stopped and turned to her. "Sadie just quit, Beth. Do you know what that means? Do you know how hard that was for her to do? Have some compassion."

Beth stiffened and tried to free her hand. "I am aware of that, but—"

I'm not letting go. "But what?" *Her eyes are definitely green.* He dipped his chin. Several seconds passed.

"It isn't right. You wouldn't understand." She leaned against the wall.

He stepped closer. "You didn't let Sadie finish."

"I'm sorry about that, but it isn't proper, a boy and a girl together alone without a chaperone."

Ethan raised a brow. "Sadie will live with Bella. She was trying to help." He shortened the gap, mingling his fingers with hers. "Do you really believe that Bella, Russ, or I—for that matter—would leave Michael's recovery in the hands of a fifteen-year-old girl?" *No, her eyes are most certainly blue.*

"Ethan, this isn't your burden to bear. I am responsible for this family. It's my duty—"

He put his other hand on the wall behind her. "Beth Yates, you need help. You can't do it all by yourself."

She straightened and then shrugged.

He tipped up her chin, and a tear fell down her cheek. "We want to help you. You don't have to be alone in this." *What would it be like to kiss her? He'd imagined it too many times.*

"You don't understand. I—"

His lips silenced her. She pushed against his chest, breaking the kiss. "Ethan, please." She even smiled.

The gesture was all he needed. He kissed her again. This wasn't part of his original plan—the ranch, his horses—but he didn't care. This time, she didn't push him away but rose to kiss him back. He pressed in and pulled her closer. The fists that once pushed now clutched his shirt. Breaking the kiss gently and softly, he trailed his lips across her cheek, smoothing her dark curls away to make way for a single kiss on her forehead. She sighed as her heels touched the floor. He held her close.

She nodded against his chest. "I've wanted you to do that for a very long time."

He studied her. "Me too." Cradling her face, he kissed her again. "You and I might need a chaperone pretty soon."

She slapped his chest.

* * * * *

Ethan pushed through the big door to the livery, and Beth slid beside him. His very presence warmed her. She smiled at the new feelings inside her. Right now, she believed Michael would heal, Maggie wouldn't starve, and she could really live again.

"What?" Ethan said, toying with her fingers.

"Nothing," she said, unable to stop smiling.

"Afternoon, Ethan," a man called from the back room. "Be right with ya."

Ethan smiled. She smiled too. They watched each other, no doubt, still trying to make sense of what happened in the stairwell. *Ethan Dawson had kissed her.*

"What can I *do* you for?" The blacksmith stopped. "Oh, pardon me, miss. I thought you was alone, Ethan."

"No." Ethan looked at Beth and smiled. "Not anymore."

Beth cleared her throat in scold.

"I need the largest wagon you can spare, Sam." Ethan lifted her fingers to his lips and kissed her knuckles.

Beth yanked her hand to their side and tried to hide her embarrassment, but her smile wouldn't go away.

"Sure thing, Ethan. I got me a mighty fine flat, if ya wanna take a gander." Sam was a large man with big hands and feet to match.

Ethan turned to Beth. "Stay here, I'll be right back."

"All right."

"Stay here," he repeated and narrowed his eyes.

"All right, I will," she smirked.

When they were gone, Beth hugged her hands to her chest. Excitement rose from her feet and exploded in her heart. She was ten years old at a birthday party. She was a girl at her first dance. She was eating ice cream and drinking lemonade. Every dream she'd ever dreamed came true in that moment.

Voices grew closer. She calmed herself. Ethan and Sam were discussing the weight of the load when reality hit. She hadn't considered the cost of a wagon. She barely had enough for the rent after paying the doctor. She shook her satchel. The small jingle told her the balance. What was she thinking? She couldn't afford a wagon, but how else could she get Michael home?

Ethan appeared in the parlor, and Beth ran to him. "Ethan, I can't afford—"

Sam walked in, cutting her short. "Here's the receipt, Ethan. Paid in full." Sam offered him a piece of paper. "I'll bring her around front for ya."

"Ethan, I can't afford this," Beth said, pointing to the paper he'd tucked into his pocket. "I should've said something before."

"I took care of it." He took her hand, but she refused to move.

She promised herself she'd thank him properly. "This might be hard for you to believe, but I've wanted to thank you for a little while now."

He lowered his head. "I wanted to help."

"No, please. Let me finish." She took a quick breath and closed her eyes. "It was you." She opened her eyes and tucked a curl behind her ear. "It was you in Billings, the day I fell off the boardwalk. You had mud on your face."

He smiled. "Yes."

Her chest tightened. "And it was you—" she sighed, "—who put the money in my apron pocket."

"Yes."

Beth reached up and caressed his cheek. "I don't know how to thank you."

He cradled her face, pushed back several curls, and kissed her. "You just did."

* * * * *

"Easy now. I'm not as brave as I was yesterday," Michael instructed as Russ and Ethan carried him down the stairs. Every movement threatened to bring back the fever.

Ethan heaved. "Bravery is overrated."

"Beth, I don't know how you're going to put up with him," Russ said to her. "They say that heroes are the worst."

"Hey—"

Michael started to complain but stopped midsentence. No need to prove Russ correct. "I'll be the perfect invalid."

Sadie and Bella carried several boxes down and placed them at the back of the wagon. The wagon easily fit him and all of Sadie's belongings. Beth fussed with his blanket as they hoisted Michael onto the flat. Sadie climbed in by his side. Beth and Sadie hadn't spoken since she and Ethan returned. He'd speak with Beth once they were alone.

"Bella, how 'bout you and me walk on over to the boardinghouse," Russ proposed, and she agreed.

"See you there." Ethan lifted Beth into the wagon next to Michael. Ethan winked at him. Something was going on, but he couldn't put his finger on it. Maybe it was the morphine. Michael raised an eyebrow, seeing Ethan and Beth smiling at each other. No, something is going on.

"Up you go, Maggie." Ethan lifted her into the seat and then pulled himself into the wagon.

Maggie scooted next to him. "Are you going to marry Beth?"

"Maggie!" Beth exhaled.

Maggie grinned. "Because if you are, you should probably know that—"

"Maggie, please." Beth scowled.

Tugging at Ethan's shoulder, Maggie whispered in Ethan's ear, "Her biscuits are hard as agates, and her gravy tastes like...you know what." Ethan chuckled and snapped the reins. "Oh, and Beth cries when she sews."

Beth tapped Michael's shoulder. "She gets this from you, you know."

Michael managed a weak smile, watching the exchange. He hadn't seen Beth this relaxed for months, maybe years. Tilting his head, he saw Ethan smile at Beth, and Beth smiled back. He wouldn't have missed that for the world.

Beth patted Sadie's hand. "Sadie, I could use your help taking care of Michael. He can be quite a handful."

"Yes, I know." Sadie squeezed Beth's hand.

Michael shook his head and closed his eyes. "Women."

300

Chapter Thirty-Two

Beth stepped into the café kitchen and lifted her apron from the hook. The smell of bacon and eggs filled the air. And this morning, the aroma seemed sweeter. Clinton stood at the sink. Jane spun from the stove. "Well, well, well. What do we have here? Miss Fancy Pants herself."

Beth fiddled with her buttons and tucked a curl into place. "I don't know what you mean." *I hope I didn't overdo it.*

Clinton whistled and wiped his brow. Beth stepped back. He'd been drinking again. "Quite a looker." Clinton hung a pot on the wall rack, his breath heavy with whisky.

Smoothing her skirt and hair, she stared at them. She had worn her best blouse and skirt and let her hair down again. Much too fancy for Calamity Jane's café, she realized now. She'd even colored her cheeks.

"What's got into you? This ain't a dancin' parlor, girl." Jane threw several potatoes into a boiling pot.

Shaking her head at Jane's reaction, Beth knew she'd overdone it. She hoped to see Ethan today, but it wasn't Sunday, and he rarely came to the café, except on Sundays. She tied her apron, sought her reflection in the back window, and rubbed the color from her cheeks. She shrugged. Her skin was redder than before.

"Russ. Ethan. Didn't expect you this mornin', it not bein' Sunday and all," Clinton called out, obviously for her benefit. She took a deep breath and smiled. *He came.* Clinton winked and snapped a towel at her as she peeked into the dining room.

Her heart beat out of rhythm. Ethan sat near the front window. His presence thrilled her and scared her all at the same time. How would he be? Did he regret kissing her? Biting her lip, she hoped not. Ethan laughed, and she took it as a good sign. Besides, he came, didn't he? She stepped into the dining room. "Good morning, Russ." She poured his coffee and added, "Ethan."

"Good morning," they replied.

Russ dumped sugar in his cup, but Ethan's gaze lingered. Beth tucked a wayward curl behind her ear. His eyes didn't look confused or sorry. Ethan swallowed, and his jaw twitched. "How's Michael?"

"Dr. Ownings seems pleased." Leaning down on the table, she added, "Says it's a miracle." Ethan took her hand. Their fingers locked. She glanced at his hand, so rough yet so perfect.

"It is a miracle." Ethan squeezed her hand.

Russ cleared his throat. "We did come for breakfast, right?"

Ethan played with her fingers. "Among other things."

Russ whistled and looked the other way. "No need for hot sauce today."

* * * * *

Maggie halted, seeing the schoolhouse beyond a row of pine trees and rocks. She prayed to be sick or something else awful, but God hadn't answered her prayer yet. "Why can't I stay with you, Bella?" *I don't want to be eight anymore.* "You didn't go to school. I'm so *apprehensous.* What if my tooth falls out?"

"Honey, school is important. There will be a lot of children your age." Bella straightened the ruffle on Maggie's dress and retied the bow of her left braid.

Maggie scratched at the ruffle around her neck. "It itches. I'm about to have a stomachache. Please, can't I stay with you?"

"You'll be fine." Bella squeezed her hand and pushed her in the direction of a group of girls. "Mind your manners and your dress." She waved and smiled.

Maggie stared at the group. Most of them taller and meaner, she decided. *Girls don't like me very much.* Maggie approached the group, but they didn't let her in, just tightened the circle and giggled. Maggie glanced over her shoulder. Bella's bright yellow dress swayed, saying goodbye for an eternity.

"I'm Maggie." She tried to squeeze inside the circle. "I'm new here."

But the leader snubbed her, and the rest of the girls copied.

Maggie searched the schoolyard for the boys. Surely, she'd fair better with the boys. "Don't mind Jo. She just Jo."

Maggie turned. A girl with fire-orange hair folded her arms and stuck her tongue out at Jo.

"Jo?" Maggie said.

"Josephine Marks. But we call her Jo, and she's the boss of everyone. If she don't like you, no one does. But I like you just fine. I'm Clara Beets, but Jo calls me 'Pig Face'. Call me whatever you want, I don't mind. Besides, all Jo talks about is knitting, and I rather die than knit. I'm for adventure. How about you?"

Maggie grinned. Clara could talk a hind leg off a mule, as Chaz put it, but Maggie didn't care at all. "I'm Maggie Yates. Your hair is awful orange. I like rocks."

Clara shrugged. "Rocks can be adventurous, I guess."

The school bell rang, and Clara grabbed her hand. "Come on, you can sit by me."

The teacher wrote "Miss Buttery" on the chalkboard in fancy letters, all connected like. With a name like that, she must be nice. She had pretty hair and wore plain clothes, and her voice wasn't at all squeaky, not like she'd imagined.

Maggie decided to like Miss Buttery, even though she wore a skirt. And she had a friend, like Bella said.

"Lucy Aimes?" Miss Buttery called out.

"Here."

"Clara Beets?

"Here."

Maggie tried to pay attention as each name was called, but two boys sitting behind her began to unravel the ribbon on her braid. She yanked it away and sat up straighter. Beth's words ringing in her ears. *Mind your manners and stay away from the boys.*

The boys whispered and snickered, tugging each braid one at a time. After Josephine Marks and the mean girl gang, she'd already had enough.

She focused on Miss Buttery, but at this rate, she'd be the last name called.

"Fritz Lloyd."

"Here."

"Jonas McCoy."

"Here," the boy behind her said.

Clara nudged her and slipped a peppermint into her hand under the desk.

Jonas leaned between them. "Aren't you the girl who lives at that whorehouse?"

Maggie turned and scowled. *Jonas McCoy.* She didn't know what a whorehouse was *exactly*, but it sounded simply awful. Jonas McCoy was older—taller anyway. His white hair stuck out in every direction, and he had big ears too. Clara said his father ran the town or something like that.

Rolling a strip of paper into a tight ball, she stuck it in her mouth. She watched the teacher. Jonas McCoy would have a spitball in his face first chance she got.

Maggie heard her name and spit out the wad into her hand. "Here." *You're lucky, Jonas McCoy.*

Lunchtime didn't come soon enough. Her stomach growled so loud, the entire classroom heard it. The children poured out the door and scattered. Maggie opened her desk and gathered her lunch, simple as it was. Jo led the girls to a bench situated under a large tree. Jo sat on the bench, the other girls on the ground. She and Clara climbed on a rock to eat. She'd been called a "ninny," a "horsetail," and something else she couldn't repeat, or she'd have to say sorry.

Jonas jumped up from behind them. "My mama says you're an orphan and that you live with a prostitute."

"Leave her alone," Clara said.

Maggie stood. "You are the stupidest boy I ever saw, Jonas McCoy." She grabbed a handful of dirt and threw it at him. "Stop 'arassing me."

Jonas retaliated, throwing dirt and rocks square at her face.

"Jonas McCoy, I'm gonna pay you for that." Maggie dropped her lunch.

Clara grabbed her arm. "He's just a McCoy."

Jonas blew his tongue, and she took after him like a raging bull. He zigzagged while the other boys cheered. Maggie clamped the back of his overalls and pulled. He tumbled to the ground. She landed on top, balled her fist, and smacked him in the eye. Maggie felt her body lift into the air and saw the shock on Jonas' face. Without a doubt, Miss Buttery had apprehended her.

"What is going on here?" Miss Buttery held Maggie by the back of her neck and lifted Jonas to his feet.

Maggie pointed. "He started it."

Jonas shrugged. "I did."

Miss Buttery marched them into the schoolhouse to the chalkboard, the entire class spying beyond the front door. Miss Buttery vigorously wrote words across the chalkboard and then turned to them. "You will write this twenty-five times." She tapped the chalkboard with a piece of chalk. With a flick of her wrist, she held out two pieces of chalk.

Maggie stood, staring at Jonas then at the board. *I'm going to be in so much trouble when Beth hears about this.* She glanced at Jonas, who had already begun, stiffened her chin, and started writing. The race was on. Normally, she preferred boys, but today, she decided she'd never talk to Jonas McCoy again.

Jonas leaned close. "I just wanted to—"

"Shhh." Maggie wrote the last word and slammed the chalk down loud enough for Jonas to notice. He wrote his last word and put his chalk down quietly. Smug, she returned to her seat only to find it filled. Clara shrugged.

"You two will share a seat for the remainder of the day." Miss Buttery narrowed her eyes. "I will not tolerate this kind of behavior in my class. And on the first day of school, no less."

Maggie saw the teacher's lips move but hoped she'd imagined the words wrong. Sit next to Jonas? Miss Buttery motioned, and Maggie and Jonas sank into the bench. Maggie scooted to the opposite end of the seat. As class ended, she glanced at Jonas and smiled. His eye had turned black and blue.

The bell rang and children began to exit. "Ah. Beth Yates, I presume," Miss Buttery said, and Maggie slowly turned, fearing the truth. Beth stood at the doorway.

This is gonna end badly. Maggie stood like a post, listening to Miss Buttery tell of her behavior. She rolled her eyes. *Jonas started it.*

"I don't allow this kind of behavior in my classroom, Miss Yates."

Beth scowled. "Miss Buttery, I can assure you, this kind of thing won't ever happen again. Isn't that right, Maggie?"

Maggie nodded. *Beth looks really mad.*

Miss Buttery smiled. "Good. Maggie is a bright girl."

You're a teacher. You have to say that.

Beth grabbed Maggie's hand and lectured her on good behavior all the way home. "What would Mother and Father say, Maggie? What a way to behave on your first day of school."

"He called me an orphan, said I lived with a protestant." Maggie hung her head.

"You don't even know what that is."

Maggie pulled back. "Yes, I do. It's a lady with lots of husbands."

"Sticks and stones, Maggie. People will say what they want to say. You can't go punching noses every time."

"Michael does."

Beth growled as they climbed the stairs. "I don't know what to do with you." Beth opened the door. Bella sat at Michael's bedside.

Beth dropped her purse on the table. "Maggie gave the mayor's son a black eye today."

Bella gasped. "Oh, honey."

"A black eye?" Michael said.

Maggie nodded, and her lips began to quiver. She ran to Bella. "He said the most *awfulest* things. The girls are mean. Well, except one." *Please, don't make me go back to school.*

"Come here, Maggie." Beth took Maggie's hand. "I will say this once and hope I never have to say it again. You'll go without supper if you ever do something like this again."

Maggie nodded. *Go without supper?* She could handle that.

"And tomorrow, you will apologize to Miss Buttery and to the mayor's son."

"What?" Maggie hoped after Beth's lecture, she'd never see Jonas McCoy or Josephine Marks again. Going back to school was a thousand times worse than starving to death. She wrinkled her nose and gritted her teeth when Beth showed no sign of changing her mind. "And what are my other options?"

Chapter Thirty-Three

Paisley's General Store seemed bigger than Sadie remembered. Since she'd left Hawk, everything seemed different—the sun brighter, the mountains taller.

"Beans and Peas. On sale today," Chaz called out, cutting herself off as the door closed. "Why, Sadie, haven't seen you in here in ages. People been talkin' about you. Is it true?" Chaz was inches from her face. "I heard it from Mrs. Tilts, who heard it from Ms. Alice. I simply must know the truth of it."

"Well," Sadie stepped back and straightened, "depends on what you've heard." Bella said this was a good idea. *I'm not so sure.* Only a couple of weeks had gone by since she'd quit.

"Hawk kicked you out. That's the word." Chaz punched a fist to her hip.

Sadie tensed. "I quit, and I ain't never goin' back." Sadie shook her finger. "That is the truth of it."

Chaz patted her cheek. "Glad to hear it." Leaning in, she added, "I slipped laxative powder into his coffee beans yesterday." She raised her chin. "From what I hear, he had it comin'."

Sadie smiled as the bell announced another customer.

"Beans and Peas. On sale today only," Chaz said.

A young man tipped his farmer's hat and nodded as he scanned the store. "Good day, lassies." His Scottish accent and pressed jeans said he wasn't a local.

Sadie offered Chaz the list Bella had written. "Bella needs a few things, and I'd like to have a look at your cotton prints, if you have some."

"Have we got cotton? Hank, you hear that? Of course, we have cotton prints. This ain't Corvallis."

Fingering the reams of cotton Chaz laid out, Sadie remarked, "They're beautiful." Bella had been teaching her household duties—sewing, her latest lesson.

"You'll need to know these things if you are to marry and settle down," Bella said. *A girl like me…married? Michael would never—*

"That one's fair." The voice made her jump.

Sadie patted her chest.

"Didn't mean to scare ya, little lass." He removed his hat. "Name's Ian McCann."

"Sadie Simone," she said, he towered her by a foot. "You're not from around here."

"Just in town for a short time. Over from Philipsburg. Do ya know it?" His deep accent made understanding his words difficult.

She shook her head but then remembered. "The mining town?"

"That's right." He fidgeted with his collar. "Got myself a fine buggy outside. It'd be my pleasure to take ya for a ride."

"I don't know, I—" Sadie searched for Chaz, who seemed to disappear.

"I don't drink, smoke, or chew tobacco. I attend church regularly. Don't have a girl, not yet anyway. Got myself a job, a house, and two little brothers. No parents."

Sadie's head spun. Ian was bold and straightforward. "And you have a buggy."

"A fine buggy. Would be finer with a lady such as yourself sitting inside. One o'clock tomorrow, if you're willing."

Chaz suddenly appeared. "Out of striped candy today, but you tell Bella we expect some in on Tuesday." Chaz turned to Ian. "We have everything but striped candy."

Ian donned his hat. "Nice to meet you, Sadie Simone. One o'clock, tomorrow?"

She smiled. "All right."

"Tomorrow then." He tipped his hat.

Chaz puckered her lips as he left, and Sadie grimaced.

* * * * *

"We know nothing about this Ian McCann. I don't think you should go riding with him." Michael watched Sadie adjust her bonnet and fasten it tightly around her chin, her blonde curls too fancy. *He might get the wrong impression.*

"I think he's nice, and it's just a buggy ride."

Michael adjusted. "Correction. It's a second buggy ride." He grit his teeth. *This bed is a prison.* He'd be chained to it if Beth had her way. "You could've said no."

Sadie smirked in the mirror. "But I didn't. Besides, Bella says it is good for me to be with a *true gentleman.*"

She meant that as a jab. The idea of Sadie going out in a buggy with a strange man wasn't right, but what could he do, stuck here in this bed. *Doctor's orders.*

"It's too soon for you to be alone with a man." He wanted to say, "With a boy."

"I'm alone with you all the time." Sadie cocked her head with her hands on her hips.

The gesture usually made him smile. "That's different." *I would never…Ian McCann might.*

"If you'd ask me for a buggy ride, I'd go with you," she said.

"I don't have a buggy."

"Exactly. Ian is a friend. He's heading home in a few weeks anyway."

Good riddance, Ian McCann. Leave tomorrow. Today wouldn't be too soon.

Sadie rolled her eyes and patted him on the head. "You be a good patient while I'm gone. Call for Bella if you need anything. Beth and Ethan should be back soon."

He swatted her hand away.

"Get some rest, Michael. You're a grump." Sadie smiled before she closed the door.

Heart pounding, Michael stared at the door and then slammed his book onto the bed, nearly missing his bad leg. *I have to get out of this bed.* Determined to do whatever it took, he yanked off the blanket.

* * * * *

Sadie closed Michael's door and put her back against the wall. She covered her mouth and held her breath. *You're in love with him.* She sighed. *Who are you kidding?* She couldn't tell him. *He thinks of me as a little sister. He wouldn't ever—couldn't ever love me without thinking of me as a whore.*

A loud thud interrupted her thought. She heard bed-springs squeal. Pulling herself together, she listened. *He's going mad stuck in that bed.* The sound of horse hooves stopped in front of the building. She had no business going for a buggy ride. *I don't deserve to be happy.* Michael was right. *But I want to be happy.*

* * * * *

Michael shimmied to the edge of the bed and slowly tugged his leg with him. *I can do this.* He'd done it before but never alone. Logic kicked in. *The bone is intact, it's nerves telling you it hurts. Don't believe them. Ignore the pain.*

His good leg would bear most of his weight. Pushing himself up, he wobbled to the left, then to the right. He grasped the bedpost and a chair to steady himself. A couple of deep breaths and he was ready. *Just take one step...*

"Ouch." Pain ripped from his foot to his hip. The room tipped to one side as he started to fall.

* * * * *

Eli removed his spectacles and rubbed his forehead. What a day. He'd die a young death at this pace. Gladly, he retired before the other men. His guest room at the Daly Ranch was simple, no marble floors or tall arched doors, just patterned carpet and painted wood. A small fireplace adorned with a pastoral picture sat cold. Eli pulled at his collar.

A knock at the door brought him to his feet to open the door. The footman held out a piece of paper. "Sorry for the hour. A letter for you, sir. The rider is waiting."

Eli opened the note. *Blank.* He looked up. "Yes. Tell him to wait outside."

"But he's in the parlor now, sir."

Donovan. "Have him wait outside. I'll be down shortly."

The young man obeyed. Crumpling the paper, Eli threw it into the empty fireplace, but then thought better of it and searched it out.

* * * * *

"This is quite the show," Donovan said as Eli dismissed the footman from the Daly courtyard.

"I specifically wrote for you to wait in town." Eli poked him in the chest and scanned the yard. Torchlights flickered. *Yes, we're alone.*

Donovan cowered, patting his horse. "You said we had some unfinished business here and to come right away."

"Correction, *you* have some unfinished business here." Eli checked several open windows and pulled Donovan into the shadows.

Donovan narrowed his eyes and adjusted his leather glove. "What do you mean?"

"Miss Elizabeth Yates has landed here, of all places. Works at a pitiful little café on Main Street."

"That Yates girl is here?" Donovan chuckled. "I see. She's that much of a problem for you?"

"Get rid of her this time."

"Oh, I'll get rid of her. I've got a score to settle." Donovan pulled himself into his saddle.

"Get out of here, and I want you on the next train out of town when it's done," Eli whispered and then slapped the horse on the hind. Dirt and gravel stirred up in the courtyard as Eli returned to the house.

* * * * *

"Ethan." Beth locked the front door to the café. "What are you doing here?"

He folded his arms and leaned against the brick wall. "Waiting for you."

She smiled. The face she'd seen on every customer today was here in person. "Shouldn't you be working out at your ranch?" She gasped. "Your horses came in today."

"Tomorrow, but we're ready for them. I had to pick up a few things in town." Ethan pushed himself from the brick and put his arms around her waist. "Besides, I wanted to see you."

She smirked. "You've eaten at the café every morning this week and"—she shook a finger at him—"you've walked me home every day too. You can't do this. I won't let you."

He kissed her nose. "What if I told you I'm here on business?"

Beth narrowed her eyes. "Business? Can't imagine what kind of business that might be." She blushed, realizing how that sounded.

Ethan pulled her close. "You're teasing me."

"Maybe." She smiled. *All right, this has to stop. People are staring.*

He must have read her thoughts, for he released her and offered his arm. "Come on. I'll walk you home."

Walking past the café window, Beth saw Jane nudge Clinton, grinning. Beth cleared her throat. "What business have you with me?"

He swung her from the boardwalk to cross Main Street. "I'd like to give Michael a job."

Beth halted in the middle of the street. "What?"

Ethan urged her across. "Not right away, of course, but I've been mulling things over. Ranching is hard work. I haven't said anything to Michael yet."

She covered her heart. "Ethan." She dreaded Michael going back to work at the Big Mill.

"I'll pay him a good wage if he agrees…and if you agree."

"I don't know what to say." What an honor to love this man. She memorized the contour of his face. Did she love Ethan Dawson?

"There's one condition," he said and faced her.

Movement beyond the alley caught her eye, but no one was there. Probably just a cat. Beth lifted a brow. "A condition?"

"I don't want you to work on Sundays. Michael's income will more than make up for it."

Thrilled, she replied, "All right, Ethan."

Ethan took her hand, swinging it as they walked. She smiled, for she'd already asked Jane for Sundays off three days ago.

* * * * *

"What did you just say?" Sadie stared at Ian as he shifted in his seat. Going for a buggy ride was one thing, but marrying him? *Out of the question.*

"Will ya marry me?" His Scottish accent deepened, as did his brown eyes.

"I heard you the first time. What I meant was…why?" Her lace gloves felt tight all of a sudden. Her mouth went dry. *You don't even know who I am—what I was.*

Ian took her hand. "I'm sure of my decision." She pulled away, watching ducks swim across the millpond. "I'll be good to ya."

She faced him slowly. "Yes, I believe you would. It's not that."

He pushed his hat back and wiped his brow. "There's someone else."

Yes. No. Michael would never…could never love—

"No." She squeezed his hand.

"What is it then?"

Sadie bit her lip and sighed. "I've done things, Ian." Tears stung her eyes. "Things I'm not proud of."

He wiped her tears away. "Leave the past where it belongs, lassie. The devil'll have a heyday if ya don't."

You don't know the half of it. "Ian, you have to know the truth." She exhaled. "I am—I was a prostitute." She turned away.

"I know, little lass, and I want ya to be my wife."

* * * * *

Still shy on his feet, Michael watched Ian McCann approach Sadie after Sunday service. Bella and Russ talked with Ethan and Beth near the door. He eyed Bella and motioned to Sadie with his cane. *Bella, do something.* Bella must have misunderstood his glare, for she smiled.

Sadie giggled, and Ian laughed. Michael didn't. "Excuse me." Michael pushed his way through the crowd, his cane tapping the wood floor. "Pardon me." His leg grew stronger, but he still felt the handicap and the pain, especially in a crowd with obstacles aplenty. Currently, however, he felt nothing—nothing but pure satisfaction of rescuing Sadie from a decision she would regret for the rest of her life. "Mr. McCann, Sadie has no intention of riding in your buggy today," then added for clarity's sake, "Or ever."

"What are you doing?" Sadie glared.

"Ya must be Michael." Ian offered a handshake. "I've heard a lot about ya. Seems I owe ya a debt of gratitude."

British brut. Michael refused to shake his hand. *I'd rather kiss a cow.*

"Come on, Sadie." Michael took her hand and pulled her through the crowded aisle, ignoring the pain that intensified.

"Michael, what was that all about?" Sadie squirmed, but Michael tightened his hold.

Beth and Bella jumped as the church door swung open, banging the handrail. Russ let out a whistle.

"Michael!" Beth called out.

"Young people's quarrels are quick to heal," Russ said.

Michael paused for a moment, hearing Russ' words, and then continued.

"Michael, let go of me. You're hurting me." Sadie slipped from his grip. "Ian was just offering to take me home." Sadie glanced back at the church. "You had no right to be so rude."

"I have every right." Michael wiped his hand over his face. *That came out wrong.* "You can't do this." He had to think.

Her face reddened, and her eyes filled with tears. "Why? Why can't I do this? Why can't I be happy?"

He was breathless. "Not with him."

She stared at him. "With you?"

His eyes jerked, and he shrugged. "No." *Maybe later. I don't know.*

She stiffened. "Why not?"

"Because." *Because I'm poor, I'm lame, I'm not good enough.*

Michael heard voices behind them and then footsteps. He reached for her, but she pulled away, her chin quivering. "Sadie, please."

She tipped her chin and shook her head. "I'm fine, really." She cleared her throat. "You're friendship has meant more than you'll ever know." She turned and ran.

"Sadie." He tried to grab her.

"Michael, let her be," he heard Bella's voice. "Give it some time."

Michael dug the end of his walking cane in the dirt and shook his head. Russ squeezed his shoulder. "Son, you can't fix everything."

Chapter Thirty-Four

Donovan should have taken care of Miss Yates by now. I certainly pay him enough. Maybe too much. Eli patted the pocket of his coat before stepping into the carriage across from Ulysses Schwab.

Schwab whipped up his collar and turned to the driver, muttering something about the distance. Eli grinned when Schwab adjusted in his seat. "How's business in Portland?"

"No business today, Sands. Let's enjoy the scenery, shall we?"

Eli's lips twitched as he forced a smile. Schwab had been snubbing him all week. *No one snubs Eli Sands.* Eli cleared his throat and surveyed the mountains as the carriage lurched. The open carriage might as well have been closed. The air was so thick, Eli couldn't take it in. Warm wind hit his face as a bead of sweat dripped down his spine.

Schwab talked casually with the driver. Except for an occasional nod, he ignored Eli for most of the ride. What did Eli care? He'd be richer than Schwab before the year's end. He pushed his nose into the air, silent payback to the man sitting across from him.

Hamilton was as busy as it could be for a town its size, nothing to his great Chicago. Eli clamped his hand on the buggy wall. *Donovan.* The sight of Donovan leaning against a brick building made his blood boil. Donovan pushed himself from the wall and kicked at something on the boardwalk.

Was the deed done? Was Miss Yates no more? He had no way
of knowing.

* * * * *

Beth looked up from clearing a nearby table. Marcus
Daly held the door open and silenced the bell. "There she is.
Calamity Jane in person." He motioned toward the kitchen.
A trail of dark suits filled the café. She smiled. It wasn't every
day that Daly graced them with his presence.

Jane appeared in the dining room, wiped her hands,
and yanked off her greasy apron. "Don't be bashful, boys."
Jane offered a solid handshake, and the men surrounded her.

Instantly, the men became little boys, begging for their
moment of fame. *The famous Calamity Jane.* Beth was used
to the show. "Would you mind signing my son's comic book,
ma'am?" asked a taller gentleman.

Jane took the book. "It'd be my pleasure, but if you call
me *ma'am* one more time, I might have to shoot you." Silence
befell the group. Beth shook her head as Jane winked, and
the men reluctantly laughed.

Beth pushed through to the kitchen as Clinton came
out, carrying a stack of clean plates. The door jammed in the
middle. Clinton cursed as the plates tipped and slid from his
arms. No time to apologize. Beth lunged for them. Clinton
scrambled too. His breath reeked of whiskey.

They caught them—all of them. There they stood, fro-
zen in an awkward position, plates teetering in their arms,
both breathing hard. He swayed, barely able to stand. A
weary smile lit his face. One by one, she set the plates on the
counter. Clinton wiped his brow. His eyes fogged. "That was
a close one." His words slurred.

She nodded, considering how the presence of one man
could have such an effect on a person.

"Have a seat boys," Beth heard Jane bellow. "Meal's on the house."

"If she keeps that up, we'll be broke by winter, and you'll be out of a job." Clinton left the dishes on the counter, huffing. "I'm going to the saloon."

"What about the food?" Beth called after him and sighed. She'd be waitress and cook but thankful that men in the company of Mr. Daly would be gentlemen, men of wealth and position to be sure. Anyone in the company of Daly had to be. The tips would be good if she managed herself well. She checked her appearance in the window. How she wished Anne-Marie hadn't gone home. Beth flipped her pad and lifted the short, stubby pencil from her pocket.

She could handle this. Pushing through to the dining room, she froze. Her pencil dropped to the floor. The pad in her hand fell to her side. *Eli Sands. Here?* The only question that dared to enter her mind.

Run. Every beat of her heart screamed it. She stepped backward, stumbled. Perhaps he hadn't seen her.

But his eyes found her. The power in his gaze held her like a prisoner. She tried to look away but couldn't.

"Pick up your feet, girl. We've got customers," Jane yelled.

Heat rose to her throat, every nerve in flames. *He's found you. You'll never be free of him or the debt.* Eli's beady eyes narrowed like a vice around her neck.

Suddenly, she snapped out of his trance. Turning on her heel, she tore through the kitchen like Ethan's horse in the café. "He's here." Ripping off her apron, she searched frantically for her satchel and yanked her coat from its hook. Several cans of beans fell across the floor as her coat snagged the corner table.

She stole a careful glance through the back kitchen window into the alley, tried to get Jane's attention but couldn't.

No one can save me but me. Then she saw Eli Sands stand beyond the ticket counter.

"How did he find me?" Beth muttered as she pushed through the back door. *Run.*

The back door slammed and caught her skirt. She yanked it hard and fell onto her knees. As she scampered to her feet, she knocked over a pile of crates in the alley.

Suddenly, a shadow lunged at her. The blow sent stars in her line of vision. Pain shot through her ribs. She wanted to scream but had no breath. A gloved hand clamped over her mouth as her assailant pulled her to her feet.

Her head spun. She kicked and wriggled. She struggled to see his face. She scratched at his hand over her mouth. *I can't breathe.* She bit down hard, and he released it. She drew a breath, then another before he covered her mouth again.

She kicked, tried to scream, biting, struggling to be free. But his hold was too tight. *This can't be the end. Not now. Not when everything—*

"Shut up," he whispered hard and threw her against the wall and pinned her. Then she saw his face. *Donovan.* Terrified, she stared at his eyes. Darkness loomed inside. She thought of Michael and Maggie. Ethan. Courage rose, and determination fought his vise-like grip. She tried to push him away.

She readied her knee, hoping to repeat her escape, but Donovan swerved, pinned her legs, and clutched her face. "Not this time. This time, there is no escape."

Tears filled her eyes. *God, help me.*

"I'm going to enjoy this." Donovan made her look at him. "You see, you've caused me a lot of trouble." He pressed his nose against hers. "But that all ends now."

Her skin crawled, every last inch. She forced a muffled scream. He clamped down. He slammed her body against the brick and pressed the side of her face against the rough brick. Vibrations sailed threw her nerves.

With his full weight against her, he pulled a knife from his pocket and pressed it on her cheek. "You and I are gonna take us a nice…little…walk."

He slammed her up against the wall again, giving a physical demand. She dug at the brick and mortar behind her, reaching at anything that might save her. He ran the point of his knife along her bottom lip as he pulled his hand away, and she felt blood run down her neck. "Not a word. Not…a…peep. Understand?" His eyes darkened.

She nodded, hoping movement would be her rescuer. He smiled with his accomplishment.

Suddenly, a gunshot rang out. Beth jumped. Donovan's eyes jerked to one side, black and glassy. He faltered and drew a long breath. His grip weakened as his hands crawled down her blouse and skirt. She took a deep breath as he slumped to the ground, blood pooling at his back.

Jane wiped the barrel of her gun. "Knew something wasn't right 'bout him last night at the saloon."

With her hand at her throat, Beth stared at Donovan as he drew a gurgled breath—his last. Footsteps grew close. Daly and his men flooded the back door of the café, halting, one behind the other.

Jane eyed the crowd, lowered her gun, and spit. "'Sides, ain't nobody gonna be stealin' my chickens." She belittled the scene, no doubt for Beth's benefit.

Seeing Sands coming through the crowd, Beth gathered her things and ran.

Chapter Thirty-Five

"Michael!" Beth shouted long before she reached the steps and the door. Main Street and Fourth Street were a blur. Her throat burned. Her voice skipped as she screamed his name again. "Michael!" Remembering the blood on her face, she wiped it away.

Heart pounding, she pushed the door open so fast and hard, it hit a wall hook and bounced back at her.

"What is it?" Michael was at the window.

Bella came running down the hall. "Is it Maggie?"

"He's here. Get your things." Beth heaved a large suitcase above the closet, dropping it to the floor. The room shook.

"Who's here?" Michael's eyes widened. "Your lip is bleeding."

She waved both he and Bella away. "Eli Sands. He's found us. He's at the café right now. Probably followed me. And Donovan—"

Her hands trembled and she closed her mouth. She'd just seen a man killed.

"Slow down, honey. What's this all about?" Bella grabbed Beth's shoulders and dapped the blood from her lip with a handkerchief.

"He's a horrible, terrible man. He'll stop at nothing. We have to leave. Now."

Michael's face registered the grave truth of the situation and yanked a suitcase out from under the bed and threw the top open, emptying a dresser drawer into it. Beth threw another bag on the table, knocking over a chair.

"Calm down, Beth. Michael, who's this Sands fella?" Bella turned to Michael. "Surely—"

Michael started to speak, but Beth cut him off. "Bella, please. There isn't time. I'll explain later." *If there is a later.* Beth paused for a split second to take a deep breath. "We owe him a lot of money, and there's more."

Bella put her fists on her hips. "This is about money? Surely, we can reason with the man."

Beth buckled her case and pushed it toward the door. "You don't reason with Eli Sands." Sands was probably gathering his men right now. Donovan couldn't have been his only man. "The stage leaves at noon."

Michael cocked his head, his pause annoyed. "Bella's right. None of this makes sense to me."

"Pack." Beth ordered and then exhaled. "We must get Maggie from school without him seeing us."

Bella tried to hug her. "Beth, please."

Beth pulled away and searched around the room. *We'll go to Missoula. From there, who knows?* Eli Sands would never find them in Missoula. *Perhaps Seattle.* She closed the case, fastened the straps, and yanked it up by its handle.

"What about Ethan?" Bella raised an eyebrow, hip fisted.

Beth gasped. *Ethan.* She could hardy breathe with the lump in her throat. How could she even tell him? There wasn't time. Things between them had happened so fast. Still, she should have told him.

The door slowly cracked. Michael jumped in front of her. Had Sands followed her to the room? Sadie peeked inside. "What is going on?"

Beth sighed. Bella pulled Sadie inside. "We're leaving town," Michael said.

Sadie shook her head. "What? Why?"

"We're leaving now." Beth scanned the apartment, kissed a confused Bella, and gathered the suitcases. "Thank you for everything, Bella. I'll write and explain once we've settled…somewhere."

"Honey, please. There must be another way."

Beth shook her head. "It isn't safe here anymore." Beth took one last look around the room, the room she'd called home for so many months. Tears filled her eyes as she hurried to the stairs.

Silent, Sadie held the door open. Michael paused with her for a moment. "I have to go. I wish I'd—"

"We have to hurry, Michael," Beth called from the bottom of the stairs. She searched the street. *Quiet.* Just the usual crowd. Her mind traced an alternative route to the schoolhouse. She was bound and determined to keep them safe, even if it meant giving up on her hopes and dreams again.

* * * * *

"Ethan!" Bella's horse came to a sliding dusty halt. Ethan dropped the gate latch into place and rushed to her. He didn't even know she could ride, let alone ride like that. She reached for his hand and tried to catch her breath.

"Something's wrong." He saw it on her face.

"Beth is leaving town." She patted her chest and continued, "She's trying to catch the afternoon stage."

"What? Why?" Ethan looked for Russ, who was already saddling their horses near the barn.

Bella shrugged. "Something about a Sands fella and owing him a lot of money. She's running scared, Ethan. I've never seen her like this. I think he's tried to hurt her before. And now there's a dead man at the café."

Ethan motioned to Russ as Buck Reardon came out of his cabin. His wobbled gate not fast enough for Ethan. Ethan mounted Jax and met Buck halfway, Russ and Bella in his tracks. "I have to go to town. Man the fort." Ethan pulled up, dust in his wake.

Buck spit to the ground. "What do I tell this Rowlan fella when he gits here?"

Ethan rubbed his forehead and adjusted in the saddle. The California horse breeder was due within the hour. "Tell him to wait."

"And if he doesn't?"

Jax sidestepped with anticipation. "Then he doesn't." Ethan shook his head and turned Jax toward town in a single motion, dust whirled into the air.

* * * * *

Beth waved at Maggie's teacher, Miss Buttery, who stood at the top of the school steps, confused at their quick departure.

"Is it true, Beth?" Maggie pulled at Beth's hand. "I don't have to go to school anymore?"

Beth shook her head and dragged her beyond the schoolyard toward State Street, scouring side streets before crossing. They had to stay off of Main Street.

Maggie beamed. "This is the best day ever. Are we really gonna ride a stagecoach? Can Bella come too?"

"We have to hurry." Beth glanced back at Michael, who lagged behind, his pace hindered by too many cases and the need of a cane.

"What about my rocks? My legs hurt." Maggie let go of Beth's hand. "I didn't get to say goodbye."

Beth exhaled. "Maggie, there isn't time."

Maggie frowned and pulled from her hand. "I don't want to leave. I like it here."

"We can't stay here. It isn't safe." They had to leave, she told herself—kept telling herself. She thought her running days were over. She adjusted her suitcase and sighed. Sands would find her again, keep coming for her.

The edge of the train station sat up ahead. The stage-coach had arrived at the south end of the platform. If they timed it right, they might make it. "Come on. Hurry." She shifted the cases in her hands and looked up as three horse and riders came into town.

Ethan slid Jax to a stop several yards away, dismounted, and embraced her. "What's this all about?" Tears came without permission. Sobs followed. She threw her arms around his neck. "I'm so afraid."

"You're not leaving me," Ethan whispered in her ear and tightened his grip. "Ever."

She nodded in his embrace and glanced at Bella. "I didn't think I had a choice."

Bella patted her arm and smiled as Maggie and Michael joined them, exhausted.

Ethan caressed her face. "Why didn't you tell me about this Sands fella and the money?" He pulled his handkerchief from his vest pocket and dabbed her lip. "No more running."

"He was my problem, not yours," she gained her composure to speak.

Russ came close and put his hand on her back. "Your problems are our problems, and we'll have no more of this runnin' business."

She nodded as Ethan released her and took his handkerchief to dry her eyes. "I thought we were free of him. Montana seemed worlds away. I thought we'd be safe here, but he's here right now at the café, and a man named Donovan came here to kill me. He tried to, but—"

Bella pulled Maggie into her arms and covered her ears. "That the dead fella down at the café?"

"Jane shot and killed him right in front me."

Ethan pulled her close again. "You're going to tell us everything, and then we—all of us—are going to see this Sands fellow together.

Chapter Thirty-Six

"I can't face him again." Beth stared at Ethan.

Ethan took her hands. "*We're* going to face him." He dipped his chin. "And we're going to face him right now."

Russ and Bella joined him. "That's right, sugar. The good Lord never intended you to bear this burden alone."

Beth nodded. She knew that now, but it didn't make facing Eli Sands less terrifying. "What if he has proof of the debt?"

"Sugar, if you owe this scoundrel a blessed dime, I'll eat my hat—both hats."

Beth managed a smile, and Ethan squeezed her hand. "Even if he does, we can manage it."

She sighed, tears filling her eyes. *I don't deserve you.*

Maggie tugged on Bella's sleeve. "Does this mean I have to go back to school?"

"Oh, honey." Bella leaned down and kissed Maggie's cheek. "Yes, but you'll be brave like your sister, won't you?"

"I'll try, but I can't make any promises."

* * * * *

Beth cleared her throat, seeing Eli Sands as they entered the café. He leaned back in his chair and pulled his spectacles to the end of his nose. Jane rushed from the kitchen and wiped her hands on her apron. "Girl, you left me high and dry."

Ethan squeezed Beth's hand and whispered to Jane. "We'll explain later."

Russ and Michael stood in the doorway with Sheriff Irvine in tow. Bella and Maggie stood outside the front window, Maggie nose-pressed against the glass. They approached Daly's table of men, and Daly rose. "What's this about, Ethan?"

"I apologize for the interruption, Mr. Daly. I assure you this won't take long. We need to speak with Mr. Eli Sands." Ethan put his arm around Beth's shoulders.

Beth tensed. Daly motioned to Sands, and heads turned. Sands straightened and rose. "We'll speak in private. My business is nobody's business."

Beth jumped as Ethan slapped his hand on the table. "No, we'll speak now."

Jane stepped to their side, lifting her apron to reveal her pistol. For once, Beth relaxed at the gesture. Sands' scowl flattened as he found his seat. "I'm not sure what this is all about."

"Explain to me, sir, why you forced Miss Yates to work off a debt she did not owe."

Eli jumped to his feet. "How dare you accuse me, whoever you are." He studied the men around the table. "Surely, there has been some misunderstanding. I've never seen this girl before."

Beth jumped in. "That's a lie." Russ, Michael, and Sheriff Irvine closed in around her. Her courage rose. *Now. Speak your mind now.* "You said my parent's debt was far more than our home was worth. You made me believe I had to work to pay off the balance." She straightened, fists at her side. "You deceived me, sir." She glanced at Ethan, whose strength gave her courage. "You forced me to work at a brothel…owned by you." She glanced at Micheal, hoping the truth didn't hit him too hard.

"That is absurd." Sands' face flared red, almost purple. Eli scanned the room from Mr. Daly to Calamity Jane, who made no effort to hide her pistol.

"You said," Beth continued, "a pretty thing like me would make you a lot of money." She thought of Annie Parker's words.

Ethan smiled and held her hand firm.

"I've never been so insulted." Eli kicked his chair backward.

Daly cleared his throat and nodded to the rest of the group but didn't speak.

Sheriff Irvine stepped in. "Sands, can you show proof of this debt?"

Eli's gaze shifted as he hurriedly grabbed his belongings. "Surely, this is all a misunderstanding." He spread out his fat fingers on the table. "My colleagues know I own a reputable banking firm. I would never force a child to pay off a parent's debt, nor do I own a brothel. This is a disgrace." He wiped his mouth and threw the napkin on the table. "Quite unsettling."

"Then you release Miss Yates and her family from any obligation to you or your firm in front of these witnesses?" Ethan pointed to Mr. Daly and the others. Daly stood.

"Miss Yates owes me nothing." Eli excused himself. "Never seen her before in my life." The doorbell announced his departure. Jane followed him out. Bella tucked Maggie behind her as Sands stormed by. Beth relaxed.

Daly tipped his head. "Seems my suspicions about Sands were correct."

"Never cared for him myself," another man added.

Daly shook Ethan's hand. "Best of luck to you, Ethan. We were sorry to see you leave our ranch. And to you, Miss

Yates. Hope things settle down for you. Seems you've had your share of troubles."

"Thank you, sir," Beth forced, still in disbelief.

Ethan kissed her hand. "You were great."

"I was terrified."

Daly and his men gathered their things. "Miss Yates, you let me know if Sands causes you any more trouble. Name's Schwab." He handed her his card.

Beth nodded and sighed. Her very next breath held more hope than she'd ever known.

Suddenly, a gunshot rang out, then a second. Everyone ducked. Jane stepped into the café. "Just scarin' him off." She spun her gun into its holster. "Sheriff, what do you want me to do with the dead body I got out back?"

"Never a dull day 'round here." Russ and Michael, along with Daly and his colleagues, followed Jane and Sheriff Irvine out back. A dead body was still a novelty.

Ethan waited until the door closed, until they were alone. Tucking a curl behind her ear, he cupped her face. "There's something I've been wanting to ask you."

She looked down, toying with the buttons on his shirt. Something shiny and gold caught her eye. Her fingers traced the gold chain to his vest pocket, a chain familiar yet lost to her. "Where did you get this?" She lifted it from his pocket.

He seemed confused. "My pocket watch?"

"Yes." Beth smiled and caressed its markings. "It was… my father's watch." She flipped around to read the inscription, "In His Time."

"In His time, indeed." He started to pull the chain free.

"No. Keep it." The watch held a piece of her heart. *No, much more than that.*

Ethan hesitated. "Are you sure?"

She put her hand over his heart. "I want you to have it."

He slipped the watch in his pocket and held her close. "About that question—"

"Whatever it is, the answer is yes." She threw her arms around his neck, and he kissed her.

They may have been standing in a tiny café owned by the infamous Calamity Jane in a not-so-famous Montana town, but to Beth, they were in a world of their own.

* * * * *

Eli leaned against the wall at Hamilton's insignificant tiny train station. With a train ticket in one hand and his bag in the other, he awaited the next train out of this God-forsaken town. He cursed it. *Nothing but dirt clods and dust.* Didn't hold a candle to his great Chicago. Curling his fingers around the ticket, he checked his watch.

The train wasn't due back through Hamilton for half an hour. He mumbled to himself. Shrinking into the shadows in the corner of the station, he watched Marcus Daly and his colleagues mount their horses and head for the river. He hated fishing anyway. Too many bugs. He would forget about his time in Montana eventually, but for now, it ate at him. First, there was the hunting excursion. Sure, he'd held a gun before but wasn't skilled. His colleagues joked and jeered at his inadequacy as he fumbled with loading the contraption, nearly shot a huntsman's foot when he jerked the trigger prematurely. *Faulty trigger.*

The riding expedition proved less dangerous but no less humiliating. Riding a horse seemed simple enough, according to his guidebook, but when his horse veered from the group, he couldn't turn the beast the right way. He cursed the horse to a complete stop where, at once, it bent down to graze. Affording his colleagues a sideshow laugh and an even heartier one when the guide grabbed the reins and offered him a riding lesson. *Weak specimen of a horse.*

Spilling red wine on Mrs. Daly's dining rug was a mid-week disaster, but no one knew he was the one responsible. There was one unfortunate, embarrassing incident after another until the final incident in town.

Eli shook his head to clear the memory. He kicked his boot against the building, knocking off the dirt and patted the telegram in his pocket, reminding himself of his one success. "This is not over, Miss Yates…" the whistle of the train sounded in the distance, "…until I say it's over."

* * * * *

A quiet knock at the door woke Beth suddenly. She shot up out of bed. Darkness covered their little apartment. Only the moon peaked through a crack in the curtains. *Who could it be at this hour?* Michael stirred but didn't wake. Maggie was still sound asleep.

Beth pulled on her robe and flipped her hair over her shoulder. She opened the door. "Bella?" Beth rubbed her eyes and stared at the letter Bella held in her hand. "What time is it?" Stepping into the hall, confusion forced her awake.

Without answering Beth's question, Bella whispered, "Sadie's gone."

"What?" Beth quietly shut the door behind her as not to wake Michael and Maggie. "What do you mean she's gone?"

"She wasn't here when we got back. I thought she needed some time alone." Bella dabbed her cheeks with her handkerchief and offered Beth the letter. "But then I found this on my dresser."

Beth scanned the note. Her eyes, no doubt, revealed her shock. She dropped the letter to her side. "She's married?"

Bella blew her nose and nodded.

"When?"

"Today—tonight?" She shrugged. "Ran off with that Ian McCann fella."

"I see that." Beth snapped the letter.

"She didn't even say goodbye." Bella rubbed her forehead. "This is my fault."

"It's not your fault." *Probably mine, more than yours.* She'd cautioned Michael to give Sadie time, assuring him that time would heal the wound after their little spat.

Beth wondered, especially in light of recent events, if perhaps there was more to Michael and Sadie's friendship than even Michael dared to admit, but it was too late now.

"Bella?" Beth bit her lip. "What are we going to tell Michael?"

Chapter Thirty-Seven

Three months later

Beth studied her reflection in the mirror, a large stained glass window and tall bookshelves filled the background. *You've changed. Yes, yes I have.* She twisted and turned. Certainly talking to oneself was allowed on a day like today. Her laced fingers rolled the tiny pearl at her neckline. Mother and Father should have been here. *You would have loved Ethan.*

Tilting her head, she gently touched and smoothed her hair.

"The pins will hold," Bella promised.

Several curls hung around her face. Beth tucked one behind her ear, a task Ethan liked to do himself. The ivory gown she wore was like something out of a dream. How could something so old be so beautiful? Still as fine as the day it was made, she supposed. A Dawson heirloom, Ethan's mother said.

Organ music began to play, its muffled melodic tones echoing down the church hall and seeping into the reverend's study. Footsteps welcomed the sound of Bella's voice.

"Maggie, stop fussing. You only have to wear it for one day."

Audible truth of what was about to happen. The door opened, and the music instantly grew louder. Her heart skipped.

"They are ready for you, honey."

"Bella," Beth sighed, "is this really happening? I've pinched myself so many times, I've made a mark." She showed Bella her wrist.

"You look beautiful." Bella squeezed her arm. "Now, come on."

Beth nodded. "I don't deserve to be so happy."

"None of us do, sugar."

"When do we get to eat the cake?" Maggie said, pulling at her collar. "It itches."

"Oh, Maggie." Beth grabbed her dress and whirled. "This will be you, someday."

Maggie wrinkled her nose. "I'd rather die to death. Is the cake before or after the kiss?"

Beth rolled her eyes, and Bella smiled.

"Is there going to be a wedding today or not?" Michael stood in the doorway, handsome as ever in his new suit and tie. *So much taller now.* More in character than in height.

"Maggie's wantin' some cake, so best be going." Bella said.

Michael offered his arm. "Shall we?"

Beth gathered her gown with her lacy gloves. "I'm ready."

"Mother and Father would be proud." Michael smiled.

Beth beamed. *Don't cry.*

Bella led Maggie ahead. "Now, Maggie, remember, walk slow. And don't *throw* the flowers. Just drop them gently."

Reverend Burkhart nodded to Mrs. Williams at the organ. The music began. Heads turned, and Ethan looked up. Their eyes met.

"Now? Do I go now?" Maggie whispered.

Bella gave Maggie a push into the aisle. "Go, honey."

Russ and Peter stood beside Ethan, patting his shoulder. Ethan shifted. Maggie hurried down the aisle. So stiff and fast, she completely forgot to drop the flowers. Bella glided down the aisle. Ethan's family sat in the front row—family so dear, it seemed she'd known them all of her life. Maggie quickly snuggled with Ethan's mother.

She took a deep breath as Michael walked her down the aisle. Ethan took her hand as she reached the front pew, pulled her close, and stole a kiss.

Bella cleared her throat, and someone whistled. Several more joined in. With their fingers entangled, Beth and Ethan shared a smile. Who would've guessed things would turn out so wonderfully?

"Dearly beloved, we are gathered here today in the sight of God and in the presence of these witnesses," Reverend Burkhart squeezed their hands, "to join this man and this woman in holy matrimony."

The End

Book Club Questions

1. What was the most memorable scene in the book to you and why?

2. In *Runaway River*, each character faces a challenging situation and deals with it in their own way. How does each character deal with their circumstances? How do you deal with difficult or challenging situations?

3. *Runaway River* opens with a pivotal and heart-wrenching scene where the characters lose their parents in a horrific fire. What situation in your own life created a pivot point that left you forever changed?

4. Rev. Biggs said several things to Beth at the funeral. Beth had a strong reaction to his words. Have you ever been told clichés at a difficult moment in your life? Have you ever offered clichés to someone else going through hard times? What is the best thing to offer someone going through a difficult time?

5. Bella was afraid to attend church because of her former lifestyle. What were her reasons for not attending church? Were those reasons justified? What is the church's responsibility when it comes to someone like Bella?

6. Most of our lives are spent interacting with people we know well. Annie Parker did not play a major part in *Runaway River*. Nonetheless, the role she played in helping Beth was huge. Do you look for ways to help people you may not know well?

7. The Infamous "Calamity Jane" did own a café in Hamilton, Montana. She deserved the title, but Beth saw a heart of gold. Who do you know that has "calamity" written all over them but has a side others don't often see? Have you told them lately what positive things you see in them?

8. First impressions abound in *Runaway River*, from how Beth views Ethan to how Michael views Sadie and how Bella views the church, etc. What first impressions in your life have you found to be inaccurate?

9. God spoke directly to Beth, Michael, and Sadie. Both His words and tone were different in each scenario. Why was His approach different with each person? How does God to speak to you? Why does He speak with you that way in that tone?

10. Beth went to the river and prayed (yelled) at God. Is it okay to have this kind of reaction toward God? Can God take it? Was God's response to Beth in keeping with His character?

11. The inscription on the back of the pocket watch read, "In His Time," from Ecclesiastes 3:11, which reads, "He has made everything beautiful in its time. He has also set eternity in the human heart; yet no one can fathom what God has done from beginning to end." How was this scripture essential to the story of *Runaway River*? How is this verse integral to your life?

About the Author

Kim D. Taylor lives in Washington State with her husband, Glenn, and two teenage sons, Cameron and Reid. She enjoys gourmet cooking, table settings, entertaining guests, and a cup of tea with family and friends. Kim has over twenty years of business, real estate, and pastoral ministry experience. Runaway River is the first book of the Bitterroot Mountain Series in the Mountains of Montana Collection. The second book, Stubborn Creek, is coming soon.

Visit www.kimdtaylor.com for more information.